CUFFS AND CUPCAKES

BLACK FOX SECURITY DOMS

BOOK TWO

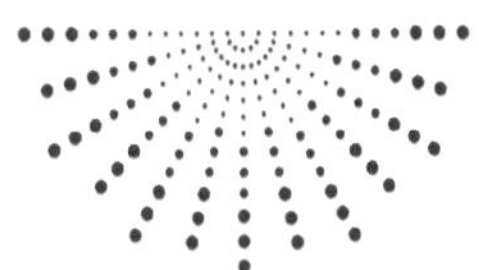

GOLDEN ANGEL

CONTENTS

PROLOGUE

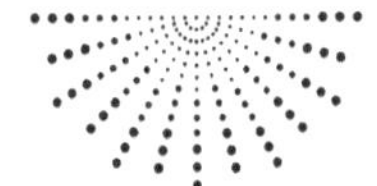

AUDREY

What am I doing here?

It wasn't the first time such a thought had popped into her mind while at one of her parents' parties, but it was the first time she felt like she might actually do something about it. Her fingers tightened around the champagne flute she was holding as she kept the smile plastered on her lips. At least the champagne was good.

Of course, it was. Her mother would accept nothing less at one of her parties.

The ultimate hostess. That was her mom. Or at least what her mom aspired to be among their social set. Audrey eyed the dessert table across the room. None of the women was venturing near it. If she dared to, she would have to listen to some targeted comment about her weight. Either a direct one from her mother or an underhanded one from someone else, about how 'brave' she was to eat sugar.

At least her boyfriend, Cash, was smart enough not to make a comment, not after that one time. Audrey didn't lose her temper often, but that had been their first and only fight.

The men didn't have that problem. They got to eat as much as they wanted at these things, regardless of their size.

Audrey just wanted to know if the little bite-sized delectables were good or not. If they were, she might have a few questions for the caterer... but how to get to them without notice?

Easing her way to the side of the room, smiling and nodding, she slowly crept closer to the dessert table. Profiteroles, petit fours, macarons, and something she thought might be a stickless version of a cake pop. If it was, she was curious and also amused that the caterer had gotten any kind of cake pop past her mother.

Cake pops were not up to Francie Bower's standards.

Not much was.

"Hey, Audrey."

Audrey turned, trying not to feel guilty. She hadn't done anything wrong, after all. Yet. She hadn't even gotten to the dessert table.

Beside her was the rebel of their social set. Lorelei was Cash's older sister and Audrey's favorite of his family. Unlike Cash and his younger sister Emily, Lorelei didn't toe the family line. She rarely showed up at these events, and when she did, she had a tendency to drink too much, talk and laugh too loudly, and call the old men out when they said something misogynistic. The older generation shuddered to see her coming.

"Hi, Lorelei, I didn't know you were here." Audrey felt her smile relax into a more natural one. Lorelei could be very judgmental of the people around them, but she'd always been nice to Audrey. Often, Audrey had the thought that Lorelei and Audrey's brother, David, would get along well. Neither of them fit in with their parents' plans and social maneuvering. Of course, David had moved away from their parents and this whole social scene and had a new girlfriend he seemed to be enamored of. Lately, Audrey had been envying him more and more.

"Yeah, well." Lorelei huffed, looking around and flipping her dark hair over her shoulder. She looked uncomfortable in the conservatively cut dress she was wearing. Whenever Audrey had seen her casually, she tended toward ripped jeans and vintage t-shirts. If she dressed up, it was in more of a pin-up style. In fact, she'd been the one to show Audrey how to do her hair and makeup that way when Audrey had wanted to try it. "Your mom always throws a good party. But what happened to the crab puffs?"

"Mom switched caterers."

"Damn. The crab puffs were good."

"I can give you the caterer's contact information if you want," Audrey offered.

"Sadly, I don't think I'll have an occasion to use a caterer anytime soon," Lorelei said dryly.

"I can ask her for the recipe."

Lorelei's expression lit up. "Yes, please." She hesitated, the light in her hazel eyes dimming. "If you still want to pass it on to me after this."

"After what?"

"You should go to the coat closet. Well, I don't know if 'should' is the right word. But I know that if it was me, I would want to know. If you don't want to know, or if you already know and you're fine with it, then don't go."

"Know what?" Audrey's confused question was asked to no one, though, because Lorelei had already turned and darted off through the crowd.

An unhappy, sick feeling started to rise in Audrey's stomach.

Because she did know. At least, she'd suspected. But she hadn't *known*. Hadn't had proof. She hadn't gone looking for it because it was going to throw everything into upheaval.

Her stomach twisted.

Audrey didn't want to go look. She didn't want to know. She didn't want to think about what she would have to do once she *knew*.

Or she could do nothing. She could stand here and sip her champagne while the party moved around her. The people moved around her. She could stand and smile and wait for Cash to reappear. She could ignore the signs that she'd seen before. The slightly rumpled shirt. The way his lips looked freshly kissed, even though she hadn't been kissing him. The scent of someone else's perfume hanging in the air around him.

She could pretend she didn't notice.

Pretend she didn't know what Lorelei had told her.

Just like her mother did with her father.

But she had never wanted to be her mother.

Turning felt like an out-of-body experience. Like someone else was in control of her body, moving her like a puppet through the crowd. The smile on her lips felt brittle, as if it might crack at any moment. No one stopped her. They moved around her like pretty decorations, flowing without purpose.

By the time she reached the door to the hall, there was no turning back. She knew it deep in her heart, even though part of her was still begging her to turn around. To walk away. To go back to the party and back to pretending. Because this was going to change everything.

CHAPTER ONE

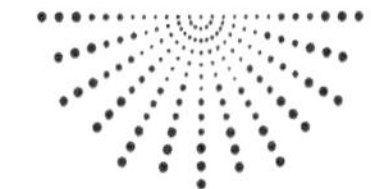

Six Months Later

Audrey

Looking around the lobby of Black Fox Security while she waited for her brother, Audrey felt a rush of exhilaration. She was really here and not just to visit. No longer under her parents' thumb. No longer dodging Cash's calls and impromptu visits. No more pretending.

The lobby of the security firm was spacious and quiet since it was a Saturday. No one was working. She was looking forward to meeting his team, though, at the welcome party he and his girlfriend, Cassidy, were throwing for her tonight. It looked like a regular lobby—not that she knew what security firm lobbies were supposed to look like. But she hadn't been expecting something like an accounting firm.

She was leaning her elbow on the counter of the receptionist's desk—it was two-tiered, with the desk part lower than the counter side where she was standing—facing the hallway David had gone down. There were a few small piles of fliers and cards for local businesses on the counter. Audrey wasn't sure how much foot traffic security firms got, but maybe she should bring something in for her bakery once it opened.

At the very least, it wouldn't hurt to go around to other businesses in the area and see if they would let her leave some kind of flier or card. It was a good idea. The kind of thing she needed to be thinking about now that she was opening her own business. She needed to make it work. While her grandfather had left her a hefty trust fund, she only had access to a small part of it right now. The rest would come to her after her parents passed. As frustrated as she was with them right now, that wasn't a day she was looking forward to.

Which meant she had a safety net for the future, but it wouldn't be there to catch her in time if she was one of the businesses that failed in its first five years... which was something like fifty percent of businesses. Almost twenty percent failed in the first year.

Stop thinking about that. Visualize success. Visualize people loving your baking and coming in regularly. Visualize all the special event cakes you're going to make and how happy you're going to be here in your new life.

Yes.

She could do this.

She was a damn good baker, and she knew it. She was smart. She could figure out the business stuff.

"I can do this," she muttered under her breath as the door to the office beeped, the same sound it had made when David had used his keycard to get in. Audrey jumped, straightening and turning. She felt her eyes widen as one of the most gorgeous men she'd ever seen in real life came through the door.

Even though he must have seen her through the glass, he still looked surprised to see her there.

Tall, broad-shouldered, with a swimmer's muscled build that made his body look like an upside-down triangle. The grey turtleneck he was wearing hid whether he had that hot little 'v' at his hips, but Audrey would bet her bakery that he did. The wire-rimmed glasses did nothing to detract from the handsomely sculpted lines of his face. Tanned skin, black hair, black piercing eyes... he looked like a model, not a former military turned security guy.

But that's exactly what he was.

It took a moment for her floundering brain to recognize him from the pictures David had sent her of his team. He looked different out of uniform and with the hair on top of his head grown longer.

Mason. That was his name. The one who liked baklava.

"Mason?" She beamed at him, trying to cover up her immediate reaction—which would have been full of drool if she hadn't controlled herself—with the bubbly excitement of meeting one of David's team members. In fact, David had often referred to Mason as the closest thing he had to a best friend. "Oh my God, it's so nice to finally meet you!"

Taking several steps forward, Audrey flung out her arms. If she hugged him, he wouldn't be able to see her expression, and she could have a moment to control herself. Sure, she'd seen plenty of handsome men in real life, but there was something about *this* man that was affecting her in an entirely different way. Cash had never made her feel an immediate surge of lust when she looked at him, and he was incredibly handsome.

If looking at Mason had been good, touching him was electric. He was taller than her, even in her heels, and rock hard. Granted, her brother was rock-hard muscle when she hugged him, too, but this was nothing like hugging her brother. Mason was slimmer, with leaner muscles, and it felt like her entire body lit up.

Touching him might have been a mistake. Now, she didn't need to just get her face under control; she needed to get her whole damn body under control.

"Audrey?" He didn't sound certain, and she realized he hadn't immediately recognized her.

Giving him another squeeze as cover to give her a moment to get herself together, Audrey released him and stepped back. She tilted her head back to smile up at him, her brain frantically reaching for the first thing she could think of to say. Baklava. David had passed on the message that Mason had particularly requested baklava at the bakery because it was his favorite.

"I didn't know I was going to be seeing you here, or I would have brought your baklava—I made three different kinds, so you can tell me which one you like the best." Oh crap, she was babbling. Of course, she hadn't known she was going to see him here. No one was supposed to be here right now. She and David had been just stopping by so he could pick up something.

She must sound like a complete idiot.

Also, admitting she'd made three types of baklava made her sound way too eager to please. That's what her mom would have said. She was trying too hard. As usual. Maybe it was good to tell him now, though. She'd made them before she'd met him, so he couldn't misinterpret it as her meeting him, then trying to impress him because she was attracted to him or something.

Even though she was.

Wildly.

But she didn't want to look pathetic. Or desperate.

Because she wasn't.

"Thank you." Mason smiled at her, and Audrey did her best not to melt. Good grief. Did he know how lethal that smile was?

Of course, he did. Guys like him always did. But he probably didn't mean to use it on her that way. She was just… needy and pathetic.

Get out of my head, Cash.

"Sorry." She wrinkled her nose, stepping back. Her hand drifted up to the end of her ponytail, giving it a little tug, hard enough to sting a little. "I know I come on kind of strong. I'm trying to get better about it."

"I like how you come on. I didn't mind." The smile still seemed genuine, not as if he was trying to placate her. Audrey relaxed a little.

Mason was nice. Of course he was.

She wasn't back home with her parents and their friends and their expectations. If she'd reacted this way to one of their friends' sons, they would have been horrified and embarrassed. Audrey wouldn't have had the chance to apologize because her parents would have been pulling her back and apologizing for her brashness. And then she would have been scolded about improper behavior and minding her manners and not making such a show of herself.

But she wasn't in Philly anymore; she was in Pittsburgh, and Mason was nice. And insanely hot.

"Hey, Audrey, ready to go?" David's voice almost made her jump, because for a moment she'd forgotten she was waiting for him. She wasn't sure whether she was relieved or disappointed he'd interrupted the moment. "Oh, hey, Mason. What are you doing here?"

"Uh, I just had to pick some stuff up." Mason's focus was now entirely on David, and she was not feeling bereft just because he wasn't looking at her anymore. Nope. Because that would definitely be pathetic.

"Same." Her brother came up beside her, slinging his arm around her shoulders as he held up a folder in his other hand. Audrey smiled up at him. She was so glad she still had some family and that he'd been welcoming to her, even though she'd been trying to get him to talk to their parents for months after he'd cut them off. "Audrey and I are headed over to brunch with our grandmother now. Cassidy is driving her and meeting us there."

"I love Cassidy," Audrey chimed in, because she loved seeing the happiness on David's face every time she said it. She truly did love Cassidy. She hoped David and Cassidy got married and lived happily ever after. If anyone deserved it, it was the two of them. "So does Grandma. We stayed up 'til two o'clock last night talking. I adore her."

The poor girl had been worried about whether Audrey would hate her, since her stalker ex-boyfriend had shot David while trying to kidnap her. As if that was Cassidy's fault.

Now her stalker ex was dead, and they could live happily ever after without him hanging over them.

That was a big part of what they'd talked about last night, and Audrey had been happy to reassure Cassidy that she didn't blame her at *all.*

"She's pretty great," Mason agreed, making Audrey want to melt even more. She just wanted to stand here and stare at him. Which meant she needed to get away from him right now. She couldn't be lusting after one of her brother's team members. She had a bakery to get up and running. She wasn't looking for a relationship.

"She's so great. But we do need to go so we can meet her." Audrey smiled. "Will you be at Jensen's tonight?"

She hadn't met Jensen yet, but that's where her welcome party was going to be. David's apartment wasn't big enough to hold everyone comfortably, according to him, and Jensen's was where they usually gathered. Apparently, the house was incredible. Audrey was looking forward to seeing it.

Something changed in Mason's expression, his smile faltering. Audrey felt her heart falter, too.

"Yeah, he's coming," David said, frowning at Mason when he didn't answer right away.

"Yeah, I'm coming," Mason echoed.

Something was going on there, and Audrey wasn't sure what. Maybe it wasn't any of her business.

"Great." She smiled brightly. It couldn't have anything to do with her; that was one thing she was sure of. She'd just gotten to town after all. There was something else going on, and it must have to do with him. "See you there!"

"See you there," Mason said as she and David walked out of the office.

The elevator arrived right away, and Audrey turned inside, hoping to catch another glimpse of him, but he'd already moved out of the lobby and gone to do whatever he'd shown up to do. She sighed internally. It was only natural to be disappointed when the eye candy disappeared.

The elevator started to move.

"So, that's Mason."

"He was nice." She smiled at David. "I'm looking forward to meeting the rest of the team."

"They're all nice. Well, mostly." David frowned. "Zeus is a little stand-offish. I don't think he's coming tonight, anyway."

"He's the new one." Which was easy to remember because he was the only one who hadn't been part of David's team when David was still enlisted.

"Yeah, he has a thing with his girlfriend tonight that she wants him to go to instead."

"That's okay, I'll meet him later."

"If he even lasts on the team."

"Why wouldn't he?"

The doors to the elevator opened, and David shrugged as he started to walk out.

"Not everyone makes the cut."

Audrey had a feeling there was more to it than that, but she didn't want to push. If David wanted to talk about it, he would. Things were good between them right now, despite the fact that their parents were reaching out to him again now that Audrey had moved here, and she didn't want to mess with that.

"Well, if he lasts, then I'll meet him," she said teasingly, tucking herself under David's arm again and giving his hard body a squeeze. Yup, definitely not the same as Mason's. "In the meantime, we'll have fun tonight."

"Yes, we will. You and Mick will be able to trade baking tips—although make sure that his doesn't include adding weed to the brownies," David added a little grimly, making Audrey laugh.

Mick was Jensen's cousin, who also baked, mostly as a side hustle for the local farmers' market on weekends. She'd heard the story about how Cassidy had eaten two of his special brownies before going to the job interview where Grandma had hired her. She'd been high, David had been pissed, and Grandma had been delighted.

"As long as you're not trying to set me up with him." She was looking forward to meeting him, but not like that.

"I pinky promise I'm not." David held out his free hand with his fingers tucked in except his pinkie. Audrey curled her pinkie around his, and they shook on it. She couldn't keep the smile from her face. When they'd been kids, pinkie promises had been the ultimate agreement, and she loved that David remembered that.

It wasn't that she'd sworn off men or anything after Cash. She did want to date. But she wanted to get the bakery open first, and *then* she'd think about dating.

And it was just a coincidence that Mason's face flashed through her mind again.

CHAPTER TWO

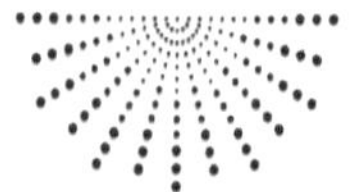

Fuck.

Mason gave himself a shake as he walked through the hall of Black Fox to his office, feeling unsteady on his feet. He had never in his life been hit like a lightning bolt when it came to a woman. Sure, there had been times in high school that he'd experienced an instant reaction to something.

But nothing had prepared him for Audrey Bowers' effect on him.

Her curves.

The pin-up style that was hotter than it had any right to be.

He hadn't even known he liked pin-ups.

If someone had asked his type before this moment, he would have told them that he liked elegance. Smoothness. Calm. Serenity. That he preferred brunettes over blondes, though he wasn't going to reject anyone based on something so superficial.

He would not have pictured bubbly warmth and chirpiness, with miles of curves packed into polka dots. He would not have pictured bright red hair and redder lips that curved into a beaming smile.

"Fuck," he muttered under his breath, stopping outside his office to press his head against the wall. Closing his eyes, he took a deep

breath. "You are a psychologist. You know your reaction is just a combination of a dopamine, norepinephrine, and serotonin release. It doesn't mean anything."

The only thing it meant was that she was the first person to make him react in such a manner.

He suddenly had a much better understanding of what others had gone through. Even though he understood the process, there had always been a part of him that felt sure people exaggerated when they described how they felt. Secretly, he'd worried there was something wrong with him that he'd never felt that way, and it was easier to attribute it to others' exaggerating rather than him being different.

Well.

Turned out he wasn't that different.

Why now?

Why not a year ago? A month ago? Hell, why not yesterday, before Yasmine and I agreed to get married?

Before he'd asked his parents to arrange his marriage would have been even better, but definitely before he and Yasmine had agreed to it.

His phone buzzed in his pocket and immediately buzzed again. He pulled it out to see who was calling. His mother. Of course. As always, her timing was impeccable.

It occurred to him that the description he would have given for his 'type' when it came to women closely matched the description he would give of his mother. *Take a break, Oedipus. We like what we know.*

Taking a deep breath, Mason straightened up and answered the phone.

"Hello."

"Mason, sweetheart! Your dad and I are putting together the list of people to call about your engagement, and we wanted to know if you wanted us to call Asad and Cyrus, have their parents tell them, or if you wanted to speak with them yourselves." His mother's smooth, low voice was laced with unusual excitement.

He suddenly wished he hadn't answered the phone.

This was what he got for letting his parents arrange his marriage. They were far more involved than they would have been otherwise.

If only he'd been a little less impatient to get his life started. A little less impatient to 'catch up' to Asad and Cyrus, his cousins, who were more like brothers. Cyrus had gotten married last year, and Asad was planning his proposal to his girlfriend, and Mason…

He'd gotten jealous. He was man enough to admit that.

Jealous and worried he was being left behind. He'd had no girl-friend, no one he was interested in dating, and nothing about his past relationships made him think he was going to suddenly find 'the one'. Letting his parents arrange his marriage had seemed practical.

Logical.

Easy.

"Mason?"

"Sorry, Mom. Um, I'll tell them myself." Otherwise, they'd be calling him as soon as they heard the news, anyway. Plus, he needed to think of the best way to phrase it. To explain.

"Okay. We're planning to start calling tomorrow. You're still telling your friends tonight, right?"

"Right."

Because his parents had done the impossible and managed to find a woman who wanted the same things out of life that he did, was also willing to have her marriage arranged, and she was even his described type. And kinky. They'd had several long talks about what they wanted from a marriage. She checked all the boxes on paper.

And she was even friends with a lot of his friends.

They'd never tried dating before for a myriad of reasons, but once their parents set them up, well… it just made sense. They were both ready to be married. They got along well. Mason liked her. A lot.

But he'd never felt like he'd been hit with a brick by her.

It was a weird chemical reaction in my brain. Tonight will be different. It's probably a completely, if unexpected, natural reaction to knowing that I'm announcing my engagement. A lot of people have second thoughts before making a major life change.

I don't even know Audrey.

My brain is just playing tricks on me because making a lifelong commitment is scary. It should be scary. This just proves that I'm taking it seriously.

That was exactly the advice he would give any client who came to him with this problem.

"We're telling our friends tonight," he said firmly. "You can start calling everyone tomorrow."

"Wonderful, we're so excited. Yasmine is such a lovely girl."

"She is."

She really was. And now that he'd gotten a little space from his sudden, shocking reaction to Audrey, he could see it for what it really was. An aberration. A natural response to knowing he was taking the first step toward the rest of his life this evening. Marriage was serious. He took the commitment seriously.

Perhaps he should have expected to be tested. A lot of people struggled, and that was when they were in love with their intended. Mason was approaching marriage a little differently, with a well-thought-out, practical plan for his life. It shouldn't be surprising that his brain would react with a roadblock that was purely emotional and physical.

Now that he'd gotten past it, everything would be fine.

AUDREY

Jensen's house was everything that had been described and more.

"This is amazing!" She stared in awe at the front. Three stories up. A massive front porch, which was still covered in Halloween decorations. She assumed those would be coming down soon.

"It is, isn't it?" Cassidy beamed as she stood on the other side of Audrey's grandmother, letting Grandma lean on her arm as they went up the steps. The house had double doors. Huge, dark, heavy wood doors that were ornately carved. The doorknob looked like brass. "Living here felt like being on a movie set."

"I want to get one of those flowy robes and appear in the windows at random to passersby," Audrey said enthusiastically. She could already picture how cool that would look. This kind of house was made for a dramatic robe. The kind widows wore in movies when they'd killed their husbands, and the police showed up to question them. "Do you think they'd let me do that next Halloween?"

Grandma and Cassidy both laughed.

"Just wait till you see the inside; you're going to want to just walk up and down the main staircase in that robe. Maybe lounge around the furniture," Cassidy teased.

"It would make a great movie set." Grandma looked around. "You could do horror. Or a historical movie. Or maybe a porn."

"Grandma." David groaned as he joined them on the porch. His arms were loaded with boxes of desserts Audrey had made for tonight, including all three kinds of baklava she'd made for Mason to try. She felt a little guilty looking at her brother's overloaded arms, but he'd insisted he could carry everything and wouldn't let her take any.

"I'm just saying."

"I wish you would stop."

Audrey giggled as she rang the doorbell. It hadn't taken her long to realize that Grandma liked to say outrageous things just to make David react. Granted, she also just liked to say outrageous things, but she was a little worse when David was around. It was highly entertaining.

A handsome man with brown hair opened the door. Very handsome, with a boyish face and a beaming smile. Yet she didn't have the same reaction to him that she'd had to David's other teammate earlier.

"Hey, hey, everyone. Come on in."

They all piled inside, David immediately heading deeper into the house with the boxes of food while Audrey stood awestruck in the foyer. There was an actual chandelier above her head. A real crystal chandelier. The inside of the house somehow managed to be even more impressive than the outside. She felt like she'd stepped back in time. Everything was carved wood, stained glass, marble, and covered in ornate wallpaper.

"Holy crap... this house is *amazing*."

"Thanks." Jensen, who had been introduced before David took off, looked around, shoving his hands in his pockets. "We can't take credit for it. The guy who owned it before had it restored to what it looked like when it was originally built in the twenties."

"Don't ever change it."

He chuckled.

"We don't plan to. Come in and meet everyone who's here already, then I'll give you the tour." He said it in a completely non-smarmy way, so Audrey didn't have to worry that he meant it the way her parents' friends' sons had when they'd offer a 'tour' of the premises and really meant a tour of the inside of their pants. She wouldn't have expected any of David's team to be smarmy, anyway.

"Sounds great."

Inside meant moving to the left, where she did her best not to be distracted by the gorgeous living and dining rooms and focus on the people instead. Most of whom were standing around the dining room table where food had been laid out. David rejoined them, sticking close to her side as he introduced her to his boss, Lincoln, and Lincoln's wife, Ashley.

There was a pretty big age difference between them, but it was clear from the way they looked at each other that the love was real. Audrey was used to seeing some big age gaps with her parents' set; what she wasn't used to was thinking that the couple looked completely in love. She was used to more transactional relationships. Which she didn't judge anyone for, but it wasn't what she wanted for herself.

It was nice to see that love still existed and not just for David and Cassidy.

Drew, another member of David's team, and his wife, Naomi, were also clear examples of a couple who were happily married and in love. The moment after Drew shook Audrey's hand, his arm went immediately around Naomi's waist again, tucking her close against him, and she leaned into him. Good grief. Audrey was surrounded by happy couples.

Thank goodness for Jensen and his brother, who came out of the kitchen with trays bearing the treats Audrey had made for the party, so she didn't feel so alone in her singledom. She and her grandma.

After being introduced to Mick, Audrey was given the promised tour by Jensen. The house was truly amazing. The stained glass went through all the upstairs rooms, the bathrooms had clawfoot tubs, and the wallpaper was constantly changing, yet somehow always fitting the space. Whoever had designed the place had a real talent. The decor was overwhelming in the best way possible.

"This is amazing, thank you for showing me around," she said as they made their way back down the main staircase. She absolutely understood what Cassidy meant about sweeping up and down it in a dramatic robe. Heck, she wanted to run around the whole damn house in one.

"Absolutely. I enjoy showing it off, even though I had nothing to do with it, other than having the good sense to buy it." Jensen grinned at her, his head cocking to the side as the noise from downstairs increased again. They'd heard several people arriving while he'd been giving the tour. "Sounds like another one has arrived. I think that must be everyone."

They turned the corner, heading from the second floor down to the first. There was a landing on the staircase before the final set into the foyer, with a bench seat and a massive stained-glass window. It looked like the perfect place to sit and read, and Audrey was wildly jealous.

Not as jealous as she was a moment later when they turned the corner and started down the stairs, and she saw who had just come in.

Mason.

And his arm was around a beautiful woman.

An *incredibly* beautiful woman. One who looked like a model.

A woman who was the opposite of Audrey in every way.

Tall. Not quite as tall as Mason, but only an inch or two shorter. Slim with perky breasts that would probably never sag, even as she aged. Pointed cheekbones that were definitely not from Maybelline. Long silky black hair that flowed over her shoulders and down her back and probably never experienced a moment of frizz. Tanned skin that had probably never turned lobster red under the sun. Her eyelashes looked too long to be real, yet Audrey was willing to bet good money they weren't fake.

It's not fair.

Of course, Mason wasn't single. Of course, his girlfriend was a goddess.

And yet, when his gaze lifted and met hers, her heart still skipped a beat.

"Jensen. Audrey." He hesitated as the woman next to him smiled, which made her even more beautiful, as impossible as that should be. "Audrey, this is my fiancée, Yasmine. Yasmine, this is David's sister, Audrey."

Audrey forced an answering smile onto her face even though the inside of her chest suddenly hurt so much, it felt hard to breathe.

"Hi!" She hurried forward, reaching out with her hand to greet Mason's fiancée, and managed to trip on something because she wasn't looking where she was going. Instead of a calm, collected handshake and welcome, she face-planted right at the golden couple's feet.

I hate my life.

CHAPTER THREE

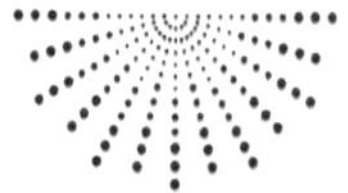

MASON

"Holy shit, Audrey, are you okay?" The words burst out of him as he let go of Yasmine's waist, both of them immediately bending down to help her up. Was she hurt? Why wasn't she moving?

"Nope." Her muffled answer made his blood run cold, but then he relaxed at her next words. "Just leave me here to die, please."

Yasmine laughed, sliding her hands under one of Audrey's arms as he did the other. Jensen was already hurrying up, too, a horrified and slightly guilty expression on his face.

"Shit, Audrey, please tell me you're not hurt," Jensen said as Mason and Yasmine got her up. Mason tried to ignore the way his palms felt warmer where he touched her and how his pulse started racing as he felt the softness of her skin.

He'd thought the weird reaction to her would have already dissipated, but apparently, it was going to take a little longer. Maybe after he and Yasmine made their announcement and his brain accepted that yes, he really was getting married and committing himself to one person for the rest of his life. This was just an early, unexpected version of cold feet.

As soon as she was on her feet, he dropped his hands and stepped away from her. It was wrong to be this attracted to another woman when his fiancée was standing right there, even if their relationship was an arranged one. While he couldn't help the attraction, he could at least keep his distance and not touch the object of it.

"Just my dignity," Audrey said, brushing her pants and avoiding everyone's gaze as several others started coming in to see what all the noise was about. She was wearing the same outfit she had been in earlier that day, her bouncy ponytail drawing his attention as she moved.

Stop looking.

"Don't worry about it, we all trip sometimes," Yasmine reassured her, smoothing things over exactly the way Mason would have expected her to. Her kindness was one of the things he really liked about her. "It's nice to officially meet you."

"You, too." Audrey's cheeks were a hot, bright red, and she groaned as her brother came in, wanting to know what the 'thud' they'd heard was.

Mason couldn't help but feel sorry for her. He wanted to tell her that even her fall had been cute, but he didn't think that was appropriate.

"Hey, Mason, did you just call Yasmine your fiancée?" Jensen asked. Since the rest of the team—sans Zeus—was all now gathered in the foyer, as well as David's grandmother, Mason guessed they were making the big announcement. Jennifer, Black Fox's receptionist/office manager, gasped as she looked back and forth between him and Yasmine.

"Yes," he confirmed, lifting Yasmine's hand to show off the ring. They'd gone the other day to pick it out together. "We're getting married."

A round of 'congratulations' was immediately offered, some of them sounding a little confused. Which wasn't a surprise. Other than David, Mason hadn't even told any of the team that he was letting his parents arrange his marriage. It had felt too weird.

"You guys were dating?" Jensen asked. He turned to Claudia, who was their team's sniper as well as being one of Yasmine's friends. She was also a Dominatrix at the BDSM club they all belonged to. "I didn't know they were dating. Did you know they were dating?"

"Well… I knew what was going on." Claudia raised her eyebrow at Mason. "I don't know that I would call it dating since Mason asked his parents to arrange his marriage, and they picked Yasmine. There wasn't much dating involved. And I didn't hear anything about it from Mason, just Yasmine."

"You didn't tell them we were getting engaged?" Yasmine elbowed him in the side, looking a bit exasperated. Mason covered the spot protectively before she could do it again. "I gave all of my friends a heads-up."

"I figured it would be easier to tell them all at once." Because then he wouldn't have to explain it over and over again.

"But this party is to welcome Audrey to Pittsburgh."

"Yeah, but everyone's here for it." From the look she was giving him, that did not excuse not telling them. "I didn't think it would be that big a deal."

"Men." Yasmine rolled her eyes. She directed another smile at Audrey. "Sorry. I knew Mason wanted to tell everyone that we were officially engaged tonight, but I thought he'd prepped them all. We didn't mean to steal your thunder."

Oh. *Oh.*

He hadn't thought about it that way. It just seemed practical to make the announcement when everyone was gathered. Plus, he'd figured the focus would be on Audrey's arrival, so that there would be less attention paid to him and Yasmine.

It hadn't occurred to him that they might pull attention from her that was supposed to be hers.

"Sorry, I definitely didn't mean to do that," he said, feeling chagrined now as he looked at Audrey. "I was hoping we'd kind of fly under the radar since tonight is about you."

"Oh, thanks," Yasmine teased him. "Under the radar is exactly how I always dreamed of my engagement."

Mason threw his hands up in the air. "Sorry, sorry. I've never been engaged before. I don't know how to do this."

"It's fine, I'm just messing with you." Yasmine snickered, and he mock-scowled at her.

See? This was why they worked. They were comfortable with each other. They got along. The fact that she didn't make his skin tingle and that he was hyperaware of another woman when he was beside her... well, that didn't have to mean anything. It was just a strange version of cold feet.

"I'm confused," Audrey said, looking back and forth between them, hesitation all over her face. She wasn't the only one.

"Right. Let's go into the other room and get some food, then we'll explain everything." He put his hand on the small of Yasmine's back, turning her toward the living room.

Touching her in front of Audrey shouldn't make him feel weird. Or wrong. If anything, it should be the other way around. His brain needed to get back on board with what was happening.

Everyone dutifully followed them into the other room, some of them taking the time to grab their own plates and drinks before arranging themselves around the living room. All together, they filled up both of the couches and the chairs that were available, leaving some standing room.

Audrey was across from him, allowing him to see her every expression, as much as he tried not to look.

Audrey

An arranged marriage? That's what Claudia had said, though she hadn't realized those still existed outside of books. At least, not in the sense that Mason and Yasmine had done.

Although when she thought about it, hadn't that been what her parents had done with her and Cash? They'd been the ones to introduce them. They'd been incredibly encouraging of her and Cash dating. They'd been dropping hints about marriage. They'd been the ones trying to push her and Cash back together after she caught him cheating red-handed. Them and his parents, although he'd been on board for all of it, too.

She might not have asked them to arrange her marriage, but wasn't that exactly what they'd tried to do?

There were a lot of marriages 'arranged' among their group, when she looked at it that way.

"So, you're just marrying who your parents are telling you to?" Mick asked, looking horrified.

Audrey dipped her head, lifting her drink to her lips to cover her smile. At least she knew she wasn't the only one feeling that way. While her parents might have done their best to maneuver things, the idea of *asking* them to take control of her life in such a way was terrifying.

"No." Mason shook his head.

She tried not to look directly at him because when she looked directly at him, it was hard to deny how attracted to him she was. Knowing he wasn't in love with Yasmine, that it was arranged, made her feel a little less like an awful person, but the fact remained that he was still taken, and lusting after him was wrong.

"I just realized that I've never had thoughts of marrying any of my girlfriends, but I am now ready for marriage, and I want kids and a partner, and I figured my parents know me really well, and they might do a better job of setting me up for that than I was doing for myself."

Mick still looked horrified at the explanation.

Grandma nudged Audrey with her elbow.

"You should let me arrange your marriage," she whispered gleefully, a rather frightening look in her eyes.

"No, thank you," Audrey whispered back. Her grandmother would probably do a better job than her parents, but she'd just gotten full control over her life for the first time in her life. Giving it away again was not on her to-do list.

"Come on, I bet I'd be good at it." Grandma lifted her hands from her lap, spreading them apart as if to describe the size of something. "I'll get you one with a giant—"

"Brenda," Cassidy whispered repressively from Grandma's other side, cutting her off at what was probably exactly the right time. Despite interrupting, she was still grinning in amusement.

Leaning against the arm of the couch on her other side, David had his arms crossed, and he was glaring at Grandma, who either didn't notice or was really good at pretending not to see him.

Which was when Audrey realized everyone was listening to Brenda's whispers and that Mason and Yasmine had stopped talking. Which meant everyone had heard Brenda's offer to find Audrey a man with a giant *something*.

As if her dignity hadn't already fallen flat on its face tonight.

She could feel her cheeks turning red again.

"So, um, what about you?" she asked Yasmine. "If it's okay to ask."

"It's okay. You're probably the only one here, well, and maybe Mick, who doesn't know I'm cursed."

Cursed?

"You're cursed?" Mick threw his hands up in the air. "Jensen never tells me anything."

"I told you about her curse."

"Did not."

"Did too!"

"Um, how are you cursed?" Audrey asked, trying to ignore the brothers' back and forth, as distracting as it was. The fact that no one had reacted like Yasmine was joking was very intriguing. Even her grandma didn't bat an eye at the statement.

"My dating life is cursed. Everyone I date since college or even get involved in a serious relationship with, not only does it not work out, but after we break up, they find 'the one.'" Yasmine made the statement completely matter-of-factly.

"The first time, I was kind of happy for them. It hadn't been a bad breakup, and I was glad he'd found what he wanted. The second time seemed like coincidence. By the sixth time, it was hard not to feel cursed. After the tenth time, I'd given up, so when my parents said they knew someone who was looking to arrange their marriage, and they thought we'd be a good match… well, it seemed like maybe this is the way to break the curse."

"No dating, straight to marriage. Do not pass go, do not collect two hundred dollars." Everyone laughed at the moment. Sitting in one of the armchairs was the gorgeous Black woman who'd made the comment. She'd come in while Audrey was getting the tour, and they hadn't been officially introduced yet, but from that joke alone, Audrey was pretty sure she was going to like her.

"I don't need two hundred dollars anyway," Yasmine retorted. "I need the curse lifted."

"Here's hoping," Ashley said, lifting her glass as she leaned into her handsome husband.

The group talk broke apart again into smaller groups, and David pulled Audrey up so he could introduce her to the young woman who'd made the Monopoly joke since she was the only person there that Audrey hadn't met yet. Her name was Jennifer, and she worked as the receptionist at Black Fox, though David immediately said that she was more of an office manager. She was working there while getting her Masters in Human Resources Management, which sounded incredibly intimidating to Audrey.

"Hey, Jennifer," Jensen called over, interrupting the conversation. "Did you see that we found some new spicy pickles?"

Immediately, Jennifer brightened up and then pulled back, wary. "Not your crazy hot spicy like you like it, right?"

"No, normal people spice," Jensen reassured her, making several people who overheard his remark laugh.

"Excuse me," Jennifer said, smiling at Audrey to take the sting out of her departure. "It seems I have a pickle to try."

"That's not the pickle he wants to give her," Grandma muttered under her breath as Jennifer walked away, headed for the dining room where Jensen was waiting. He had a plate with a pickle on it, and the way he was looking at her, it did seem like he might be interested in her.

"If Jensen ever offers you food, ask for a heat level before you take a bite," Cassidy advised Audrey, ignoring Brenda's comment.

David was dragging his hand down over his face, looking as if he wanted to groan but was trying to hold it in so Grandma wouldn't think that she was getting to him. If he was going to be such a drama queen, he might as well make the noise, too, but that was just Audrey's opinion.

Since Jennifer was now preoccupied, David pulled her over to say hi to Claudia, who Audrey *had* met before, but it had been over a year ago. The slender brunette was as intimidating as ever. She was also, unfortunately, talking to Mason and Yasmine, which meant that Audrey couldn't *not* look at them.

Yasmine was so nice, Audrey couldn't even dislike her. She immediately started asking Audrey questions about the bakery, how the move was going, what her plans were, and she was really listening.

"I'm a financial advisor, certified, so if you ever have any questions about the financial side of the business, please come to me. If I don't know the answer, I'll at least know who to send you to so you can get one," Yasmine offered.

"Oh, thank you, that's amazing."

"Absolutely. It's important for business-minded women to stick together." Yasmine smiled at her. "I help Naomi with the non-profit and give financial literacy courses to the women there."

"I'm taking one," Cassidy said, raising her hand a little. "Yasmine is a great teacher. Don handled everything for us, so I'm having to learn everything from scratch now."

"And you're doing great." Yasmine grinned at her. She glanced down at her watch. "Speaking of, I really should get going. It's getting late, and I have an early morning class to teach tomorrow at a church before their service."

"I'll walk you out," Mason said immediately.

They really did look perfect together. Like they'd stepped right out of a magazine ad. Even their energy matched. It might make Audrey's heart ache a little because she already had a crush on Mason, even though she'd just met him—silly to deny it—but obviously, Yasmine deserved happiness. She hoped this arrangement gave them both everything they wanted.

"Thanks." Yasmine smiled back at him.

"You aren't leaving together?" Claudia asked.

"No, we drove separately because Yasmine knew she had an early morning tomorrow."

"I didn't want to make Mason leave the party early with me," Yasmine explained. "He shouldn't have to adhere to my schedule, especially when it's a gathering with his team." She turned to Audrey, reaching out her hand, which Audrey automatically met with her own. "Audrey, it was so nice to meet you. I'm sure I'll be seeing more of you."

"Same, it was great to meet you," Audrey said. Other than the fact that she'd been attracted to Mason before she knew he was taken and then face-planted in front of both of them, it really had been nice to meet Yasmine. She liked her. She'd push past this attraction to Yasmine's fiancé thing. It wasn't like she really knew the guy. Once she got to know him, the whole intimidating *'He looks like a god, and I can't stop staring at him'* thing would go away.

"You should come to game night. And book club." Yasmine grinned as she walked away, Mason at her side.

"Game night? Book club?" Audrey turned to look at Cassidy and her brother, expecting they must have an explanation.

"Game night is at my place every Thursday," Claudia said, though her attention was on Yasmine and Mason, watching them walk away. Her expression was completely neutral, making it impossible to tell what she was thinking. "Ladies only."

"And book club?"

Cassidy groaned and looped her arm through Audrey's. "Your grandmother roped us in. Come on, I'll let her tell you about it."

"I'll… I'll be elsewhere," David said immediately, backing away and following after Mason and Yasmine, who were headed toward Lincoln, Ashley, Drew, and Naomi. The quartet was standing on the opposite side of the room from Grandma, who had cornered Mick and was discussing something with him rather enthusiastically. He looked interested in whatever she was saying, bending his head so he could hear her better. If he wasn't forty-some years younger than her, Audrey would have thought they were flirting.

"Why doesn't my brother want to hear about book club?" Audrey asked, amused.

"Again. I'll let your grandmother tell you about it. Although... do you know what hucows are?"

"What *what* are?"

CHAPTER FOUR

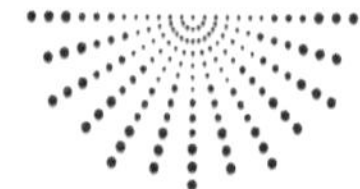

"That was fun," Yasmine said, as Mason closed Jensen's front door behind them. "Audrey seems really nice. Is David excited to have her here?"

"He is. It's hard to read him sometimes, but I know he's glad she came, although I think he's a little worried about what it means for interactions with his parents. She's still in touch with them even though he's not." Mason walked over and held out his arm for Yasmine to take so he could help her down the stairs.

The heels she was wearing weren't very high, but it would still be easier for her to get down the stairs of the front porch with someone to lean on. Plus, that's what he should do as her fiancé. Make sure she was being taken care of and make sure she was safe.

"Well, hopefully, it will turn out okay. Do we know if she's kinky?"

Fuck. Mason hoped not. The only thing worse than seeing her casually at events like this would be seeing her at the club.

"I have no idea."

Yasmine snickered, glancing at him as they reached the bottom of the stairs.

"You should see the look on your face. Are you worried David would freak out?"

"Yes." That was something he was worried about now that she'd brought it up. It was definitely a consideration. "Not freak out, maybe, but I'm not sure how he'd handle it."

"You know it's not your job to handle everyone's emotions and reactions just because you're the team therapist, right?" she teased.

"Then what else are they paying me for?"

They both laughed.

But it felt weird. Something felt strained now that they'd made their announcement to their friends. Things felt off between them, instead of comfortably settled as they had been before.

"So," Yasmine said as they neared her car. "We did it. We announced it."

"Yeah. Does it feel a little odd to have it out in the open?" he asked hesitantly. He didn't want to make her feel bad about it, but her demeanor made him wonder if she felt the same way.

Her shoulders sagged with relief when he said it.

"Okay, so it's not just me? It feels more awkward now than it did before?" she asked, turning to face him and searching his expression. Her dark eyes were wide, her face lit by the streetlamps above the line of cars. She was stunningly beautiful. Gorgeous, in fact.

The kind of woman who turned heads when she walked down the street.

But he'd never felt the same surge of desire for her that he'd felt the moment he'd laid eyes on Audrey.

Maybe it was time to try to correct that.

"It'll get better," he reassured her in a murmur, bending his head down to press his lips against hers, reaching to put his hands on her hips and pull her body toward him.

They'd kissed before. A peck on the cheek, a perfunctory brush of the lips. Both of them knew they weren't getting into this because of some mad passion or love. That wasn't what they were expecting. It wasn't what they'd agreed upon.

But they'd just announced their engagement. They should do

something to level up this relationship. Especially if it would help him stop thinking about a certain redhead.

Yasmine stiffened as he pulled her against him, and their lips met. Mason did his best to kiss her with all the passion he saw David kiss Cassidy with. That Drew kissed Naomi with. But she remained stiff against him, though her lips parted. Their tongues touched.

It was…

Not passionate.

That was definitely not the word for what he felt.

He was pretty sure she wasn't feeling passionate, either.

Swiftly ending the kiss, Mason lifted his head, trying not to let the disturbance he felt show in his expression. He liked Yasmine, dammit. He didn't want to hurt her feelings. But it was a relief to see that she looked concerned as well.

"Um."

"I just thought we should try a real kiss," he explained. "Now that we're out as engaged."

"Right. That was a good idea. I don't object, I just think I wasn't prepared." She didn't move away from him, but the awkwardness between them was growing. Standing with his arm around her felt odd. As though they were invading each other's space rather than enjoying the closeness.

"Should we try again?"

"Um."

Dammit. If he wasn't feeling so guilty about his attraction to Audrey, he might be insulted that Yasmine clearly wasn't excited about kissing him again. Then again, even if Audrey didn't exist, he wasn't feeling excited about it, either. Mason didn't have a sister, but he imagined this was what kissing his sister might feel like. Except he would never kiss his sister with tongue.

Obviously, this was something they were going to need to get past. Just not tonight. They couldn't force things.

"Maybe tomorrow?" he suggested. "We should start trying to get used to the physical side of the relationship."

"We should. I think I just need to readjust my mindset," Yasmine agreed quickly. "I know we've been talking about marriage and talking about having kids and everything, but we haven't... done anything. It's just a shift, going from thinking of you as a friend to, um, romance."

"Yeah, it is. Like I said, we'll get better at it." He dropped his hands from her hips, easing back. The distance eased some of the awkwardness between them, to his relief, the expression on her face echoing how he felt. "It's a shift for both of us. Maybe next Friday at the club we could try a scene?"

Even though they were both kinky and both had been members of the Outlands for a long time, they'd never scened together. Although he wouldn't have said he had anything against scening with her, Mason hadn't wanted to risk the curse. He wasn't interested in marriage until recently, and the idea of dating her and then accidentally ending up in a relationship that required settling down hadn't appealed.

"Yeah, that sounds good. We should do that." She smiled, her shoulders relaxing. Mason wasn't sure if she was relaxing because he had suggested a scene and she thought the kink would help, or if because they had a week before they had to try romance again.

He was a good kisser. He was a good Dom.

Next week, he'd be able to prove that to her.

Holding the door open for her, he waited until she was in her car to close it. She gave him a little wave through the window, which he returned before returning to the sidewalk. Watching her drive away, he let out a long sigh.

Maybe he should just head home.

But if he did that, it would be admitting that Audrey had gotten under his skin; the only reason he wouldn't be going back inside to spend time with his friends was her. Or, more accurately, the guilt he felt over his reaction to her. Maybe what he needed wasn't distance from Audrey—which he'd gotten plenty of all afternoon, and it hadn't helped—but exposure therapy.

Most people tended to annoy him after a while. If he spent more time around her this evening, surely she would do something annoying, then he could get back to his planned future with Yasmine without Audrey taking up space in the back of his mind.

AUDREY

As Cassidy and Audrey came up behind Audrey's grandmother, to her shock, Mick pulled up his shirt. Not that he was looking at her and Cassidy. Nope. He was looking at her grandmother and grinning as he showed off an admittedly impressive set of abs.

"Ooh, you really do have a six-pack!" Grandma said, reaching out and putting the hand that wasn't holding her drink on them.

"Brenda!"

"Grandma!"

Cassidy and Audrey reacted at the same time. Grandma lifted her head away from Mick's abs, turning to look at them, but she didn't move her hand.

"You two should come feel these; they're great," she said, grinning widely. "Mick has a very impressive body."

"Thanks, Brenda," Mick replied, winking at her, still happily holding his shirt up for her convenience. Audrey was starting to have more sympathy for David's dramatics about their grandmother's antics.

"Mick, pull your shirt down and find someone else to talk to," Cassidy ordered. "We want to talk to Brenda about book club."

"Maybe I can talk about book club, too," he said, obediently lowering his shirt. "I can read."

Grandma pouted and shot Cassidy a dark look as she was forced to remove her hand from his stomach.

"Her book club is all women."

"Oh, okay then." Mick shrugged and winked at Brenda again as he started to walk away. "If you want a ticket to the gun show later, just let me know."

"The gun show?" Audrey asked, confused.

Immediately, Mick halted and lifted his arms, curling his fists in to show them off—although since he was wearing a long-sleeve shirt, it didn't have quite the same effect as if his arms were bare.

"These guns."

"Mick, what the hell are you doing?" Jensen called from across the room, causing Mick to chuckle and drop his arms, heading for his brother.

"I'm definitely going to the gun show later, and you can't stop me," Grandma told Cassidy.

"You know he's, like, at least thirty years younger than you, right?"

"I'm a cougar. Rawr." Grandma made a clawing motion with the hand she'd been feeling Mick up with before taking another sip of her drink. She was still giving Cassidy a dark look. "You'd better be careful, Cassidy. I'm starting to think David passed his butt stick on to you."

"His what?" Audrey felt like her brain was melting.

"I think Audrey should come to book club," Cassidy said, ignoring Grandma's diversions, which was probably the best way to handle things. And it gave Audrey a moment to realize that Grandma probably meant David had a stick up his butt, and he'd passed it on to Cassidy.

That seemed like something she would say.

Thankfully, Cassidy's statement had the exact effect she'd probably intended. Grandma perked up immediately.

"You absolutely should come to book club. Our next meeting is in two Sundays—not next Sunday, but two Sundays from tomorrow. How fast do you read?" Grandma's entire focus was on Audrey now, eagerness lighting up her expression.

"Um, it usually takes me a few days to finish a book, but I'm going to have a lot going on with the bakery opening soon—"

"Oh, don't worry about that. *Milking Mina* isn't too long."

"Milking what?" Yup, back to her brain melting.

"*Milking Mina*. It's a hucow romance." Grandma said it so matter-of-factly that Audrey was starting to feel like the crazy one for not knowing what a hucow was. She looked at Cassidy, who shrugged.

"I wasn't joking about the hucow thing," Cassidy said, giggling.

"But what does being a human cow mean?" Audrey asked plaintively. She really had thought Cassidy was kidding, so she hadn't asked for more details.

"Like pet play but with cows."

"What's pet play?"

Cassidy and Grandma exchanged a glance. Grandma appeared amused, while Cassidy was more concerned.

"Um, how much do you know about kink?" Cassidy asked gently.

"Kink?"

"Oh, dear," Cassidy muttered.

That began a very quick discussion of the kind of romances Audrey's grandmother liked to read. Audrey had heard of *Fifty Shades of Grey*, briefly, but she'd never read it. Her mother didn't approve of reading romance, although Audrey had managed to sneak a few into her repertoire now and then.

None that had sex in them, much less the kind of things Cassidy and Grandma described.

Pet play was people actually pretending to be pets. Crawling around on hands and knees, acting like animals, and wearing plug tails. Audrey decided not to ask what a plug tail was. If it was what she was picturing, that was not a discussion she wanted to have with her grandmother. She could ask Cassidy later. If it wasn't too awkward to ask the woman, she was pretty sure would be her future sister-in-law.

"Great. Okay." Book club with her grandmother talking about kinky books. Sounded… interesting.

"Claudia and Naomi have joined, too," Cassidy told her, a little smile on her face like she knew what Audrey was thinking. She probably could guess pretty easily. "Brenda is still working on trying to get Ashley and Jennifer to join."

"Who else is in it?"

"Some of my friends." Grandma smiled serenely. "They're fun, you'll like them."

"Great. So, um. What was the name of the book again?" Audrey pulled out her phone to order it. It turned out it was part of a series, though she was reassured she didn't need to read the whole series to jump into that one, which was good because it was a long series.

As she was putting her phone away, the front door opened, and Mason walked back in. Alone. His gaze scanned the room and clashed with hers, and Audrey's traitorous heart did a little flip.

Dammit.

He's taken, stop it.

Tearing her gaze away, she looked over at the dining room. It was definitely time for a cupcake.

CHAPTER FIVE

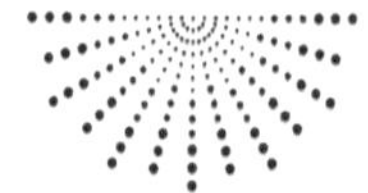

Cupcake acquired, Audrey found herself pulled into conversation with Naomi and Claudia, who were thrilled Audrey would be joining them for book club. Her grandmother had apparently already run around telling the rest of the women that Audrey would be joining them. Which meant she really had no choice but to read the hucow book.

"I've never really read romance before," Audrey admitted, though she didn't tell them why. She felt too embarrassed about being a grown woman who cared about her mother's opinion of her reading choices.

As she spoke, her gaze drifted over to where Mason was looking at the desserts, which meant she caught the exact moment he saw all the baklava. Did her heart do a little flip again as he began to load up his plate? Yes, yes, it did.

"Neither had Claudia," Naomi said, snickering as she cast a glance at the bossy brunette, who didn't seem bothered by Naomi's amusement.

"I still don't know what I'm doing as part of this club; these books make no sense."

"The hucow thing?" Audrey asked, jerking her attention back to the other two women and away from Mason, who had just taken a bite of baklava and was just standing there with his eyes closed, chewing. She turned toward Naomi so she couldn't see Mason anymore. Watching him was going to give her heart palpitations.

"No, the heroine thing." Claudia scowled at Naomi's answering snicker and focused on Audrey, who knew her confusion was showing on her face. "These heroines make no sense. I started getting book suggestions I'd never gotten before, thanks to book club, and some of them sounded pretty good, so I figured I'd read them."

"The fact that you like the smutty parts has nothing to do with it," Naomi quipped, skillfully stepping sideways as Claudia reached out to poke her.

"That doesn't hurt, but the heroines." Claudia threw her hands up in the air, one more gently than the other since it was holding her drink. "They drive me nuts!"

She pointed a finger at Audrey.

"If you were drowning in debt from your mother's medical bills and she needed another procedure done, and your billionaire boss was dating you and wanted to pay for your meals and clothing and give you a place to live, wouldn't you be relieved? Wouldn't you say yes?"

"Um… probably." Audrey had a feeling that was the right answer. And it did make sense. "Does he know I'm drowning in debt from my mother's medical bills?"

"Sometimes." Claudia waved her hand. "It doesn't really matter either way. The number of heroines who refuse to let this crazy rich man pay for *anything* for them, even if they're only eating one meal a day, is freaking unrealistic. If I was dating a rich guy, he'd be paying for *everything*."

"Sure he would," Naomi murmured, winking at Audrey and ignoring Claudia's glare at her. Which was impressive because it was a really intimidating glare.

"They don't let the hero take care of them. Ever. He usually has to force his way into her rundown apartment with a shoddy lock so he can care for her when she's too sick to stand, much less cook for herself and eat it. But oh no, I'm Miss Independent woman." Claudia snorted. "And that's just the beginning of the too-stupid-to-live actions."

"Yes, because you're such a joy and so cooperative when you're sick."

Claudia waved off Naomi's remark.

"I've never been sick enough that I can't stand and make my own meals, but if I was, I would absolutely let someone else cook for me."

"Uh huh." The significant look Naomi gave Audrey and Cassidy said she felt otherwise.

"*Anyway*, my point is that the books make no sense a lot of the time."

"And yet, she keeps coming back and reading more of the genre, even when she's not doing it for book club." Naomi smirked. A quick glance at Cassidy, who was grinning, confirmed to Audrey that these two often needled each other like this.

"She likes the sexy scenes," Grandma chimed in. "That's why I read them, too."

"I'm not sure I needed to know that," Audrey muttered.

"You should be happy to know that life isn't just for the young." Grandma shook her head.

"It's not that; it's that you're my grandmother," Audrey protested. "I try really hard not to think about what Cassidy and David get up to. And I try really, really, really hard not to think about what my parents do or don't do. Or what my dad does with women other than my mom."

There were sympathetic looks all around, and Audrey winced a little, but no one here knew her mom. And it was nice not to have to censor herself completely. If she'd said anything like that back home, it would have definitely gotten back to her mom, who would be horribly hurt. Even if it was true and Audrey wasn't the one doing the actual action, her mother considered being told about her husband's indiscretions to be worse than the indiscretions themselves.

At least, that was how it always seemed to Audrey.

"Your mother could do with reading a romance or two," Grandma said, her voice softening slightly as she spoke of her stepdaughter. The complete opposite of Audrey's mother, who couldn't mention her stepmother without sounding brittle and disapproving. "And removing her buttstick."

"So, I always wondered," Audrey said loudly, before her grandmother could go down the buttstick road, "what do you do with the books when you're done with them?" When everyone looked at her, no one answering immediately, she frowned. "Like, do you donate them to the library…"

"Oh, you're reading paperbacks… got it." Naomi smiled. "I think we all use e-readers at this point or an app on our phone."

"I… never considered that. I've never read anything but a paperback."

"I like it because I can adjust the font to be bigger," Grandma said. "And I can leave little notes for myself at my favorite spots to go back to. I like to mark out the sex scenes for future re-reads."

"I just don't want to carry a book around everywhere." Claudia shrugged. "I don't always have time to sit down and read, but I can get in a few pages whenever I have a minute since it's on my phone."

Naomi nodded in agreement. "Same for me."

"I still like reading both, but it's easier to carry around my e-reader," Cassidy said, shrugging.

"Okay, so… if I'm going to do it on my phone… how does that work?" Audrey pulled out her phone, and the others crowded around to help her figure things out. While they were doing that, the front door opened again, and another couple walked in. There was a moment of hesitation from everyone, which had Audrey's alarm bells ringing in her head. For some reason, people weren't as happy to see him as they had been to see each other.

The man was definitely former military, like her brother and the rest of the team. He moved just like they did. Though he was completely bald, he had a full beard and mustache. An earring dangled down from one ear, like a chain with a little knife hanging from the end of it. The woman at his side was a pretty blonde, and her dark eyes were bright and wide as she looked around the foyer with interest, seemingly indifferent to the people to her left in the living room, all staring at her.

"Hey, Coriander, we weren't sure you were going to make it," Jensen said, coming forward. "Hi, Noelle, welcome to my house."

"His name is Coriander?" Audrey whispered to Claudia, who was standing the closest to her and watching the couple greet Jensen through narrowed eyes.

"His name is Zeus—I'll explain the spice thing later—and we don't trust him," Claudia murmured back.

Well, coriander was an herb, not spicy, but okay then.

***

MASON

The arrival of Zeus and Noelle shifted the mood of the party. Not a lot. Some people might not even notice. But Mason was always attuned to the group and watched people's behavior more closely than the average person. That was his job, after all.

He watched as David took Zeus and Noelle over to introduce them to Audrey and Brenda, a lot more formally than he had for anyone else. If they were ever going to integrate Zeus into their group, they needed to put a better foot forward. Zeus was trying. Just showing up here tonight was proof of that. They'd run into him at the BDSM club they all frequented, but this was the first team social event that he'd shown up to.

Mason shifted closer. Not because he was trying to get closer to Audrey, of course; he was just doing his job of keeping an eye on the group and how well Zeus was integrating into it. Exactly like Lincoln had asked him to. Their boss had chosen Zeus, after all, even with his past. He wanted Zeus on the team. If Mason could help ease the way, all the better.

"Hey, Clove," he said amiably when Zeus caught his eye. For just a moment, he thought he saw a flash of amusement in the other man's face, but it was quickly covered up by his usual, stoic expression.

"Mason."

"Okay, seriously, can someone explain the name thing to me?" Audrey complained with a cute little scowl, looking around at everyone in their circle. "Why are you calling him by spices instead of his name?"

"It's our call signs," David explained. "I'm Ginger. Mason is Posh, Drew is Sporty, Claudia is Scary, and Jensen is Baby."

While he was talking, Brenda, Naomi, and Claudia started to drift away, which made sense, since they all knew this already. He got the impression that Claudia preferred watching Zeus interact from afar. She was headed in Jennifer and Ashley's direction, both of who were openly watching Zeus and Noelle. Naomi went to join her husband in the dining room, and Brenda made off to the kitchen.

"So, we're trying out random spices on Zeus until we find one that fits," Mason chimed in, and was rewarded with a delighted smile and laugh from Audrey. The sound of her laughter made him feel strangely warm inside, especially knowing that he was the reason for it.

Dammit.

He shouldn't be feeling this way.

He should move away from her.

But that would look rude to Zeus, and he was trying to help Zeus become more a part of the team.

"Why not call him Sexy? Or Spicy?" Noelle suggested, giggling as she leaned into Zeus' side. This time, he didn't bother to hide his amusement as he looked down at her.

"I'm okay with never hearing David call me Sexy, actually."

That made David crack up, which was good. Mason didn't hold back his laughter, either. Where he and David led, the others would eventually follow. Seeing them laughing at something Zeus said could only help the cause. It didn't surprise him when he took a quick glance around the space at everyone else, and Lincoln caught his eye and gave him an approving nod.

"Well, I'll just have to call you that then," Noelle said, but there was a little edge to her tone which had Mason eyeing her. Zeus didn't seem to notice. Then again, he was a lot harder to read than most people.

"There was someone else on the team before—I'm blanking on her name right now, Abbey or something—why can't Zeus use her call sign?" Audrey asked. "Or something like it."

"No, everyone gets their own call sign. Besides..." Mason glanced at David. He wasn't sure how much David wanted to reveal about his *other* life to his sister. Did she know? Would she understand? "Well, there are other reasons for the names, but they're kind of private."

As in, the nicknames actually came from the submissives at the BDSM club who had dubbed their group the Spice Doms and given them the names that they'd used for their call signs. Abigail, their former IT person who was now with the NSA, had never been part of the kink scene with them. Though they'd irreverently called her Smarty, which meant that she'd fit in with the general theme.

"I thought the subs at the club called you the Spice Doms and that's why you have girl names," Noelle said, her brow furrowing as she looked between Zeus, David, and Mason. "Did I hear wrong?"

"Subs?" Audrey asked, her gaze darting between all of them. Fuck. "Club?"

David tilted his head up toward the ceiling, and Mason got the impression he was doing his best not to glare at Noelle. Because he wouldn't want to glare at a submissive, even one who had just outed him to his sister. It wasn't like she'd done it on purpose. She was apparently just terrible at reading the room.

"Oh... was I not supposed to say that?" Innocence dripped from Noelle's voice as her eyes went wide. She put her hand up in front of her lips. "I'm so sorry, I assumed everyone... well..." She waved her hand around as if that provided her full explanation.

Zeus' grip tightened around her shoulders as David's head dropped down to look at her in disbelief.

"Hey, Noelle, let's go get something to eat. And drink. And then we can have a real quick conversation about privacy and what 'private' means," Zeus said grimly, moving her along before David could snap at her. The fact that Noelle immediately began protesting as he moved her didn't stop him, but it also didn't bode well for the relationship.

A girlfriend who couldn't keep her mouth shut or read the room wasn't going to be a good match for any of them.

Silence fell in their little corner as Audrey looked between him, David, and Cassidy.

"So, um… subs? I'm assuming she doesn't mean a kind of boat or a sandwich. Or a teacher."

Well, great. Exactly the conversation he didn't want to have with a woman his brain was all too eager to fantasize about. That was exactly how his day was going.

CHAPTER SIX

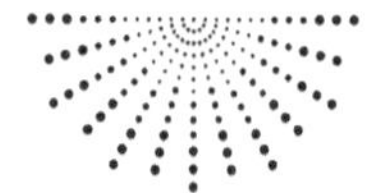

It was clear that asking about subs was making everyone really uncomfortable, and Audrey almost backed off, but she wanted to know what Noelle had meant. Not knowing made her feel left out, like there was some big secret that everyone knew that she didn't. Even Noelle and Zeus, who didn't seem to be accepted by everyone in the group, knew. So, why shouldn't she?

"She's probably going to find out, eventually," Cassidy said to David, patting his shoulder sympathetically. "At game night, if not at book club."

"Find out what?" Audrey wasn't used to being pushy, but sometimes, a girl just had to know. It didn't hurt that whatever it was, Mason was obviously involved, too. Maybe it would be something that would turn her off from him, since being engaged to another woman hadn't fully wiped out her reaction to him. Knowing that their relationship was arranged made some part of her feel like it was okay to be attracted to him, even though if she could make a conscious decision about it, finding out he was engaged would have cut that off cold turkey.

"You know how I explained that hucow is a kink? Well, there are other types of kinks, too, and we all belong to a club where people can explore those kinks," Cassidy said quickly.

Beside her, David groaned and put his hand over his face. He could be a bit of a drama queen sometimes. Grandma was right about that. Beside him, Mason was shifting in place uncomfortably and looking anywhere but at her, which she tried to ignore.

"The submissives at the club call them the Spice Doms and gave them the nickname."

"Doms?"

"Dominants. As opposed to submissives."

"And the submissives are the hucows?" Audrey was so lost, but she was trying to understand, she really was, and also trying not to show any judgment on her face. She wasn't judging, she was just… surprised. Uncertain. But she didn't want to make them feel bad, especially Cassidy, who had already been so nice and was trying so hard. David groaned.

"No, well, yes, a hucow would probably be a submissive, but that's just one type of kink. There are lots of submissives who aren't into that." Cassidy blew out a long breath. "I feel like I'm doing a bad job of this. Mason, you're a psychologist, how would you explain it?"

Mason froze. Audrey got the impression he kind of wanted to run. She should probably let him off the hook, but she was intrigued now, as well as confused. And, honestly, it would be nice to have someone other than her brother or her brother's girlfriend explaining this kink stuff to her.

"Ah, well… different strokes for different folks, first of all," he said, flashing a grin at Audrey as he reached up to run his fingers through his hair. The tone of his voice had changed to more of a lecturing one, so he was giving off a sexy professor vibe. "There are all sorts of reasons people get into kink, and there have been some studies that give us reason to believe that genetics do play a part in it."

"I'm out. I can't be here while he talks about kinks being genetic to my sister," David said, throwing his hands up in the air and stalking away. Cassidy followed him, her voice low and chiding. While she couldn't hear exactly what Cassidy was saying, Audrey got the impression that she was scolding him.

And now she was alone with Mason.

Sexy, unavailable, engaged to another woman, Mason. Audrey looked up at him as he watched Cassidy and David go.

"You don't have to keep talking about this with me," she reassured him. Did she want to hear what he had to say? Yes. But he was uncomfortable. And engaged. Maybe it would be different if he was single, but he wasn't. "I can look it up later. Do my own research."

"Well, there's a lot of information out there, and not all of it is correct." He cleared his throat. "If you have any questions, feel free to come to me. Or any of the women. Well, maybe not Noelle. But Cassidy, Claudia, Naomi, Yasmine… they're all members of the club, too. Jennifer is also in the scene, although she doesn't go to the club, and she'd be able to answer questions as well."

"They're all submissive?"

"Oh, no." He practically choked on his drink, laughing and coughing as he slapped his hand against his chest. "Claudia is definitely not submissive. She's one of the Spice Doms, too, and there's a reason the subs chose her to be Scary. Trust me, you do not want to be on that woman's bad side."

"Well, I wouldn't want to be on Naomi's bad side either," she muttered. But apparently, Naomi was submissive since Mason didn't name her as another dominant. "So, the dominants are in charge? But Naomi and Claudia seem like they're both in-charge personalities."

"They are, but what someone wants inside the bedroom—or in a platonic kink relationship—might not match up with how they are in their day-to-day life. There are some people who are in charge all day who want nothing more than to give up control to someone else when they get home. And there are some people who are extremely passive outside of the club, but they're dominant in their kink life. Everyone is different, and so is every couple. Or throuple. Or polyamorous group."

Well, she wasn't in Kansas anymore.

She wondered if there were kinky people in Kansas. In which case, saying she wasn't in Kansas anymore wouldn't really make sense. Not that she'd ever been to Kansas.

And why she was focusing on this inane thought cycle, she had no idea.

"Claudia is a dominant. The rest of the team are also dominants?" She tried to ask it as nonchalantly as she could since his answer would also be personal to him.

"Yes, the whole team is, although that's not indicative of anything. The other Black Fox team has a submissive with them. Anyone can be submissive or dominant, or completely vanilla and not interested in kink at all."

"Vanilla means not interested in kink?"

"Yeah, you know. Vanilla. Basic. Nothing unusual."

Audrey stared at him.

"You know that vanilla is the second most expensive spice in the world, right?" she asked. "It's incredibly labor intensive. It only grows in a very specific warm climate; it can take up to *three years* before the vanilla orchid even starts producing the flowers that become a bean, and it takes another nine to ten months before it'll produce a vanilla pod. Every orchid has to be pollinated by hand because the vanilla bean bee is now extinct, and there's a really small window of time for that pollination process, and even if you get it right, the orchid will only produce one single vanilla bean. And *then* there's the whole harvesting process, which is an ordeal in and of itself!"

Holding up his hands in front of him, Mason was smiling at her in a way that made her blush. Partly because she hadn't meant to rip into him, but also partly because, well, his smile did melty things to her insides that she should absolutely be ignoring.

"Hey, I didn't coin the term. Although I'll admit, I also had no idea that vanilla took all of that. Especially considering how it's everywhere."

"Artificial vanilla is," she admitted. "If you want to call artificial vanilla basic, I can live with that. Not real vanilla though. Real vanilla is… it's not basic at all."

"I can see that."

He was still smiling at her.

Dammit.

Why did he have to be taken?

Mason

Watching Audrey get flushed and passionate about vanilla was far more interesting than it should have been. Part of him knew he should walk away. Find someone else to talk to.

But he couldn't do that without bringing her over to someone else. Leaving her alone in the corner here would hardly be welcoming. Everyone else had already abandoned them. Besides, surely the more they talked, the more the luster on her would dim.

Exposure therapy, remember?

They'd been talking about kink. Of course, his brain had gone straight to his attraction to her, to wondering if she'd like a demonstration. He wasn't proud of it, but now that he had the opportunity, he could change the conversation. If they moved onto more mundane topics, more boring topics, then surely the attraction would go away.

She was just another woman, after all. They didn't really know each other. They just happened to have met at a time when he was settling down and committing to someone. Once he got to know her, he'd know that she was just like every other woman he'd met before, regardless of his initial reaction to her.

"Is vanilla your favorite flavor?" he asked.

"No, chocolate is," she admitted. "I do like vanilla, though. As long as it's real vanilla. I am a bit of a vanilla snob."

"Well, now I don't know if I've ever had real vanilla." He'd had vanilla ice cream and such, but now that she'd gone into a description of what it took to get the real stuff, he was pretty sure the ice cream at the store didn't contain it.

She laughed. Mason didn't want to admit how much he liked making her laugh. Knowing she was laughing because of a joke he'd made. Especially since he didn't think anyone would ever call him 'the funny one' on his team. But he wanted to be funny for her.

"I'll make sure you get to try some sometime soon." She grinned at him. "How do you feel about crème brûlée?"

"I'll try anything once. Your baklava was amazing."

"You still haven't picked a favorite."

"It was too difficult. I think you'll just need to keep making all three for me until I can decide." He rubbed the bottom of his chin, doing his best to hide his smile and knowing he was failing. Which was fine since he wanted her to know he was joking, so she didn't feel obligated.

Though if she made them, he'd eat them.

He wasn't kidding about not being able to decide.

Audrey laughed again. "I can do that."

The way she was looking at him as she said it sent little tingles all along his spine, and he realized he was grinning back at her. Not hiding it at all.

Fuck.

Were they flirting?

This felt like flirting.

Fuck. He couldn't flirt with her. He had to stop this.

Mason cleared his throat, forcing his lips to stop smiling. He never smiled this much. It should have felt natural to stop, but it didn't.

What had they been talking about before they got off track?

Shit. Right. Kink.

That was not a better topic.

Books. That's where this had all led from.

"Anyway, since you'll be reading books with kink and around people who are kinky, the only other thing you should probably know about is that the main rules are Consent is King and kink-shaming is deeply frowned upon."

Audrey's smile had faded, too. He hated to see it go, but it was for the best. If she kept smiling at him, he wasn't going to be able to stop smiling at her.

"Well, I know what consent is, and I know what shame is, but I feel like you mean something specific by kink-shaming."

"Yeah, it's nothing too complicated. Just as long as everyone involved is a consenting adult, we don't shame people for what they want to experience. It's very much 'well, that's not for me, but you have a good time'. Or just not commenting at all if it's not something you're interested in because there's no reason to bring down someone else's enjoyment."

"Ooh." Audrey's eyes lit up. "I like that. Instead of saying 'why would someone want to do that' or 'I would never do that'?"

"Exactly." He nodded. Not that he thought Audrey would have had a problem with that. She seemed like the type to err on not hurting anyone's feelings. But there were people in the world whose intentions were fine, but they spoke thoughtlessly. The number of people who felt like it was okay to be derogatory about something they weren't interested in to someone who was obviously finding enjoyment in that thing always boggled his mind. It was best to say it explicitly, just in case, since she was new to the scene.

"No! I'm leaving!"

Both of them jumped as a woman's voice echoed around the room. Noelle went stomping by, Zeus following quickly after her, heading for the front door.

"Noelle—"

"No, I'm not going to stand here and be humiliated by you! You can't boss me around outside of the club. You're a fucking jerk!" She darted out the front door as her words stopped Zeus in his tracks, as if he couldn't believe she'd said that to him.

All the rooms were dead silent, watching him, waiting for his reaction to his submissive cursing at him and name-calling. Mason wasn't sure what had just happened, but he would bet money that Zeus hadn't done anything that violated what he and Noelle had negotiated. That this was Noelle's reaction to being scolded about talking club stuff in front of a newcomer.

Did everyone else realize that?

Shit.

Mason stepped away from Audrey. It might be rude to leave her alone, but Zeus was already struggling to fit into the team. This was only going to make things harder on him, especially if they believed he was being a jerk to his girlfriend.

"Hey, Juniper, you okay?" he asked, clapping Zeus on the shoulder. He deliberately used a spice to address Zeus, so that the other man would know nothing had changed in how Mason saw him, keeping him part of the team. Zeus jerked in reaction. Clearly, he hadn't realized Mason was coming up behind him, which showed how distracted he was.

Zeus let out a long, slow breath, and Mason could actually watch him regaining his usually centered, calm demeanor.

"Yeah. She didn't like being told that she can't just talk about club stuff in front of people that aren't part of the club—" Before he could continue speaking, the front door opened again and Noelle reentered.

She was sniffling, shoulders hunched in, an expression of regretful contriteness on her face.

"I'm sorry I freaked out like that," she said immediately, looking directly at Zeus, holding out her hands as she walked toward him. He immediately opened his arms for her to walk into them. "I just... you know my past. I get so triggered when people say I did something wrong. I'm afraid of being kicked out again." Now she tearfully turned her attention to Mason.

"The last club I was part of, my best friend—my ex-best friend now, I guess—spread the most awful rumors about me in the club, and when I tried to defend myself, they kicked me out. I really didn't mean to do something wrong, it just slipped out, but I freaked out, feeling like I was going through that all over again."

Everything she said made a kind of sense. Everything in her demeanor said she was sincere. Conversation began behind him again, people getting back to whatever they'd been talking about before Noelle's outburst.

"I get it," Zeus said, stroking his hand over her hair. "Come on, let's go home. We can talk more there."

"Okay." She sniffled again and looked at Mason with big eyes. "Bye, Mason. I'm so sorry. Again. Please pass my apologies on to everyone."

"I will," he reassured her. But as he watched them leave, a feeling of foreboding settled over him.

CHAPTER SEVEN

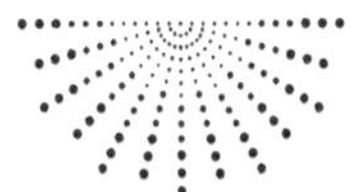

Watching the interplay between Zeus, Noelle, and Mason, Audrey couldn't deny that she was more than a little disturbed. She drifted to where Cassidy and David were. Both of them were frowning at the trio near the front door and talking quietly, and she wanted to know what they were saying.

Yeah, she was nosy like that.

Both of them looked up when they saw her coming.

"What's up?" she asked quietly, glancing over to where Zeus and Noelle were now walking out the front door, Mason closing it behind them.

Cassidy sighed, keeping her voice low, even though Zeus and Noelle had left the room, indicating she didn't want everyone else to hear what she was saying either. Most of them had gone back to their own conversations now, anyway.

"You heard what she said about the club she was kicked out of?" Cassidy asked, and Audrey nodded. "That's my old club, too."

"Ooh, so you know what happened?" Audrey had to admit she was curious. She might not entirely understand this whole kink thing, but she was fascinated by it. And she wanted to know more.

To her surprise, Cassidy shook her head.

"That's the thing, I don't. When everything was going on with her, I was dealing with Don. I wasn't going to the club much, and I definitely wasn't paying much attention to any gossip or anything." She glanced at David again, her concern clear on her face. "I do know that there was a whole bunch of drama around her eloping with a friend's fiancé, but I don't think that's the same friend she's talking about. The thing is, when I saw her up here, I thought maybe she needed a fresh start. Like me. So, I never asked anyone back home what happened. Now, I'm wondering if I should."

"I'm sorry, back up, she eloped with her friend's fiancé?" Audrey was horrified. That sounded like something straight from Reddit, not something that would happen to someone she actually knew in real life. Even with all the drama that sometimes occurred in her parents' social circle.

Cassidy made a face.

"Yes. Apparently, it didn't work out, so they got the marriage annulled, and she moved up here, looking for a fresh start. Just like me. It's a crazy coincidence that we happened to move to the same place, but stranger things have happened." Cassidy shrugged. "There haven't been any problems with her until now, and I don't know that this is any of my business, but this is the first time she's said anything about being kicked out of the club. If she really got kicked out, instead of moving up here to start over... well, I'm wondering why."

"Well, I'm wondering now, too, and I'm not a part of any of this."

David's hand was on Cassidy's back, and she could see his arm moving as he rubbed her soothingly.

"It's up to you," he told her. "Or, if you want, I can talk to Gavin and have him reach out."

"Gavin?" Audrey asked.

"He owns the Outlands, the club up here, but he's got a good relationship with Master Patrick, who owns Stronghold, the club I came from." Cassidy glanced at David, biting her lower lip as though she was trying to figure out what to do. "That's the thing. I know if someone gets blacklisted at Stronghold, Master Patrick sends out a heads-up to everyone else. He sent one about Don."

It was really weird to hear Cassidy call someone 'master', but Audrey did her best to keep her expression neutral. She didn't want to accidentally kink shame someone. She loved the idea of not being judged, but that meant participating in being nonjudgmental.

But her list of questions was piling up higher by the minute.

"To be fair, Don was a possible danger and a definite abuser," David pointed out. "If her stuff was just relationship drama…"

"Master Patrick would never kick someone out for relationship drama. You have to break one of the rules. Relationship drama isn't that. There's been plenty of people with relationship drama, with his closest friends, who didn't get kicked out." Cassidy sighed. "It feels like I'm intruding into her business, though."

"She kind of shouted her business out to everyone here," Audrey pointed out. "It wasn't like you went looking for it. And she said something different from what she'd said before, or you wouldn't have thought twice about it."

"That's true." Cassidy glanced at David again. "I'm going to think about it."

"I don't think she's a danger to anyone, or you would know," he said. "Well, maybe dangerous to Zeus emotionally if he's falling for her, but I don't think she's physically dangerous."

"Yeah." Cassidy didn't look entirely convinced, but she put a smile on her face as Mason came over to them.

"Sorry for abandoning you," he said to Audrey with a grimace. "I wanted to make sure Zeus knew he had backup."

That just made her like Mason even more. Thoughtful. Caring. It was amazing to her that he'd needed someone to arrange his marriage. He was a bona fide catch.

"No problem. I thought it was nice of you to support him."

"Mason, you're the therapy guy. Thoughts on Noelle? And Zeus?"

Instead of answering immediately, he hesitated.

"I think Zeus is trying to fit into the team. I don't think he has the most open personality, but he's trying. I think it's a good sign he came here tonight."

"What about Noelle?" Cassidy pressed when Mason stopped there. It was hard to read his expression as he shrugged a shoulder.

"I think… I think she's hard to get a read on. I don't really know her, and I've only interacted with her a few times."

"Right. Well." Cassidy looked at David again and shrugged. "Maybe we'll hear something from Zeus later."

Audrey did notice that Cassidy didn't say anything about asking her friends from D.C. about Noelle in front of Mason, or anyone else, as the night wore on. Not that anyone brought up Zeus and Noelle. It was like there was a silent agreement between everyone not to discuss them.

Poor Zeus. She hoped he had an easier time fitting into the group over time.

The rest of the night passed without incident until it was time to go. As she got into the backseat of their car, she saw Mason a little ways down the street ahead of them, and her stupid heart fluttered again.

If she was going to have a crush on one of her brother's team members, why couldn't she have a crush on one who was available? Or Mick. He was hot, if kind of a himbo. Of course, the fact that her grandmother had monopolized most of his time this evening would have put a damper on that crush, anyway.

Still. Jensen was hot. Even if he did seem into Jennifer.

Okay, maybe there really wasn't a good alternative on the team.

Why couldn't she just *not* have a crush on anyone on her brother's team?

"Well, that was fun," Grandma said brightly as she buckled her seatbelt. She'd taken the seat behind David, while Audrey had gotten in behind Cassidy. She leaned forward to pat him on the shoulder. "Thank you for inviting me. I had a great time. That Mick boy is very cute."

David glowered at her in the rearview mirror.

"Leave Mick alone, Grandma."

"Why?"

"He's too young for you, and I know you're just… flirting… with him to get under my skin."

"Maybe I'm flirting with him because I want him to get under my clothes."

Groaning, David pulled out into the street, while Cassidy and Audrey choked on laughter. She didn't know if she was more horrified or amused. God, she wanted to be her grandmother when she grew up. She'd forgotten what hanging out with her was like. The fact that she was actually their step-grandmother wasn't the only reason Audrey's mom had stopped talking to her; if she'd been a different kind of woman, the two would have had a different kind of relationship. But Audrey's mom would not have been torn between horror and amusement; she would have just been horrified and possibly in need of fainting salts.

"Thanks for throwing me a welcome to my new home party," Audrey interjected before Grandma could give David an aneurism.

"You're welcome. I just wanted you to know that we're glad you're here." Even though it was dark and his back was to her, she could tell he was smiling. "I hope we didn't overwhelm you."

"You didn't, it was fun. I hope everyone else had fun, too."

"I know Mick and I did," Grandma said with a snicker.

"I think they did," Cassidy spoke over Grandma, talking a little louder than normal to drown her out. "It's nice for them to get together outside of work. I'm glad Zeus made it, although I wish he maybe hadn't brought Noelle and he could have stayed longer."

"Me, too," David agreed, apparently on board with Cassidy's plan to ignore Grandma.

Audrey glanced over at their grandmother, who had narrowed her eyes and was glaring at the back of David's headrest. She looked like she was plotting.

"Is there something going on between Jensen and Jennifer?" she asked. Maybe some gossip would help distract Grandma from hassling David. At least while Audrey was in the car. Afterwards, David would just have to deal.

"Not really. They like each other, but she started dating the doctor who did the surgery on David after he got shot," Cassidy said. "I don't think they're exclusive, though."

"Not yet. Jensen needs to make a move if he wants to keep it that way," Grandma said. "You snooze, you lose. He keeps trying to give Jennifer the wrong pickle. That's why I make my intentions clear. I told Mick exactly what kind of pickle I want him to give me."

They were at a red light, thankfully, so it wasn't dangerous when David leaned forward and rested his forehead on the steering wheel. His shoulders moved as he took in a deep breath. Cassidy reached over and sympathetically patted him on the back.

"Mason seems happier now that he's engaged," she said, clearly trying to steer the conversation away from pickles. "He was smiling a lot more tonight than he usually does."

"He doesn't usually smile?" Since today was the first time she'd ever met him, Audrey didn't really have a baseline. David had described all his teammates to her in the past, and he'd said Mason was serious, but that could really mean anything coming from David. Especially in comparison to some of his other teammates—Jensen seemed to never stop smiling, and Drew was usually smiling as well.

"When he's watching other people do something, not usually in the conversations he's having with other people," Cassidy explained. "If that makes sense. He was definitely smiling more tonight, even when just talking. I noticed it while you two were chatting, right before Zeus and Noelle arrived. He wasn't just smiling, he was laughing."

"Maybe being engaged has him loosening up a little," David said, straightening up and glancing over at Cassidy. With the light of the streetlamp from overhead, Audrey could see the sappy smile on her brother's face. "I know falling for you loosened me up, and now I feel like smiling all the time."

Aw. Well, that was adorable.

"Good line," Grandma said approvingly. "You'll definitely get laid tonight."

Audrey snorted, reaching up to cover her mouth with her hand and stifle her laugh. Poor David.

At least this was distracting her from the little bit of hurt that she felt that Mason hadn't been smiling at her, necessarily. He was just more smiley because he was engaged.

Which is good. He shouldn't be smiling because of me. He should be smiling because he's engaged.

Right.

She really needed to get her head on straight.

Just because it was an arranged engagement didn't mean he wasn't really happy about it.

She was probably just on the struggle bus because she was new to Pittsburgh, she hadn't had a chance to meet many men yet, and when she'd met him this morning, she'd thought he was single. It made sense that she'd felt an immediate attraction.

Now that she knew he was engaged, her little crush would go away quickly. She was just getting over the shock of that discovery, and her brain and emotions were catching up with the reality of his unavailableness.

After David dropped her off at her apartment building, Audrey went straight inside to her new home, feeling exhausted now that the evening was over. It wasn't entirely unpacked yet, but she had all the basics. She definitely didn't have the energy to do more unpacking tonight.

But she couldn't fall asleep right away, either, when she got into bed. She tossed. She turned. Her thoughts kept whirling around the whole evening.

Mason.

Mason and Yasmine.

Hucows.

Mason.

Kink.

Mason.

Zeus and Noelle.

Mason.

Eventually, she decided she might as well get started on her new book if she wasn't going to sleep.

Grabbing her phone, she rolled onto her back and turned it on.

Within half an hour, she was wide freaking awake and more turned on than she'd ever been in her life, but also more horrified by her arousal than she'd ever been. She shouldn't like this. Right?

Human cows. Not something that she would have ever thought she'd find sexy. Though she didn't think it was the cow part she found sexy. It was the couple. The way the hero was so bossy but caring. The way he made the heroine feel when she submitted to him.

The way he took charge of her completely, and she let him.

Dammit.

There was no way she was going to be able to fall asleep when she was feeling like *this.* Her nipples were hard, her pussy was wet, and she had an itch between her legs like never before... and she had no idea where her vibrator was. Somewhere in one of the boxes.

"Fuck," she muttered, as she kicked off her covers and shoved her hand down her pajama pants and underwear.

Slick wetness met her fingers the moment they got past her mound. She'd definitely never been this turned on before. She dipped her fingers between her folds and circled them around her clit, which felt like it was throbbing.

Closing her eyes, she shuddered as she started rubbing hard and fast, too turned on to try to take things a little slower. She just needed to come.

Thinking about a man who tied her into place and ran his hands all over her body. Who took control of her completely. Who pinched her nipples until they hurt, then used her for his pleasure, causing her own as he did so.

A man with Mason's face.

She cried out as she came, shuddering and clenching, panting for breath as the strongest orgasm she'd ever had rolled over her in a hot wave of pleasure. And as soon as the sweet ecstasy receded, the guilt set in.

But it wasn't like he or Yasmine knew who she was picturing while she got herself off. Audrey let out a long breath as she lay there in the darkness, staring up at the ceiling.

Tomorrow. Tomorrow, she would get her head on straight. Focus on her bakery. And maybe think about dating. Clearly, she needed to do something about lusting after a taken man. That wasn't who she was, and she refused to be that girl.

CHAPTER EIGHT

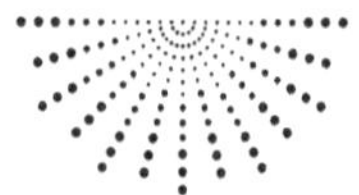

Mason

"What do you think, Mason?"

Mason jerked in his seat around the conference table, his gaze going to the picture of Royce Macleod and Marshall Devlin that was on the screen in front of the team. They'd been talking about Royce MacLeod entering the race for governor and hiring Devlin as his head of security.

Devlin, who used to be the third partner at Black Fox Security, before Lincoln and Harris realized he was sleeping with Lincoln's first wife and stealing from the firm. They'd taken back control of all the business and financial aspects he'd been handling and removed him from the firm at the same time Lincoln had served his first wife with divorce papers.

He had practically announced he was coming for Black Fox over the past few weeks by badmouthing them, trying to poach team members, and then—after getting nothing but refusals—sending black roses to everyone's house in the lead-up to the announcement of his new position. A huge bouquet of them had been delivered to the office on that day.

Since then, nothing.

But they all knew it was a threat.

Which they were currently trying to assess.

As Mason stared at the picture, he could not for the life of him remember what had actually been said before his opinion was requested.

"Um…" he said, trying to stall, which caused a round of snickers from the rest of the team. Even Lincoln, who had asked the question, smirked at him. "Sorry, I missed what we were talking about."

"He's too busy dreaming about his wedding already," Drew teased, making everyone laugh.

Jensen raised his eyebrows.

"Shouldn't that be his wedding night?"

"It can be both."

"Focus, gentlemen," Lincoln chided them, though he was still smirking.

Mason let out a long, slow breath. He hadn't been thinking about Yasmine at all. He'd been thinking about a certain redhead and wondering what she was doing. How setting up her bakery was going. If she'd done any research into kink yet and what she thought. It was Tuesday morning after the party. She probably had. Unless she wasn't interested at all.

Focus, Mason.

It didn't matter to him whether or not Audrey was interested in kink. He needed to start working on dreaming about his wedding. And his wedding night. Because right now, all he pictured was him and Yasmine sitting and talking, the way they'd done when they'd gotten together to talk about marriage.

"Lincoln pointed out that Devlin is not normally known for his patience and wondered if it's possible that MacLeod is reining him in. Or possibly keeping him too busy to come for us," David updated Mason.

Beside him, Claudia played with a pen between her fingers, staring at the screen on the wall with such intensity, it was amazing it didn't catch on fire.

"It's always possible," Mason said. "On the other hand, I think it's also possible he's more patient than we ever gave him credit for. He was doing a lot of work behind the scenes we never knew about, after all. Though he did get rushed and sloppy toward the end, we can't judge him solely on that."

"True." Lincoln nodded. His smirk had faded, and he tilted his head as he looked at the screen, his eyes dark as he studied the face of his ex-best friend and business partner. "Any thoughts on what's motivating him?"

That was something Mason had been considering ever since they'd found out Devlin was behind the black roses being sent to the team and that he had a new, powerful employer. Even before that, Devlin had been trying to poach staff and clients and badmouthing them around town.

Keeping quiet and above it all was doing them some good with the people who weren't into dramatics, but of course, there were always the people who leaned into the drama.

The fact they hadn't lost any staff, despite Devlin's best efforts, while they'd actually hired one of his old team members, helped as well. Zeus had left the firm before Devlin had been kicked out, but the point was still made. They'd kept all their staff and most of their clients, plus added one of his old team members.

Which was why not everyone trusted Zeus.

"I think jealousy of you," Mason said. Shifted his gaze to meet Lincoln's. "Not just professionally, but personally. That's why he went after Janet first." They'd confirmed that Devlin had been the one to approach Lincoln's now ex. Of course, it was still her own decision to cheat on Lincoln, but Devlin had initiated it. "I think he's also jealous of your and Harris' relationship. Because Harris took some of your attention."

"So, what, he's in love with Lincoln?" Jensen looked confused.

"No, obsession and possessiveness don't necessarily equate to romantic love or sexual attraction," Mason replied, glancing at Baby. He still looked confused. "You can be obsessed with someone without wanting them romantically or sexually. But I do think that Lincoln is Devlin's focus. I think he initially stole from the company because it was like taking something of Lincoln's when he couldn't have all of Lincoln's focus. Deep down, he knew he couldn't have all of Lincoln's attention, not when he and Harris were so close."

"He did try to pit you two against each other several times," Claudia chimed in, directing her statement at Lincoln. "It never worked, but… he tried."

"Yes, I know." Lincoln rubbed his hand over his face, appearing tired. "I always thought it was regular misunderstandings. I didn't think it was deliberate."

"It might not have been," Mason said. "His subconscious desires and fears could be driving his actions without him really realizing what he was doing. He might have told himself that he was doing the right thing, for some unknown-to-us reason. Or he might have even convinced himself that what he was saying was true."

"So, he seduced Lincoln's wife because he wants to be Lincoln? Like, replacing him in Janet's bed and pretending he's Lincoln?" Drew looked utterly disgusted and horrified. Not surprising. While David was in a serious relationship now, Drew was the only other married member of the team.

"In effect, yes."

"That's sick, man," Jensen said, getting a round of nods from everyone at the table, including one from Zeus, who had been mostly silent and motionless for the meeting. His expression was stoic as usual, but Mason thought he appeared disturbed under that stony exterior.

Unfortunately, picking apart what was going on with Devlin didn't offer them much in the way of action. They discussed some options for shoring up their reputation and agreed that silence would continue to be the best answer. MacLeod's opponent, Senator Marlin, had used them as additional security for one of her events, and she wanted to use them again in the future. Just being an Indian-American woman running for governor had increased the threats being sent to her, far more than she had gotten as a senator.

While Devlin had done his best to badmouth them among their own community, any kind of retaliation might have some blowback on them at a time when they needed to be discreet and completely circumspect.

Which meant they had to sit back and do nothing about it.

Not the most satisfying conclusion to a staff meeting, and both Claudia and Jensen were grumbling by the end of it. Normally, Drew would be, too, but he seemed to be inward focusing. As usual. Mason eyed Sporty. He looked like he'd lost some fat and increased his muscle mass, which meant he'd probably been working out a lot more.

When David had been shot, Drew had blamed himself. There had been no way to know that Cassidy's ex had found her, but he'd been the sober one at the bar when Don had shown up and dragged Cassidy into the back alley. Mason was pretty sure that Drew felt like he should have realized Cassidy was missing sooner, that he should have acted sooner, then David wouldn't have been shot.

Not that Drew would talk about it with Mason, so this was all theoretical, but he was pretty sure he was right.

Mason caught up to him and clapped him on the shoulder as they walked down the hall.

"Hey, we should have lunch together. Soon."

"Sure, sure." Drew avoided his gaze, reaching up to adjust his dreadlocks, the movement forcing Mason to move his hand off Drew's shoulder. It could be coincidental, or it could be exactly what Drew meant to do. Mason would be willing to bet money on intentional. Drew didn't do many things by accident. "Soon."

"Eventually, I'm going to have to force the issue if you don't decide to come chat with me on your own," Mason said.

Drew's jaw tightened, but he nodded. He was still avoiding Mason's gaze, though, and he couldn't tell if Drew was nodding agreement or just to get Mason off his back. They rounded the corner to the lobby. Mason's stomach was already grumbling, and he was ready to go grab some lunch, so there was no point in going back to his office first. He ground to a halt as soon as he saw who was standing at the front desk, talking with Jennifer.

"Hey, Audrey," Drew said as he moved past her. He didn't slow, much less stop, unlike Mason. He was too flummoxed by seeing her there, so unexpectedly, as if his thoughts in the meeting had manifested her presence.

"Hi, Drew!" She smiled brightly as Drew headed out the doors to the elevators before shifting her gaze. "Good morning, Mason."

Was it his imagination, or were her cheeks a little pinker than usual? Maybe she was just cold from being outside. She was wearing an olive green peacoat, and her hair was pulled up in a high ponytail with a black-and-white polka-dot scarf tied in it. The day wasn't freezing outside, but it was definitely cold enough to have put some pink in her cheeks on the walk over. Maybe she'd just arrived.

"Hey, are you here to see David?" he asked, looking between her and Jennifer. Jennifer was seated in her usual position behind the desk, smiling genially.

"That and drop off some fliers," Audrey said, reaching out to tap a small stack. "Grand opening is Saturday, so I wanted to put some fliers out at the local businesses. And also to tell everyone here that the soft opening is Friday, and you're all invited."

"What's a soft opening?" Jensen asked from behind Mason. He shifted over to let the other man into the conversational grouping.

"It's like a practice run," Audrey explained. "I've hired two staff members, and this will be our first time actually doing all the things for real customers, so a soft opening lets me limit the number of people coming in. That way, we can do everything for people who will be forgiving if there are any screw ups." She grinned widely, her excitement obvious. As she spoke, she was practically bouncing.

"Awesome, I'll definitely be there." Jensen leaned his arm on the counter of Jennifer's desk, cocking his head to the side as he looked down at her. "Hey, Jennifer, want to go with me to Audrey's soft opening?"

Jennifer, who had been putting a stack of files together, froze for a moment. So did Mason. He felt like he shouldn't breathe or he might mess something up for Jensen. If Baby was doing what Mason thought he was doing, it had taken him a long time to get here, and he didn't want to mess it up for him.

"I... ah... like, together?" Jennifer's confusion was obvious as she stared at Jensen, still holding the files between her hands. On the other side of the desk, Audrey's eyes had gone wide with interest, and Mason had to wonder how much she knew about the situation and if she understood how monumental this was.

"Yes. Like a date." Though Jensen kept his voice casual, his shoulders and body were tense as he waited for her answer. "Unless you and Dr. Dick are seeing each other exclusively."

"His name is Richard." Jennifer's voice sharpened.

"Fine. Richard. Are you seeing each other exclusively?"

"No. We haven't discussed that."

"Then do you want to go with me to Audrey's soft opening?"

"You don't care that I'm seeing someone else?"

Mason bit his lip against telling her that the competition was likely what had driven Jensen to finally face his own feelings and act. When it had been just the two of them dancing around each other, he hadn't been risking anything by denying his attraction to her. Now that there was someone else interested, he risked losing Jennifer, and he couldn't wait any longer.

Whether that would lead to a successful relationship was debatable, but he was glad to see that Jensen wasn't just sitting on his ass and letting what he really wanted slip through his fingers.

Something about that thought sent a tingle down Mason's spine, but he ignored it, too caught up in the drama playing out before him.

Jensen shook his head in answer to Jennifer's question.

"Not as long as you're also seeing me."

Finally letting go of the folders, Jennifer crossed her arms over her chest, leaning back in her chair and facing Jensen full on with her eyes narrowed.

"I've done some scenes with him. Do you have a problem with that?"

"Nope. Although I hope you'll let me scene with you, too, eventually. Probably not at Audrey's soft opening." Jensen glanced at Audrey, grinning at her. "Unless you're opening a kink-friendly bakery."

"Um, no." Now, Audrey was definitely blushing, and she glanced at Mason before her gaze darted away.

He would pay so much money to know what she was thinking right now.

"Right. So. Friday?" Jensen returned his attention to Jennifer, who had lifted her chin and was looking a little more confident.

"Sure. It's a date." *Finally.* The unsaid word hung in the air.

Not that Jensen seemed at all bothered by it. He grinned widely as he straightened up.

"Great. It's a date." Shoving his hands in his pockets, he sauntered back toward the offices, proving that he'd come out for one reason and one reason only. He might not have known about the soft opening before he saw Audrey, but he'd taken full advantage of the event.

"Well, I guess I'll have two customers, at least," Audrey joked. Jennifer nodded, though now that Jensen had disappeared, she looked a little shell-shocked. To say that was unexpected was an under-statement.

"You'll definitely have more than that, I'm sure the whole office will come," Mason said to reassure her. "It's not like you're far, and we all love baked goods. Plus, you're David's sister."

"Right." Audrey glanced at the watch on her wrist. "Well, I should get back. You guys were my last stop, and I have employees to train this afternoon."

"I heard you hired Ashley," Jennifer said. "She's excited."

"Good, I'm excited to have her."

"Ashley… as in Lincoln's wife?" Mason asked, surprised. He hadn't realized she was looking for a job. She didn't need one if she didn't want one.

"Yeah, she said she loves the idea of working in a bakery. Person-ally, I think David said something to her, because I was having trouble finding a second employee." Audrey shrugged, looking a little sheep-ish. "I'll take what I can get, and she seems enthusiastic."

"Right well, I was headed out to get some lunch, so why don't I walk you back?" Mason suggested.

"Oh, you don't have to do that."

"Well, the place I was going to go to grab something is right past your bakery, so either I'll be walking beside you, in front of you, or behind you." It was all true, which was why he'd asked. Otherwise, he might seem like a creeper, leaving with her and going in the same direction. This way, where he was going and why he was walking with her was at least out in the open.

"Well, okay then. That makes sense." She smiled at him, though it seemed a little guarded.

Or maybe he was imagining things because he felt a little guarded. He could be projecting. This was just a coincidental run-in, but some of his thoughts about her were not the kind of thoughts someone who was engaged to another woman should be having. He needed to be on his guard when she was around because he wanted to eradicate those thoughts, and he sure as hell wanted to make sure he didn't accidentally act on any of them.

"Great. Let's go." He gestured in front of him, and she turned, the skirt of her coat flaring out a little as she did so, showing off her shapely legs and the tight jeans she was wearing. Which he was definitely not looking at. He looked at Jennifer instead, who appeared lost in her own little world; she wasn't paying any attention to him or Audrey. "Jen, I should be back in about a half hour."

She jerked upright, coming out of the reverie she'd sunken into.

"Right. Half an hour. See you then."

Hiding his smile, Mason followed Audrey out the door and to the elevator. His smile faded a little as he realized they were basically going to be alone together, even if it was just walking down the street.

It would be fine.

Everything was fine.

CHAPTER NINE

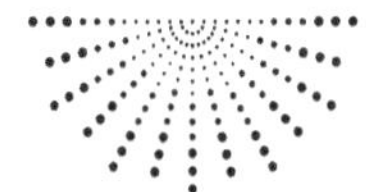

AUDREY

Had she been hoping to run into Mason when she'd gone into Black Fox?

No.

She was pretty sure she hadn't.

In fact, she'd almost avoided going in because she'd wanted to avoid running into him. Then she'd talked herself into it because she did want to invite everyone to the soft opening, and she had wanted to say hi to Jennifer. She'd told herself that she probably wouldn't see him, anyway, because she wasn't going farther than the front desk.

When Jennifer had told her that everyone was in a meeting, she'd been relieved. Okay, maybe a little disappointed, too, but mostly relieved. And her disappointment could be attributed to missing a chance to see David.

But now Mason was here, and he was somehow even more handsome than she remembered, but he was also still taken, and she needed to get past this stupid crush.

"How's your day going so far?" she asked brightly to cover up how uncomfortable she was being alone in an elevator with him. It wasn't his fault she had a stupid crush.

Besides, the more she pretended they were just friendly, the easier it would be to think of him as a friend.

Just pretend he's Jensen.

She liked Jensen, but she hadn't been attracted to him at all. She was happy for him that he'd asked Jennifer out and got a yes. Just like she was happy for Mason that his parents had found a bride for him.

Yup.

Just like that.

Fake it 'til you make it.

"Not bad. Meetings aren't my favorite things, though, which is why it's nice to get out of the office afterward. This afternoon, those of us who are in the office will be training."

"But not everyone will be there?"

The elevator doors opened, and Mason gestured for her to step out in front of him, leaving his hand up to hold the doors at bay even though it probably wasn't really necessary. It was still a nice gesture. Gentlemanly.

As soon as they were both through the doors, he ended up beside her as they left the building, and he gave a little wave to the security guards they passed on the way out.

"No, Claudia and Drew have a job this afternoon for a jewelry show that's happening downtown."

"Oh, well, that's fun." Audrey shook her head. "I knew David did security, but well, he doesn't talk about the job much. He mostly tells stories about things on the job, but sometimes, I don't know what he's actually doing. I always pictured bodyguard services."

"We do some of that, too. Sometimes, we consult with companies looking to beef up their own security."

Mason grinned, and when she glanced up at him, his eyes had unfocused, like he was remembering. She was still surprised that Cassidy said he didn't smile much. Then again, she'd met him on the day of his engagement, so maybe he was just smiling more all the time now.

"One time, we got to break into a company's headquarters because they wanted an assessment on their current system. That was a lot of fun."

"Fun and hopefully not dangerous." She shivered as they stepped out onto the street, not from the idea of danger but because a cold blast of air hit them the moment they stepped outside. Mason didn't seem bothered, even though he wasn't wearing a coat, just another sweater similar to the one he'd worn on Saturday.

Her brother always denied when he was cold, too. Maybe it was an ex-military thing.

"Not dangerous at all, since they knew it was going to happen. But they didn't know when or how we were going to do it. It was a good exercise for us as well because it helped us see things from the other side of things and gave us ideas on how to prepare."

"Makes sense." The sidewalk was far from empty, but Mason stuck by her side as they moved past some people walking dogs, a few harried-looking workers rushing past, and several other couples.

Not that she and Mason were a couple. They weren't. They were a pair of people walking together, side by side, because they were going in the same direction.

"Are you excited about your grand opening?"

"Yes and no," she admitted. "Excited but terrified is more accurate. What if nobody comes? What if my business is a bust?" *What if everything her parents had said was right? What if she'd ruined her life by moving away and trying to set up her own business?*

What would she do then?

"Well, first of all, even if no one came on day one, that wouldn't be an indication that no one will *ever* come," he pointed out.

Audrey frowned. That seemed… but he was right.

"That might be true, but I would still rather have a huge rush of people at the grand opening. It would feel like I'm getting off on the right foot."

"But what if you have a huge rush on day one and then no one shows up on day two?" he teased.

She ground to a halt, her jaw dropping open. She hadn't even considered that. It felt as if day one went well, then so would every-thing after that. But if it went poorly, she'd never recover. But he was right. She could do all this work for a grand opening, get everyone in the door on day one, and then nothing.

It suddenly felt hard to breathe.

"Woah, Audrey, I was teasing. I'm sorry." Mason had quickly real-ized she wasn't right beside him and turned so that he was facing her. His hands came up to hold on to her shoulders, giving her a bit of extra stability, which she appreciated. "I shouldn't tease you like that. The only reason I did is that I *am* that sure that your bakery is going to be a wonderful success."

Looking up into his dark eyes, framed by his glasses, feeling his hands on her shoulders, she suddenly felt very, very warm. Warm enough that a blush started to creep across her cheeks in response to it.

There was something incredibly intimate about standing this close, meeting his gaze like this.

"Okay," she said, because her brain had gone on the fritz, and it was the only thing she could think of to say.

"Have you run a business before?"

Audrey snorted as Mason released her and stepped away, his ques-tion shaking her out of her frozen state.

"No. I studied business in school, but I think my parents always expected me to use that to help whoever I married. They didn't want me actually working." At least, not more than a cushy, nepotism posi-tion at her dad's company, where she didn't have any real responsi-bilities.

At the time, she'd thought that he was being supportive and putting her to work so she could get some experience and start moving up in the company. It had quickly become clear to her that she wasn't there to actually work, just to get a paycheck and meet 'the right kind of people.'

Which was not what she wanted.

"Well, jumping into having your own is definitely one way to go," he replied. "Sink or swim, right?"

"Unfortunately, yes. I've had to use most of the money that's currently available to me from my trust fund to set it up. I have enough to live on for this year even if I make nothing, but after that… well." She sighed. "And twenty percent of businesses fail in their first year."

"That many?" He sounded surprised, then shook his head. They were coming up on her bakery now, the pink and white awning sticking out from the building was a nice, cheerful landmark. "Yours won't."

He sounded so sure of it, Audrey almost believed him, even though he couldn't guarantee any such thing.

"I hope not. I have high hopes, but it's scary."

They came to a halt in front of the glass door to her bakery, where Cupcakes & Crumbs was printed in large letters above her logo—a cupcake with pink frosting in a green and cream striped liner, adorned with a little red heart on top, and several large crumbs scattered around the base. The pink frosting matched the pink on her awning and the upper half of the walls inside the store. It made her happy just to look at it.

"Anytime you do something new, it's scary. The important thing is that you do it, anyway." He smiled at her. "It's going to be great, Audrey, I believe that."

Taking a deep breath, Audrey let it out on a huff and nodded.

"Thank you."

If she could find half the confidence that he had in her, she would be in a good spot. But first, she had to get things ready and train her new employees. And Mason had lunch to get to. And a fiancée.

"Thanks for walking me. Tell Yasmine I say hi."

He blinked, then nodded his head.

"I will. Have a good rest of the day."

Turning, Audrey unlocked the front door and let herself in. She deliberately did not look to watch him walk down the street. That man was firmly off the market.

Mason

Walking away from Audrey, Mason gave himself a little shake.

He'd almost forgotten about Yasmine until Audrey had said to tell her hi. Because, of course, he would be speaking to his fiancée on a regular basis and be able to tell her hello.

The fact they hadn't done more than send a couple of texts since Saturday...

Well, it wasn't like they were pretending to be a love match. Still, he was pretty sure he wasn't supposed to forget about her completely while he was talking to another woman.

I'm a fucking awful fiancé.

Or maybe he was just engaged to the wrong woman.

No. He put the mental brakes on that line of thinking.

Absolutely not.

He wasn't going down that path. There was no way he was going to hurt Yasmine like that. She already believed that she was cursed, based on her dating history. The whole point of doing this arranged thing was to find a compatible person with the same goals to have as a life partner. Chemistry was a bonus, not a necessity.

Having incredible chemistry with someone else did not mean he was making a mistake.

Just like with Audrey's bakery having no guarantee of success based on opening day, there was no guarantee that initial chemistry would last beyond the first interaction. *Similarly, there's no guarantee it would be a failure beyond that.*

Scowling, Mason dug into his pocket and pulled out his phone.

He might not be able to control who he felt chemistry with, but he *could* control his actions. He *could* control his choices.

Right now, he was choosing to call his fiancée and let her know he was thinking of her. Which was true. He just wouldn't say exactly how or why. Maybe he couldn't force love to grow, but connection was something that could be encouraged by taking specific steps.

"Hello? Mason?" Yasmine's smooth tone was tinged with confusion. "Is everything okay?"

"Yes, everything's fine." Crap. His own fiancée thought he wouldn't call her unless something was wrong. He really was failing at this fiancée thing. "I was just calling because I was thinking of you."

"Oh. Oh! Well, that's very nice to hear." She sounded pleased but also a little guilty, which actually made him feel better. Maybe she sounded guilty because she also had not been thinking of him. "Um, anything specifically?"

"Uh, not really. Although David's sister's bakery is having a soft opening on Friday. Do you think you might be able to get away from work for a bit to go with me?" Surely the more time he spent with Yasmine, the better. Especially when Audrey was around.

He wasn't sure if chemistry was transferable, but it couldn't hurt to try, right?

"Sure, I could take some time around lunchtime. We could eat and then go there for dessert?"

"Perfect." He turned the corner and smiled as he saw the food trucks that were his destination, already feeling more relaxed as he put a plan into place and prepared to reward himself with good food. "And then Outlands in the evening."

"Right."

Was it his imagination, or had she hesitated just a little? Did she sound excited or reluctant?

"Right then. I'm about to get lunch now."

"Okay. I will see you on Friday then."

"Great."

"Great. Bye."

Hanging up the phone, Mason grimaced as he pushed it into his pocket. He didn't think he was imagining how awkwardly the call had ended. They would get better at all of this. They'd jumped from acquaintances to engaged very quickly. They just needed practice.

But he'd done the right thing, and he could feel good about that.

Now. Was he in the mood for gourmet grilled cheese or *birria* tacos today?

A cool gust of wind blew past him, making him shiver. The tacos.

He needed a little bit of heat. Getting into line for the Rojo Fondo Taco truck, Mason tilted his head back and stared up at the sky. It was very blue today, with puffy white clouds. A gorgeous day. A perfect day. And he was making good choices, taking steps toward the future he wanted and improving his skill at being a good fiancé.

So, why did he feel like something was very wrong?

CHAPTER TEN

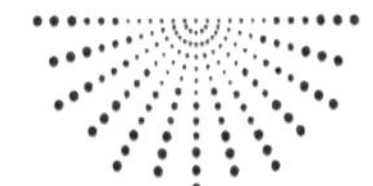

AUDREY

Game night with the girls. Audrey couldn't remember the last time she'd done such a thing. She was glad it was happening, though, because otherwise, she would be spending tonight alone in her apartment, an absolute nervous wreck because her bakery was opening tomorrow. Sure, it was the soft open, but she was just as nervous about that as the grand opening.

If the soft open didn't go well, how could they possibly handle a grand opening? They couldn't. Unless no one showed up. But she didn't want to hope for no one showing up to her grand opening.

"Stop it."

Audrey jerked in surprise, the seatbelt tightening across her chest at her sudden movement, and looked at Cassidy, who was driving.

"Stop what?"

"Stop thinking that you're going to fail." Cassidy glanced at her and smiled. "It's going to be great. Everything's ready. Ashley texted me that you're all set."

"We are. Although…"

"No."

"You don't even know what I was going to say!"

"The whole reason I'm driving tonight is so you can't try to sneak away to go back to the bakery." Cassidy gave her another stern look before refocusing on the road. "Everything is set. I know you're going to be there crazy early tomorrow morning. You've been working like mad all week. Tonight, you're going to relax and have fun and be with friends."

Audrey huffed. "For someone who hasn't known me for very long, you do a much better job of reading me than people I knew for years."

"Yeah, well, trauma will do that to you," Cassidy joked, although it wasn't really a joke. "I'm always paying attention to people's moods."

"Sorry. I didn't mean to remind you of that." Audrey immediately felt terrible that she'd brought it up. She and Cassidy hadn't talked much about what Cassidy's abusive ex had been like, but she was sure the other woman's memories were terrible. Audrey knew he'd been abusive while they were together, stalked her after they broke up, harassed her friends, put trackers in her shoes, then tried to kidnap her, before finally shooting David… after which he got a knife to the throat, as David had so charmingly put it. But those were just the facts, not what it had been like to live through all of that.

"It's okay. Some days, everything reminds me of him. Other days, I'm totally fine. It's all part of the healing process." Cassidy's voice was remarkably calm, considering what they were talking about. "The important thing is that I got away. A lot of women don't."

That part, Audrey could relate to, at least a little. Not that what Cash had put her through was anything like what Cassidy had gone through, but… she'd escaped the life that had been laid out for her. A life that had been slowly smothering her.

"I'm really glad you got away."

"Me, too. Your brother saved me in more ways than one." Cassidy shook her head in wonderment. "Not just him, either. My friends in D.C. gave me faith in people again. They supported me when I couldn't do anything for them in return. Got me to safety up here. Then everyone here continued that. I really wasn't looking for love, ever again, but your brother is the one who made me realize I could still have that part of my life, too."

Audrey felt tears spring up in her eyes.

"That's so beautiful."

"Sometimes, it feels like I was headed toward a terrible fate, then the universe intervened and sent me to a different destiny." Cassidy sighed. "Which sounds very dramatic, but that's how it feels sometimes."

"You went through something pretty dramatic, so that's fair."

"Dramatic *and* traumatic," Cassidy quipped, making them both giggle. "It's kind of wild that I can laugh about it now, but… some days I can. And I feel like that's healthy."

"Definitely healthier than drowning in melancholy," Audrey agreed.

"Yeah, I did plenty of that already. Okay, here we are." She pulled to a halt, parking in front of a stone house that looked straight out of a fairy tale. Audrey blinked in surprise. It even had a little turret on the left side.

"That's Claudia's house?" Audrey pointed. Maybe Cassidy meant the next house over.

"Yup. Unexpected, huh?"

"Definitely." Audrey got out of the car, looking at it. She would have expected Claudia's somewhere more like David's home, with clean modern lines and lots of dark colors. Not a Thomas Kinkade painting. Even without anything blooming in the flowerbeds or on the bushes, it was a picturesque little house. A romantic dwelling. She went to the back car door and opened it so she could pull out the tray of extra goodies she'd made for tonight—an assortment of cookies and cake pops.

She followed Cassidy up the path to the front door. Cassidy knocked, but didn't bother waiting for someone to come to the door, just opened it and stepped back so Audrey could pass through in front of her. The inside of Claudia's house matched the outside. It was soft. Cozy. Neither of which were words she would have ever used to describe Claudia, which made the dichotomy all the more fascinating.

"Hello, come on in," Claudia said, even though they already were in. She was standing behind a large table where Ashley and Jennifer were seated. Both of them smiled and waved. "Naomi and Yasmine should be here soon. I think it's just the seven of us tonight. Brenda's not coming, right?"

"She sends her regrets," Cassidy said, and shook her head as she closed the door behind her. "I'm not sure what she's up to tonight. She told me it's none of my business. Not in a mean way, but she didn't want to tell me what her plans were."

"We'll probably find out eventually," Ashley said cheerfully, hopping up from her seat at the table to come around and take the tray from Audrey.

"Oh, I've got it... Well, thank you." Apparently, Ashley wasn't taking no for an answer; she'd already taken the tray from Audrey before she could finish her sentence. Bemused, she looked at her suddenly empty hands.

"No, I've got it, boss," Ashley said, winking at her as she turned and headed toward a smaller table that was adjacent to the kitchen and already piled with food. There were two coolers on the ground to the right of it. "You're going to have to get used to being in charge and bossing me around."

"I feel like I'm being the one bossed around," Audrey muttered good naturedly, although she wasn't entirely kidding. Ashley seemed to have decided that her job was to handle everything but the baking and the books this week, and she was constantly shooing Audrey away from everything else.

"Go A-Team!" Ashley cheered, using one hand to move aside a bowl of chips and salsa, squishing it in with the other platters, to make room for the baked goods.

"A-Team?" Jennifer asked, raising her eyebrows and leaning forward to rest her weight on the table.

"That's what we're calling ourselves," Audrey explained. "My other new employee's name is Alexis, so all of our names start with A. The A-Team."

"Or Triple A, but I like A-Team better," Ashley said, returning to the table and sliding back into her seat.

"I think Seven Wonders tonight," Claudia said, looking over the boxes she'd pulled out. "Since there are seven of us."

"Imagine my surprise," Jennifer muttered and smirked when Claudia shot her a look.

"Have you played before?" Claudia asked, and it took Audrey a moment to realize the other woman was directing the question at her.

"Um, no."

"That's fine, it's easy enough to learn; it's the strategy that's hard," Claudia said, nodding her head and starting to pull the other boxes off the table. "Go ahead and grab something to drink—the blue cooler has non-alcoholic options, and the red cooler has the booze."

With her soft opening tomorrow, Audrey opted for the blue cooler. She was just picking out a sparkling water when there was a knock on the door. Like Cassidy, there was no wait before opening, and Naomi and Yasmine came in. Both of them were smiling in anticipation of the evening, bright-eyed and happy to be there.

"Hello, hello," Naomi said, unwinding the scarf from around her neck as she looked around the room. Her eyes landed on the table where Claudia was standing. "Oh, Seven Wonders. Imagine my surprise."

"That's what I said," Jennifer replied with a snicker, while Claudia glared.

"It's the perfect game for seven people."

"The fact that it's your favorite has nothing to do with it," Naomi teased, making Yasmine laugh. Even her laugh was pretty. Delicate. The kind of laugh Audrey had always wanted.

Cut it out, green-eyed monster.

Audrey let out a slow breath and pushed a smile onto her lips. It wasn't Yasmine's fault that she made Audrey feel inferior by her very existence. Or that she was engaged to the first man Audrey had been attracted to since finding her ex in the coat closet with another woman. That was all on Audrey.

Thankfully, no one seemed to notice she was a little out of sorts. That, or they chalked it up to it being her first time hanging out with all of them without her brother around as a buffer. Though Cassidy did step into that place pretty quickly and sat beside Audrey. Of course, that left the other side open, and as fate would have it, Yasmine took that seat.

Which meant that Audrey got to experience firsthand how *nice* she was.

Despite what Claudia said, the game was definitely confusing to start. There were so many different cards and symbols and ways that the scoring worked. As they played, Yasmine kept explaining in a low voice what everything was and the different strategic options. Most of that went over Audrey's head, but she still appreciated the effort.

She needed to kick her attraction to Mason.

She liked Yasmine.

She was *not* going to be *that woman.*

Mason hadn't shown any sort of interest in her, and Audrey would never touch a man who was in a relationship with someone else, much less engaged… but she also didn't want to be the kind of woman who lusted after someone else's man. Even if he had no interest.

"So, Yasmine, how's the wedding planning going?" Jennifer asked as they paused for Claudia to start doling out the cards for the second phase of the game.

"Oh, we haven't really started yet." Yasmine was looking at the layout of cards in front of her, as if she was studying them and thinking of a strategy. "I have a vision, of course, but we have to figure out the details."

"Something big, something small?" asked Naomi.

Yasmine opened her mouth. Closed it, frowning.

"I… always wanted a big wedding, but I don't know. Is that appropriate for an arranged marriage?"

"I don't see why not. It's still a wedding and a marriage, right?" Jennifer said encouragingly.

"I've been to a lot of weddings that were basically arranged marriages, even if they didn't call it that," Audrey offered, determined to do her part as a girl's girl. Yasmine was really sweet. She deserved to be reassured and supported. And Audrey was telling the truth. Her wedding to Cash would have been like that if she'd given in to her parents' pressure after she'd caught him cheating. "All of them were huge weddings."

"I guess." Yasmine sighed, fiddling with one of the cards even though it had been perfectly lined up with the others.

"Yasmine." Naomi's voice was gentle. "Do you *want* to marry Mason?"

"Yes. I want marriage and kids, just like he does. I think our parents did a really good job setting us up. I've finally broken the curse." She lifted her head, smiling, though her voice was more matter-of-fact than excited.

"You also always wanted romance."

"Well, two out of three isn't bad." Yasmine laughed, garnering a few smiles, though no one laughed along with her.

Audrey's stomach churned with sympathy that she was sure the other woman wouldn't want. She couldn't help it, though. Even though Yasmine was joking and laughing, she could practically feel the other woman's pain emanating from her.

"Is Mason at least trying to be romantic?" Jennifer asked. "I'll kick his butt for you if he's not putting in the effort. You two might just need a little spark to light the fire."

"Well… he kissed me."

That got a round of silence, and Audrey had to metaphorically sit on the little green-eyed monster in her head again.

"Um… had you two not kissed before?" Claudia asked after a long moment with a frown. The whole night she'd been pushing the game forward, making sure they didn't slow down for too long, but now she was making an exception. Everyone had their cards, so they could start Phase Two, but she wasn't moving things along.

"We'd done pecks on the cheeks, but we hadn't kissed-kissed," Yasmine explained.

"And that's supposed to be romantic?" Jennifer wrinkled her nose. "I feel like the romance is supposed to come before the kiss."

"Yeah, Jensen kept buying Jennifer pickles even though he refused to ask her out," Naomi said. "Has Mason gotten you anything other than the engagement ring?"

"Well… no." Yasmine sighed.

"How was the kiss?" Cassidy asked.

"Um…" Yasmine appeared to be searching for words, and the expression on her face was not encouraging.

"Oh, dear. That bad?" Cassidy made a face.

"The subs at the club are always all over him; I feel like we'd have heard if he was a *bad* kisser," Jennifer said.

That made Audrey's stomach flip over for a different reason. Great, more unwanted jealousy.

Maybe she needed to start dating. She'd wanted to focus on her bakery, but if she was dating, maybe her brain would stop focusing on a man she couldn't have.

Even if his fiancée didn't seem super enthusiastic about him, which was a travesty in her opinion. But feelings couldn't be forced. They were still getting married, regardless.

"It wasn't *bad,* it just… I don't have a brother, but it's what I imagine kissing my brother would feel like," Yasmine explained. Jennifer immediately recoiled, and Claudia made a retching noise that Audrey felt compelled to echo. The idea of trying to kiss-kiss David… blech. Yup, that was the noise. "Things will get better. They have to." If the level of determination in someone's voice could affect outcome, Audrey had no doubt that things would get better for Yasmine and Mason.

And she was happy for them.

Really.

"Right well." Claudia cleared her throat as she looked down at their completed Phase 1 of the game. Apparently, there were three in total, and even after playing through the first one, Audrey still didn't feel like she knew what she was doing yet. "Let's start Phase 2."

Putting her head down, Audrey focused on the game. Tomorrow, she'd download a dating app. Or maybe she'd wait until after tomorrow night. Cassidy and Ashley had convinced her to go to the

Outlands tomorrow night to celebrate her soft opening, just to see what it was like.

Maybe she'd meet someone there who would help this unwelcome attraction to Mason dissipate.

CHAPTER ELEVEN

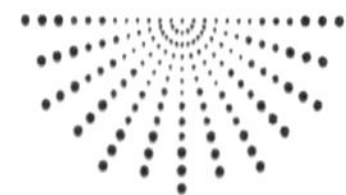

Lunch with his fiancée. Easy enough. Or so he'd thought.

But she wanted to talk wedding plans, just like his parents, and he'd been ducking his mother's calls for the past few days, much to her annoyance. Wasn't it the job of the bride and her family to plan the wedding? He thought he was just supposed to take care of the honeymoon.

Although, to be honest, he hadn't started making any plans toward that, either.

"Okay, so a year out works for you?"

"Yeah, that should be good."

"Or maybe we should make it a year and a half so we can have a spring wedding. Or a June wedding." Yasmine dragged her teeth over one side of her lip as she stared down at her tablet, which she had open to a calendar.

"Does it matter?" Part of him wanted to get it over with faster, but another part of him wasn't unhappy with the idea of pushing it off farther. Another symptom of the proverbial 'cold feet.' Making a major life change was always accompanied by resistance in one way or another.

Yasmine's head jerked up, and she stared at him across the table. Shit. Maybe it did matter.

"I mean, whatever you want is fine with me," he said hastily. "Are weddings supposed to happen at a certain time?"

"May and June are really popular for weddings, but that means it's also when everything is the most expensive. People like spring weddings. There are really beautiful things for fall weddings, too. And winter weddings. I don't think I would want to do a summer wedding past June, though, or a winter wedding, just because of the unpredictability of the weather. Though if everything's inside, the summer weather won't matter as much."

"But the winter weather will?"

"Well, yes, because there can be icy conditions on the roads and things like that." She tapped her finger against the table, then smiled at the server, who appeared with their food. "Thank you."

The poor guy looked like he'd been hit by lightning and stammered out a hasty 'enjoy your meal' before backing away. He still sent a yearning glance Yasmine's way over his shoulder as he turned to head to another table, though she didn't appear to notice.

She really was stunningly gorgeous.

So, why wasn't he attracted to her?

With tonight's scene looming closer by the hour, he was doing his best to notice everything attractive about her, but... he might as well be trying to find Naomi attractive. Or Cassidy. Or Jennifer. All attractive women, and all women he'd never been attracted *to*.

The attraction would come. They just needed to work on it a little. And he needed to stop letting his brain distract him.

"Would you like a big wedding or a small wedding?" she asked, sliding her tablet to the side but not turning it off as she picked up her fork.

"Ah, small, I would think. Close friends and family." Mason hadn't ever really thought about it before, but a big production sounded awful. Especially since this was an arranged marriage. But the expression on Yasmine's face, although she did her best to keep it neutral, shifted. Shit. He was fucking this up again. That clearly wasn't what she wanted. "Did you want a big wedding? What if we do something in the middle, a medium-sized wedding?"

"So, like, a hundred to a hundred fifty people?"

"That's medium sized?" The words were out of his mouth before he could stop them; that sounded like a big wedding to him. He tried to remember how many people had been at his cousin Cyrus' wedding because that had been huge, but he honestly had no idea how to gauge the crowd. He would have to ask Cyrus.

Yasmine pressed her lips together.

"Maybe we should come up with our guest lists of the people we want to be there, then we can see how many people that is. You should ask your parents if they have people they want to invite, too."

If he let his parents have their say, they'd end up with three hundred people in attendance.

Maybe Yasmine had a point about a hundred to a hundred fifty being small.

"Maybe we could elope," he suggested, and Yasmine's lips immediately flattened in obvious displeasure. "That was a joke." It had been. Sort of.

"I don't think our mothers would ever forgive us," she said, the edge of her mouth curling up in a smile, but the amusement didn't reach her eyes. If anything, she looked exasperated with him right now.

He couldn't blame her.

"What's your favorite color?" she asked, apparently ready to move on from the guest lists for now. Mason made a mental note to make his list over the weekend, although he didn't think it would be very long. His team. His parents. His cousins and aunts and uncles.

"Um. Grey?" He looked down at the shirt he was wearing. It was grey. Like most of his shirts. Did that make it his favorite color?

When he looked up again, Yasmine was staring at him in dismay.

"Your favorite color is grey?"

"I don't think I have a favorite color. I like all colors." He just didn't like wearing very many colors. "Why?"

"Because we need to choose colors for the wedding." She sighed when he stared at her blankly. "That determines what the bridesmaids and groomsmen wear, the color of the table linens, the bouquets, that kind of thing. Although I guess we should decide if we're doing fall or spring before we choose colors. We can't do a fall wedding with spring colors or vice versa."

"Right, that would be terrible," Mason agreed, even though he had no idea what she was talking about. Yasmine narrowed her eyes at him. "I'm happy with whatever you choose."

"I want us to choose this together, though," she said plaintively. "I don't want you shut out of the decisions about your own wedding. We should both have a say."

Well, when she put it that way… Mason sighed inwardly. This was clearly important to her. He should make an effort.

"Right. Um, what about blue? Could that go with fall or spring?"

Immediately, Yasmine brightened. "Yes, depending on the shade."

"Well, I like blue."

Beaming, she switched to a notes app on her tablet to record his preference, and Mason felt a surge of relief. Finally, he'd done something right.

"What's your favorite flower?"

Fuck. This was torture.

Somehow, he got through the meal, doing his best to give Yasmine some kind of answer for everything. But the further they got into the questions, the more he felt off-kilter.

He asked for the check and a box, and Yasmine frowned again as she noticed his mostly full plate.

"Was it bad?" she asked in a low voice, presumably so none of the workers would hear her.

"No, I just wasn't very hungry. Plus, I want to make sure I still have room for the bakery." The truth was, his stomach had started feeling queasy over the questions and had gotten worse with each one she'd asked. He wasn't sure he'd be able to eat anything once they got to the bakery, either.

"Right." She smiled again, but it looked forced. "So. Tonight. Is there anything specific I should wear? Or prepare for?"

"Ah, no. Wear whatever you want. I figured we'd start with basics and see how that goes."

"That makes sense."

Was she disappointed? Her expression hadn't changed, but Mason was getting the sense he'd disappointed her. Again.

Shifting in his seat, he tried not to let his discomfort show. They were engaged. There were things they were going to have to work through. Everything had moved very quickly thanks to it being arranged. They were still getting to know each other.

That's all.

The server came, and Mason paid for their meals, quickly boxing his up. His stomach still felt tight and uncomfortable. As did the rest of him. Getting to his feet, he rolled his head around, trying to loosen the muscles in his neck and shoulders.

Heading to the door, he was going to try to hold Yasmine's hand, but she was walking too far ahead of him. He settled for holding onto his leftovers, which at least gave him something to do with his hands as they left the restaurant. Once they were outside, she had one gloved hand tucked into her pocket while the other held the strap of her shoulder bag where she'd stored her tablet. It was too big for Mason to call it a purse.

"The day is turning out nice," she said, turning her face up to the sky as they walked down the street. The House of Starrett, where they'd had lunch, wasn't too far from Audrey's bakery, thankfully. The air was nippy, but not so cold that they'd be miserable walking.

"It is," he agreed, happy to have an easy answer. The tension in his stomach eased a little now that they were away from the restaurant and past all the wedding talk. "I think we've got a few good weekends left before it gets too cold to enjoy walking."

"I can't say I ever really *enjoy* walking, but I do like the nice weather," she joked with a little smile.

"Oh, I love going for long walks on the weekends. Around the city, maybe doing some hiking on trails. I'll probably be doing that tomorrow during the day, trying to get in the good weather before it's gone. You could come with me—you might like walking better with someone."

"Not really." She shook her head. "I've done the group thing before; it doesn't make a difference other than making me feel bad if I can't keep up. Besides, I have a yoga class tomorrow afternoon. I was thinking about stopping by the bakery at some point, just to support Audrey on her grand opening day as well as today."

"Oh, me, too. The whole team is planning on going in the morning."

"I was going to go after my class," Yasmine replied hesitantly, and he got the sense she didn't want to tell him no right after rejecting his invitation to go hiking, but that she also didn't want to go in the morning.

"Okay, well, it's probably good to spread it out some. Keep her busy all day." Mason smiled. Yasmine really was a thoughtful person. He liked her. They were good together. If he made a list of everything he wanted in a life partner, she would check all the boxes. That's why he'd agreed to this arrangement in the first place.

Was it weird that physical chemistry hadn't been one of his boxes?

Maybe. But in his defense, until he'd met Audrey, it hadn't played that big a part in any of his relationships.

Though there had always been a little spark previously. More than he and Yasmine had. But those relationships had all come about naturally, not through his parents. It made sense that this one was different.

"What do you do on weekends once you can't go hiking?" Yasmine asked as they turned onto the street for the bakery. Mason could see the pink-striped awning immediately, despite the distance. It was a good way of standing out from the buildings and other businesses around it.

"Hang out with friends, watch movies… sometimes I read. Or take a class. I do winter hikes too, when I start feeling too cooped up. What about you?"

"Friends, of course. And my yoga class. I also have a belly dance class that I'm starting soon. I prefer reading or listening to podcasts over television or movies. I usually like to do my podcasts or audio-books while I'm doing something else, like cleaning or my laundry."

"Ah, I can't really do the audio stuff. It's kind of in one ear, out the other." Mason shrugged sheepishly. "I need something visual to hold my attention."

They'd reached the bakery, and it was clear they were not the first ones to arrive. The inside of the small space already had quite a few people milling around within it. Mason pulled the door open for Yasmine to enter in front of him. Despite stepping back in order to do so, he was immediately hit with a warm blast of air, scented with cinnamon, chocolate, and that soft smell that always came with anything freshly baked.

It smelled like Audrey. Or, he supposed, Audrey smelled like her bakery.

Either way, his body immediately reacted, interest perking up, blood humming in anticipation. He felt more awake, more aware.

None of it made sense, and it was driving him a little nuts that he was still reacting like this.

"Wow, that smells amazing," Yasmine said, walking past him.

"It does." Mason let out a long, slow breath as he followed her inside.

Pretty much the entire team was there. Ashley's mom and stepdad were there, sitting with Lincoln at one of the tables, eating and watching Ashley as she moved around behind the counter. Naomi, Drew, Cassidy, and David were at another. The visual of Drew and David's large, muscular frames seated on the delicate-looking chairs was highly amusing.

In line in front of the counter were Jennifer and Jensen, standing awkwardly beside each other as they picked out their treats. Mason wondered if Jensen had considered the fact that their head boss was also going to be here when he'd invited Jennifer to accompany him.

He would guess not by the way Jensen kept shooting little glances over at Lincoln to see if he was paying attention to the fact that their receptionist/office manager was there with one of his team members. At least, Mason assumed that was what Jensen was worried about—it wasn't like Lincoln had any room to talk when it came to age gaps in a relationship.

Behind Jennifer and Jensen was Claudia, her brother Manuel, and her brother's best friend, Ian. They were occasional regulars in the office, stopping by to visit Claudia. Ian's grandfather had been their client a few times, but it was really his relationship with Manuel that got him inside the office. Manuel had a pass to see Claudia, and Ian could show up with him.

His attention came to rest on the redhead behind the counter.

Hair pulled back in a high ponytail with a navy and cream striped bow adorning it, Audrey was wearing either a navy dress or shirt to go with it, with a creamy apron atop it. Between the apron and the counter, Mason couldn't tell whether it was just a top or a dress.

Her eyes were bright with excitement, and she was beaming at everyone and everything, happiness practically spilling out of her. There was just something about her that drew his attention, even though he was trying to focus on the woman who'd walked in with him.

As if his thought summoned her gaze, Audrey looked straight at him, and the moment their eyes met, his heart did a little triple beat in his chest.

Fuck.

CHAPTER TWELVE

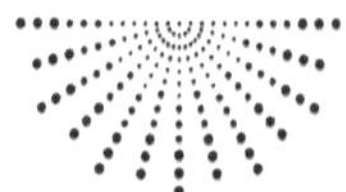

AUDREY

The Outlands looked like a regular building from the outside, though the curtains were drawn over the front window so no one could see into it. The window looked like it was tinted as well, adding an extra layer of privacy.

Trying to hide her nerves as she got out of the backseat of Ashley's car, Audrey brushed her hands over her borrowed skirt. Her legs were getting cold because she wasn't wearing anything but a thong and fishnets underneath, and she was starting to regret her decision to wear heels instead of boots. Even if they were her favorite, most comfortable pair of heels that were also incredibly cute. At least she had her coat on for now, which helped with both warmth and confidence.

She was going to have to take the coat off once they got inside, though, and she was a little nervous about that. While she wasn't a stranger to low-cut necklines, she'd never worn anything like a corset before, and her boobs were pushed up so high, they practically made a shelf.

"You look fantastic," Ashley, the owner of the skirt and corset Audrey was wearing, reassured her. She was the closest in size to

Audrey and had offered to let her borrow an outfit for tonight. While Audrey might not be entirely comfortable with how her boobs were being shown off, she did love the emerald green of the corset and the way the black skirt flirted around her thighs.

Ashley also looked gorgeous; her royal blue peacoat covered most of her outfit, but she was wearing really cute black stockings with seams up the back that were still visible. The coat set off her ivory skin and pink cheeks nicely. Her long brown hair with its blonde highlights spilled over her shoulders and down her back, gleaming even in the lamplight.

"You really do," Naomi agreed. She was getting out on the passenger side, wearing a fuzzy black-and-white coat of faux fur. Her hair was freshly done in long microbraids that were pulled half back away from her face, in a half-up, half-down style. "New things are always scary, but once you get inside, you'll see there's nothing to worry about."

"Thanks. And thanks for coming with me." Audrey took as deep a breath as she could with the corset gripping her so tightly. Every breath like that meant her boobs went up again because she couldn't expand her belly the way she normally would for a deep breath.

Cassidy had offered to have Audrey come with her and David, but Audrey felt like she was already taxing her brother's sensibilities enough just by showing up. She wasn't sure he would be able to handle the getting-ready process or actually taking her there. In his head, she was still his baby sister who he had to protect.

"Of course. I had to make sure you would go through with it," Ashley said with a wink, closing her car door. She looked over at Naomi. "She's been a bundle of nerves all day. She even started hiding in the back of the bakery with Alexis at one point."

It turned out Alexis was shy around large groups of people, and she'd hide in the back for most of the day. Which was fine, since her job was decorating, and she had plenty to do to get ready for the grand opening tomorrow. With everything going on, it would be easier to introduce her to everyone on another day.

"I wasn't hiding, I was helping," Audrey protested. "Alexis had a lot of chocolate work to do for the decorations for tomorrow's cupcakes."

That and when Mason appeared, she'd lost her head a little. He'd come in, and they'd locked gazes, and she'd barely been able to breathe... and then she'd seen Yasmine beside him. Remembered he was completely off limits. And hid in the back with Alexis, helping with the chocolate decorations for tomorrow, until he left.

Yeah, she wasn't proud of that, but it was better than making a fool of herself in front of everyone.

If she didn't meet someone new to crush on tonight at the club, she was downloading a dating app on Sunday. Not tomorrow because she was going to be totally focused on her bakery. Though she didn't have high hopes for tonight, either, just because she was a little nervous about meeting Doms.

After finishing *Milking Mina*, she'd asked Cassidy for a recommendation for something a little more realistic and without the hucow aspect, and Cassidy had started her on the Suncoast Society Series by Lesli Richardson. The kink was a lot more up Audrey's alley, though she wasn't sure about the two men thing in the first book. She liked the idea of one person for herself. If more than one person was what someone else wanted, she was happy for them as long as they were happy, but it wasn't what she wanted for herself.

She wanted something like what Cassidy and David had. Probably. Not knowing exactly what they were doing behind closed doors—and not wanting to know—she might not want to do all the things they did. After reading a few Suncoast books, she was pretty sure she'd like to try bondage and maybe some spanking and flogging... canes and whips sounded far too scary.

The whole thing was pretty intimidating, really. But it was exciting too. Alluring. It made her shivery and scared, the way a really good horror movie did, and she'd never avoided those.

"Let's go," Ashley said, sliding her arm through Audrey's and pulling her forward. Naomi came in on the other side, doing the same. Even if she'd wanted to run, she wouldn't have been able to. Although she didn't want to run. Mostly.

"Again, thanks for coming with me tonight. Especially since both of you have men you could be coming with."

"Lincoln has too much to do this evening," Ashley said with a shrug. "He's just happy that I have something to keep me out of trouble."

"Same with Drew. He's been working a lot lately." Unlike Ashley, Naomi didn't sound nonchalant, though she was trying.

"Really? Lincoln doesn't usually work late; this is an exception." Frowning, Ashley leaned forward to look around Audrey at Naomi. The other woman shrugged, turning her head away, like she was looking down the street... or avoiding Ashley's gaze.

"He's been overworking ever since Don. I think, no... I know he's blaming himself." Naomi sighed. "It's fine. He'll get past it eventually, and it's not like I don't have plenty to do. There's *always* something to do."

"Let me know if you need help with anything," Ashley said immediately. "Just because I have a new job doesn't mean I can't help."

"I know." Naomi smiled.

"I might be able to help eventually, too, just... right now I'm kind of crazy busy," Audrey said.

"You're already helping, just by sending over the end-of-day stuff to us instead of throwing it in the trash," Naomi reminded her as they reached the door to the club. "Which is very appreciated."

"I'm glad to." Especially when she'd found out the number of kids at the shelter Naomi ran. Poor kids. They deserved treats, considering everything they were going through.

Remembering the women Naomi helped on a daily basis, Audrey shook off some of her blues. The worst thing a man had ever done to her was cheat on her. Those women and kids were going through much worse things. Cassidy had been through something much worse.

Even Ashley. She couldn't imagine what it felt like to have her dad cheat on her mom with her best friend, let alone said friend becoming her new stepmother... it was one of those things where truth was stranger than fiction. If she'd read that in a book, she would have said it was too unrealistic because who would even do that?

And yet Ashley's ex-best friend had done just that. The double betrayal had to have been awful.

Of course, she'd also gotten her ex-bestie back... Ashley's husband, Lincoln, was Rebecca's father. So, she'd become her stepmother's stepmother. It was brutally efficient karma.

"Here we are." Ashley stepped forward and opened the door to let Naomi and Audrey inside. Despite having been betrayed in such an awful way by her best friend, she hadn't let the experience jade her. Maybe she'd been different right after it happened, but she was clearly incredibly happy and secure in her friendships now.

Audrey was happy for her and happy to be included in them.

Naomi also let go of Audrey's arm, letting her walk in first. She would have rather followed one of them in, but since they were practically pushing her ahead of them, she wasn't going to kick up a fuss.

It turned out the entryway wasn't all that impressive. At least, not in terms of being a kink club. It looked like a regular room with a front desk and a coat check behind it. There was a bouncer standing next to the door that must lead to the main club, and to the right of him were two more doors labeled as bathrooms. One of them had a dragon carved into it, and the other had what looked like a die with too many sides.

"Um, which one are we supposed to use?" Audrey asked in a whisper, turning to Naomi, who was right behind her, and pointing at it.

"Whichever one feels right to you today." Naomi smiled at her. "They're for everyone. Though there are locker rooms inside the club, too."

Audrey nodded and followed Naomi over to the front desk, trying not to feel too much like a puppy. Ashley looped her arm through Audrey's again as they moved, which helped a little... unless Ashley was acting as a leash?

"Hi, Eben. We've got a friend with us tonight," Naomi said, greeting the woman behind the desk. She was another beautiful Black woman, with straight black hair that brushed the tops of her shoulders. The corset she was wearing was black with a white collar, making it look almost like business-wear if one ignored the very low neckline and the way her cleavage filled it.

"I heard. You're David's sister, right?" Eben asked, smiling brightly at Audrey. "He and Cassidy are already inside."

"That's me." Nerves bubbled in her stomach, but she pushed them down so she could return Eben's smile.

"And you just opened a bakery, right?"

"Grand opening is tomorrow, but yeah. I had the soft open today, so that might be what you're thinking of. It's called Cupcakes and Crumbs, and it's on Liberty." Great, now she was babbling.

"How exciting! I'll try to stop by this weekend if I can. I'm a sucker for a really good chocolate chip cookie." Eben grinned. "Especially if it's gooey in the middle."

"She makes *great* chocolate chip cookies," Ashley said immediately, giving Audrey's arm a little squeeze as she advertised for her. "You're going to love them."

"Awesome. I can't wait." Eben even sounded like she meant it.

"Thank you." Audrey could feel the blush starting on her cheeks. Taking compliments was not her forte, but she'd discovered that Ashley only doubled down if she tried to dismiss it.

Eben got them checked in, had Audrey sign off on some paperwork, took their coats to hang up, then wished them a good night. It was all surprisingly mundane.

That ended when they walked past the bouncer and through the door into the main area of the club. It was a bar, but Audrey had never seen bar patrons dressed like this before. The corset and skirt she was wearing, which had felt so very risqué, suddenly seemed very tame by comparison to some of the outfits on display. Her eyes widened as she took in the scene.

A woman wearing nothing but a full body fishnet stocking that covered her from neck down to where her feet disappeared into stiletto heels, was kneeling on a cushion beside another woman who sat on a barstool. The woman on the barstool was dressed head to toe in what looked like black leather, completely covered. Sitting across from her was a man wearing shiny black short shorts, calf boots, and silver piercings glinting from his nipples. There were three drinks on the table, and Audrey watched, fascinated, as the woman picked up one and lowered it down in front of the woman kneeling beside her, allowing her to sip through the straw.

"Keep moving, and try not to stare *too* much, though obviously you don't have to look away," Ashley murmured, pulling her along. On Audrey's other side, Naomi chuckled, as she was close enough to hear Ashley's comment. "Oh, look, there's Cassidy and David."

Audrey's head jerked around, although she had the belated thought that maybe she didn't want to see what her brother was wearing...

Thankfully, he was wearing more than he did at the beach. No shirt, but he had on pants. The fact that they were leather and a little tighter than the pants he normally wore was something she could easily ignore. He was looking back at her, though, for only a moment, before covering his eyes and groaning. Next to him, Cassidy was giggling, her eyes bright with amusement.

Claudia stepped out to peer around David and grinned when she saw Audrey. While Cassidy was dressed more like Naomi, Audrey, and Ashley, Claudia stood out for the simple fact that she was far more covered. While she was wearing a corset and a short skirt, her boots were thigh high, nearly to the hem of her skirt, and had viciously spiked heels. Her dark hair had been pulled back into a severe bun high on the back of her head, and her makeup was smoky, with sharp cat's eye eyeliner.

She gave Audrey a little wave, and Audrey waved back at her.

The presence of so many of the women who had befriended her was helping to settle her nerves.

Then Claudia's focus went beyond her, and she waved again, still smiling. Audrey turned to see who Claudia was looking at, and all those nerves that had just started to settle zipped right back up and started to swoop all around her.

Mason had just walked in, and just like her brother, he was wearing nothing but leather pants... but her reaction to seeing *his* upper body was very different. She was so distracted, she almost didn't notice that Yasmine was at his side until Mason offered Yasmine his elbow to help steady her on the towering heels she was wearing.

Audrey's heart sank into her stomach.

Coming tonight suddenly felt like a horrible mistake.

CHAPTER THIRTEEN

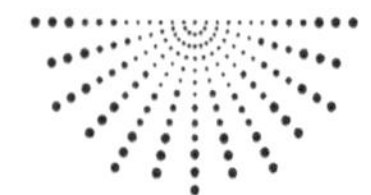

MASON

Fuck.

He had his fiancée on his arm, and she looked amazing in a tightly fitted PVC top and skirt that hugged her body like a glove, but the difference between his reaction to seeing her versus Audrey was hard to ignore. While he could aesthetically appreciate Yasmine's beauty and ensemble, it didn't cause the spark of hot need that one glance at Audrey did.

Audrey, with her red hair finally down, curling around her pale shoulders, her breasts plumped up by the corset that nipped in her waist to give her an exaggerated hourglass. Mason had never really thought of himself as a curves man... until now. He'd never really cared what a woman's body looked like enough to have a preference.

Until now.

But he had a feeling it wasn't a preference for a body type.

It was a preference for Audrey.

Fuck. Fuck. Fuck.

Taking in a deep breath, he tore his gaze away from the new complication in his life, forcing himself to focus on the woman leaning on his arm. The one he was engaged to.

They were going to scene tonight, pushing their relationship forward. If his subconscious was already balking at the idea of such a massive change in his life, it made sense that continuing to move forward would cause more resistance. There was nothing inherently special about Audrey other than she'd shown up at the exact right time—or wrong time—for his brain to latch onto.

Staying away from her hadn't worked, trying his version of exposure therapy hadn't worked… so, from here on out, he was going to stay away, even though it didn't seem to change his reaction to her. Because that was better than being around her. It wasn't fair to Yasmine.

Yasmine was now frowning at him. He pushed a smile onto his lips.

"I already reserved a private room for us, but we have a minute to say hi to everyone, if you'd like." If she didn't, he would count his blessings; it would be a lot easier to ignore his reaction to Audrey if he didn't have to stand very close to her, but he also wasn't going to keep Yasmine from her friends.

She hesitated for a moment, then nodded. "Let's go say hi, real quick."

Great.

He led her over, giving everyone a genial smile while the women greeted each other with hugs and compliments. He and David did the manly nod thing, jerking their chins up at each other.

The fact that Jensen wasn't here didn't entirely surprise Mason. He didn't think that going to the bakery together meant that Jennifer and Jensen were suddenly an exclusive item, but he couldn't see the other man showing up at the club tonight after having a date with her. It did surprise, and worry him, that Drew wasn't here but Naomi was.

They were definitely going to need to have that talk soon.

"How's your day going?" Mason asked David, who was doing everything he could to avoid looking in his sister's direction.

"Terrible. First, my grandma shows up at the bakery with Mick as her date, and now I have to see my sister like this."

Mason almost choked.

"Your grandmother and Mick?" Geezus, the age gap on that was worse than Lincoln and Ashley.

"I don't think they're actually *doing* anything other than annoying me, but I'm not sure they're *not* doing anything either. Grandma told me it was none of my business and started threatening to take my butt stick out herself so she could whack me with it." David's tone and expression were so direly grim, Mason could hardly contain his amusement.

"What did Audrey think?" he couldn't help but ask. It was only natural to ask since she was Brenda's other grandchild.

"I don't think she realized they were on a 'date'," David said, using his fingers to make air quotes around the word 'date.' "She was busy because that was around the time Harris and his team came in, just after you left."

"Ah, gotcha. Well, the more Brenda knows it bothers you, the more she's going to do it."

"What if I manage to make it stop bothering me, and it turns out she wasn't doing it just to bother me?" The pained expression on David's face made Mason press his lips together.

It wasn't nice to laugh at a friend's pain, but the situation was genuinely hilarious. Especially the way David was reacting to it. Mason was ninety-nine percent sure Brenda and Mick were just messing with him. That was exactly the kind of thing they would both do.

There was that other one percent, though...

"Mason, should we go?" Yasmine asked, turning toward him.

He glanced over at the clock on the wall.

"Yeah, our room should be ready." He swept his gaze across everyone with a small smile as he held out his arm for her to take again, deliberately not letting himself focus on or linger on any singular person. "Have a good night, everyone."

Leading Yasmine away to the sounds of everyone else wishing them a good night, they headed over to the opening at the back of the bar, which looked over the lower floor. That's where both the Dungeon and the private rooms were. When they reached the lower floor, something made Mason look up. Audrey was there, flanked by Ashley and Naomi, with Claudia hovering protectively just behind them.

So, she was well taken care of.

Still, his stomach twisted at knowing there were probably any number of Doms who would jump at a chance to introduce her to the scene, even with her brother around.

It would be a good thing if one did. Maybe then my brain would get on board with reality.

Thankfully, because of the overhang, he couldn't keep looking up at her without being obvious. A few moments later, he and Yasmine were walking out of view of the balcony and to the side, where the private rooms were, his name on the board outside the second one.

"Here we go," he said with forced cheerfulness as he escorted her into the room. His club bag had already been brought down and was waiting for him on one of the chairs. The room was richly furnished and decorated. There was a bed as well as a St. Andrew's Cross, a spanking bench, and an assortment of implements in case he didn't have something he wanted to use. Gavin, the owner of the club, made sure the rooms were always fully stocked. "Everything is already set up. Do you need to use the bathroom or anything before we get started?"

Rather than answering right away, Yasmine walked over to the bed. Mason frowned as he watched her, wondering what she was doing. Sitting down on the edge, she rested her elbows on her knees, hands clasped in front of her.

With a sigh, she looked up to meet his gaze.

"We need to talk."

***

Audrey

Forcing herself to watch Mason and Yasmine walk out of sight, so that maybe her stupid brain would get the hint and cut it out with this wild crush, Audrey felt her stomach churn nauseously. She didn't want to hang out or scene or find a Dom to flirt with. She wanted to go home, eat some ice cream, and maybe cry a little. Which was a ridiculous way to feel because it wasn't like there was anything between her and Mason, other than her own imagination.

She didn't want anyone to realize *why* she was leaving, though, which meant she had to stay at least a little longer.

Her gaze drifted over the activities below, and her stomach did another flip. There was a man spanking a woman bent over a bench. Her cheeks were a bright, hot red, yet every time his hand came down, she moaned so loudly, it was audible where Audrey and the others were standing.

Another section had a woman standing against a large wooden X shape, leaning against it while a man used a flogger on her upper back and buttocks, both of which were exposed. Her darker-hued skin didn't show the color of impact the way the woman being spanked did, but from the undulations of her body, it was clear she was enjoying it just as much.

Arousal stirred, clashing with the unhappy envy bubbling inside her. It was hard not to picture Mason doing the same things with Yasmine. Even if Yasmine hadn't particularly liked kissing him.

Thanks to watching the scenes below, it took her a few minutes to realize that Claudia and Naomi were having a conversation off to her side.

"What's wrong?" she asked, leaning toward them. They both looked concerned. It might not be any of her business, but she was dying for a distraction.

"Mason and Yasmine," Naomi said, the side of her mouth quirking.

Welp. So much for a distraction.

"Oh, yeah, you noticed that, too?" Ashley said from Audrey's other side, trapping her in the middle of the conversation.

"Noticed what?" Audrey asked. If she had to hear about Yasmine and Mason, she might as well understand what they were talking about.

"She had her dumping face on," Claudia explained, which made Audrey blink.

"Her what?"

"Yeah, so when she talks about being cursed, she tends to leave a few things out." Naomi leaned against the balcony, elbow propped up on the bar, and she sighed loudly. "Like the fact that she's the one who has dumped every single one of her boyfriends *and* pointed them in the direction of the person she thinks they're going to end up with."

"To give her credit, she's got a knack for matchmaking," Claudia said. "Even if it does cause her to sabotage every relationship she's ever been in."

"So, she's not really cursed?"

"Cursed by self-fulfilling prophecies, maybe." Ashley sighed. "I don't know whether to be happy or not. She wants marriage and kids so badly, but she and Mason just don't fit right together in my head. I wasn't going to say anything because it seemed like a done deal, but..." She shrugged.

"He's too reserved for her," Claudia agreed. "She needs someone who will be passionate about her. I don't think I've ever seen Mason be passionate about anything. It's not that he doesn't care, but... it's like he's always watching things happen around us rather than being a part of them."

Audrey had noticed that, although she wouldn't say he was completely removed from everything. And both Yasmine and Mason seemed reserved to her, so why was it bad for Yasmine if he was also reserved? She didn't know why she felt the urge to defend Mason; it wasn't like anyone was saying anything *bad,* exactly. But she also didn't know either Mason or Yasmine as well as Claudia, Naomi, and Ashley did.

"Do you think she'll really go through with it?" Naomi asked. "Maybe they'll just talk about it. They've already announced the whole engagement thing to all of us. It makes it a lot harder to back out now."

"I just don't understand why they didn't test their chemistry before deciding marriage would work." Claudia shook her head. "I guess that's what they're doing now, but it feels a little late."

As much as Audrey wanted to defend Mason and say that he was a good match for Yasmine—for any woman, really—her stomach flipped over at the thought of them testing their chemistry. Doing the things that she was seeing on the floor below.

"You know how Yasmine gets. She probably thought it would work out. Check all the boxes and everything should run smoothly." Ashley sighed. "If only it was that easy. I don't know what to hope for. I don't want another relationship not to work out, especially now that she's engaged, but at the same time, can you imagine marrying someone who you have no chemistry with?"

"Especially since she said kissing him was like kissing her brother." Claudia shuddered. "And not in the Cersei and Jaime way."

"Oh, bleh." Naomi made a gagging noise.

"Who?" Audrey asked, frowning. All three women turned to stare at her.

"You haven't seen Game of Thrones?"

"Or read them?" Naomi asked, right on the heels of Claudia's question.

"Um, no." Definitely not the kind of television or books her mother would approve of. Just like romances. In fact, Audrey was starting to realize exactly how many things she'd missed out on that she actually liked because she was trying to do the things her mother approved of. "I guess I'll add that to the list of things I need to do."

"Absolutely." Claudia beamed at her, eagerness lighting up her eyes with anticipation. "We're going to have so much fun. There are so many things that you get to experience for the first time."

"And she gets to live vicariously through you as you do," Ashley teased. "Just watch out, she'll have you watching Lord of the Rings next."

"I haven't seen those movies either, though I did read The Hobbit for school," Audrey admitted.

"You poor deprived baby," Claudia put her arm around Audrey's shoulders, making her laugh. "Don't worry. I'm making a mental list in my head of all the fun things we're going to do."

"Fun, nerdy things." Ashley snickered.

"You enjoyed them, don't lie."

"I did say they're fun. I don't mind being a nerd."

Naomi leaned over the balcony railing again, looking down at the activities below before glancing back at them.

"Do you want to go downstairs?" she asked, directing the question at Audrey. "We could get a closer look at everything."

"Um…" No. She didn't. Not really. Because downstairs was where Mason and Yasmine were. Doing… something. Maybe breaking up. But maybe trying to make the chemistry work between them.

Which was something she really didn't want to think about, much less face head-on. How would she feel if they walked out of the room, disheveled and smiling?

Jealous.

Envious.

Like crying.

Definitely not anything she wanted any of the people here to witness her feeling because she had no right to it. So, she had a crush on Mason. He was *taken.* Even if he and Yasmine broke things off tonight, she couldn't justify acting on her crush right after they broke up, if ever.

She liked Yasmine. They were becoming friends. And she was becoming friends with all of Yasmine's friends.

Ruining that by dating Yasmine's ex wasn't something she was willing to do. No matter how attracted she was to him.

"We don't have to," Naomi reassured her. "That can wait 'til next time, if you're interested. I just wanted you to know it's an option."

"I think I'm more comfortable up here for right now, if that's okay." Audrey smiled weakly. It would be easier to hide her reaction up here if Yasmine and Mason appeared any time soon.

Though her goal was to stay long enough not to arouse suspicion, then leave before they came out. Either way. Because she didn't want to look devastated if they were happy or happy if they had broken up.

"It's absolutely okay," Claudia reassured her, while Naomi and Ashley nodded in encouragement. "This is a lot to take in, even if you're interested. If you decide you want to go down, we can go down. If you want to stay up here tonight, we can stay up here. And if you see someone you want to talk to, we can introduce you. Whatever you want."

"Thanks." She wished Claudia's reassurance made her feel better, but unfortunately, the thing she wanted was the one thing none of them could offer her.

Because he was one level down in a private room with the woman he was going to marry.

CHAPTER FOURTEEN

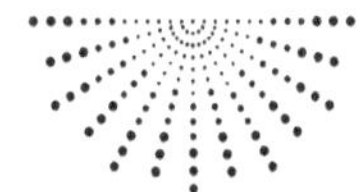

MASON

Making his way over to the bed where Yasmine was sitting, Mason settled next to her. Whatever she wanted to talk about, he got the feeling it wasn't the scene he had planned.

"Okay," he said slowly. "Let's talk then."

"Are you attracted to me?" she asked bluntly, lifting her chin to meet his gaze, more than a touch of defiance in her demeanor. Her dark eyes weren't accusatory, but they were filled with some kind of emotion he couldn't read.

Fuck.

He didn't want to hurt her.

"I think you're an incredibly attractive woman," he replied with complete honesty.

The look she gave him told him that he wasn't fooling her.

"Yes, but are you attracted _to_ me?" she repeated with emphasis. "There's a big difference between finding someone attractive and actually being attracted to them. Maybe I should preface this by saying, I find you a very attractive man, but I think I'm lacking in feelings of actual attraction."

Mason let out a long, slow breath. He didn't want to hurt her feelings. Even though she acknowledged that she felt a lack of chemistry, that didn't mean she wouldn't be hurt if he acknowledged the same.

But he also couldn't lie to her.

"I'm not sure I'm attracted to you," he admitted. "As I said, I find you very attractive. I feel as though being attracted to you is the next natural step since we're engaged. We might just have to work at it a little more than a couple who began their relationship with attraction."

She looked at him for a long moment.

"I suppose that makes sense." But she didn't sound entirely convinced.

Taking her hand in his, Mason wrapped his fingers around hers and covered both of them with his other hand.

"I'm sure every arranged marriage starts off a little awkwardly. We know we want the same things out of life, though. We've had a lot of good discussions about what we want our lives to be, and we're compatible in every way when it comes to that. The attraction might be coming slower, but that doesn't mean it won't happen. We're just... doing things a little differently than everyone else. What their relationships look like will be different from what we look like."

Slowly, Yasmine nodded her head.

"That's true. I just... I don't know. I thought things would fall into place once we were engaged. But when we kissed, it just didn't..." She waved her free hand, trying to explain in a gesture what she couldn't find the words for.

Mason understood what she meant because he'd felt the same. That hadn't changed things for him, though. Neither had his attraction to Audrey. He'd already made his choices before he'd met Audrey. Getting engaged to Yasmine hadn't been a spur-of-the-moment, impulsive jump; it had been a well-thought-out decision he'd considered from all sides before making.

He wasn't going to let that all go for a flash of attraction, of chemistry, that could very well disappear as easily as it had come on. What he and Yasmine had together was important—respect, affection, the same goals.

"Once again, we're on the same page," he joked, getting a very brief smile from her. "But I don't think that was a fair test either. We hadn't kissed like that before. I surprised you. Neither of us knew what to expect."

If he was being completely honest, part of the reason he'd kissed her like that was in reaction to *his* reaction to Audrey. Which wasn't good motivation. He'd wanted to know the difference, though.

He couldn't help but compare the lack of attraction he felt for Yasmine to the instant attraction he felt every time he saw Audrey. But he'd come in tonight planning to work on their chemistry, ready to make it work. So, maybe it was different from when he'd kissed her before.

His eyes dropped down to her lips.

Full. Pouting. Red from her lipstick.

They should be tempting, but he could easily resist because there wasn't anything to resist.

If she was Audrey…

Stop it.

Obviously, this was a case of wanting what he couldn't have. For all he knew, if he ended things with Yasmine, his attraction to Audrey would end just as abruptly. Once he could have her, he wouldn't want her so much.

And then he'd have let Yasmine down for no reason, he'd have to tell his parents and her parents and all their friends… the feeling of admitting such a big failure to everyone because he'd leapt before he looked roiled in his gut. No thanks.

"Should we try kissing again?" Yasmine sounded uncertain.

"It can't hurt, right?" He smiled and leaned forward, forcing himself to focus on the woman in front of him. The woman he had agreed to marry.

Lowering his lips to hers, he kissed her gently at first, then began to lean in… but she pulled away and jumped to her feet. Mason stared at her as she began pacing back and forth.

"Yasmine?"

"Just… just give me a minute." She came to a halt, staring up at the ceiling with her hands fisted at her side, taking a deep breath before meeting his gaze again. "This just. It's not what I thought it would be like."

"What did you think it would be like?" he asked, and she narrowed her eyes at his reasonable tone.

"Well, I didn't think it would be like talking to a therapist, for one," she snapped at him.

Mason put his hands up in surrender. This was the first time he had ever seen a flash of Yasmine's temper. He didn't want to fight with her about this.

"Sorry, it's hard to turn off sometimes. But I also can't meet your expectations if I don't know what they are."

Unfortunately, something about what he was saying, or maybe how he was saying it, seemed to be frustrating her even more. She started pacing back and forth, shooting him unhappy little glances.

"I thought we'd find a way to make things more romantic." She rubbed her forehead. "Crap. I can't believe this is happening to me again."

"Nothing is happening to you again." Mason patted the bed next to him, where she'd previously been seated. "Come sit down, and we'll talk through this."

"If we're trying to find passion, should we be talking through it?" she asked him. "Why not leap up and take me in your arms? Or pull me over your lap and spank me for overthinking?"

"Is that what you want me to do?" He was floundering, and he knew it, but he didn't know how to fix it.

"I don't know!" She stomped her foot. Actually stomped her foot. "Maybe I want you to just *do* something. Anything. Not talking, but *doing*."

Mason stared at her. He'd never seen Yasmine like this before, and he didn't really know what to do now that he was. If she was on the team and in his office for a session, they'd talk through what was frustrating her. What was making her feel this way. Why she was reacting this way.

But she'd made it clear she didn't want him to talk to her like that... and he didn't know what else to do.

What did she want him to do?

Sighing, her shoulders dropped into a slump.

"Maybe this is something we should have worked out before getting engaged."

"Probably," he admitted. "I think we can still work through it, though."

"Can we?" She shook her head. "I keep feeling like you're not attracted to me, but you are attracted to someone else."

The thoughts in Mason's brain came to a screeching halt, and he suddenly felt like he couldn't breathe. The expression on her face went from almost accusatory to dropping.

"Shit. I knew it." Tears gathered in her eyes. "Why do I keep doing this to myself?"

"Hey, hey, Yasmine..." Mason got to his feet, but once he was there, he wasn't sure what he should do. Pull her into his arms? But in a non-romantic way? Hold his arms open so she could come in for a hug if she wanted? Or maybe he shouldn't have gotten to his feet at all. "You haven't done anything to yourself. I asked my parents for help with finding a wife; they reached out to your parents, and they matched us up. I think they did a good job, too."

"On paper, sure," Yasmine replied bitterly, starting to pace again. This time her arms were wrapped around her upper body like she was hugging herself.

Crap. He should hug her or something.

When she paced back his way, he did exactly that, gently pulling her into a hug. When she didn't resist, he decided it must have been the correct move. Thankfully. She leaned her forehead against his shoulder, her arms still around herself, keeping her distance but also accepting his comfort. He felt her shoulders slouch again as he rubbed his hand up and down her back.

"Haven't you ever heard the saying that marriage takes work? Or that love isn't an emotion, it's a series of choices?" he asked. "I've chosen you. Or, well, my parents chose you, but I agreed. I'm willing to work on this. We just keep choosing each other and working on it, and we'll figure it out."

"That doesn't sound bleak to you?" She lifted her head to look at him plaintively, turning her arms within his embrace, so her balled fists were placed against his chest. "Especially if you're attracted to… someone else in a way that you aren't with me."

"I don't have to act on any attraction that I don't want to act on." Even as he said the words, he felt his chest tighten. They were true, but it also felt wrong. He was more than his instincts and reactions, though. He had control over what he did. "We can choose each other."

It made sense to him, but Yasmine was shaking her head. His heart sank in his chest, and at the same time, tension slowly released from his muscles. He hadn't even realized how much tension he had been holding in his body until it began to dissipate.

"I don't want to marry someone who doesn't want to be with me with their whole heart. Can you honestly say that person is you?"

He hesitated.

"That's what I thought." She dropped her head back down and pressed her forehead against her fists.

"Yasmine… we have to be sensible about this."

"No."

"What?"

This time, when she lifted her head, she pushed with her arms as well, and he let her break his hold. Let her go. Let her step back. Her chin held high, there were unshed tears in her eyes, but her expression was calm. Determined.

"You're the one who isn't being sensible." She shook her head and took another step back. "It's not sensible to get married when we aren't attracted to each other. It's even less sensible when you *are* attracted to someone else, especially someone we'd be seeing on a regular basis."

Mason opened his mouth.

Closed it.

Felt his jaw pop as he clenched his teeth together.

"We can't get married," Yasmine concluded sadly. "It's not sensible."

"It's not sensible to give up a future we both want because of something that's a chemical reaction in my brain. It will go away."

Her eyes widened as she met his gaze again, her surprise evident. Then she laughed, a short, sharp sound that snapped through the air before cutting off as abruptly as it began.

"Oh my God. You actually think that's true."

"We are more than our impulses."

"We are, but that doesn't mean we can ignore them, either. Especially when we're about to make a life-altering decision. I don't want to be married to someone who isn't attracted to me but who is attracted to someone else, Mason. I don't want to be married to someone who has to *work* to be attracted to me." She sighed. "Maybe it's my fault. Maybe I was foolish for thinking everything would fall into place once we were engaged. I thought I could trick the curse, but I should have known better."

"You're not cursed." He didn't want her to keep thinking that.

Maybe he wasn't attracted to her, but he cared about her. She deserved to be happy. He wanted her to be happy. When they'd talked about what they wanted their lives to look like, her desire for children had been palpable, and she wanted a partner in that. Someone to lean on, someone to share the responsibility, someone to build a life with.

That was what he wanted, too. They could still make it work… but only if they were both on board. And it was starting to sound like she wanted things they hadn't talked about. Things he didn't know if he could give her, especially if he didn't even know she wanted them.

"Sure. I'm not cursed." Yasmine moved over to the bed and sat down heavily. "That's not the problem right now, though. The problem is figuring out what we're going to tell everyone."

Mason followed her. He sat down next to her and put his arm around her.

"The same way we did it before; we'll tell them together. We can still be friends. This doesn't have to be some big, terrible thing." Although it felt like a failure, he wasn't going to tell Yasmine that. Not when she was so down on herself already. Yes, he dreaded going to his parents. Yes, he dreaded the jokes his friends were going to make.

Yes, he felt like his chance at a future with marriage and kids was slipping through his fingers.

But he wasn't going to drag Yasmine down the aisle.

If she didn't want to try to build that future with him, that was her prerogative.

"I feel like everyone is going to be laughing at me," she muttered. "Here I thought I had this great solution, and instead, it's blowing up in my face. As usual."

"We haven't told anyone yet. We can still get married."

The look that she sent him was half exasperation, half resignation.

"I'm starting to think we aren't as good a match as I thought," she said.

Mason did his best not to bristle. Maybe they weren't, but he was still convinced they could make it work if they tried. And he, at least, was the one willing to try.

"When do we tell everyone?"

"We could do it tonight. Most of them are here."

"And our parents?"

"Call them tomorrow."

Yasmine sighed.

"At least we hadn't started actually planning the wedding and putting down deposits. That would have made everything harder."

Mason squeezed her shoulders in reassurance. There was no rush from touching her. No heat, no sizzle. No heightened awareness. Just the warmth of her leg under his hand. Which was how he usually felt about women.

Which would have been enough except...

Yasmine wanted what he felt when he looked at Audrey. Even though it was likely to go away, especially now that his subconscious would no longer be panicking about making a major life change. Well. Perhaps once it did, he could approach Yasmine again and point that out.

"Just... promise me one thing," Yasmine said, her head dropping down to look at her lap, where her hands were resting.

"Anything."

"Give me a month."

"What?" A month for what?

She heaved a sigh.

"Give me a month before I have to see you with her. I just need some time to grieve the whole... almost getting what I want, only to lose it. I need a month."

"Yasmine... I'm not... there's not..."

"There is." She lifted her head now to give him a sharp look. "I think you two will be good together if you can get your head out of your ass and admit it. But I need a month. For dignity, if nothing else. Promise me."

"I promise."

It was an easy promise to make since he didn't have any intention of approaching Audrey about this at all. No matter what Yasmine thought. Now that the circumstances that had sparked his unusual reaction to her were being removed, his outsized attraction to her would follow.

That was the only logical outcome.

"So," Yasmine said, straightening up completely and squaring her shoulders. "How should we tell everyone?"

CHAPTER FIFTEEN

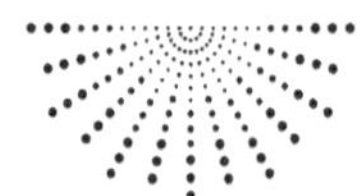

AUDREY

Walking into her bakery Saturday morning, Audrey felt both energized and oddly deflated. Going to the club last night had been a mistake, but she couldn't have known that when she decided to go.

She should have waited a week, at least, until her grand opening was over.

Now, she was excited and terrified about her bakery opening, while simultaneously feeling like a twit for having a crush on Mason.

He and Yasmine had still not come out of their private room when Audrey left. She'd claimed she was more tired than she'd realized and needed to get home to rest before the early opening of the bakery this morning. It was a really good excuse, and everyone had wished her well. Naomi hadn't seemed too sad to leave early, hopeful that Drew might be home by the time she got there. Ashley had stayed at the club; an older blonde woman named Leah had stopped by to let her know that Lincoln had called and would be meeting her there.

Audrey had left because she'd wanted to shut her brain off.

Surrounded by all the people happily engaged in scenes of pleasure and pain, she hadn't been able to stop thinking about what Mason and

Yasmine might be doing. The combination of envy and guilt that her thoughts induced had made her nauseous.

Anxiety over this morning hadn't helped either.

She'd barely gotten any sleep last night, despite leaving early. She'd been too wound up, recipes and decoration ideas dancing in her mind, alongside the sight of a woman moaning as she was whipped from behind. Nipple clamps. Leather. Latex. Crops.

A few of her ideas for cupcakes and cookies were now more bachelor/bachelorette themed… or, really, kink-club themed, but that wasn't necessarily a bad thing. Maybe the club sometimes did events where they would want themed baked goods. If not, she could always use it for Cassidy's bachelorette party. She and David weren't engaged, but Audrey knew her brother. He was locked in, and that was where their relationship was headed.

If Yasmine had a bachelorette party, Audrey could use the ideas for her, too.

Hopefully, by then, she'd be past this dumb crush.

Arriving at the back entrance to the bakery, she blinked in surprise when she saw Alexis already standing outside the door, huddled in a huge blue puffy coat. The long dark strands of her hair blew gently in the wind where it came out from the hood. The coat looked almost like a sleeping bag, extending all the way down to her ankles. Only her face could really be seen.

"Alexis? What are you doing here so early?" She was also curious why Alexis was *so* bundled up. It was cold, but not to the point where Audrey would wear a sleeping bag-style coat.

On the other hand, Alexis looked really warm, whereas Audrey was shivering slightly…

"I couldn't sleep, I was too excited," Alexis confessed, smiling shyly at her. "And then I got to the point where I was afraid that if I didn't get up, I'd end up sleeping through my alarm and be late, so I decided being early was better."

Audrey had to laugh as she unlocked the back door because she'd had a similar experience.

"I did the same thing," she admitted. "Although I must not have been up quite as early as you." She opened the door, and the blast of warm air made her sigh in relief. Maybe Alexis had the right idea with the super puffy warm coat. It wasn't stylish; Audrey's mom would throw a fit if she saw Audrey wearing something like that... but she wasn't making decisions to please her mom anymore.

Maybe this winter, she'd get a super unstylish, super warm, super puffy coat.

Alexis sighed with relief as she followed Audrey through the entrance into the warm kitchen. Warm compared to outside, at least. It would be even warmer once they got the ovens going.

"I'm still not used to the winter weather here," Alexis said, shrugging off her jacket to reveal a sensible white t-shirt and blue jeans underneath. Her body type was the opposite of Audrey's; she was petite all over, and on her, the simple clothing choices made her look like a short model. Her long dark hair had been pulled back into a severe bun, keeping all of it out of her face and pinned neatly in place. It reminded Audrey of the way she'd had to wear her hair for ballet class when she was younger, before her mother had decided she was too fat for ballet.

Audrey had told her there was no official uniform and to wear whatever she was comfortable in, but now she felt overdressed compared to Alexis. But she would also be in the front of the store today, as well as the back, so she'd wanted to make sure to dress up a little. Though she'd chosen comfortable tennis shoes to go with her black-and-white polka-dot dress and short socks over her stockings.

Hm.

Maybe the coat wasn't the only reason Alexis was warmer than her.

She'd felt like she'd needed to wear a dress today, since it was the grand opening. Was that from her mother's influence? No... she liked her dresses. She'd wanted to be a little fancy. Tomorrow, she'd wear jeans or at least some kind of pants. Today was special. Besides, her mother would have been horrified that she was wearing tennis shoes with a skirt, even if it was the more sensible option.

"You're from Savannah, right?"

"Florida, actually, but I went to school in Savannah. SCAD, the College of Art and Design." Alexis sighed. "Not that my degree is going anywhere at the moment. The Pittsburgh theater scene is only so happening."

It was a joke, but Audrey could feel the disappointment coming off Alexis at not being able to follow her dreams. She could sympathize, considering how long she'd squashed her own to please her family.

Alexis was in an even worse situation, though. She wasn't here to please her family; she was here because her only family member left, her aunt, was sick and needed someone to take care of her while she went through treatment.

"It'll get better. Your aunt has three more rounds of chemo, right?"

"Right." Alexis smiled wanly. "And then some waiting and some tests, then she'll decide if she's getting a mastectomy or not, and then we'll see."

When Audrey had hired Alexis, she'd known that it was possible the other woman would be moving away during the summer, but she'd also been the best person for the job. She baked, she was a good decorator, and she didn't mind the early hours or the pay.

"If you ever want to make something special for her here, do it," Audrey offered.

"Thanks. She's usually not super interested in food after the chemo, but there are usually some good days before the next round, so I might take you up on that."

"Please do. Okay. Not to change the subject, but…"

Alexis laughed as she walked over to the hooks on the wall where several pink and cream aprons with the Cupcakes and Crumbs logos on the chest hung. She took one off the wall and put it on as she spoke.

"Let's absolutely change the subject. Are you excited about today?"

"More like terrified." Audrey sighed, but she couldn't stop the smile that spread on her lips. "Also, really excited. I can't believe this is finally happening." She spread her arms out wide. "It feels like a dream. A really good one."

Alexis beamed at her.

"Good. That's what it should feel like." She took another apron off a hook and walked it over to hand to Audrey. "It's going to be amazing."

"I hope so. Okay. Let's get started."

They got the lights on, the ovens preheating, and the counters wiped down. Being here in the bakery made it easy for Audrey to focus on her excitement. Sure, she was still nervous that no one would show up today, but at the same time, she could easily picture a long line out the door. Especially since they served basic coffee along with a small fridge of refrigerated drinks, though she expected the coffee to be more popular on an early morning.

Humming as she went into the front to give the display cases a look over, she flicked the lights on and walked around in front of them. Empty right now, but soon to be filled with all the delicious treats she was going to sell. Her heart felt like it was going to pound right out of her chest with happiness.

Something on the outside of the front door caught her eye as she turned around, looking everything over. Frowning, she walked over and unlocked it. A piece of paper had been taped on the outside of the door, right over her logo.

Opening the door, she quickly pulled it off and let the door shut again as she stared at the message that had been left.

GET OUT.

It wasn't written; whoever had left it had used magazines and newspapers to cut out the large letters, like something from an old movie or TV show. The message was simple enough, but it also made no sense.

Maybe this was someone's idea of a practical joke?

Maybe it wasn't for her, though. Maybe it was for Alexis. Or Ashley. But that didn't make sense, either.

Maybe I'm making something out of nothing because my brother works for a security firm, and it's made me paranoid.

It was probably just kids or something. Maybe being silly on a dare. She didn't have a security camera up on the front door, only the back one and the one inside the bakery. She'd ask David about putting one on the front door later today. Not because of the note, but because the note made her think it was a smart thing to do.

"Hey, A-Team in the house!" Ashley's voice echoed in the kitchen, full of bright cheer. She was way earlier than she needed to be, too.

Audrey laughed as she shoved the note into her apron pocket. It seemed like they were all excited this morning, which took her spirits right back up to where they had been before she'd seen the note.

Quickly locking the front door again, Audrey headed back to the kitchen, where Ashley was already perched on a stool, watching Alexis as she was putting ingredients together for the cinnamon buns they were starting the morning with.

"Good morning," Audrey said as Ashley turned to look at her.

"Good morning, bakery owner!" Ashley grinned. "It's a beautiful day to open a bakery!"

Both Audrey and Alexis laughed, and Audrey went over to give the other woman a hug. Like Audrey, Ashley was dressed up in a cute blouse and skirt combo. She wasn't wearing tennis shoes, but she did have comfortable flats.

"I told you that you didn't have to dress up just to run the counter," Audrey said.

"Look who's talking." Ashley gave her a pointed up and down look.

"It's just for today."

"Well, so is this. Tomorrow, I'll be in jeans, I promise."

Alexis chuckled quietly.

"And this is why I work in the back," she said. "I got to wear jeans *today.*"

"One day, I'm going to get to see what you look like in a dress," Ashley threatened.

"Maybe one day." Alexis shook her head, smiling as she concentrated on what she was doing.

"So, what are you doing here so early?" Audrey asked Ashley. "Couldn't sleep?"

"Pretty much. I'm too excited. Mind if I make a pot of coffee to start us off?"

"Go for it." Audrey was too buzzed for any extra caffeine right now. If she had anything with caffeine, she'd probably go through the roof.

"Great. Also, you left the club way too early last night and missed all the juicy stuff. Mason and Yasmine broke up." Ashley announced the news like it was no big deal.

Audrey froze, hands on the bag of flour she'd been about to pick up. Emotions she was not proud of ran through her. Relief. Happiness. Hope. And guilt. Immediate crushing guilt because she was a horrible person.

"They're the ones with the arranged marriage… or engagement, I guess?" Alexis asked. Though she'd hidden in the back during the soft opening yesterday, she'd heard a lot about all the team from Ashley and Audrey's conversations.

"Yup, although not anymore." Ashley was busy getting the coffee pot filled with water and pouring it into the machine, so she thankfully didn't notice the way Audrey had frozen.

Forcing herself to pick up the flour and move over to the empty workspace on Alexis' left, Audrey bent her head down to hide her expression. She wasn't sure what the look on her face was because she wasn't sure how she felt about what she'd just heard.

"So, why did they break up?"

Bless Alexis for asking the important questions Audrey couldn't bring herself to voice. Whoever said curiosity was a bad thing?

"No chemistry. They were good on paper, but…" Ashley shrugged. "Maybe if they'd been down for a sexless marriage. I could see Mason going for that but not Yasmine."

"You could see Mason going for a sexless marriage?" Audrey frowned as she lifted her head, finally finding something to say. She couldn't see that about Mason at all.

"Well, maybe not without sex, but one without passion. I don't think he's asexual. But he's just not very *passionate*," Ashley corrected herself. "I can't see Yasmine living without passion and romance. And Mason is definitely not romantic."

Ashley sounded so sure of herself that Audrey bit her tongue against arguing with her. After all, it wasn't like she sounded judgmental while she was saying it. Just matter-of-fact. And Audrey didn't know him very well. Maybe he wasn't passionate or romantic.

Just because she was wildly attracted to him didn't mean that he returned the feeling. She had no idea if he was passionate or romantic. Maybe she was just making it all up in her head *because* she didn't really know him.

But she felt bad for him and Yasmine.

Getting engaged and telling everyone, then calling it off a week later, had to be difficult. Though she supposed it was easier than going through with the marriage and calling it off after that.

The fact that Mason was now single didn't mean anything to her. She didn't want a future without passion or romance either.

"I think I'm going to make some baklava cupcakes for Mason," she announced. "What's Yasmine's favorite flavor?"

That would give her something to do for both of them. Sure, baked goods couldn't fix a broken heart—or a slightly bruised one—but it was better than nothing.

"Orange chocolate, maybe?" Ashley suggested. "She doesn't eat a ton of sweets, but last year I found out she goes nuts for those chocolate oranges. She bought a whole bunch all at once since they're only sold around the holidays."

"Perfect." Maybe making the cupcakes would help assuage some of the guilt that was running through her.

She would also need to crush the hope because there was no way she was going to act on her crush. Yasmine was someone she wanted as a friend, and friends didn't date friends' exes.

In some ways, it was nice to have something to focus on other than her bakery finally opening. She could focus on condolence cupcakes instead of running into the bathroom to throw up her breakfast.

CHAPTER SIXTEEN

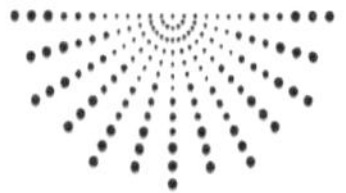

Telling their friends last night that the engagement was off had been the easy part. Telling their parents this morning, that was the hard part.

He'd gone to Yasmine's house, bringing breakfast, so they could call their parents together. Although she'd said they could do it separately, he thought a united front would be better, so their parents would know they were serious and both on the same page. Just like they'd been about the marriage, right up until the point that they weren't.

He'd brought breakfast because he was feeling guilty about the dream he'd had last night.

Despite the breakup and the fact he should no longer be experiencing any symptoms of cold feet, he'd had a dream about doing utterly filthy things with a certain redhead. And felt guilty enough that when he'd woken up with a raging erection, he'd gone to take a cold shower to make it go away instead of jerking off.

Even though it seemed like Yasmine had been pushing him in Audrey's direction last night, that didn't mean it was okay for him to dream about another woman right after ending their engagement. He handed over the sausage and egg bites she liked so much in an attempt to assuage his guilt.

"Oh, thanks." She smiled at him, though it wasn't the same smile she'd had a few days ago. It was genuine, but it didn't brighten her expression the same way.

"Breakfast tea, too." He held up the cup tray that had two drinks on it—tea for her and coffee for him. Some of the light came back into her eyes as she regarded him with amusement.

"Are you hoping that if you feed me, I won't fall apart on you?" she asked, reaching out with slim fingers to pull her tea from the tray. "I promise I won't. I'm sad, but I'm not crying my eyes out sad."

"I'm sad, too." He didn't even have to lie about that. "I really thought…" His voice trailed off because he didn't quite know how to phrase it, and he didn't want her to feel bad about deciding to end things. In a lot of ways, he knew she was right. And if she didn't want to marry him, she didn't want to marry him, and that was that.

"I know." Now her smile had turned sad again as she sat down at her kitchen table. "It's not your fault, Mason. It's just—"

"Do not say the curse." He cut her off, pretty sure that's exactly what she was going to say. "Curses aren't real."

"Okay, then you explain it, Mr. Logical. How does this keep happening to me?" She opened up the wrapper of her egg bites, raising one eyebrow as she challenged him.

"You really want to know what I think?" he asked slowly. After their talk last night, he'd done a lot of thinking about where they'd gone wrong.

Yasmine stared at him for a long moment, then shook her head.

"Let's just call our parents. It doesn't matter, anyway."

She was going to keep thinking she was cursed, regardless. Mason sighed inwardly, but he doubted he was going to be able to convince her with one conversation. He'd also rather not get into a fight right before talking to their parents.

"Okay, which of our parents do you want to talk to first?"

Thirty minutes later, Mason left Yasmine's apartment feeling like he'd been raked over hot coals. Their friends had been understanding and supportive. A few of them had even been encouraging. Not so much their parents. He was glad he'd been there for Yasmine when her mother had started lamenting that she was never going to have grandchildren at this rate. And he was glad Yasmine had been there for him when his father had started in on how important it was for a man to fulfill his obligations.

He didn't think he'd ever forget the look on his dad's face when Yasmine had coolly informed him that she would never want to marry a man who considered her an obligation rather than a partner and an honor, then offered her condolences to his mother if that was how she was treated in her marriage. He'd never seen his father stunned into silence before. That alone had been worth the discomfort of doing a video call and seeing his parents' expressions as he disappointed them.

Mason headed back to his own home to regroup. If his parents called him today, he was not going to answer.

Unfortunately, he didn't get the peace he was hoping for. Almost as soon as he got home and sat down, his phone rang. It wasn't his parents; it was his cousin Asad.

Sighing, Mason answered. He had no doubt that word had already reached his cousin, and if he didn't answer, Asad would just keep calling back until he did. Nonstop. He was annoying like that.

"Hello."

"So, what's this I hear about you breaking off your engagement?" Asad's voice, filled with the perpetual amusement it always held, also held a hint of accusation. "I didn't even know you were engaged."

"Yeah, I was going to call you to tell you, but I never got around to it." Which, when he thought about it, was an indication that maybe he hadn't really believed it was going to happen. Because Asad would definitely be one of his groomsmen in his wedding one day. If he ever got married, which at this point was looking less and less likely. "Is your mom calling Cyrus, too?"

Asad's brother would be another groomsman, along with the members of his team. Why he was thinking in terms of wedding planning now that he was no longer planning a wedding, he had no idea.

Maybe he was realizing that if he'd have been more excited about marrying Yasmine, Asad and Cyrus would have been his first calls after his parents and his team.

"Probably. She was appalled I didn't know anything about your engagement, much less you breaking it off." Asad chuckled. "I think your mom asked her to find out what I knew and why you weren't going through with it. So, Cuz, why were you getting married, and why aren't you? By the way, you're on speakerphone because Morgan is curious too."

"Hi, Mason. I don't have to listen in if you don't want me to, but I am very curious about what's going on. And Asad will probably tell me later, unless you specifically tell him not to."

"Hi, Morgan." He smiled. He'd found Morgan's bluntness charming when Asad had brought her as his date to Cyrus' wedding, and that charm remained. "It's fine, I don't mind you hearing, too. My parents know pretty much everything."

He gave them a quick rundown of asking his parents to arrange his marriage, them finding Yasmine, her 'curse', and their realization that there was not a lot of chemistry between them. Something Yasmine very much wanted and that he didn't think he could give her. They hadn't gone into detail with their parents about that; they'd just told them that once they'd become engaged, they'd realized that they weren't as compatible as they'd thought, and they wanted to end things rather than pushing forward.

"I was willing to try, but she wasn't… We talked a lot about what we wanted our lives to look like in general, and we were well matched on that, but once we got into the details, it was more difficult."

"You could have tried more romance, you know," Asad said. His voice was light, but he wasn't joking. "Women like the romance."

"It wasn't a romantic relationship; it was an arranged one."

There was a pause and silence on the other end of the line. Mason scowled, leaning back against his couch. He got the impression that Asad was face-palming or maybe that he and Morgan were exchanging looks, trying to figure out how to respond to that. Saying the words out loud… well, okay. He could see Asad's point. Maybe the arrangement had been out of logic and practicality, but once they were engaged, he could have tried to be more romantic.

"Fine," he said begrudgingly. "I probably could have tried to be romantic."

"It sounds like you two were more good friends with similar life goals than anything else," Morgan said. "But if she wanted romance, and you didn't, then you weren't going to be compatible."

"It's not that I don't want romance, I just..." His voice trailed off.

When he thought about being romantic, when he thought about being passionate, it hadn't been Yasmine he'd pictured in his head. Which officially made him the worst fiancé ever. She'd been right to dump him.

"You just?" Asad prodded. "What?"

"Yasmine accused me of being attracted to someone else, and I can't say she was completely wrong," he admitted. It felt like a relief to finally be able to say it to someone. He sure as hell couldn't tell anyone here in Pittsburgh and definitely not anyone on his team. "But it was just an attraction. I was still willing to marry her."

Someone sucked in a breath, and he was pretty sure it was Morgan.

Yeah, he was not coming off well here. He covered his face with his hand, sighing, because when he said it out loud, it really did sound pretty bad.

"I mean, attraction happens," Asad replied carefully. "You can't always control who you're attracted to. It's happened before, right? So, why was this different?"

"That's the thing, it hasn't happened before. Not like this." It was hard to get the words out for some reason. A relief. But it wasn't easy saying them. Sharing the truth. "I think it's because I met her right after Yasmine and I decided to get married. You know the whole idea of 'cold feet'? I think my brain latched onto an attractive woman because I had decided to make a big life change, and there was a part of me that balked at it."

"I think cold feet means that you get scared of the change and back away, not that you actively become attracted to someone else out of nowhere." The amusement was back in Asad's voice, but also sympathy. There was no judgment, which made it a little easier for Mason to talk about it.

"I've just never had an instant attraction to someone like this. Not such a strong one. It was like, I saw her, and…" And it was like getting hit by a lightning bolt. Which was ridiculous. "But when something comes on that fast, it's not going to last. I don't want a quick hit of excitement. I want companionship and peace and affection."

"And what, you think you can't have all that plus attraction?"

"I mean, it doesn't last, right?" He was out of his depth because he'd never experienced anything like this. "Take you and Morgan, for example. You knew each other before you got together. You didn't have an immediate attraction. It's something that built and developed naturally."

"I was attracted to her, but I think I get what you're saying. No, it didn't hit me like a lightning bolt. But there's no one path to happiness or attraction. Would you tell someone there's only one way to do kink?"

Mason scowled, his forehead moving against his fingers.

"No."

"So, why do you think there's only one way for lasting attraction to start?"

"What's her name?" Morgan asked when Mason didn't reply immediately.

"Audrey. She's David's younger sister, which is another reason it wouldn't work out. I can't date my team leader and best friend's little sister." No matter the chemistry and regardless of what Yasmine thought.

"Uh huh. I don't think that matters as much as you think it does." Asad snickered. "Although, maybe don't spank her in front of him."

"Thanks for stating the obvious." Sighing, Mason let his hand drop back down beside him, resting it on his couch. "It doesn't matter, anyway. Now that I'm not getting married to Yasmine, I'm sure this whole attraction thing is going to go away as quickly as it came. It was a reaction to arranging my marriage, nothing more."

"Prove it."

"What?"

"I'm assuming you haven't seen her yet today. So, go prove it. Go see her and see if the attraction is gone." Asad's tone shifted. "Unless you don't really think it's changed and you're avoiding her."

"I'm avoiding people in general because they're annoying."

"You picked up my call."

"Because you're somehow even more annoying when I try to avoid you."

"It is a talent I possess." Asad smirked. Mason didn't need to see him to know that his cousin was smirking. "But I'm just saying. Shouldn't you at least test your hypothesis to see if you're right? Or are you scared that you aren't, and that's why you're avoiding people today?

"I'm not scared." Because he was right. There was no reason to be worried about his reaction to Audrey, dream last night aside. They'd told their friends. Now, they'd told their parents as well. Yasmine wasn't going to change her mind. He had no doubt his dreams would be redhead free tonight.

The fear-of-life-changing fueled attraction no longer needed to exist, and so it would be gone—or at least lessened—and he was sure it would disappear quickly.

"So, you're going to go see her?"

"Sure. Her bakery is having its grand opening today. It's only polite to stop by."

"I'll be interested to know how it goes. I assume you don't want me telling my mother any of this to pass on to your mother?"

"Please." His voice was pained at the thought. That was the absolute last thing he needed.

Asad snickered.

"I'm going now."

"To the bakery?"

"Eventually. Goodbye."

"Bye, Mason!" Morgan's previous quiet meant she didn't have

anything to say, but she sounded cheerful enough saying goodbye to him.

"Keep me updated."

"Bye, Morgan." Mason hung up without acknowledging his cousin's final words.

Asad had a good point, thought. He should go to the bakery. Prove to Asad that his reaction to Audrey was an aberration that faded as quickly as it came on.

First, he was going to do some more research into 'cold feet' and the various ways it manifested, as well as the science of attraction. Just because he was interested.

Not because he was worried Asad was right.

Then this afternoon, he'd stop by the bakery and prove it to himself.

CHAPTER SEVENTEEN

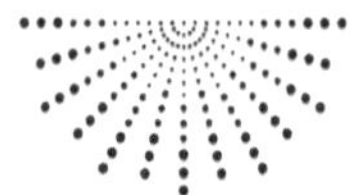

Cupcakes and Crumbs' grand opening was good. Not amazing. Not terrible. But solidly good. Solidly busy.

Was there a line down the block?

No.

But there was a line.

For three hours straight, there was a line. Sometimes, it was only one or two people behind the person ordering, sometimes, it was nearly to the door, but there was a line.

Ashley kept smiling and moving the line alone. Alexis was in the back, baking up a storm to keep up with the more popular demands. And Audrey was running back and forth between them, assisting with both. Making sure the tables were clear and clean after people left, for the few who decided to take a seat.

Several Black Fox Security team members, mostly Harris' team, came in early in the morning. Harris made sure to introduce her to Aiden, Jaxon, and Seth before they stepped aside to let others through. Zeus came in not long after them on his own. He did not have Noelle with him, and Audrey couldn't help but wonder if something had happened between them, but she didn't know him well enough to ask.

Ashley didn't ask him either, probably because that was one of the points where they did have a line to the door—he was in and back out far too fast for her to get nosy.

Finally, around lunchtime, things slowed down to a trickle, the line finally disappeared for the first time, and Audrey made her way over to the table where her grandmother and Cassidy were sitting. They'd come in mid-morning to get coffee and treats and had stayed through.

"This is quite the grand opening," Grandma said, beaming at her. "I hope you're proud of yourself."

"Proud and exhausted," Audrey confirmed. "And we still have the whole afternoon and evening to go." Since it was a Saturday, she was staying open till eight, in case people wanted cupcakes or dessert after dinner.

Tomorrow they would close earlier, at four o'clock, so she and Ashley could go to book club. One of the perks of being the owner. She could make her own hours. Right now, she didn't have hours posted because she planned to spend the first month trying to be open as much as possible to determine when it made sense to be open. Since she only had two employees, she would be doing most of the work, but that was also part of being the owner.

"It was definitely busy. A lot of foot traffic." Cassidy glanced out the window. "There are a lot of businesses here, so I wasn't sure there would be since it's the weekend."

"Well, Black Fox Security made up a lot of the business," Audrey replied, laughing as she set one foot up on her knee. "They all seem to be in and out of the office on Saturday, and it's just around the corner."

"Good point. A lot of them go there to train or work out, too."

"Ooh, can we go watch that after we're done here?" Grandma asked, her face lighting up. "That sounds fun."

"They're working out, not providing a show," Cassidy scolded.

"Why can't it be both?"

"Oh, hey, there's Yasmine and Claudia." Cassidy leaned toward the window and raised her hand in a wave, ignoring Audrey's grandmother's question. Which was probably the best way to deal with her at the moment, if Audrey was being honest.

Audrey set her foot down, feeling suddenly very awkward as the door to the bakery opened and the two women came inside. How was she supposed to act toward Yasmine now? They weren't *friends* friends, and she hadn't been there last night when Yasmine and Mason had told everyone they'd broken up. She'd gotten it second-hand from Ashley.

Was she supposed to know?

Would Yasmine be upset that Ashley told her?

She should have asked when Ashley told her if it was okay for her to know, but she'd been too distracted by the heaps of guilt caused by her initial reaction. Immediately, her gaze locked onto Yasmine's face, searching for any signs of upset or heartbreak. She looked exactly the same as she had every other time Audrey had seen her. Calm. Confident.

Stunningly gorgeous.

Either she was perfectly fine, or she was hiding it really well.

"Hey, there, I heard you and Mason called things off." Grandma stood up and opened her arms to offer Yasmine a hug. She immediately stepped into it, bending slightly because Grandma was so much shorter than her. Audrey felt another wave of relief. Trust her grandmother to immediately broach the subject, awkward or not. "I'm sorry, honey."

"Thanks, Brenda." Yasmine smiled gently as she straightened, stepping away, only to have to hug Cassidy, who had gotten up from her seat as well. "The curse continues, apparently."

Was Audrey supposed to hug her? Or not? She wasn't sure of the new friend etiquette.

"I have something for you," she blurted out, jumping to her feet, which immediately protested having to be used again. They had been enjoying the reprieve. Ignoring the soreness, she hurried to the back, circumventing the need to decide whether to hug Yasmine.

Thankfully, the orange and chocolate cupcakes were finished. She gave Alexis a reassuring smile—the other woman had been sitting down and also resting, but she jumped to her feet when Audrey appeared as if worried at being caught taking a break—and picked up the tray to take it out front. The actual cake was orange flavored, with a chocolate center, chocolate and orange-flavored icing, and decorated with a candied orange slice on top.

It was the first time Audrey had made this particular combination, but she thought they'd come out pretty well. Hopefully, Yasmine agreed. If not… well, she'd tried.

Ashley glanced over as Audrey came out of the back room, but since she was talking to a new customer at the counter, she had to stay where she was.

Yasmine, on the other hand, was standing by herself at the end of the counter nearest to the door to the back, obviously waiting for Audrey to reappear. She skidded to a halt, holding the tray out in front of her like an offering… or a shield.

"Hey." Audrey's voice squeaked. "Um, so these are chocolate orange cupcakes. Ashley said that you like that combination."

Dark eyes widening, Yasmine stared down at the tray, and a small smile curved her lips.

"I do. This is really thoughtful of you, Audrey. Thank you."

"First one is on the house." Audrey lifted the tray a little, encouraging Yasmine to take one.

"You don't have to do that."

"I know, but I want to," she said firmly. Guilt cupcakes didn't work if the receiver had to pay for them.

"Thank you." Yasmine hesitated a moment, hand hovering over the offerings, before picking one up. Once she'd chosen one, Audrey set the tray down on the counter beside them, ready to be put in the display case.

"Let me get you a plate. Do you want anything to drink?"

"I'm good. Actually, can I have a box? Claudia and I are on our way to lunch. We just wanted to stop in and see how the grand opening was going. I'll eat this for dessert later."

"Oh, right, of course." Why was she so flustered? It wasn't like

Yasmine *knew* she had a crush on Mason or that she'd been relieved to hear they'd broken up.

Feeling her cheeks heat pink, Audrey ducked behind the counter to get one of the to-go boxes.

"Here you go." Audrey set the little box down on the counter and held it open for Yasmine to place the cupcake inside.

"So, today is going well?" Yasmine asked as she gently lowered the cupcake into the box, careful not to squish it and get icing all over her hands.

"Really well. It's been a great turnout. As long as Ashley and Alexis don't quit from being overworked, I'm golden," Audrey joked. Although she wasn't entirely joking.

"I'm glad to hear that."

"And… are you okay?" She wasn't sure if it was okay to ask, but she felt compelled to.

"I am. Disappointed, of course. But a part of me isn't surprised." Yasmine smiled sadly, but Audrey also remembered what Claudia and Naomi had said about Yasmine's curse being a self-fulfilling prophecy. Maybe she wasn't surprised because she was the one who'd made it happen. "Mason isn't the one for me. I'm starting to think no one is."

Audrey's heart hurt for the other woman.

"You just haven't found the right one yet," she said. "I mean, you're gorgeous, you're smart, you're kind… any guy would be lucky to have you. You just have to choose the one you want."

"If only." Yasmine laughed, shaking her head sadly at the same time. "Somehow, I keep picking guys who aren't right for me. Ones who are attracted to someone else." There was something about the way she said it, putting a bit of emphasis on *someone else*, that made Audrey feel like Yasmine was trying to tell her something.

"Mason was cheating on you?"

"Oh, no. He would never do that. He's loyal to the bone. But we didn't have the right chemistry. I think he does have that chemistry with someone else."

Again, the little emphasis on *someone else*, and now Yasmine was looking at Audrey so intently, it really did feel like she was trying to tell Audrey something. Like that Mason was attracted to her. Or was she reading way too much into this because that's what she wanted to hear? And she wanted to think that maybe Yasmine would be okay with it?

"I've asked him to give me some time before I have to actually see him with her, although he could always make his move before then." Yasmine shrugged, like she didn't care, but the intensity of her eye contact with Audrey made it seem like she cared a lot more than her tone indicated. "The important thing is that I want him to be happy, even if I can't be."

Okay, seriously, *was* she giving Audrey tacit permission to accept Mason's advances if he even made any?

Or was she speaking in general?

Audrey couldn't ask, though, because what if she was wrong? What if she wasn't doing that at all and got pissed that Audrey would think that she was?

Thankfully, Claudia was coming up behind Audrey, looking at the cupcakes still resting on the tray. She'd unbuttoned the top of her coat, letting the collar hang open to reveal the top of a red shirt.

"Ooh, what are those?" she asked, nodding at the cupcakes.

"Chocolate and orange cupcakes," Audrey blurted out, relieved to have an interruption before she did something monumentally ridiculous, like asking Yasmine if she was hinting that Audrey should hook up with Mason. "Do you want one? On the house."

A free guilt cupcake for Yasmine and a free 'thank you for interrupting this conversation' cupcake for Claudia.

"Sure."

"Great, let me pack one up for you." Which also meant that she didn't have to look at Yasmine now.

"Thanks." Claudia turned to Yasmine. "We should get going if we're going to do lunch."

"Yes, we should." Yasmine smiled, the polite social smile that Audrey was starting to recognize as her default expression, though she wondered if it was a real smile. "It was good to see you, Audrey. Congratulations on the bakery officially opening."

"Thank you." Audrey smiled brightly as she handed the cupcake box over to Claudia. "I really appreciate you stopping by."

They both wished her a great rest of the day before heading out. Audrey sagged slightly before looking over at her grandmother and Cassidy again and frowning. Mick had appeared while she was talking to Yasmine, and he was now sitting at the table next to her grandmother.

That wasn't the problem. The problem was that her grandmother had her hand on Mick's bicep and was rubbing it, leaning toward him to say something, while his head was bent toward hers, and Cassidy was staring at them both with a fascinated and horrified expression on her face.

They weren't really flirting, were they?

CHAPTER EIGHTEEN

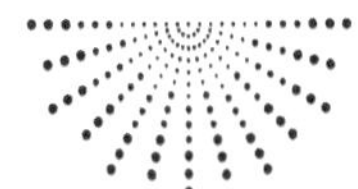

MASON

Going to Audrey's bakery was not a big deal.

It was the grand opening. He'd been there yesterday for the soft opening. She was his closest friend's little sister and now kind of his friend as well. It only made sense that he would go to support her on opening day. He doubted he would be the only one.

He was no longer engaged to Yasmine. There was no reason for the attraction to linger.

So why, as he made his way down the street, did it feel like his heart was racing? Why did his stomach feel a little queasy even though he'd had a healthy, nourishing lunch? Why did his palms feel sweaty when he wasn't wearing gloves, and his hands weren't in his pockets?

I'm being ridiculous.

Seeing the pink and cream awning sticking out over the sidewalk ahead of him, he gave himself a little shake.

He was building things up in his head; that was the problem. Talking to Asad had only helped so much, and now, he was putting all sorts of pressure on himself that didn't need to be there.

As he approached, the door opened, and Brenda came out on the arm of Mick. Cassidy followed them with a vaguely disturbed expression. Spotting him immediately, Brenda's face lit up.

"Mason!" She stepped forward, letting go of Mick to open her arms wide. "I'm sorry you and Yasmine didn't work out."

"Thanks, Brenda." He bent down to hug her gently. "I'm fine, but I appreciate that. How is the grand opening going?"

"Fantastic." Brenda beamed as she stepped back, her eyes brightly alight under the blue hat she was wearing over her white curls. "They've been busy all morning, and not just with the people who were here yesterday and came back."

"Great." He smiled at Mick and Cassidy. Unlike Brenda and Cassidy, who were both wearing warm coats and hats, Mick had on a t-shirt, no coat, and flip-flops. At least he was wearing pants and not shorts. Mick's winter clothing choices always made Mason shudder, but somehow the guy never seemed to get too cold. "What are you up to now?"

"We're going to see a movie," Brenda said, beaming as she wrapped her hands around Mick's arm again, leaning into him. "Ooh, just feel that muscle."

"I'm going home, apparently," Cassidy said, her voice oddly hollow. "I've been given the rest of the day off."

"Yup. I'll take care of Brenda, no worries," Mick said, looking down at the much older woman on his arm and giving her a wink. "*Really* good care of her."

Okay, well, Mason now understood the expression on Cassidy's face. Did David know about this?

He was going to guess not. Mason could not imagine David reacting well to Mick escorting his grandmother around town. Especially with the way they were looking at each other.

The age gap wasn't that much worse than Lincoln and Ashley's, but Lincoln also wasn't any of the team's grandfather. And Ashley wasn't any of the team's sister.

He hoped Mick realized he was getting into. If that was indeed what he was getting into. They might just be messing with Cassidy and David. If anyone was going to assist Brenda in messing with her grandkids, Mick would be at the top of the list.

Fuck, he did not want to think about this. He just needed to get into the bakery, prove Asad wrong, and get out.

"Okay, well, have fun." He gave them a little wave, shot Cassidy a sympathetic look, and shrugged when she glared at him and turned aside to let them pass. It wasn't like he could tell Brenda that she couldn't go see a movie with Mick any more than Cassidy could.

Brenda wasn't going to listen to either of them.

That would definitely bear watching, although it was not on his priority list of concerns. Letting out a long breath of air, Mason walked into the bakery. It smelled amazing, just like the day before. There was a couple sitting at one of the tables in the corner, totally engaged in their own conversation.

A tall man with broad shoulders stood in front of the counter. Mason easily recognized Grant—who held David's position on Harris' team—from behind. He was tall and broad enough that he completely blocked the sight of Audrey until she moved to the side to get something out of the display case for him.

Mason had been expecting Ashley, not Audrey, and the sight of her hit him straight in the gut, practically knocking the wind from him. She was smiling broadly, her eyes lit up from within, her red ponytail bouncing as she moved. Today, she had a black-and-white striped bow scarf tied around her head like a headband, rather than around her ponytail, and secured with an off-center floppy bow. She had on a matching polka-dot dress, which she was wearing underneath the pink and cream store apron.

When had he ever thought of aprons as looking sexy before now?

Never.

The answer was never.

What the hell is wrong with me?

Obviously, his attraction hadn't dimmed at all.

Maybe it was too soon? He and Yasmine had just called things off last night.

There was a part of him that wondered if Yasmine might change her mind. Maybe he was still clinging to hope that they would work things out, so his brain was still stuck on having cold feet.

He was tempted to turn around and run out back out the door, but just as he had the thought, Audrey's gaze moved to meet his. Her eyes widened, then she smiled and waved.

Well, fuck.

He couldn't run away like a coward now that he'd been seen.

"Hey, Mason, I have something for you. Let me just finish ringing Grant up." The smile she gave him was sympathetic.

There was no escape. He took a deep breath and walked forward, greeting Grant as the other man paid for his pastries. Grant thanked Audrey, dropped a dollar in the tip jar, and headed out, leaving Mason and Audrey alone except for the couple in the corner.

"Here." Audrey pulled a small tray out from behind the counter, something that wasn't in the display case. It was covered with cupcakes that had a sprinkling of something on the top of the icing swirl. "Baklava cupcakes."

"*Baklava cupcakes?*" His mouth watered immediately, his hand lifting to reach for one.

"Yeah, I heard about you and Yasmine and… well, I just wanted to do something to cheer you up. So, baklava cupcakes. I saved these for you, and whatever you don't want, I'll put up for sale."

"Thank you." Dammit. She really was as sweet as she was sexy. His cold feet really knew how to pick them. Even with the counter between them, he could feel the sizzle of their chemistry, of his attraction, as he picked up one of the cupcakes from the tray. "How much for all of them?" He didn't want to share the baklava cupcakes she'd made for him. Was it ridiculous? Yes. But he hated the idea of anyone else getting them.

Her eyes widened in surprise.

"Oh, they're on the house for you. I can box them up if you really want all of them."

"I do, but I also want to pay for them." If he paid for them, they would feel less like pity cupcakes. "I appreciate the gesture, but I don't want you to lose money on me when I'm fine."

Audrey's lips pursed, like she was thinking about denying him.

"I'll just put what I think they cost in the tip jar if you don't tell me, and I bet I'll overestimate what it would be," he warned her. Surprisingly, her expression turned smug.

"Go ahead. As the owner of the establishment, I don't have to take your payment, and I can't take the tips. Technically, they're for Ashley, although she doesn't need them, so she's giving them all to Alexis." The little smirk on her lips as she got sassy with him made his hand itch to spank her.

Shit. Since when did he want to spank a woman just because she was being a little bratty with him?

Since Audrey.

He should go.

But she was putting the tray on the counter and taking out a box to put the cupcakes in. Mason decided the best thing to do was eat the cupcake he had in his hand, which would at least give him something to focus on other than the woman behind the counter.

Honey, orange blossom, and pistachio flavors exploded on his tongue at the first bite, and he moaned.

"Fuck, that's good."

Audrey lifted her head to look at him, her eyes sparkling again. Behind him, he heard the sound of the door opening as the couple that had been sitting in the corner exited the bakery. He was acutely aware that it was just him and Audrey in here now.

"Really?"

"Really. And I am more determined than ever not to share them."

The pleased smile she gave him felt like it was warming him from the inside out. He wanted to always see her smiling like that.

Fuck me, I really need to get out of here.

"I'm glad you like them. I'm already thinking about making them one of the flavors of the week."

"You should." Even though he'd be tempted to buy them all. "I've never heard of baklava cupcakes before."

"It's really just the flavors." She ducked her head shyly, putting the last of the cupcakes in the box and closing it up. Pushing the box over to his side of the counter, she smiled. "There you go."

"Seriously, Audrey, you should let me pay you." Mason reached into his pocket to pull out his wallet.

"Nope." Shaking her head, she stepped back away from the counter, shoving her hands into her apron pockets as she did so. Then she suddenly frowned and pulled something out of one of them, holding it up to see what it was, and she made a face.

"What's that?" Something about her reaction to the thing had his instincts alerting.

"I... it's probably nothing. It's just a note that I found on the bakery door this morning before we opened." But she held it in front of her like she wasn't sure she wanted him to see it or not, and she'd frowned when she realized what it was.

"What does it say?"

Her emerald gaze met his, and she hesitated. Mason lifted one eyebrow. Letting out a little huff of air, she set the note on the counter and pushed it over to him.

Picking it up, Mason felt his skin prickle. The letters were large and threatening, he didn't need his reading glasses to see them clearly.

Get out.

AUDREY

Watching Mason read the note, his expression like a thundercloud, Audrey couldn't help but squirm. Then again, she'd been internally squirming from the moment he'd walked in the door, all tall, dark, and handsome. Watching his serious expression melt into pure pleasure when he'd bitten into her cupcake had done all sorts of wild things to her insides.

She didn't have to feel *as* guilty about that now that he and Yasmine were no longer together, but considering they'd just ended things last night, she couldn't entirely shake it. Especially since she also still felt relieved that he was now single. Not that she was going to do anything about it, no matter how good he looked and no matter how much she wanted to.

Although… it almost felt like Yasmine had been giving Audrey permission earlier…

That, or she was making things up in her head because it was what she wanted.

"Do you know who left it?"

"I haven't got a clue. It's probably just some kids or something."

"Have you asked Alexis or Ashley about it? Alexis isn't from here, right?"

"No, but she's living here very quietly, and I can't think of a reason why someone would want her to get out." Audrey shrugged.

"Is there anyone who would want you to get out?"

"No. Maybe it's someone who wanted this space?" She gestured to the bakery at large. "Or someone who really hates baked goods?"

That made the corner of his mouth twitch, but he shook his head.

"Can you think of anyone else who wouldn't want you here?"

"My parents want me to go back to Philly, but they wouldn't leave a note like this." She shrugged. "I really don't think it's anything to get worked up about. I'm going to ask David to make sure we have cameras on the front door as well as the back, and if it happens again, then we'll know who did it."

"Okay. You're working the rest of the day, right? I'll go stop by the office now. David should be there. I'll give him the note and handle getting a camera on the front door."

Audrey wished he'd laughed it off instead of taking it so seriously. It was making her nervous that he didn't think it was a joke. But that didn't mean she wanted her brother involved any more than he had to be.

"Oh, well, I wasn't going to tell David about the note." She wrung her hands in front of herself, bringing them together and twisting her fingers. "I was just going to ask him to set up the camera. He's just got a lot going on right now, and I don't know if this is even anything. Someone might have left it on the wrong door."

Mason raised his eyebrow at her again. Pressing her legs together, Audrey told herself that she wasn't going to squirm. Or find it sexy.

"Do you have to tell him? I don't want him freaking out after everything that went on with Cassidy if this is just some stupid prank or a mistake."

"Fine. I'll handle getting the camera installed, and I'm going to stop by regularly to check in on things. If anything else out of the ordinary happens—*anything*—you're going to tell me about it."

"Yes, Sir." She was trying to lighten the mood, but something flashed in his eyes at her response that took her breath completely away. The air between them seemed to thicken, and she felt her body tighten all over, her pulse pounding so loudly, it could probably be heard on the street. It felt like something momentous was about to happen...Then he shuttered it, the light in his gaze dimming, metaphorically stepping back as he picked up the box of cupcakes and physically stepped back.

"Okay. I'll stop back in tomorrow to check on things."

"Great. Thanks." Audrey brushed her hands over her apron as all the tension that had filled her body fled, leaving her feeling like a deflated balloon. He nodded his head and headed out the door. It was ridiculous to feel abandoned. Or disappointed. She was seeing things that weren't there.

It was probably all the romances she was reading.

Audrey was grateful that Ashley was on her break and had missed all of that. Although maybe she should mention the note to her and Alexis, to see what they thought. Make sure there was no reason they would think the note was for them. Mason taking it seriously made her feel like maybe she shouldn't be so quick to brush it off.

She would do that this afternoon.

Tomorrow, Mason would be back. He was planning to check in regularly.

And if that gave her a little thrill to know he was going to be coming by often, that wasn't something anyone else needed to know.

CHAPTER NINETEEN

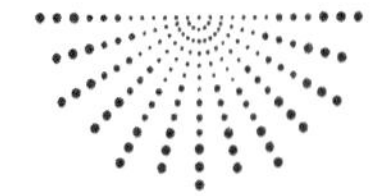

While he couldn't prove Asad wrong yet, Mason now realized that he'd had too high expectations for himself. The subconscious couldn't be controlled by the conscious mind. Expecting his attraction to Audrey to turn off just because he and Yasmine had ended their engagement had been unrealistic, though he hadn't realized it at the time.

The fact that he now felt protective of her because of the note that had been left on her bakery was probably part of why he felt so much chemistry with her right before he'd left. Heightened emotions were always going to exacerbate other emotions. And it was only natural to feel protective of her. She was David's little sister after all, and he liked her as a person.

Plus, she was a complete innocent. If someone was trying to scare her, of course, he was going to feel protective.

Step one—get that camera up.

It was possible Audrey was correct, and it was just kids playing a weird prank for some reason. Stranger things had happened. The camera would help her feel better and him as well. There was every chance that this would be a one-off thing, but just in case, the camera would be there.

Step two—see if any fingerprints showed up on the note. It was unlikely, considering that both he and Audrey had touched it, the surface wasn't all that large, and it had been in her pocket for most of the day, but he should at least try.

Step two point one was to tell her that if anything else showed up, not to touch it without gloves on.

Step three—dig into Alexis' background to make sure this note wasn't aimed at her. He didn't know anything about Audrey's employee, and it was possible there was something Audrey didn't know, either.

The chance that it was connected to Ashley seemed the least likely because he knew the most about her. While she had an enemy in the form of her ex-best friend and current daughter-in-law, Rebecca wasn't going to make trouble for her and risk being cut off from Lincoln's money.

Which meant that step four was to do some digging into Audrey's background. Her parents didn't want her in Pittsburgh, and from what he knew about them from David, they were used to getting their way. On the other hand, he also knew that they were more than willing to cut their children off if they weren't getting their way— which was what had happened to David.

Why should Audrey be any different?

But he was still going to dig.

For her safety.

Not for his own interest.

Heading straight for the office, Mason felt a lot more energized than he had this morning. Having a mission, even a small one, could do that to a man.

Walking into the lobby, he was surprised to find David and Lincoln there, chatting. Both of them looked up when the elevator doors opened, and David raised his hand in greeting as Mason stepped off the elevator. Trying not to feel like the note was burning a hole in his pocket, Mason waved back, using his key fob to open the doors.

"What are you doing here?" David asked as he walked in. "I thought you were taking today off."

"I am, I just was in the neighborhood and decided to swing by to grab a few things. Is something going on?"

David and Lincoln exchanged a glance.

"Has Marshall reached out about trying to hire you away again?" Lincoln asked, a small scowl forming, as it always did when he had to talk about his ex-best friend and business partner.

"What? No." Mason shook his head. "Not that I would take it even if he did. He doesn't seriously think any of us are going to jump ship, does he?" Marshall Devlin was smarter than that, surely. Especially since he'd already tried that tactic once.

"Not everyone, but he's reaching out to a select few," Lincoln replied grimly. "Zeus and Jensen on our team and Darcie and Jaxon on Harris'."

Mason let out a low whistle, shaking his head at Marshall's temerity and persistence. The man did not know the meaning of the word 'no'.

"I haven't heard from him, but if he does contact me, you'll be the first to know."

"I still think he's up to something," David said, shaking his head. "I don't think he really thought anyone would accept his offer. I just can't figure out why he'd try again. Jensen said that he was trying to push the idea of being up close and personal with the next governor of Pennsylvania, and he did not appreciate Jensen pointing out that we've been hired by the other candidate, and that MacLeod does not have a lock on the race."

"Maybe he truly doesn't believe the senator can win," Mason suggested. "We all know that he's a misogynist."

"I am surprised he reached out to Darcie," Lincoln admitted.

"He might have done that just to piss Grant off."

"Why would that piss Grant off more than approaching Jaxon?" Lincoln asked, frowning.

David and Mason both looked at him incredulously. Had he really never noticed the way Harris' team leader panted after Darcie? It was Grant, so saying he panted after anyone was an exaggeration, but anyone who knew him could see that he treated her differently.

Lincoln looked back and forth between David and Mason, slow understanding dawning on his expression. "Oh, really? Well, that's interesting."

"Maybe he's trying to distract us from something else," Mason suggested. "If we think all he's doing is try to poach team members, it gives him some cover for other things."

Could he have something to do with the note left on Cupcakes and Crumbs?

That seemed far-fetched.

And yet, he'd been behind sending black roses to all the team members. Because the first house to receive them had been Jensen, in the middle of everything that was going on with Cassidy's ex, they'd assumed Don had been behind the flower delivery. It had quickly become clear that he wasn't, but they still hadn't known that it was Devlin until the day that Royce MacLeod had announced that he was running for governor and introduced Devlin as his head of security.

Still, why would he go after David's sister instead of Lincoln directly? So far, all of his efforts had been focused on Black Fox—either by bad mouthing them or attempting to poach their clients and team members. Thankfully, he hadn't been very successful.

That might mean that he was trying something new.

A note on a bakery door that was only tangentially connected to the firm didn't seem likely, but… that would be something else to look into if they weren't already watching Devlin and his current team closely.

"Is there anyone on his team we can approach who'd maybe let some information slip?" Mason asked. He wasn't surprised at the face David made; he was an ultimate do-gooder, like a redheaded Captain America, but Lincoln nodded slowly.

"I'm not sure. Most of them are just there for the money, but…"

"But that means there's an opening, depending on what you're willing to offer them." Mason shrugged. "The fact that Devlin is trying to poach people means he probably thinks his own people are poachable. Even if they're not, if someone reports to him that you tried, he's going to become paranoid that someone did say yes." Mason paused, sudden realization hitting him as he spoke. "That might even be why he didn't approach everyone on the second go-around. He thinks it'll make you paranoid that someone said yes and didn't report it because actually trusting his team never occurred to him."

"Every accusation is a confession?" David asked dryly.

"When it comes to someone like Devlin, yes."

"So, maybe I shouldn't approach all of them, but just a few," Lincoln said slowly. "The one I think is most likely to say yes and the one I think is most likely to report back to Marshall."

"Possibly. Or just one of those. If you do the latter, he'll spend as much time investigating his own team as he does anything else. And it won't hurt for him not to completely trust them."

Unlike Lincoln. It didn't surprise Mason at all that Lincoln wasn't suggesting that any of his own team might have taken up Devlin on his offer.

Trust was what had always bonded them together. Even with Zeus. They all might be wary of him, but Mason also trusted that Lincoln had done a deep dive and come up with no reason not to hire him. That meant that he was willing to build trust with him.

"Also, to that point, we should anticipate that we're going to receive evidence that Zeus spoke with Devlin sometime soon." Which was why it had been smart of Zeus to tell Lincoln about it ahead of time. Another point in Zeus' favor.

Or, if Mason was super paranoid, a brilliant psychological move by Zeus and Devlin to ensure Zeus gained more trust with the group. Personally, Mason didn't think Devlin was that brilliant, especially not when it came to building relationships. If Lincoln reached out to one of Devlin's team members, and that member reported it to Devlin, Devlin was going to be incredibly suspicious of that person. He was not going to trust him more because he'd reported the contact.

"You think Devlin was setting Zeus up?" David frowned. Obviously, he was going to be sensitive to anything that might disrupt his team, and the addition of a new team member had already done that.

"I think Zeus left Devlin's team before we discovered everything Devlin was up to here, so there's no way Devlin would think he had a chance at hiring Zeus back after everything that went down. Especially now that Zeus is on our team, which was a coveted spot." Mason paused. He really didn't think this next part was the case, but it would be irresponsible not to bring it up. "That or this is a seriously long game by both of them, and Devlin is a hell of a lot smarter than I've been giving him credit for."

Both Lincoln and David grimaced.

"Marshall is smart as hell, don't underestimate him," Lincoln said. "At least, I have to tell myself that, given how long he was fooling me."

"It wasn't for as long as he thought he was fooling you," David reassured him, clapping his hand on their boss' shoulder. "And you fooled him in the end."

"There is that." A glimmer of a smile slid over Lincoln's lips before disappearing. "I don't think Zeus is working for Devlin or that this is a long game."

"I don't either, but I have to acknowledge it as a possibility, just in case I turn out to be wrong." Mason shrugged.

"Okay, well, we're headed out." Lincoln glanced at David. "I guess we have a lot to talk about over cupcakes."

That made David chuckle.

A feeling of guilt squirmed inside Mason. It wasn't that he was trying to keep things from David, but he was well aware that the note in his pocket was probably something David would want to know about. Even if it turned out to be nothing.

But as Audrey said, David had a lot on his plate right now. Not just the Devlin thing, but also security for Senator Marlin. And eventually, he was going to find out about his Grandma and Mick. So did Lincoln. There was no reason to worry them with a random note that might be nothing more than a prank. If it turned out to be something more, obviously, he would tell them then.

Mason would do the work to make sure that the note was nothing and that Audrey and the bakery were protected. That way, David wouldn't have to worry at all.

The fact that it gave him an excuse to go by the bakery more often… well, that was just going to help him wear out his attraction to Audrey.

CHAPTER TWENTY

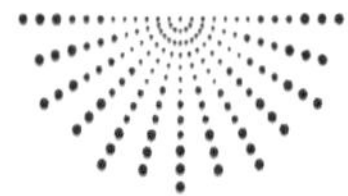

AUDREY

What a day.

A really good day.

Audrey couldn't keep the grin from her face as she sat down in one of the chairs, looking at the now-empty and gleaming display cases. She'd sent Alexis and Ashley home, with her thanks, and a bunch of tips for Alexis—who had tried to refuse them, but both Ashley and Audrey had pressured her into taking them. Ashley didn't need them, and it wouldn't be right for Audrey to take them.

Besides, she didn't need them right now.

Maybe one day, but not right now. Hopefully, not ever if things kept up the way they had today.

Sitting back in the chair, peace settled over her as she lifted her feet to rest on the seat across from her. The chairs were plastic, so they weren't as comfortable as an armchair, but there wasn't anywhere else she'd rather be right now.

My bakery.

All hers.

Pride and happiness welled up inside her, and tears stung at her eyes. She blinked quickly, raising one hand to wipe them away. She just couldn't remember the last time she'd been this happy.

Which, of course, meant that was when her mother called. Impeccable timing, as always.

Staring at her phone screen, Audrey made a face. She didn't have to pick up. But she should. She'd been dodging her mother's calls most of the week. Her parents knew her bakery was opening today. At some point, her mom was going to throw a fit if she didn't start picking up the phone. The longer she waited, the worse it would be.

Might as well get it over with. She was in a great mood, so that was better than trying to talk to them when she was in a bad mood, right?

Audrey swiped the call button, rolling her shoulders back as she tried to reduce the sudden tension between them.

"Hello?" She did her best to sound chipper, upbeat, and hide the exhaustion. Her mom didn't need any ammunition when it came to her choice to open a bakery.

"Audrey! Finally! Why haven't you called me back?" Her mother's tone was unusually strident, and it made Audrey wince.

"I texted you that I was overwhelmed with getting the bakery ready to open," she reminded her mother and got a snort in return.

"Texts. That's hardly a respectful way to interact with your own parents. You should have called us back. Or, at the very least, picked up the phone one of the many times that we called."

It had only been three times, but a bit of guilt lodged in Audrey's chest, knowing she could have called back.

She just hadn't wanted to.

Which was why she'd texted. She knew her mother wouldn't text back. So, guilty as charged. The tension between her shoulders was getting worse and working its way up into her neck. She switched sides for where she was holding her phone and rolled her head around, putting one hand on the back of her neck and digging her fingers into the muscles to try to loosen them.

"Well, I picked up now. I just finished up the grand opening of the bakery."

"I see. Does that mean you'll be less busy in the future?"

Audrey didn't know why she'd hoped for a 'congratulations' from her mother, but some part of her had, and it hurt not to receive it.

"Probably not. There's going to be a lot of long hours until I can afford to hire more employees."

"What on earth are you using your trust fund for if not to make your bakery a success?"

"That's exactly what I'm using it for." Audrey didn't bother to try to explain to her mother—again—that she wasn't spending it all at once. Her mother knew how businesses were run, but it felt like she'd been encouraging Audrey to spend as much money as possible, as quickly as possible.

Probably because her mother spent money like that, but also possibly because her mother realized that if she overspent and ran out of her trust fund... she would need her parents' help.

"Were you calling about something in particular, Mother?"

No 'mom' or 'mama' for Francie Bowers. She only answered to 'mother'. Audrey couldn't even remember calling her 'mommy' as a child.

"What, I can't call to congratulate my only daughter on the day she opens a new business?" The strident tone had given way to a more tearful one, quick as a snap. Even though Audrey knew that her mother could turn it off just as quickly, it always made her heart squeeze. "I've already a son who refuses to take my calls. Now, I'm going to lose you, too."

"You're not losing me, mother." She softened her tone because that had sounded like sincere upset on her mother's part. "I just needed some space."

"Space from your own family?"

Audrey didn't point out that she'd moved closer to two of her family members. Her mom didn't consider Grandma to be part of their family.

"Space from Philly," Audrey explained gently. "Space from the social scene. I wanted to do my own thing. I promise, it was something for me, not against you."

Although technically, moving away from her parents' influence had been for her. But she really wasn't doing it to spite them or because she didn't love them. She'd just needed to get away from the way they tried to control what she was doing and the constant pressure to get back together with Cash.

Her mother's hints that Cash was going to propose in order to win her back had been the final straw.

"Well, when are we going to see you again?"

"I can't leave any time soon after just opening the bakery... would you and Dad like to come visit me here? Maybe we could even have a meal with David." Audrey crossed the fingers of her free hand that her brother wouldn't explode at hearing that she'd suggested such a thing.

"I'm not having any meal with that boy until he apologizes for the absolutely disrespectful way he treated me and your father." The sharp anger in her mother's voice was cutting. "We raised him. Fed him. Clothed him. Gave him whatever he wanted and needed. And how does he repay us?"

He joined the army instead of going along with their life plan and taking over their father's business. Audrey inwardly sighed. Time to change the subject before her mother could really get started on a rant. More than her shoulders and neck were hurting now, all the joy from the day being sucked away through the phone.

"I'll be home for Thanksgiving, but I probably won't be able to get away before then," Audrey said, rather than answering her mother's question.

"So now, we're only going to see you on holidays?" Her mother's voice was becoming rather shrill.

"No... I just..." The sound of someone tapping on glass made Audrey's head jerk up. Mason was on the other side of the front window. He raised one eyebrow at her and tilted his head toward the door. "Mother, I'm so sorry, but I have to go. Someone I need to speak with just showed up outside the bakery."

"Of course, because everyone else is more important than your own family. Good night, Audrey. I hope you don't one day have cause to regret treating your own mother like a second-rate citizen." Her mother hung up before Audrey could respond.

The peace of her empty bakery had been shattered, but strangely, she didn't feel as bad as she normally did after speaking with her mother. Maybe it was because there hadn't been time to talk to her father, too, and get the double guilt trip. Or maybe it was because starting off from a place of happiness meant she didn't end up as low.

Or maybe it was because there was a hot man standing outside her bakery door waiting to speak with her.

Audrey's feet and legs protested as she stood, but she smiled anyway and didn't even need to force it as she went to let Mason inside. The night was dark, lit up only by the streetlamps, and he was finally wearing a coat. The black material blended with the darkness around him. If she didn't know who he was, the effect would have been dangerously intimidating.

As it was, she felt her cheeks flush with heat in reaction to how sexy he was as she opened the door to greet him.

"Hey, what are you doing here?" Casual. Good. That was casual. Nonchalant. She definitely didn't sound like she wanted to throw herself at him the day after he'd gone through a breakup.

He shifted his arm, holding up a box that had been tucked underneath it. The box was also black, which was why she hadn't seen it before.

"Camera. I figured I'd walk by and see if anyone was here tonight, and if not, I'd come back tomorrow." His gaze swept over her, and she had the unsettling feeling that he could see far more than just what she was wearing. "If you're too tired, I can either do this and lock up for you after, or I can come back tomorrow. Whatever you're more comfortable with."

Audrey only hesitated for a moment.

"I would like to have the camera up tonight, if that's okay. I'll probably sleep better. And I don't mind staying. I don't have an extra key for you to close up with because I gave them to Ashley and Alexis, but I'm aiming to be the first one here tomorrow."

"Got it." He flashed her a smile as he stepped inside, and Audrey felt her pulse pick up as she realized she was now going to be alone in the bakery *with Mason.*

Down girl. He's not here for you; he's here to set up a camera.

<u>M*ASON*</u>

Close proximity to Audrey was only making his attraction worse. Knowing they were here alone…

He should have waited until tomorrow.

But it had made sense to stop by and see if he could do it now. After all, if he waited until tomorrow and someone left another note tonight, he'd be kicking himself for waiting. Plus, he'd been nearby. It was on his way.

It had nothing to do with wanting to see her again, unless it was to ask how the first real day had gone.

Which was exactly what he did once they figured out where she wanted the camera located and what she wanted it to pick up—basically the whole front window and door.

"So, how was your grand opening? Are you feeling reassured?"

"Sort of." She sat down at a nearby table, watching him intently as he got to work. He could feel her eyes on him, making him hyper-aware of his every movement and how he might appear to her. Even though it didn't matter what she thought of how he looked. "It went really well, but see, I talked to someone who pointed out that a good grand opening day doesn't guarantee future days."

Her tone was teasing, but Mason still felt bad. He hadn't meant to put a damper on things for her.

"It definitely doesn't hurt." He glanced over at her. Thankfully, she was smiling at him.

"It doesn't. And a lot of people said they were happy a bakery had opened up here, and they'd be sending their friends."

"No one who seemed like they wanted you to get out?" It was a joke, but also not. If someone did want her out of this space, there was every chance they would have stopped by to see how today was going.

"Not that I could tell—at least not of people who came inside." She hesitated. "You think the person who left the note might have stopped by?"

"If it wasn't a prank, it would make sense. They might want to see how the grand opening was going or if the note had affected your attitude at all. If you seemed anxious."

"Well, I didn't see anyone like that, but it was really busy. And if they wanted to see any of that, they would be able to do so from outside the window." She gestured toward it, turning her head and staring at the front of the bakery with a pensive look on her face. "That's another thing the camera will be good for."

"Absolutely. Okay, it's in place, now let me get it hooked up to the system." Thankfully, that didn't take him long either. While he was working, Audrey remained seated, doing something on her phone. Mason didn't mind. He imagined she'd been on her feet for most of the day, and here he was keeping her here even longer.

Maybe he should offer her a foot massage as an apology…

No. Stop it.

If there was anything he could do to make his situation worse right now, it would be to start touching her; he wasn't sure he would be able to stop.

He cleared his throat, and she jumped in her seat, head coming up in surprise, eyes wide with… something. The way she looked at him.

Fuck.

The air suddenly felt heavy. Tight. So did his chest. His dick perked up. He felt like a fucking teenage boy again, with no control over his body. Which didn't make sense. He always had control.

Why wasn't this going away?

"I'm all done," he said, his voice deeper than usual—the voice he used at the club when he was scening.

Heat flushed over her pale skin, turning her cheeks bright pink, and she hastily turned off the screen of her phone and got to her feet, shoving it into a pocket in her skirt.

"Great." Unlike him, her voice had gone higher. Squeakier. "Thank you so much for doing that."

"Sorry, I didn't mean to interrupt whatever you were doing."

"I wasn't... I mean... I was just reading." She stumbled over her words, and the blush on her cheeks got even redder.

Mason would be willing to bet she was reading something for Brenda's smutty book club. Had she been reading about kinky sex while he was hooking the camera up?

Maybe it wasn't his fault it felt like the air between them was simmering. Maybe she'd been reading, and she knew he was a Dom, and it was just an aftereffect. Maybe it was coming from her, and he was picking up on it, and for some reason reacting more strongly than he normally did.

Maybe I'm going to need to start thinking about the fact that Occam's razor says the simplest explanation is that I'm just attracted to her.

Even Yasmine was pushing me toward her.

But I told Yasmine I'd give her a month.

There was no way the strength of this attraction could last a month. He just had to get through it.

"Right." He cleared his throat again. "Well, I should get going. Let me give you my phone number so you can call me in case something happens—and I do want you to call if there's another note tomorrow. I'll want to see the camera footage."

"Yes. Okay. Great." She was practically scarlet as she picked up her phone and cleared the screen before bringing up her contacts and handing it over to him. "Thank you."

"Of course."

The phone was still warm from her hands, and Mason did his best not to think about that as he quickly filled out his name and number and handed it back. Audrey bent her head over it, and Mason felt his phone buzz in his pocket. She peeked up at him, a small smile on her face, despite her red cheeks.

"I texted you, so now you have my number, too."

"Great. Thanks."

"Thank you. Um, I'm just gonna go get my coat and head out now."

"Did you drive?"

"Yeah."

"I'll walk you to your car."

For a moment, he thought she might protest, but then she nodded. It wasn't that late in the evening, but it was very dark out, and he would have insisted even if she'd argued. Hell, he'd have followed her if she'd rejected his offer just to make sure she got there safely.

David would expect no less.

All he had to do was get her to her car, not touch her, then keep resisting this attraction until it went away.

CHAPTER TWENTY-ONE

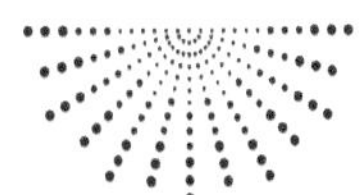

Audrey: No note this morning.

Mason: Glad to hear it. I'll look at the camera footage later today, just in case.

Audrey: Even though there was no note?

Mason: Someone could have stopped by, intending to leave one and seen the new camera.

Audrey: Wow, and I thought my brother was paranoid.

Mason: It's not paranoia if they're actually out to get you.

Audrey: That doesn't help. You know that doesn't help, right?

Mason: That's why I'm going to check the feed and be paranoid for you.

Audrey: Thanks? I think?

Mason: You're welcome.

AUDREY

"My favorite part is when she's hooked up to the milking machine, then he puts it in her butt."

If Audrey had thought her own grandmother was outrageous, she was unprepared for Grandma's friend Karen. In her defense, she wasn't sure that anyone *could* be prepared for Karen. She was a tall, thin woman with thin features and long, thin silver hair that went down to her waist in a French braid, and she was wearing a pink sweatshirt with a kitten on it... enthusiastically talking about anal sex and milking.

They were all sitting in a big circle in the middle of Grandma's living room. Dining room chairs had been pulled in along with the rest of the furniture to give them enough seating. Grandma, Naomi, and Claudia were on the couch, while the other two older women present took the armchairs. Audrey was beside Cassidy on one side of the room, while Yasmine, Jennifer, and Ashley were on the other.

"Of course it was." Mary, Grandma's other friend who was part of the book club, rolled her eyes. A beautiful black woman with light brown eyes, close-cropped gray curls, and a sleek, elegant style, going by her clothing, she wasn't as enamored of the hucows as Karen and Grandma.

"Karen likes it whenever the heroine gets it in the butt," Cassidy whispered, leaning over to make sure Audrey was the only one who could hear her.

To be honest, Audrey did, too. She wasn't sure she'd be so willing to admit that, but she'd read a book during the past week where it didn't happen and had found herself disappointed.

She'd always thought she didn't like reading that much, but it turned out she just hadn't been reading the right genres. Reading books where she knew the couple was going to get together in the end and be happy, she actually read quite quickly. And enjoyed it.

Plus, it was a nice break from putting together the bakery.

If a certain real-life man's face kept popping up in her mind when she was reading them and picturing certain scenes... well, now that he and Yasmine weren't together anymore, she didn't have to feel quite so guilty. Audrey peeked over at where Yasmine was sitting between Mary and Jennifer.

The other woman didn't look like she was heartbroken or like she'd spent the weekend mourning the end of her engagement. She looked like she had every other time Audrey had seen her. Calm. Sophisticated. Like a supermodel who didn't have a care in the world.

"Did anyone else also read the book that inspired Mina to try the hucow stuff?" Jennifer asked. "I didn't think I'd be into the kink, and I don't think I'd want to do it myself, but it made me want to go read more."

"*His Favorite Hucow*? Yes, that was really good." Naomi grinned. "It made me understand why Mina wanted to try the hucow thing."

"I read it, too. I liked that there was a real story behind it," Claudia said. She was lounging on the couch with Naomi and Grandma, who were to her left with Naomi in the middle. "She did something bad, and she wanted to atone. Plus, she didn't do anything stupid. I hope something shitty happens to Lily, though. That heifer has it coming. Is there a book about her where we can find out what happens to her?"

"Unfortunately, no, but there's always hope for the future." Grandma sighed. "The rest of the series isn't hucow. There's an age play planet, a pet play planet, and a pony play planet. I'm hoping for more hucows; this one was my favorite, although the pet play planet was really good."

Things Audrey had never thought she'd hear from her grandmother's mouth. She didn't know whether to be more amused or appalled.

"It was. I liked the hot puppy dog in that one," Karen said, her expression getting even brighter somehow. "Brutus. That one was filthy."

"And some of us haven't read that series, so let's refocus." Mary made a little twirling motion with her finger. "We're supposed to be talking about *Milking Mina* and *Rawhide Ranch*."

"I didn't think the kink was for me, either, but I ended up enjoying reading about it a lot more than I thought I would. I would have liked to know more about the ranch and the petting zoo," Yasmine said. "The other characters seemed fun, too."

"They are. You should read *Rawhide Ranch* if you get the chance," Naomi told her. "There are actually two series, the *Rawhide Ranch* series, which is all age play and Daddy Dom and the *Submissives of Rawhide* series."

"Unfortunately, I don't read as fast as you," Yasmine said ruefully.

"I don't think anyone reads as fast as Naomi." Ashley grinned, apparently unbothered by her slower reading speed. "It's good, though, because Naomi can read all the books and then tell us about the best ones."

"Damn right." Naomi eyed her. "Have you read *Burn for Me* yet?"

"I'm just going to wait 'til it's your turn to choose the book."

Naomi made a frustrated noise and looked up at the ceiling, raising her hands slightly as if she wanted to shake something. "That's not for months still! I need to talk to someone about Mad Rogan!"

"Well, at least you'll like my pick for this month," Ashley told her. "It's Daddy Dom."

"Can't you read both?"

"No, because unlike some people, it takes me a week or more to read a book, not a couple of hours."

"Fine. But when it's my turn..." Naomi pointed at all of them. "Mad Rogan. If you have time to read *His Favorite Hucow*, you have time to read *Burn for Me*."

"That's not true. *Burn for Me* is a lot longer book, and it's the first book in a trilogy," Grandma said, shaking her head. "I need time to read all three. You know I have to finish a series once I start."

"Naomi's been pushing for *Burn for Me* since we joined the club," Cassidy whispered to Audrey. "So not very long, despite the way she's acting. But she wanted us to read it before the club, too."

Good to know. Audrey was enjoying watching all the dynamics between the group, even though she was sitting back and not interacting much.

Once the book discussion was over, Grandma brought out food, and the group ended up in smaller groups to talk about things.

She could hear her grandmother telling Mary and Karen about the 'hot young thing' she was hanging out with, and she decided she did not need to be part of that conversation. Similarly, she wasn't sure how she felt about talking with Yasmine—just looking at the other woman made her feel guilty. Especially when she thought about how Mason had been at the bakery last night and the thoughts that Audrey had been having about him while he was there…

It hadn't even been twenty-four hours since he and Yasmine ended things. Sure, they were over, but it still felt wrong.

Thankfully, she ended up with Cassidy and Jennifer, while Yasmine was on the other side of the room with Naomi, Claudia, and Ashley. And once Jennifer had asked how the grand opening of Cupcakes and Crumbs had gone, Cassidy took the opportunity to interrogate Jennifer, which meant Audrey was out of the hot seat.

"Does Richard know you went on a date with Jensen?"

"Yes. We're not exclusive, so I didn't *have* to tell him, but it felt weird not to." Jennifer made a face, taking a sip of her water. "He pointed out that we're not exclusive and that I shouldn't feel bad."

"Mmm. Is he seeing someone else?"

"Not that I know of. I feel like he would have told me, since I brought it up." Jennifer tilted her head to the side. "Or maybe not. Maybe that's why he told me it's fine and I shouldn't feel bad."

Dating multiple people at once was something Audrey didn't really understand. Jennifer seemed way too calm about the idea that one of the guys she was dating was seeing someone else. On the other hand, she'd be a hypocrite if she was upset.

Audrey couldn't imagine dating two men at once.

She definitely wouldn't want the man she was seeing to be also dating other women, either.

"So, you're going to keep seeing both of them?"

"For now." Jennifer made another face, then sighed. "I'm not so sure Jensen's really interested in me or if he just asked me out because someone else had. It might be nothing more than competition. So, I'm not putting all my eggs in one basket. Plus… I really like Richard. A lot. Enough that I don't like the idea of him dating someone else, even though I know that makes me a horrible hypocrite."

Okay, so scratch that about Jennifer being totally calm about sharing. That made Audrey feel a little better.

"And Richard's kinky."

"Yes, although we haven't had sex yet. We've been to a few house parties, but we keep things platonic there." Jennifer looked at Audrey. "My parents are heavy into the scene, and they have a lot of friends in it. I'm way too paranoid about someone I know showing up and seeing me butt naked or worse."

"That's why you don't come to the club, right?"

"Yup. My parents are members, and I've got a bunch of aunties and uncles who are members. The owners of the club were basically my aunt and uncle growing up." Jennifer shook her head. "I would need a whole lot of people to go on vacation at the same time for me to even be tempted to step foot in there. It's not just about them seeing me at that point; it's about me seeing them."

That made sense to Audrey. It was one thing to go to a book club where they were talking about sex with her grandmother; it would be an entirely different thing for her to walk in on her grandmother doing some of the stuff they were reading about.

"So you can scene without sex?" Audrey was fascinated by the concept, which was so different from the books she'd been reading. It seemed like all they did was have scenes that ultimately led to multiple orgasms.

"Oh, yes. It's not like the books where all the couples have sex all the time. They're like that because we're reading romances. There are plenty of people who scene platonically," Jennifer explained. "Richard and I do, though, of course, there's lots of chemistry, and he's a lot more hands-on than the fully platonic scenes. He's *very* good with his hands."

Her eyes took on a dreamy-eyed look that Audrey envied. Cash had been fine. She'd occasionally orgasmed with him, but she'd never looked like Jennifer did right now.

Thinking about him didn't make her get all dreamy-eyed.

The fantasies that she had about Mason, on the other hand...

Stop it. Yasmine is RIGHT THERE.

Maybe Yasmine really had been hinting at Mason and Audrey getting together, but it still felt disrespectful. It was way too soon.

"Hey, so what are we talking about over here?" Grandma elbowed her way into the circle, grinning.

"The Jennifer, Jensen, and Richard love triangle," Cassidy said, making Jennifer huff.

"It's not a love triangle; neither of them is in love with me."

"I don't know, Mick says his brother has it pretty bad for you." Grandma grinned. "He calls your other beau 'Dr. Dick', did you know?"

Jennifer sighed as Audrey stifled a giggle. Poor Jennifer.

SUNDAY NIGHT TEXT MESSAGES

Mason: I went over the footage from today and didn't see anything suspicious.

Audrey: #relieved—thank you for looking.

Mason: No problem. I'll keep checking throughout the week.

Audrey: You don't have to do that.

Mason: I think I'll feel better if I do. Just in case.

Audrey: If you insist. Thank you.

Mason: How was book club?

Audrey: Educational. My grandmother's friend Karen is even worse than she is.

Mason: I'm not sure that's possible.

Audrey: You can ask Claudia about it tomorrow. Retraumatize her.

Mason: Well, now I'm scared.

Audrey: You should be. This book club is very eye-opening. I hope I'm just like them when I get to their age.

Mason: I'm sure your brother will love that.

Audrey: I need to go to bed; it's a really early morning tomorrow.

Mason: Of course. Good night.

Audrey: Good night!

CHAPTER TWENTY-TWO

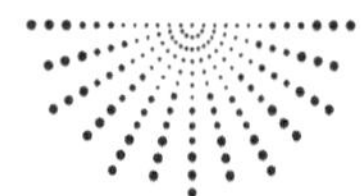

Looking at his phone one last time, Mason shoved it back into his pocket as Lincoln and David entered the meeting room. No texts from Audrey this morning. Which was a good thing because that meant she hadn't found any new notes. He shouldn't be disappointed.

He didn't want her to have any problems.

And of course, she wouldn't reach out just to say hi.

He definitely shouldn't be thinking any of these thoughts with her brother right there.

"Morning," David said, sliding a large pink and cream striped box onto the table in front of him, along with a small stack of paper plates and napkins. He'd obviously stopped by the bakery on his way in to pick something up for the meeting.

Dammit.

Mason should have thought of that.

"Morning." Leaning forward, he opened the box and smiled at the assortment of pastries inside. "Wow. These all look amazing."

"The muffins are blueberry, orange and cranberry, and banana walnut. That's coffee cake. And, obviously, these are cinnamon rolls." David pointed as he spoke. Mason went for a cinnamon roll, while

Lincoln took a piece of coffee cake—probably to go with the coffee he'd brought in with him. David picked up one of the blueberry muffins and sat down at Lincoln's right hand.

It was a heck of a spread. Something Audrey should be proud of. They all looked and smelled incredible, and Mason knew they would taste that way, too. The cinnamon roll was still warm. And sweet. Just like her.

For fuck's sake, get over yourself.

A moment later, Zeus came in to hook up the projector and was given the same offer. He grabbed one of the orange and cranberry muffins and set it off to the side while he did the hook-ups.

As he was in the middle of that, and the rest of them were unusually quiet because they were eating, Drew came striding in like a man on a mission, drawing everyone's eyes to him. He ground to a quick halt when he saw Zeus, his expression darkening, and lifted the laptop he had tucked under his arm.

"I need you to hook this up." The stilted way he said it was almost antagonistic, and Mason frowned at him as Zeus raised one eyebrow.

"That's what I'm here for," the bald man said, nodding his head at the table. "You can put it in the center there."

Drew scowled and put it down, seating himself next to Mason with a small huff. They were there to talk about Devlin with the whole team. Drew had been on surveillance this weekend. The fact that he was now behaving in a hostile manner toward Zeus… suspicion rose up in the back of Mason's mind.

He didn't want to not trust Zeus, but…

If Lincoln was worried, it didn't show in his expression, which remained bland as he glanced at his watch.

"Two minutes 'til the meeting starts, which means—" He cut off as Claudia came in, coolly regal, and holding a coffee in one hand with a file tucked under her opposite arm. "Good morning, Claudia."

"Morning." She took the seat between Lincoln and Mason, so he was now between her and Drew. Drew was still glaring balefully at Zeus, who was ignoring him as he finished hooking up the laptop.

"Muffin?" David asked, nodding his head at the box next to the laptop.

Claudia considered the offerings for a long moment before taking a cinnamon roll instead.

"Thanks."

She was a woman of few words this early in the morning.

"Everything ready?" Lincoln asked Zeus, who nodded before taking his seat next to David. Drew leaned forward to pull the laptop near him, opening it so he could get it started and find the files he wanted.

"Wait for me! I'm here!" Jensen came skidding into the conference room, just barely making it on time as usual. He grinned at everyone. He'd been grinning ever since Friday when he'd taken Jennifer to the soft opening of the bakery, so Mason took that to mean their date had gone well. Jensen quickly rounded the table to take a seat on the other side of Zeus, looking pleased with himself.

"Great. Everyone's here, so we can get started." Lincoln folded his hands on the table. "Drew, you told me yesterday that you have something big to report, so we'll let you start."

"Oh, I definitely have something big to report. As you all know, I was doing surveillance on Devlin this weekend, and he was on the move quite a bit." Drew glanced up at the screen on the wall, where he'd pulled up some photos of Devlin with MacLeod, which wasn't surprising. He flipped through several photos of them together at different events.

Devlin was being a lot more hands-on with MacLeod than he'd ever wanted to be at Black Fox, when he'd left most of the actual security work to Lincoln and Harris. Previously, he'd been content to be the behind-the-scenes guy, probably because it had given him more opportunities to embezzle. Apparently not anymore.

"It wasn't until last night when he was done with his official duties for MacLeod that I hit paydirt, though."

The picture on the screen changed to one of Devlin embracing a woman with long blonde hair, though her face was hidden. Then it changed again, as she stepped back away from him, beaming up at him with an expression of intimate enjoyment.

"Holy shit!" Jensen's expletive expressed what they were all thinking. "Isn't that—" He cut off, and they all looked at Zeus, who was still staring up at the screen where his current girlfriend was embracing his ex-boss.

If someone hadn't been paying attention to Zeus before, they might not realize that he'd gone tense all over. A muscle in his jaw ticked. Otherwise, his reaction was pure stoicism—that is to say, no reaction at all.

"Shit," David muttered.

Drew clicked through to the next picture. Devlin and Noelle kissing.

Next picture. Next picture. Next picture.

It was a slide-by-slide account of them kissing, then going into a motel room.

The meeting room was entirely silent. Mason had stopped watching the slideshow and started watching Zeus. He wasn't the only one. Drew was as well, with suspicious hostility still emanating from him. It wasn't like him to ambush someone the way he just had Zeus, even someone he didn't like.

Something was going on with Drew, and Mason had a feeling there was a lot more to it than the issues he and Naomi were having at home. On the other hand, something at work would likely give Drew a focus outside of where he felt like he was failing his wife with their infertility struggles. And something to focus on other than feeling like he'd failed David and Cassidy—Mason knew that Drew blamed himself for David being shot by Cassidy's ex.

They were going to need to have a session soon, no matter how Drew kept trying to avoid him.

Zeus was incredibly hard to read, which wasn't helping his case with the rest of the team. Or with Mason, if Mason was being completely honest. He didn't like being able to read one of the tea members. Zeus didn't appear distressed, angry, or hurt. Just... neutral.

Blank. Tense. But he could be tense because his connection to Devlin had just been discovered.

Or he could be tense because he'd just found out in a meeting of his co-workers that his girlfriend was cheating on him with their enemy. Really, it could go either way.

"So, Zeus. I suppose you didn't know about this?" Drew asked when he reached the end, a picture of Noelle and Devlin leaving the hotel room, their hair mussed, Devlin now missing his tie and clearly freshly fucked. The smug smile on Devlin's lips was impossible to miss. Drew, on the other hand, stared suspiciously at Zeus, as though he was trying to read his mind.

Good luck to him. Mason sure as hell couldn't figure out what the man was thinking or feeling.

Zeus was still staring at the screen. Slowly, he turned his head— just his head—to look at Drew, his expression implacable.

He raised one eyebrow and said absolutely nothing.

"Dude... he just found out his girlfriend was cheating on him, what's he supposed to say?" Jensen asked, swiveling around in his chair to face the table rather than the screen.

"Did he? Or is Noelle the conduit you use to pass information about Black Fox on to Devlin?" Drew continued scowling at Zeus, leaning forward with his arms braced against the desk. He was clearly ready for a fight.

And it looked bad.

It really, really did.

Jensen had jumped straight to the conclusion that Zeus was innocent, that he hadn't known about Devlin and Noelle, but Drew made a good point. No one would expect that Zeus would use his girlfriend to stay connected to Devlin. If he was still in contact, if they were working together, it would be a brilliant ploy.

Maybe she wasn't even Zeus' girlfriend. Maybe she was Marshall's, and that's why there had been tension between them. Maybe that's why they'd never scened publicly at the club.

Zeus turned his head again, away from Drew, his gaze drawn back to the screen where the picture of post-coital Devlin and Noelle was still up. The muscle in his jaw jumped again.

Because he was upset at his girlfriend? Or because he was upset he'd been found out?

Mason glanced at Lincoln, who was sitting back in his seat, arms crossed over his chest, his gaze darting back and forth between Drew and Zeus. He appeared torn. Beside him, David was also frowning, though he couldn't see Zeus' face because Zeus was facing directly away from him.

Not that the man's expression was giving anything away.

"Aren't you going to say something?" Drew demanded, leaning forward, one hand curling into a fist, resting on the table.

"What do you want me to say?"

"Something. Anything. Aren't you going to defend yourself?" Not just angry, Drew was confused. He'd done the shock and awe tactic to elicit a reaction—often a good way to go—but Zeus was giving them nothing.

Beside Zeus, Jensen looked uncertain.

"Is there something I could say that would convince you I knew nothing about this?" Zeus gestured at the screen.

Drew opened his mouth. Closed it. Frowned.

"You could try."

"When someone is determined to believe the worst of you, there is no point." Zeus shrugged, getting to his feet. "Now, if you will excuse me, I have some calls to make. Unless there's something else you want me here for?"

"You can go, but don't leave the office," Lincoln said. "Find me when you're done with your calls so we can talk."

Giving their boss a jerky nod, Zeus strode from the room. His head was high, shoulders back, jaw still clenched, and there was fire in his eyes. The question was whether he was pissed because his cover had been blown or if he was pissed because he was innocent.

The door shut behind him, and everyone let out their breath at the same time.

"Drama Queen." That was Claudia, directed at Drew, right before she took another sip of her coffee.

"I am not. I was trying to catch him off guard so we could see his reaction in real time."

"And? Now what do you think?" Jensen asked. "Because I'm telling you that to me, he looked like a guy who just got ambushed in front of all of his co-workers with the fact that his girlfriend is cheating on him with the enemy."

"Possibly," Mason agreed with a sigh, taking off his glasses and running over them with a wipe, even though they didn't really need it. He just felt the need to do something with his hands.. "He's clearly upset, but it could be because of that, or it could be because he is angry that their cover is blown."

"Oh, come on," Drew said, turning to Mason with a scowl. "You don't really believe it's an either/or, do you? How could he possibly not have known?"

"Cheaters don't usually announce that's what they're doing."

"Sure, but how did she even meet Devlin? That has to be the coincidence of all coincidences if he's not up to his neck in it with her."

"Maybe both are true. Maybe he's been passing information through her, but he didn't know she was cheating on him." This was probably where Audrey would accuse him of being paranoid.

"I hate it when you 'both sides' shit," Drew muttered.

"That's literally my job," Mason reminded him. "You got a slam dunk for proving that Noelle and Devlin are connected. That's not the same as a slam dunk for proving that Zeus knew about that connection, much less was part of it."

"Well, I don't trust him. He can't say anything to make me trust him."

"Which is why he was right when he said there was nothing he could say in his defense that would make you change your mind." Mason shook his head. "Any good PR person will tell you that sometimes you just have to let people draw their own conclusions, even if they're completely wrong, because defending yourself is only going to give them something new to pick apart. Can you honestly say that you hadn't already thought of a hundred arguments for any defense he might have made?"

Drew's frown deepened, and he huffed, sitting back in his seat and crossing his arms over his chest.

"That doesn't mean I'm wrong."

"It doesn't," Mason agreed. "But it doesn't mean you're right, either. We need more information."

"Agreed," Lincoln said, effectively cutting off the argument. He sighed. "I don't think Zeus is connected to Devlin. If I had to go with my gut, I would say that he knew nothing and that Devlin approached Noelle for this very reason. He could have even targeted her, but that doesn't mean that I'm going to assume that's the case, either."

"Zeus remains on the team?" David asked. If he was against the notion, it didn't show in his expression or voice. Though he didn't sound excited about it either.

"Zeus remains on the team." Lincoln's voice was firm. "I'm not going to tell anyone that they have to trust him completely, but I also want you all to remember that Marshall has shown himself to be devious time and time again. Breaking apart trust is one of the things he's going to aim to do with this team, and I doubt this will be the first effort. I agree with Mason; he could have found out about Zeus' relationship and approached her for no other reason than assuming we might eventually discover it, and it would both hurt Zeus and our trust in him."

"In which case, firing Zeus could make another enemy or at least someone who is hurt and angry, especially if it was unjustified. If he wasn't already passing information along to Devlin, it could be the thing that pushes him to do so." Mason sighed. "If we were sure… but we can't be sure."

"Great. That's just great." Drew's voice was growly, clearly displeased with how the conversation had gone. Mason didn't blame him, but there was nothing they could do about it at the moment.

Whether or not Zeus truly was trustworthy or if he was a plant of Devlin's, they would find out in time. In the meantime, cutting him loose could cause harm just as much as keeping him could. So, they might as well keep him.

"Keep your enemies close," Claudia murmured, echoing Mason's thoughts.

"This sucks," Jensen declared, reaching into the bakery box for a muffin.

He wasn't wrong.

"It's certainly not ideal," Lincoln agreed. "Does anyone else have anything to report about Devlin?"

No one did. Other than the brief interlude with Noelle, the man had been doggedly working and making lots of public appearances with MacLeod. Schmoozing. Showing off.

Lincoln dismissed them and went to talk to Zeus. Drew stormed off to his own office. Picking up his trash to throw away, Mason felt his phone buzz and immediately checked it.

A text message from Audrey.

He glanced over at David, who was now talking to Claudia, before opening it.

Audrey: There's another note. Alexis found it taped next to the back door when she went to accept a delivery.

Shit. He glanced at David again. But Audrey had asked him not to bother David with this. It was still just another note, not a real escalation. And with everything that had just come to light about Zeus, David had even more on his plate.

He would handle this for him, and David wouldn't have to worry about it at all.

Mason: I'll be right there.

CHAPTER TWENTY-THREE

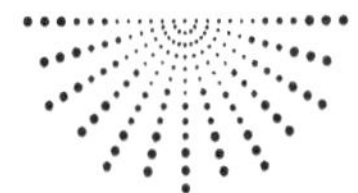

AUDREY

Although she was tempted to text Mason back that he didn't have to rush, feeling bad about interrupting his day, Audrey was too relieved that he was hurrying over to actually send a message telling him not to because she was kind of freaking out.

She glanced down at the paper in her hand again.

Bitches.

Very original.

Drawing a deep, unsteady breath, she put her hand over her heart, as if pressure on her chest could help slow its racing pace.

Audrey had no idea what to think about it.

It was hard to write off a second note as a mistake. Even harder to think that this was kids messing around, especially since the location of the note had moved. Someone had slipped it on the back door this morning after she and the other women had arrived.

Kids would be in school at that time.

Most people were at work.

There had been a small rush right after she opened—people coming in to grab something for breakfast before going to the office—but it had slowed pretty quickly. Audrey had already made a note about that for when she figured out what her permanent hours were going to be.

Right now, she was grateful for the lack of customers since it meant she didn't have to try to pretend everything was fine in front of an audience.

When a large shape appeared on the other side of the front door, she felt her chest seize up before she realized it was Mason. Her breath rushed out with relief as he opened the door, and she felt the tension she'd been holding inside her release.

He came in like an avenging angel, darkly handsome, with a serious expression. The long grey coat he was wearing only added to the effect as the bottom flared out with his movements. Their gazes met immediately, and she felt a blush creeping onto her cheeks as usual; that was just the effect he had on her. Smoothing her hands over her apron, she just barely managed to keep herself from reaching up to check her hair. That's not what he was here for.

"Hey. I'm sorry for calling you over like this, I'm just… freaking out a bit." Reaching into her pocket, she pulled out the paper, holding it by the very edge so as not to get her fingerprints on it too much. It already had Alexis'. "Since this is the second note and all."

"Can you put it on the counter?" Mason nodded at the open spot in front of her, and she put it down where he'd indicated as he came forward. Just his presence made her feel safer, she realized.

While she was competent at a lot of things, dealing with semi-threatening notes was not one of them.

Mason leaned over and read it, a thunderous scowl darkening his expression as he saw what it said. Dammit. That shouldn't be so hot. But it was.

"Original," he muttered.

"That's what I said." She tried to smile, but she knew it was forced.

"Did you check the camera footage already?"

"I did." She made a face. "They were wearing a hoodie and something over their face. I think it's a man, but I can't be entirely sure. It could just be a really tall woman with broad shoulders. I'm hoping you might be able to get more from it than I could."

"I'll take a look."

"I'm sorry for dragging you out here. I know there's not a whole lot. It's probably not even that big a deal, I just… panicked."

The look he gave her cut off her babbling immediately, and she gripped the edges of her apron, dropping her gaze.

"You absolutely did the right thing," he said, his voice gentle but firm. "I want to know immediately when anything happens. And if I can't come running myself, I'll send someone else on the team. Even if it's just someone playing a prank, you deserve to be here without worry or fear."

Audrey shifted her weight awkwardly, shrugging one shoulder, not knowing what to say to that. She wasn't afraid exactly. Or maybe she was a little. But it wasn't like they were *real* threats.

Nothing like what Cassidy had dealt with, with her ex.

"I just hope I didn't take you away from something important."

"This is important." He pulled on a plastic glove, taking a plastic baggie out of his other pocket. "You're David's little sister, first of all, and second of all, no one deserves to be dealing with creepy notes." Picking up the note in his gloved hand, he bagged it. "Unfortunately, I don't have the results of fingerprinting back from the first note yet, but we'll add this one to the queue just in case there's nothing helpful on the first note."

"Oh, that's something! The person who left it was definitely wearing gloves." Audrey perked up at being able to give an additional bit of information. "It's kind of cold out, so I know that doesn't mean they were always wearing gloves when handling it… but, ah crap, that's bad, isn't it?"

"It might be." He sounded amused. "But, like you said, they might not have worn them the whole time while handling it. If they did, that also tells us something about them."

"What does it tell us?"

"That they're smart enough to think ahead and worry about their prints being taken, which would likely mean their prints are on file somewhere."

Audrey's breath caught in her throat.

"So, a criminal?"

"Not necessarily. A lot of people have to have their fingerprints taken, even if they've never been arrested. Government jobs, teaching jobs, all sorts of things." He hesitated as he pocketed the baggie with the note. "But yes, one of the reasons would be if they'd been arrested before. It doesn't mean a violent crime, though. It could have been for something like marijuana possession."

"Right." Audrey released her apron and flattened it out again. "Well, I should show you the camera footage and see if you can get anything from it." Scooting from around the counter, she found she was hyperaware of him as she moved to the front door and flipped the sign that said she was on a break and would be back soon.

They had about an hour before people would start looking for lunch. She wasn't sure they'd get much of a lunch crowd anyway, though she was hoping for people to stop by for dessert *after* lunch.

When she turned around again, Mason was still standing by the counter, watching her. Her heart did that weird little flutter thing as she met his dark eyes and felt the heat bloom on her cheeks all over again.

"Um, this way." She tried to ignore the way all the little hairs on the back of her neck stood up as she led him through the door to the back.

As they walked in, Alexis' head came up like a startled prairie dog, then she relaxed when she saw it was just Audrey. Poor Alexis. She'd been very concerned when she found the note. Audrey hoped she didn't quit over this.

"Hey, Alexis, this is Mason. Mason, this is Alexis. Mason works with my brother at Black Fox Security. I've given him the note, and he's going to take a look at the camera footage."

Pure relief slid over Alexis' expression as she wiped flour off her hands and came forward to greet him, holding one hand out for him to take. Her sleek black hair was pulled into a high ponytail, and she was wearing a t-shirt and jeans under her apron, as usual.

"Oh, great. I'm so glad to hear that. It's so nice to meet you, Mason." She beamed at him.

Mason smiled as he reached out to accept her handshake.

"It's nice to meet you, Alexis. I'm sorry it's not under better circumstances. Hopefully, we can get this squared away."

"I hope so. I like it here. I can't imagine why anyone would have a problem with a bakery." Alexis shook her head, letting her hand drop.

"Is there anyone that's been bothering you anywhere else? Or anything weird happening at home?" he asked her.

Alexis immediately shook her head again.

"No. Nothing like that. And I don't really get out much, so I can't imagine anyone who would leave a note like that."

"Audrey said that you moved here from Savannah. Was there anyone back there who had a problem with you?"

"Not that I can think of." She shot Audrey a worried glance, her brow furrowing. "Is there some reason to think this is because of me?"

"No, I just want to eliminate all the possibilities. I know of at least one person who has a major grudge against Ashley, for instance." Mason smiled reassuringly. "That doesn't mean she's behind this, but in order to find out who's leaving notes, I want to eliminate all the possibilities."

"Notes?"

"Sorry I didn't tell you earlier. Yes, there was another note left before we opened Saturday morning," Audrey said in a rush. Part of her kind of wished Mason hadn't mentioned it because she didn't want to freak Alexis out, but he was right. Now that there was a second one, both Alexis and Ashley needed to know. "It just said 'get out'. I thought it must be a prank or kids or maybe even left mistakenly."

Alexis frowned, but it didn't seem like she was frowning at Audrey or like she was upset with her, which was a relief. More like she was frowning because she was thinking.

"Yeah, I can see that. But now that there's another one…"

"Now, I'm not sure it's kids or a prank, which is why I'm getting Mason involved. Especially since this one seems more aggressive." Audrey sighed. "He's going to look at the camera footage to see if there's anything I missed when I looked at it."

"Can I come, too?"

"Sure, maybe you'll see something."

Plus, that way Audrey wouldn't be alone in the small office with Mason. Not that she thought anything would happen.

But this way, she could be sure nothing would happen and that she wouldn't do anything foolish like act on her ridiculous crush. He probably wasn't interested, anyway. Even if Yasmine had been hinting that he was. Audrey had probably just imagined that she was hinting that. She'd read way too much into it.

And she did not want to have issues with her new friends because she did something wild, like kiss one of their recent exes.

They gathered in the office, around the computer, and Audrey pulled up the footage, stepping back to let Alexis and Mason lean in and observe. There was not a lot to see. It took less than a minute for the person to approach, glance quickly around, tape the note to the doorframe, then leave.

Audrey had already watched it five times in a row, so this time she watched Mason and Alexis' reactions. Well and maybe just a bit more of Mason. There was just something about his seriousness as he put on his glasses and then focused on the computer screen. Even if she couldn't touch, she could still look and enjoy. No harm in that, right?

Both of were equally intent on the footage, though Alexis was far more nervous. Her fingers tapped against the desk as she watched, whereas Mason was completely still and wholly focused. The intensity of his attention would have been intimidating if it was directed at her. Whoever was leaving notes, they'd better hope Mason didn't get his hands on them because he looked kind of scary now.

Which was also hot.

What is wrong with me?

Mason hit the button to play it again the moment it finished. After a second run through, Alexis straightened up, shaking her head, and glanced apologetically at Audrey.

"I can't see anything, I'm sorry. If it's someone I know, I don't recognize them."

"Thanks for looking anyway," Audrey said with a smile.

"I'm going to get back to work." Alexis hesitated. "Do you want me to go up front until you're done in here?"

Although she'd been trained on the register, in case she ever needed to take over, she'd obviously never liked the idea, and it was clear from her expression now that she desperately wanted Audrey to say no.

Well, it's not like Audrey was needed back here, anyway.

Plus, someone did need to be at the front.

And this way, she wouldn't be back here alone with Mason.

"No, that's okay, I'll go back up," she said, and Alexis smiled, her shoulders coming down. She really had not wanted to go to the front. "Mason, stay as long as you want."

"Okay."

He was so focused on watching the footage again, she wasn't sure he'd actually heard her, but apparently, she was superfluous, anyway. Trying to decide if she was relieved or put out, Audrey followed Alexis out of the office and headed back out front.

Thankfully, almost as soon as she flipped the sign back, a customer appeared, which helped distract her.

It didn't take long before Mason also returned to the front, his expression serious. He was no longer wearing his glasses. Audrey felt her heart sink a little as she looked at him. He really didn't look like he thought it was just kids or a prank this time, which meant she had to take it more seriously, too.

Which was not at all what she wanted.

All she wanted to do was bake things and sell them. Who could have a problem with that?

Well, other than her parents, but if she was sure of anything, she was sure that whoever was leaving notes was neither her father nor her mother.

They wouldn't be caught dead in a hoodie, for one.

"There's really not much to go by," Mason said, returning to the front of the counter and resting one hand on it. Audrey tucked her hands into her apron pockets to keep herself from doing something silly, like reaching for his. "I took a clip of the footage and sent it to my email to see if I can get more off of it with one of the programs we use, but I don't have a whole lot of hope."

"That's okay. Thank you for looking at it, anyway."

The look he gave her resembled the one he'd given her earlier when she'd apologized for dragging him out. It did all sorts of weird flippy things to her stomach when he looked at her like that, all stern and brooding and protective. Was that a Dom thing? It kind of seemed like it might be from the books she'd been reading.

Cash had certainly never made her feel like this before.

"I haven't really done anything yet, but I will," he said, and the way he said it carried all the weight of a promise. "I'm not hopeful about the fingerprints, but we could always catch a lucky break."

"What are you going to do?" She couldn't imagine what else he could do, unless something miraculous happened with either the fingerprints or the footage. Neither of which seemed very likely.

"I'll figure it out. Don't worry." He nodded his head, and her stomach did that swirly, loopy thing that she felt all the way down between her thighs again. "I'll see you later, Audrey."

"Bye, Mason."

It shouldn't feel like a caress when he said her name, but it did. She watched him walk out the door, her body all sorts of tingly and swirly.

Yeah, she was definitely reading more of her romance books tonight. Even if she couldn't have it in real life, a girl could dream.

CHAPTER TWENTY-FOUR

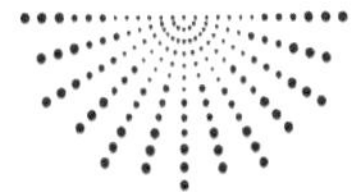

TUESDAY MORNING TEXTS

Audrey: All's quiet on the bakery front.

Mason: And back?

Audrey: And back. To my relief.

Mason: Glad to hear it. Unfortunately, the notes came back with no fingerprints but ours.

Audrey: Should I be worried?

Mason: I'm going to be around as much as possible, and I'm keeping an eye on the live feed from the camera when I can.

Audrey: Okay, thank you.

TUESDAY NIGHT TEXTS

Mason: I didn't see anything on the cameras today.

Audrey: I should be relieved, but I'm not. It's hard to think they're not coming back. I wish it was sooner rather than later.

Mason: That's understandable. They skipped one day this past time; it's possible they'll be back tomorrow. I should be able to keep a close eye on things.

Audrey: I appreciate that, but I feel bad. I'm not taking you away from anything important at work, am I?

Mason: You understand that you are important, right?

Mason: David would murder me if anything happened to you under my watch.

Audrey: It's just notes, though. It's not like anything really bad.

Mason: And we won't let it get there.

Audrey: Ashley thinks we should lay a trap for whoever it is, but I have no idea how we would do that.

Mason: Has she told Lincoln?

Audrey: Not yet. I told her I didn't want the team distracted while they're dealing with all the Marshall Devlin stuff, and she agreed.

Mason: But you don't mind distracting me 😉

Audrey: That's why I'm trying to make sure I'm not taking you away from anything important!

Mason: I was just kidding. It's not a problem at all.

Audrey: Promise?

Mason: Promise.

Audrey: Okay, I'm going to bed. If I can manage to fall asleep.

Mason: Sleep well. I've got this.

***

WEDNESDAY MORNING TEXT

Audrey: Help!

***

MASON

When Audrey's text came, only a few minutes after he'd gotten into the office, Mason didn't bother to check the camera feed. He just went running.

Down the stairs—he wasn't waiting for the elevator—and out onto the street. The brisk air nipped at his cheeks and hands as he dodged the people out on the street, ignoring the looks he was getting. His adrenaline was pumping, his heart racing, and the last time he'd felt like this… well, he'd been overseas, not in Pittsburgh.

He wasn't under attack now, but that one cry for help from her, and he felt like he might as well be.

When he came bursting through the front door, he knew immediately what the problem was.

Several customers were in the corner, mouths hanging open. One of them had their phone up and was recording everything. Audrey was behind the counter, just behind Ashley, her face pale against the black-and-white striped scarf she was using as a headband. She was wringing her hands, like she didn't know what to do.

Which was understandable, because Ashley's stepdaughter, who was also her stepmother, was standing in front of the counter, screeching at the top of her lungs, and Ashley was yelling back at her just as loudly. It was difficult to make out what either of them was saying, but he could very clearly hear Rebecca call Audrey and Ashley "Bitches."

Mason stepped up behind the raven-haired virago and put his hand on her shoulder. They'd met before, often enough that he felt comfortable touching her to get her attention.

She turned, flushed, furious, and blinked after a moment in recognition. Her face went very pale, then flushed hot red again.

"Rebecca," he said formally, keeping his tone even, despite the desire to shake her for putting that expression of forlorn horror on Audrey's face. "What brings you to Cupcakes and Crumbs this morning?"

What he was *not* expecting was for Rebecca's eyes to fill with sudden tears and for her to throw herself at his chest.

"Wiley is divorcing me!" The wail was heartfelt enough that he felt bad for her, despite the circumstances and despite the fact that she shouldn't be surprised. Wiley was Ashley's father, and he'd cheated on Ashley's mother with Rebecca. Their wedding had been the day after the divorce was finalized.

A stand-up guy he was not.

Mason had always pegged Rebecca as spoiled, mostly by her mother, and completely self-centered. He would not have expected an outburst of real emotion over losing her husband, especially this particular husband.

He patted her shoulder, trying not to be too obvious about his desire to peel her off of him.

"Um... I'm sorry to hear that?"

Ashley rolled her eyes, arms crossed in front of her chest.

"I don't know what she expected. I could have told her my dad was going to cheat on her, eventually. The relationship is ending exactly how it started."

Rebecca whirled, and Mason managed to get a grip on her to keep her from lunging toward the counter.

"You're a homewrecker!"

"Takes one to know one." Ashley smirked. "Besides, your mom was cheating on your dad first. My mom and I know how to stay faithful."

"I was faithful to Wiley!"

"Sucks to suck." Ashley shrugged.

"You're a fucking bitch! You can't talk to your customers that way. I demand you fire her!" The second sentence was directed at Audrey, and now Mason thought he understood why Rebecca had been calling them both bitches.

"Rebecca, you need to go," he said, moving around so he stood between her and the counter, his hands on her shoulders, keeping his space from her but also keeping her from being able to attempt violence. "How about I take you back to Black Fox, and you can talk to your dad? Ashley can't do anything about her father."

Rebecca's eyes were still full of tears, and she sniffled, sagging now that she didn't have the object of her ire to focus on.

"But it's her fault. Her dad is just divorcing me to make her happy."

"No, he's doing it because he's a selfish asshole you were dumb enough to believe loved you," Ashley called out over Mason's shoulder, and Rebecca's expression twisted into a snarl. "I don't care if you two stay married or not. I don't give a shit what my dad does."

The snarl fell as Ashley's words hit home, and Rebecca looked lost again.

"Come on," Mason urged gently, turning her away from the counter. "We can go to Black Fox and see your dad. This isn't helping anything."

He lifted his gaze as he got Rebecca turned around and headed for the door, and saw a man on the other side of the window, looking around inside the bakery. Maybe he'd just heard the commotion when he was walking by, but there was something about his stance that set alarm bells ringing in his head.

Blue coat with a darker blue collar, made of a rough canvas material. He had a white and navy checked scarf wrapped around the lower half of his face and a black hat pulled down low over his brow, though a lock of light brown hair peeked out on the right side.

Their eyes met.

The man's eyes widened… and he bolted.

Mason didn't stop to think; he just let go of Rebecca and ran after him, ignoring the shouts coming from behind him.

Having to get through the door slowed him down just a moment, and the man was *fast*. Mason noted his blue jeans and sneakers with one part of his mind as he gave chase, but he was already behind.

The man hopped onto the back of a motorcycle, and it roared to life as Mason cursed under his breath, trying to put on an extra burst of speed… but the bike slipped out of its parking spot and barreled down the street. There was no license plate on the back, which was illegal, but obviously, the guy didn't care.

All of Mason's instincts were pricking at him that this was their note leaver, not Rebecca, but who the man was and why he was targeting Cupcakes and Crumbs… that was something they'd have to learn. At least now, Mason had hair color and the fact that he rode a motorcycle—a Yamaha. Neither of which meant a whole lot—there were probably a lot of brown-haired men who rode motorcycles in the area—but at least it was more than he'd had before. Even knowing the make and being able to guess at the model wasn't going to help much.

Puffing from trying to catch up, Mason leaned forward with his hands on his knees, staring at the street even though the motorcycle was long gone.

Who was messing with Audrey's bakery? And why?

Should he say something to David now?

"Mason?" Audrey's voice echoed slightly as she called down the street to him. Mason straightened up and turned around. The chill in the air was clinging to his damp skin under his shirt, where sweat had beaded, making him feel even colder. He trotted back to where she was standing in the doorway of the bakery, so she still benefited from the heat inside the store.

He glanced into the area, but Ashley and Rebecca appeared to be ignoring each other now.

"Was it him?" Audrey asked, tilting her head back to look up at Mason as he approached.

"I can't prove it, but I think so," Mason replied grimly. "I don't know why else he would have bolted like that when I did nothing more than look at him."

"So, he knows who you are, too." Audrey dragged her teeth across her lower lip, frowning as she stepped back inside so he could follow her and they could close the door.

"It seems that way." Which meant whoever the man was, he'd been watching. He knew who Audrey's connections were.

Yet he'd come back for a third time.

Maybe it *was* tied to Devlin. Maybe the connections were the problem.

He would have to look into whether any of Devlin's team had light brown hair and a motorcycle.

That would give him an excuse to talk to Zeus and show the other man an olive branch of trust. Ever since the meeting where Noelle's connection to Devlin had been revealed, Zeus had been keeping to himself completely. Granted, Mason didn't completely trust him, but if he was going to stay on the team, something needed to be done.

Lincoln wasn't firing him, and Zeus hadn't quit. Which meant it was Mason's duty to go digging and try to figure out where Zeus' loyalties lay.

"Is something wrong?" Audrey asked worriedly.

Mason refocused himself. His arms started to move up—the urge to take her in his arms and hug and reassure her was that strong—but he stopped himself just in time.

"No, I was just thinking. I've got some ideas. If I come up with anything concrete, I'll let you know."

"Okay." She nodded and sighed, her shoulders dropping. "I wish this wasn't happening."

Again, he felt the urge to move closer to her, to wrap his arms around her shoulders.

"Me, too." Although even as he said the words, they didn't feel completely true. It wasn't that he wanted her in danger or that he liked that she was anxious or stressed… but he didn't hate that it gave him an excuse to check on her. The attraction he still felt to her was strong because he was feeling protective, but surely that would even out, then go away soon.

Because he really needed to get past it.

"Mason, are you going to take me to my dad?" Rebecca asked, coming up and moving between him and Audrey. He stepped back to give himself more space because she had moved right into his.

"Ah, yes. Come on." At the very least, he could separate her and Ashley, and that was something Audrey wouldn't have to deal with. She didn't seem to enjoy any level of conflict, much less the kind Ashley and Rebecca had when occupying the same space. "Let's go see your dad."

He turned to go, and the next thing he knew, she was tucked against him, her arm through his.

Mason sighed inwardly.

He really didn't like being touched by people he didn't know that well, but Rebecca was his boss' daughter. It wasn't that far back to the office. And since he didn't have a coat, maybe having a bulwark on one side wasn't the worst thing.

Glancing over his shoulder, he gave a little wave to Audrey and

Ashley. Audrey still looked upset, and he was once again struck by the desire to go comfort her… but he needed to offload Rebecca onto her father, then he wanted to look into Devlin's team. That was the best way he could help her for now.

"I'll be in touch," he said, and she nodded.

It felt wrong to leave her there, but what else was he supposed to do?

CHAPTER TWENTY-FIVE

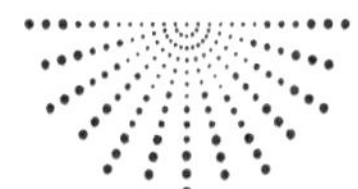

AUDREY

Watching Mason exit her bakery with a dark-haired beauty on his arm made Audrey's stomach do all sorts of unhappy flips. They made a good-looking couple. Just like he had with Yasmine. What was it about him that attracted model-gorgeous women?

Okay, so it wasn't like they were a couple. Rebecca was married. Although getting divorced.

She needed to stop the green-eyed monster inside her because it was making her crazy.

"Don't worry, there's no way she's going to get her hooks into him," Ashley said from behind her. Audrey whirled around to face her friend/employee. Out of the corner of her eye, she could see Alexis peeking out from the back, just for a moment before she disappeared again.

"What?" Audrey stared at Ashley, who smiled at her as she leaned against the counter. If she was bothered by the showdown with her ex-best friend, it didn't show on her face or in her demeanor. She looked like it was just another day; meanwhile, Audrey could still feel her hands trembling, her stomach still hurt, and her throat felt clogged.

Having Mason swinging in to save the day had made her want to throw herself into his arms.

"Rebecca. She's not his type." Ashley's smile didn't diminish, and she winked at Audrey. "You don't have to worry about her."

"Well, of course not. Why would I worry about her and Mason?" Audrey brushed away invisible crumbs from her apron as she went back around the counter, summoning up a smile and a wave for the small group in the corner who was now leaving. Goodness only knew what they'd thought about Rebecca's meltdown.

"Uh huh. Well, you don't have to, is all I'm saying."

Was she that transparent? Maybe. Audrey could already feel the blush rising in her cheeks, and she ducked her head.

"I'm not… we're not…" she muttered.

"Don't worry about it." Ashley patted her shoulder. "No judgment. Maybe I'm just imagining things."

Except that she wasn't, but Audrey didn't know how to say that.

She was trying to get up the courage to ask Ashley if she really thought the group would be okay if she had a crush on Mason, but before she could get herself there, the front door opened again, and it began the rush of people for the afternoon. A massive rush. Audrey wasn't sure where they were all coming from at first, although Ashley eventually asked one of the customers what brought them in.

A video had gone viral of Rebecca in the bakery, Ashley and Audrey's reactions, and "the hot guy" swooping in.

Whether they were there hoping for more drama, a glimpse at Mason, or because they thought Ashley was hilarious was up in the air, but the bakery was absolutely flooded by customers for the rest of the afternoon. Ashley stayed later than she'd originally planned because they were so busy.

Which totally screwed up her attempt to track what hours were going to be busy, but she wasn't sad about the new customers.

By the time they closed up, she was almost completely out of inventory, and all of them were exhausted.

Mason texted her that night that there were no updates, and she sent him a thumbs-up before she crashed into bed.

The video had gone even *more* viral overnight. Thursday was absolute insanity, and she sold out of stock again. Ashley joked that she would have to send Rebecca a thank-you note.

She was tired enough that she was tempted to skip game night and go home and crash again, but she didn't want to miss out on new friends. Plus, she wanted to see how Yasmine was doing. Although she felt a little guilty because, while she absolutely cared, there was also a part of her that wanted to know for purely selfish reasons. Which made her worry that she was a bad person.

Mason and Yasmine *were* broken up, though.

And Yasmine had been the one to end it.

And Audrey could almost swear that Yasmine had been encouraging her in Mason's direction.

But she needed to be *sure* sure.

So, game night it was. Hopefully, they wouldn't be playing anything super complicated.

"Hey, I was wondering if you were going to be coming," Claudia said, appearing pleased when she opened the door and saw Audrey. Today she was wearing black leggings and a grey oversized sweatshirt that went down to mid-thigh, her long hair up in a messy bun, and somehow she still managed to look intimidating. "Ashley called to say that she was too tired after the day at the bakery."

"It was pretty crazy. I almost didn't come, and my brain does feel kind of mushy right now," Audrey admitted as she walked in, taking her coat off as the warm air of the house enveloped her. "I'm hoping you'll take it easy on me tonight."

"We can do that," Yasmine joked, waving at Audrey from the other side of Claudia's table. "I think it's going to be a small group tonight, anyway."

"I'm just going to stand here because I can see Cassidy parking," Claudia said, waving a hand at Audrey. "Go sit down."

Which meant sitting down at the table with Yasmine. Despite it being the end of the day, she was wearing a light-blue shirt under a pinstripe vest, half her hair pulled back in a clip. From the waist up, she looked like she would fit right in at any corporate office that happened to hire models. If Audrey had to guess what she was wearing on the bottom half, she would picture a pencil skirt, high heels, and hose with a visible seam going up the back.

As usual, just looking at her made Audrey feel downright frumpy.

"Why a small group tonight?" Audrey asked as she sat, sighing with relief. The short walk from her car to the front door had almost felt like too much. She wasn't sure she was going to be able to get up anytime soon. Her legs were about to stage a revolt.

Yasmine shot her a sympathetic look.

"Ashley called out because she was too tired to come after today at the bakery. Jennifer is on a date with Dr. Grande. And Naomi is on her period, which means she's not pregnant again, so she's staying home." Yasmine's lips turned down. "She and Drew have been trying to have a baby, but it hasn't been going well. She won't mind you knowing, but don't bring it up unless she does because she doesn't really want to talk about it."

Understandable. Poor Naomi.

"And Brenda's not coming because apparently Cassidy needs a break from her," Claudia said teasingly as Cassidy came through the door. Audrey twisted around in her seat to look at her—she looked almost as exhausted as Audrey felt.

She also looked comfortable, in sweatpants and a fuzzy sweater under the warm coat she was shrugging off as she came through the door.

"Sorry Grandma's giving you a hard time."

"Honestly, it's more about being caught between her and your brother." Cassidy shook her head. "He's freaking out over this Mick thing, even though I'm pretty sure she's just messing with him, and the more he freaks out, the more she doubles down."

"What Mick thing?" Yasmine asked, sitting up and frowning.

"Oh, they've been spending time together, Mick and Brenda." Cassidy groaned as she sat down next to Audrey. "I wouldn't call it dating, exactly... but mostly because I think David's head would explode, and mine might, too."

Yasmine's eyes widened.

"Mick and Brenda? That's… okay, you know, I was going to say I wouldn't have guessed that, but when I take a second to think about it, it almost makes sense."

"Which is probably why it's driving my brother crazy," Audrey said. "I'll admit, I am trying really hard not to think about it."

"Neither of them will confirm they're doing anything other than spend time together, but Brenda keeps dropping sexual innuendoes, and when David flat-out asked Mick if he and Brenda have sex, Mick said—and I quote—'a gentleman doesn't fuck and tell'." Cassidy dropped her head into her hands, and it was hard to tell if the sound she made was a laugh or a groan.

Maybe a little of both.

"Hence, the need for a break," Claudia said. "Who needs a drink, and what do you want?"

After everyone had something to drink and Claudia had put out some snacks on the table for them to nibble on until the pizza got there, they went through the game options. Since there were four of them and Audrey was so tired, the other three agreed that Pandemic was the perfect option—the game play was still on the level they enjoyed, but since it was a cooperative game, they could give Audrey plenty of help and direction.

Which worked for her.

They got everything set up and had started playing when the first question came.

"So, Ashley said something about a video going viral?" Claudia glanced over at Audrey questioningly.

She told them the story of Rebecca, which also necessitated admitting to Claudia about Mason showing up and why she'd called him for rescue—as well as him chasing the guy down the street. Game play paused, then the pizza arrived, and they all listened while she went through the whole thing. She had to backtrack to the first note and how Mason had gotten involved, which made her nervous, considering who she was talking to.

She wasn't wrong to be.

"I had no idea!" Cassidy frowned. "I can't keep this from David, can I?"

"Sure, you can," Audrey said immediately. "Please? I don't want to bother him. Mason seems to have it handled. And David's already stressed out enough between work and now Grandma and Mick."

"Well, there is that." But Cassidy still looked conflicted. "I don't know if I can lie to him, though. Especially if Audrey is in danger."

"We don't know that she really is yet. Though granted, the notes aren't good, but they're also just notes. You don't have to lie to him, just don't say anything unless he brings it up," Claudia advised. "Audrey's not wrong, he does have a lot going on right now. Mason is a good person to take point on it—he's who David would assign to do it if he couldn't handle it himself, and right now, he doesn't have the time to, so we're just skipping a step—and now that I know, I can help, too."

"What's going on with work? If you can tell me." Yasmine's expression was hard to read, even though Audrey was desperate to, especially after admitting that Mason was helping her. She was very blank, so Audrey couldn't tell if she was upset. She didn't seem outwardly disapproving or anything, but that wasn't exactly the same thing as approving.

"Devlin again. You remember Zeus' girlfriend, Noelle?"

"Sort of. I only know what I've heard; I haven't actually met either of them."

"Well, I'll have to get you a picture of Noelle, so you know who to avoid. She was cheating on him with Devlin, and Zeus found out at a meeting on Monday. That or he's been working with Devlin, and she was the go-between, and he got outed on Monday. It's kind of hard to tell which it is."

Yasmine's mouth dropped open in shock. Even that looked pretty on her.

"Wow... okay..." She said the words slowly, as if she was trying to think of what to say and coming up with nothing. Audrey could relate.

"So, either he's spying on us and reporting back to Devlin, or

Devlin's been banging his girlfriend, so we'll think Zeus is spying on us, or it's just an incredibly wild coincidence that Devlin happens to have been banging Zeus' girlfriend."

"And on top of that, David's worried that Jensen's brother is doing filthy things to his grandmother." Claudia snickered when both Cassidy and Audrey groaned.

"Did you have to phrase it like that?" Audrey asked plaintively.

"Yes. It's funnier that way."

"Maybe to you." Cassidy scowled at her, but she was fighting a smile.

"It's a good thing Mick isn't a member of the Outlands," Yasmine said. "I could see him bringing Brenda there just for the shock value—hers and David's. And Audrey's, if she's there."

"Oh. My. God." Audrey covered her face with her hands. "The last place I want to see my grandmother is a kink club."

"Are you coming back? You didn't stay long last time," Yasmine said, and now her expression was concerned. "You don't have to go just because we do if you weren't into it."

"I… I wasn't *not* into it…" Crap. This was awkward. How did one say 'I didn't like picturing you doing the things I was seeing with the man you were engaged to,' without actually saying it? "I was really tired, of course. And I had to get up early the next day. And maybe it was a little intimidating."

She'd rather admit it was intimidating, even though they might think less of her, than admit her crush on Mason had been the biggest problem.

"Okay, just wanted to make sure that you knew you can still come to game night and hang out and everything. The club is not a requirement to be friends with us." Yasmine smiled as the others nodded, and Cassidy nudged Audrey with her elbow.

"I do like the books a lot."

"If you're up to it, you should come tomorrow. I've decided to go, and I could use the support." Yasmine glanced around at all of them.

"Of course!" Cassidy was already nodding her head. "David and I can be there. You're going to jump right back into things?"

"Might as well." Yasmine shrugged. "While Mason and I were talking about marriage and everything, I wasn't going to scene with someone else. But now I'm free, and so is he."

Wait, had she just glanced at Audrey when she said Mason was free?

"Good for you." Claudia nodded approvingly. "There's no point in wallowing, right?"

"Right. Though I'm not looking for a relationship," Yasmine warned her. "I'm off of those for good. That doesn't mean I can't enjoy a good scene or some filthy hot sex, but I've sworn off relationships for right now."

Claudia arched an eyebrow, but didn't say anything. "Mmm."

"But you still want the marriage and kids thing, right?" Cassidy asked. "You're not just going to give up on it because this didn't work out? Like, if you really don't want it, that's one thing, but I don't want to see you give up on something you really want because you and Mason didn't have chemistry."

"That's not the only reason. There is a pattern after all." Yasmine shrugged. "Maybe it's time I just accept the curse. I don't need marriage to have a kid, after all. There are other options."

"Well, that's true." Claudia sat back in her chair, blinking. She looked like she wanted to say something, but she couldn't quite figure out what to say.

Neither could Audrey, but that wasn't surprising because her own emotions were all over the place when it came to Mason, and she didn't know Yasmine well enough to know what the right thing to say was.

"I think you'd make a great mom," she offered up, both because it was true and because maybe that was what Yasmine needed to hear.

The other woman flashed her a smile.

"Thank you. Now, let's get back to the game. We don't need to talk about my cursed love life anymore because I'm just not going to have a love life at all."

CHAPTER TWENTY-SIX

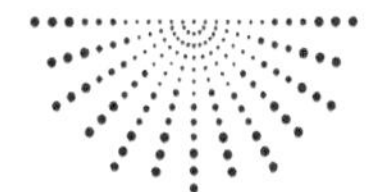

One week after his engagement had ended, he was back at the Outlands. He had not planned on coming back so soon after the breakup, but he was here tonight thanks to Claudia, who told him that both Yasmine and Audrey were coming. He told himself that he was here for Yasmine, to make sure none of the Doms were going to be worried about scening with her so soon after their arrangement ended. He wanted her to be able to scene with whoever she wanted.

Which meant he would be here tonight regardless of whether or not Audrey was going.

But yes, that was a factor, too; he couldn't deny that.

Those protective feelings he was having for her, because of everything going on at the bakery, obviously extended outside of the bakery as well.

He got there early to make sure that he was there for when Yasmine came in. She tended to be an early arrival, because she didn't like to stay out too late, so she could get her beauty sleep—as she said.

Mason took a perch in the bar on the main floor, so he could see people coming in. He was only having one beer tonight. Not because he intended to play—there was a two-drink maximum—but because he wanted to stay sharp. After this, he planned to swing by Cupcakes and Crumbs for a bit, just to keep an eye on things.

He liked to think that he had chased the culprit away, never to return again, but he wasn't taking the chance he was wrong. Not yet. It had been a few days, so if something more was going to happen, he guessed it would happen soon. He'd keep watching for a while longer.

Just in case.

As he sat, he watched the various people coming through the door, meeting in the bar, or heading downstairs. He always enjoyed being in the club, watching the members interact. Everyone was so different, yet so many things remained the same.

The respect. The warmth. The camaraderie. People coming together in a community, embracing each other for their differences, and including everyone who was willing to be a part of that.

It was nice.

He wasn't surprised when Yasmine arrived about half an hour after he got there, the first of their group. She was dressed to scene—unlike him since he was still wearing the same clothes he'd worn to work—in a black leather corset and a short skirt that hugged her body. The high heels and high ponytail were a nice touch. It was so strange how he could objectively notice what an attractive woman she was without feeling the attraction necessary to make a relationship between them work.

When she came in, she looked around, a determined expression on her face and did a doubletake as her gaze passed over him. Frowning, she strode over to the table where he was sitting. He got to his feet, leaning forward to kiss her on the cheek, then sitting back down.

For anyone who was watching—and a few people were—it was a very public manner of demonstrating that they were friendly but that she didn't belong to him.

"What are you doing here?" she asked, putting her hands on her hips, a touch of anxiety in her voice.

Mason met her gaze blandly.

"Making sure that everyone knows we're not together, and I have no claim on you." He raised his eyebrow at her. "Unless you have a problem with that."

Her snapping at him with her hands on her hips was going to go a long way toward confirming the impression he'd just given with his greeting. It wasn't like he could take out a billboard or anything, but this was as close as he could get.

"Oh." Yasmine tilted her head, obviously thinking about it for a moment. "That's nice of you. Thank you."

"You're welcome. What did you think I was here for?"

"Well…"

Giving her a firm look, he put his beer down on the coaster in front of him.

"I'm not going to be doing any scening tonight," he stated. The only woman he wanted to scene with was off limits, anyway. And not just because Yasmine had requested a month before she had to see him with someone else.

"I want you to be happy. I just want a bit of time before I have to watch you be happy."

"There's no one I'm interested in 'being happy' with."

Now it was her turn to give him a look. "Uh huh."

Mason scowled, but the server had arrived to ask if Yasmine wanted anything to drink, and by the time she'd finished giving them her order, Claudia had walked into the club and made a beeline for them. Her expression was intrigued, but she fell into easy conversation with Yasmine, while Mason sat back in his chair and sipped his beer, listening with only half an ear.

"I'm going to do a walkaround," Yasmine said, with a little twirl of her finger. "Maybe go take a peek at what's happening downstairs."

"Have fun." Mason spoke loudly, just in case anyone was listening. He was pretty sure Master Cole, who was sitting at the bar not far away, had been listening to their entire conversation with one eye on Yasmine.

Mason knew Master Cole had scened with Yasmine in the past, but then he'd scened with most of the submissives in the club. He was part of a polycule that was completely open when it came to kink, which might be exactly what Yasmine needed tonight. Someone who she could relax with and not have to think about her curse, but still get her needs met.

He smirked into his beer when, about five seconds after Yasmine left the table, Master Cole got up from his seat. The big blond caught Mason's eye for just a moment, and Mason gave him a nod. The other man grinned and ambled in the same direction Yasmine had gone.

"So." Claudia slid onto the seat next to Mason, setting her water down on the table. "That's done. Are you planning on scening tonight?"

"No. Considering Yasmine and I just ended things, I don't want any submissives getting any ideas or expectations."

Claudia snorted.

"That's one complication I hadn't thought of," she admitted. "Anyone you scene with is going to have certain expectations." She smirked in pure amusement.

"Not if I scene with two different people. I could go from person to person in one night and just keep them all platonic."

"And that's how you end up in polycule." Claudia grinned. "You and Cole."

That made Mason laugh. He was pretty sure poly wasn't for him. The idea of making one person happy in a relationship was stressful enough; more sounded nerve-wracking. He didn't know how Cole and his partners did it.

But he also didn't need to since he planned to be monogamous.

Movement caught his eye, and he glanced over at the entrance, as he had all night, every time someone came in. Red hair caught his attention, though it wasn't the redhead he was anticipating seeing—it was her brother. Which still made his senses heighten because if David was there…

Yup. Right behind David was Cassidy, then Audrey. She looked stunning in a pin-up style dress that showed off her shoulders. It had a corset top, but it was a dress with a skirt that flared out from her hips and swished around her legs as she walked. The fabric was black and covered in cherries, and she had a matching scarf tied around her head like a headband, holding her hair back from her face. Just looking at her made Mason's entire body come alive, anticipation humming along his veins.

David had the same slightly pinched expression on his face he'd had the last time his sister had come to the club. He was trying to be cool with it, but it was obviously a struggle.

Mason wondered what David would do if someone asked Audrey to scene.

The very idea sent a wave of jealousy through him.

Because he wasn't scening with anyone tonight. Which meant someone else would be the one scening with her.

And he didn't like that thought at all.

Even though he had no idea what to do about it.

"I know," Claudia murmured, jerking Mason out of his silent admiration. His brain floundered, trying to figure out what she meant.

He hadn't said that out loud, had he?

The panicked looked he gave her made her grin, and she winked.

"I know about the notes that were left at the bakery," she clarified.

Mason felt his whole body sag in relief. He had not admitted his attraction out loud. Thankfully.

"I told Audrey I'd help. David still doesn't know. But if you need anything…"

"Not at the moment, but thank you." He smiled as the other three approached, effectively ending the conversation since David didn't know.

Audrey must have said something at game night, which meant Cassidy knew, too. Dammit, how many of the other women knew?

Mason knew he couldn't keep it a secret from David forever, but he was hoping to present David with the culprit when he told him.

Hey, your sister was being harassed at her bakery, but I caught the guy who was doing it. It would be cool if I date her now, right?

He nearly choked on air as the thought ran through his head. Where the hell had that come from?

"Hey, you two," Cassidy said, stepping forward and opening her arms. Mason got to his feet to give her a hug before passing her off to Claudia, doing his best to keep his expression neutral despite the unhinged thoughts that had invaded his head.

David nodded at Mason, who nodded back. Since Cassidy was between them, it wasn't awkward to sit back down without hugging Audrey, which was good, because he wasn't sure he'd be able to hide his reaction to her if he did. It was already a close-run thing.

"Where's Yasmine? I thought she'd be here already," Cassidy said, looking around.

"She is. She went to look at the view... and yup, Master Cole is there now talking to her." Claudia smirked. "So, I'm sure they'll be headed downstairs soon."

Eyeing Mason, David frowned as he slid onto a chair. Already seated beside him, Audrey was staring at a random spot on the table.

"Are you sure you're okay?" David asked Mason.

"I'm more than okay. I'm glad she's getting what she needs. I wouldn't have been able to give it to her." Mason shook his head. "We could have gotten through a non-sexual kink scene, but I don't think either of us would have been wholly satisfied with that, to be honest. Not with the person we planned to marry."

"Mmm." David looked thoughtful as he snaked his arm around Cassidy's waist, pulling her against him. She giggled and leaned into his hold. "I guess that makes sense."

"How were things with the senator today?" Mason asked. David and Lincoln had had a meeting with her in the afternoon, so Mason hadn't seen them since the morning.

Was it wrong to start work talk while they were at the club and off the clock? Maybe, but he couldn't think of anything else to say, and focusing on David meant that he had something to look at other than the bountiful depths of Audrey's cleavage, which was on full display now that she was sitting across from them. Drooling over David's little sister's breasts right in front of him seemed pretty inappropriate.

So, it was better to concentrate on David.

It wasn't too long before Drew and Naomi came in, both of them looking a little more distant than usual as they joined in the conversation. Not just from the group, but from each other. Mason kept a close eye on them, even after a grumpy Jensen came in, alone.

He knew what Jensen's issue was, and there was nothing he could do about that little love triangle.

He was far more concerned about Drew, and by proxy, Naomi.

They seemed to relax after a while in the club atmosphere and soon ended up heading downstairs to scene. Good. That would probably help both of them. David and Cassidy abandoned them not long after that, stars in their eyes as they looked at each other. Audrey watched them go with an odd expression on their face.

"What's wrong?" Mason asked, leaning forward.

Claudia and Jensen were currently having a private aside, and he was pretty sure Jensen was getting dating tips on how to steal Jennifer away from her doctor to have her all for himself, which meant it was up to Mason to check in on Audrey.

"Just… it's not that I want to imagine my brother and Cassidy doing some of the stuff that I saw last week—or that I've read about—but I'm also having trouble imagining it." She shook her head, like she was trying to shake the thoughts off. "I shouldn't think about it too hard. Um, any updates on the fingerprints or anything?"

"Unfortunately, nothing. I just found out today before I left work. And I still haven't been able to pinpoint who the guy I chased off was."

There were two men with light brown hair who worked for Devlin, but neither of them had motorcycles. At least, neither had a motorcycle registered to him. That didn't mean they didn't have access… but it wasn't exactly a warm lead at this point.

Audrey sighed, which made her breasts heave up in her corset in a manner that had his cock perking up with interest.

Don't look, don't look, don't look.

He was staring so hard at her face, to keep his gaze from dipping down, he almost felt like he had lasers coming out of his eyes.

"I guess it was too much to hope for that it would be an easy answer." She shook her head. "I still can't figure out who would care about my bakery like this."

"If it helps, we *are* pretty sure Rebecca had nothing to do with it.

So, that's at least one suspect down." When he'd turned her over to Lincoln, he'd found out that she'd just gotten home from a trip with her mother.

Mason had very quietly run her financials, and there was no out-of-the-ordinary spending, nothing that couldn't be accounted for outside of her normal life and the trip. If she'd hired someone to leave the notes—which she couldn't not have left herself, going by the time she was on a cruise ship with her mother—she had paid for it in cash. But there were no cash withdrawals from her accounts at all for the past four months, which was long before Ashley had been hired or the bakery was even a thing.

He felt pretty comfortable marking her off the list.

"That's actually a relief. I know she's a terrible person, but I felt kind of sorry for her." Audrey traced her fingers through a wet spot on the table where someone's glass had left condensation because they hadn't used a coaster. "I think she really loved Ashley's dad."

"That or her pride is hurt, and she's worried that she alienated her former friend *and* her father for something that ultimately didn't work out." Mason shrugged when Audrey looked at him in surprise. Yes, he was a little cynical.

"It could be that. I just like to think the best of people sometimes," she admitted. "Even when I don't know them."

"I tend to think the worst. That way sometimes I get a nice surprise, and I'm rarely disappointed."

"Oh, yeah?" Her lips quirked up. "What's the worst expectation you could have of me?"

Mason met her gaze and felt his pulse pick up. His senses tingled, his nerve endings coming alive as it felt like the rest of the world melted away. The description was something he'd always dismissed as frivolous exaggeration, but right now, looking into the emerald pools of her eyes, it really did feel like they were suddenly the only two people in the world. No one else existed. No one else mattered.

"You only made the baklava so you could find out my favorite, then withhold it from me unless I do you favors."

His voice was husky. Deeper than usual. He hadn't meant it to sound like a sexual innuendo, but it came out that way. A pink blush immediately spread across her creamy cheeks, her bright red lips forming a perfect 'o' in surprise.

Fuck.

He would happily do her those *favors* even without the baklava.

"Oh, well." She cleared her throat, and her voice came out higher than usual. Squeaky. Nervous. Just like a little subbie who had caught a Dom's attention and didn't know what to do with it. "I promise I'm not looking to bribe you for anything with baklava."

"If you did, it would be a good bribe." He smiled at her, trying to joke to lighten the sudden intensity of the space around them. It didn't work.

"I'll keep that in mind." She looked down again at her wrist, where she had a black watch rather than a bracelet. "Oh, wow… it's getting late again. I should probably go."

Hopping up from her seat, she seemed about to flee, but Mason was already getting up from his. He glanced at Claudia and Jensen, who were still deep in conversation and didn't even look up. Audrey halted, wide-eyed, when she realized Mason had gotten to his feet as well.

"You don't need to wait for David and Cassidy?"

"Oh, no. I have to be up early tomorrow, and they said they wanted to stay late, so we came at the same time, but I took my own car."

"Ah. I'll walk you out."

Because he couldn't let her walk out in the dark to her car alone. It was unsafe, and David would never forgive him.

That was the only reason.

Really.

CHAPTER TWENTY-SEVEN

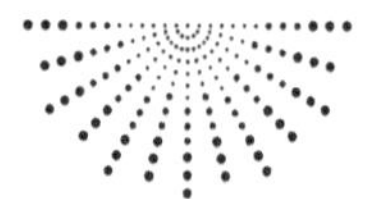

Oh God.

Mason was walking her out to her car. Just the two of them.

What do I do?

Act normal.

How do I normally act?

I don't know.

Why don't I know?

This was so much more stressful than it should have been.

But... Yasmine was doing—something—with someone else. Master Cole. Whoever that was. Did that make it okay for Mason to walk Audrey out?

Well, of course, it's okay. It's not like he's doing anything other than walking.

The only reason it didn't feel okay was because of her feelings about him. But if Yasmine was already moving on, why couldn't Mason?

Audrey cursed the cowardice that had kept her from asking Yasmine point-blank if she had been hinting that she saw Audrey's crush and was fine with it. But the thought of doing so and being wrong made her stomach curdle. Or what if Yasmine was fine with Audrey's crush, but only if she didn't act on it?

"So, is the bakery still buzzing from the video?" Mason asked as they walked out the door into the cold night. Audrey automatically hunched her shoulders in her coat, shoving her hands in her pockets, thankful she was wearing her long winter coat that covered her nearly to her ankles. Even without pants, as long as the wind didn't whip up, she was pretty warm all over.

"Yeah. It's died down a little, but there are still more people than usual coming in. All of them with their phones out and hopeful expressions on their faces." Thank goodness, she actually sounded normal when she was answering him instead of like the Hot Mess Express she was inside.

"Gotcha. So, are you leaving early because you're tired?" Mason glanced down at her, and she looked up at him in surprise. The dark shadows of the streetlamps made him look particularly dangerously handsome, especially with the sharp line of his black coat collar against his jaw, where he'd turned it up to keep his neck warm.

She looked away, focusing on the sidewalk they were walking down. Her car wasn't that far away, which she was both grateful for and suddenly wished it was a little farther.

"That's definitely part of it," she admitted, and then hesitated. "The other part is that I don't really know what I'm doing there. I don't know what *to* do."

Why she had chosen *him* to admit that to, she didn't know. Maybe because she felt comfortable with him after he'd come running to the rescue at the bakery. Maybe because she had a crush on him and felt a connection, and she was worried he felt it too, and if anything did ever happen between them, she didn't want him expecting some kind of experienced, perfect submissive.

She bet Yasmine was a perfect submissive.

"You know you don't have to do anything, right? There are plenty of people who come for the community but don't scene."

"I'm not against scening." Heat filled her cheeks. It was dark enough that he wouldn't be able to see her blush for once. "But I wouldn't know how to get into one. Even if someone wanted to scene with me, I wouldn't know what to tell them I like or don't like because I don't have any experience. I don't know. I don't know anything."

The frustration bubbling up inside her wasn't just at her lack of knowledge; it was at herself. In the few months she'd had away from her parents, she'd learned more about herself than she had in the years of living her life up to this point. Realizing how much about herself she didn't know, how much about life she didn't know, was frustrating. Especially because the opportunity had been there, but she'd never been willing to defy her parents, not even to read the kind of books they might disapprove of.

What kind of adult let their parents run their life to that degree? It was embarrassing.

They'd reached her car. The blush was still hot in her cheeks as she let out a long breath, the white cloud puffing out from her lips and dissipating into the darkness.

"Anyway. That's not your problem. Sorry."

"Don't be sorry. Did you tell the others about how you feel? Any of them, especially Claudia, would be happy to set you up with someone to walk you through different aspects of kink." His voice sounded rougher than it had before. Tinged with some kind of emotion. Jealousy? Or was she projecting because that's what part of her wanted to hear? "Heck, Claudia might offer to do it herself. You could try things out with one of them."

"I guess. I would be a lot more comfortable with someone I know and trust, like Claudia. I can't imagine trying anything with someone I just met. I don't know if I'd want to do it at the club, though… what if I did something wrong? What if I don't like it? I don't even know if I would like being spanked… what if I hate it?" The words were tumbling out of her now, and she found herself looking up at him as if he had the answers.

His face was mostly shadowed, but she could feel the light on hers and knew he could see her expression clearly, even if the reverse wasn't true. Maybe that's what made it easy to talk to him about this.

It wasn't like she could see his reaction.

"Do you want to try a spanking to see if you like it?" he asked.

That was the last thing she ever expected him to say to her. Audrey stared at him because her brain had just come to a screeching halt, trying to figure out if he meant what she thought he meant.

"Platonically, of course. Nothing sexual involved. If you're leaving because you're worried, we could go to your place or my place right now, and I could demonstrate, and then you'd know. For next time."

Oh my God.

He was actually saying what she thought he was saying.

He was asking if she wanted him to spank her.

In private.

Platonically.

"Sorry, I hope I didn't just make things uncomfortable—"

"Yes," she interrupted him, feeling suddenly breathless; what if he was about to take the offer away?

Hadn't she just been thinking about how her parents had stifled her? How she hadn't done what she wanted to do, even when they wouldn't know about it, because she'd known they wouldn't approve?

Was she turning into a horribly selfish person?

No. He was making an offer—a non-sexual one—and she was not betraying girl code by taking him up on it. He'd just said, Claudia could do the same thing. But Audrey wanted to try it. Now.

Then at least she'd know if she was into it or not, and Mason had just offered, so…

And if she was being really honest with herself, she wanted her first spanking to be done by the man she kept picturing in her head when she was reading her books.

"Yes?" His voice had roughened again, deepened, and her stomach did a little flip-flop.

"Yes. Uh, please." She cleared her throat. "Um, at my place, I guess?"

Before she chickened out.

"Okay." He nodded. Audrey had already given him her address for his contact information, just in case anything from the bakery followed her home. It hadn't so far, to her relief, and now it was coming in handy for an entirely different reason. "I'll see you there in a few minutes."

"Great," she squeaked out, before turning and getting into her car, trying not to feel like she was fleeing.

Oh God, what am I doing?

MASON

Fuck.

What was he doing?

Thinking with his dick and not with his head.

No. Not with his dick.

Platonic. He'd promised her a non-sexual spanking.

There were plenty of people who scened without bringing sex into the equation. He was doing a spanking demo, nothing more, and he'd done plenty of those over the years.

This was the same thing.

Except that he'd never felt the kind of attraction for any of the demo participants he did for Audrey.

Getting into his car, he shook his head to clear it and pulled out behind her. Why had he made the offer?

Because the idea of someone else putting their hands on her was already driving you nuts.

Because she wanted privacy rather than doing it at a public place like a club, where there will be people to help if it doesn't go well... and you know she'll be safe with you.

And the privacy was actually why he could do it.

Because Yasmine hadn't wanted to *see* him with anyone for a month.

It had only been a week, but she wasn't going to see either of them because they weren't going to be at the club. They were going to be at Audrey's house.

No one had to know. How would they know?

They'd just assume that both he and Audrey had gone home.

Which they were.

They were just both going to Audrey's home.

He followed her car, even though he had her address since he was keeping an eye on her.

That was the most important reason he had offered to demo a spanking for her, of course. He wanted to make sure she stayed safe. He was already protecting the bakery; it made sense he would extend that protection to all aspects of her life. The jealousy… that was an aberration, and it was controllable.

He was just doing the right thing.

By going to Audrey's house and spanking her.

Mason winced.

Even he couldn't quite spin that as fully altruistic as he wanted to. At some point, he was going to need to do a deeper examination of his feelings and figure out why the hell Audrey was so different and had been from the moment he'd met her.

But not tonight.

Tonight, he was finally going to get his hands on her delectable ass, and maybe if he just truly let himself go and fully enjoy the moment, she would no longer be such forbidden fruit. Maybe he'd finally get control over himself again.

Her apartment building had a front desk, where they signed him in. The bored woman behind the counter barely looked at them. They were barely looking at each other. Even though they'd agreed for this to be non-sexual, sexual tension was thrumming through the air, and he didn't think it was just coming from him.

He was going to have to be very, very careful to stick to their agreement and not confuse things for either of them.

"This way," Audrey said, smiling, then ducking her head, gesturing to the right and scurrying ahead of him.

Damn, she was cute. Mason followed more slowly, turning over in his head where the boundaries for tonight should be.

He'd offered to show her a spanking.

And he didn't have any of his implements.

She was wearing a skirt.

That was easy enough to flip up, and a bare bottom spanking didn't necessarily have to be sexual, but it would be a hell of a lot easier for him if she kept her underwear on. So, underwear on, dress on, but skirt up. That sounded reasonable.

No kissing. Obviously.

No fondling.

Of course.

Rubbing her bottom would be fine, as long as he was doing it to help soothe the burn and sting of the spanking and not for either of their pleasure. That was reasonable.

Even if his dick was already hardening just thinking about it.

But it didn't matter what his dick wanted as long as the rest of him understood that this was going to be strictly platonic.

Audrey pushed the button for the elevator, and the doors opened immediately. Stepping inside, she turned and looked up at him, and smiled nervously, all her fear, trepidation, and anticipation filling her wide eyes.

Fuck.

CHAPTER TWENTY-EIGHT

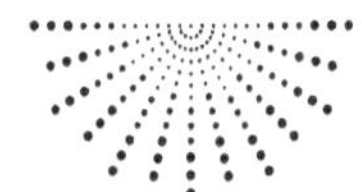

AUDREY

Awkward.

This was so awkward. Standing in the elevator was awkward because they were standing right next to each other, and she wanted to reach out to hold his hand. Her own hand felt warmer on the side he was standing on, and she felt like she could barely take in a full breath… but she also couldn't work up the nerve to reach out for him.

That wasn't what this was about.

He'd made a very kind offer to demonstrate a spanking.

Which she did want to experience with someone she trusted, and she trusted Mason.

She was also relieved she didn't have to do it in the club where everyone would be watching. The pressure to react correctly was too high there. Especially since she didn't know what the right reaction would be. A moan? Crying out? But what if she hated it?

If she did, she didn't feel like Mason would judge her. Not that they'd spent a ton of time together for her to know for sure, but she felt like she'd been getting to know him over the texts they sent. Plus, the times he'd come running to her rescue. He'd never made her feel judged once.

"I'm right down here," she said, walking quickly out of the elevator. She didn't know how she was supposed to behave. Fortunately, Mason didn't seem to mind.

Nonjudgmental.

That was reassuring since that's what she was looking for right now. The fact that she was also wildly attracted to him... well, she wasn't sure that was a good thing. He'd been very specific about it being platonic, which was a good thing, even if Yasmine was already moving on.

Audrey didn't even know if she would like kink outside of her fantasies, and Mason was a real-life Dom.

Obviously, it was something he liked. And needed. Audrey wanted a Dom—at least, she thought she did—but how could she be sure when she'd never done anything kinky before? Maybe she only liked it in her books and in her head. Maybe she would wuss out the second his hand came down on her butt.

Even though the idea of his hand coming down on her butt made her feel hot and breathless.

She was far too aware of him standing behind her while she fumbled with her keys.

"Here." His voice was calm, deep... reassuring. Warm fingers closed around hers as he gently pulled the jingling metal from her nerveless grip. "I've got it. This one?"

Nodding, Audrey stepped back as Mason put the key in her lock.

It shouldn't be sexy, having a man take over opening the door for her, but it was. She didn't like to feel incompetent or fumbling, but when she did fumble, when she was struggling, wouldn't it be nice to have someone to catch her? Cash had never, not once in their entire relationship, been that kind of guy. He probably would have laughed while she struggled with the keys, then told his friends about it later.

Not that she and Mason were getting into a relationship like the one she and Cash had been in.

But when she did decide to try for another relationship, the bar for the man she dated was going to be a lot higher, thanks to Mason.

"Thank you," she said, as he opened the door for her.

The smile that he gave her was both kind and searching, as if he was trying to read her expression.

"You're welcome." He followed her in through the door and shut it behind him, but didn't make a move to come any further in. "If you've changed your mind, you can say so. That's something you should know about kink—consent is the most important thing. Enthusiastic consent."

He was giving her an out. If she wanted it.

But if she took it, would she ever be brave enough to try again?

Audrey stood in the entryway to her apartment, staring at the beautiful, beautiful man who had offered to spank her tonight. If he walked out that door, she didn't think she would have the courage to face him again in the same way. She wasn't sure she'd be able to go back to the club, knowing she'd chickened out.

And she would be so, so mad at herself for doing so.

She shook her head.

"I want… the demonstration." Her words came out breathless, and her hands fluttered up and then back down to her sides. "I'm just nervous. I don't know what I'm supposed to do."

The smile that curved his lips made her heart pound faster and her knees go wobbly.

Oh, dear.

"Well, for the purposes of a scene, you do exactly what I tell you to."

Had his voice gotten deeper? It seemed like his voice had gotten deeper. The effect of which went straight through her and made her press her thighs together as the needy space between them was suddenly aching.

"Let's start with taking off our coats, then we'll sit down and talk through exactly what we're going to do."

Audrey nodded. Right. That made sense.

Coats off and hung up, she escorted him the five feet that took them into the main living area of her one-bedroom apartment. She hadn't had a ton of time to decorate, but she was happy with how it looked. It was comfortable, at least, even if there was still a small pile of boxes in the far corner and none of the pictures were actually hanging on the wall yet. She hoped he didn't think she was a total mess, even though it was messier than she'd want it to be to show it off.

She hadn't really thought through having him come over.

Then again, how could she have possibly planned for this?

"This is nice," he said as he made his way to the couch. Somehow, he seemed to make the entire room smaller as he moved through it. The couch now looked smaller, too, with the weight of his presence filling it. "I love the colors."

Like her clothes, Audrey liked retro furniture and designs. There was a lot of color in her home now. Things that she'd been able to choose for herself without her mother's influence. Everything in her parents' house had been beige. So much beige. With an occasional 'pop of black' to set it off. Her room at her parents' home had been the only place where there was any color, and her mom had still governed over exactly how much there could be.

Too much was gauche.

Which was exactly what her mom would think of her apartment. The unhung red and black picture frames, leaning against the walls where she planned to eventually hang them, contained pop art in colorful yellows, oranges, greens, and pinks. The couch Mason was sitting on was blue. The apartment carpet was beige, but Audrey had covered it with a large area rug that was covered in a rainbow riot of polka dots. None of her lamps matched—one was yellow and bubbly with a white shade, another was cotton candy pink with a bulbous base, and the standing lamp was Tiffany stained glass and one of the few pieces that had traveled from Philly with her.

None of it should have gone together, yet somehow it all worked. She loved it.

Her life had been beige and... well, vanilla, as Mason would say. Now it was spicy hot. Different. Colorful. Exciting.

And she had a man who was going to show her kink. Though she would not have guessed he'd be into interior decorating.

"I can't imagine you having quite this much color in your home," she admitted, sitting nervously on the green and cream striped armchair that was beside the couch. Close, but still keeping her distance. Sitting beside him on the small couch just felt too... intimate.

The whole side of her body that he was on tingled, despite the distance between them. It didn't matter that she was on a completely different piece of furniture.

She was as messy as her space.

"I don't. I wouldn't even know where to begin to put this all together." Mason smiled and waved his hand around at the assortment. It was very eclectic, she knew. "But I enjoy the effect."

"Thanks. Um, so now what?" She wasn't relaxing at all; if anything, the small talk was making her more nervous as she waited for what was next.

The wolfish smile he gave her in return wasn't very reassuring, but it was exciting. Audrey pressed her hands together in her lap.

"Now, we talk about exactly what we're going to do." He leaned forward, holding her gaze, and suddenly, it was very difficult to breathe. "Audrey. I am going to put you over my lap, flip up your skirt, and administer your first spanking. If you are wearing underwear, I will leave that on. I plan to start more gently to warm up your skin, and once your bottom is a nice pink, I will increase the force with which I'm spanking you."

Oh, fuck. She couldn't breathe at all now as she stared back at him. Every word that came out of his mouth was matter-of-fact, clearly enunciated, yet her ears were full of a buzzing noise that made her feel lightheaded.

The picture he was painting in her mind was intimate, arousing, and utterly terrifying. Especially because she was so turned on, and she wasn't supposed to be. But maybe the actual spanking would be a turn-off.

"Okay," she whispered when she realized he was waiting for some kind of response from her.

"At any time that you need to slow down, say 'yellow.' Or 'red' if you want me to stop completely." He paused again. "Do you have any questions?"

Yes. What should she do if she was about to spontaneously combust? Because it felt like she might do *that* at any second.

But she couldn't ask that. Platonic. This was platonic, and she needed to focus on whether or not she liked the kink, not on how Mason was making her feel. If that was even possible.

"Um, no. That makes sense."

"Good." The expression on his face turned wolfish as he patted his thigh. "Come here, Audrey, and put yourself over my lap for your spanking."

Oh God.

This was real. It was really happening.

Except that it didn't feel real. It felt like an out-of-body experience as she got to her wobbly feet. She'd forgotten to take her shoes off. Oh, well. It wasn't like it mattered. She didn't know why she was thinking about her shoes right now, anyway.

Maybe because it was easier than thinking about what she was doing.

Which was putting herself over a man's lap.

Not just any man.

Mason.

She'd literally fantasized about this.

The heat of his body was warm under her stomach and against her side. She could feel the hardness of his muscled thighs and... was that...

Well.

His thighs weren't the only thing that was hard.

Heat bloomed inside her, but the proof that Mason was also aroused actually made her feel less awkward. She wriggled slightly against him, partly to get more comfortable, but also partly because she wanted to feel his erection pressing against her side. It felt like a big erection. Not that she knew how to judge, but bulges were bulges, right?

Mason chuckled, and Audrey stiffened as she felt the hem of her skirt being flipped up, cooler air wafting over the backs of her thighs. She knew she was soaking wet, but hopefully he couldn't tell with the lacy black panties she was wearing. They were cheekies, so they didn't give her bottom full coverage, but they covered a lot more than a thong.

"Very cute," he commented, tracing his finger along the edge of the lace.

"Thank you?"

This wasn't sexual.

It might feel sexual because he was tracing the skin of her bottom, but they'd agreed it wasn't sexual.

If it was someone else, other than Mason, it probably wouldn't feel so sexual. She stared down at her colorfully dotted carpet, her fingers pressing into the soft fibers, trying to convince herself that this wasn't sexual and that her body wasn't humming with arousal, and it was all fine. Totally fine. Nothing anyone could be upset with her about.

"You're welcome. Ready?" His hand lifted, and Audrey nodded.

The first swat was a sharp sting that made her insides clench as she gasped in surprise at the sensation. It didn't really hurt, but it did at the same time. His hand lifted again and came down on the same spot on the opposite cheek, so she had a matching set of stinging spots.

Again, it hurt… but…

It felt good, too.

Audrey whimpered, unable to keep from wriggling as she pressed her thighs together. The throbbing sensation between them was impossible to ignore.

His hand came down again.

"Oh!"

"Still doing good?" he paused, rubbing the spot that he'd just spanked, and Audrey nearly melted on the spot.

"Yes!" She didn't want him to stop.

"Okay, then." He shifted her on his lap to hold her more securely, his arm resting across her back and his hand curling over her hip. "Remember to say 'yellow' to 'slow down' or 'red' to stop completely. I'm going to turn this pretty little bottom pink."

Audrey bit her lip against telling him that her bottom wasn't all that little. She'd read enough BDSM romances at this point to know that would not go well for her. This was supposed to be a fun demonstration, not a punishment. Besides, he thought her bottom was pretty. Who was she to argue?

His hand came down again, a stinging swat that made her want to writhe against him. Her clit was begging to be touched, and the pressure she was able to put on it as his hand began to pepper her backside with swift, crisp swats wasn't nearly enough to give her the relief her body was craving.

Shuddering, moaning, gasping, Audrey's arousal climbed higher and higher every time his hand came down to smack against her bottom. The thin fabric of her panties wasn't any kind of protection at all. She could feel the heat growing on the surface of her skin but also in her core as desire coiled in an ever-tighter grip around her.

Was his hand coming down harder?

Were the swats coming faster?

She couldn't tell.

Her body moved, undulating, rubbing her mound against his thigh, and she heard him mutter a curse under his breath.

Suddenly, she found herself hauled up onto his lap, her burning bottom against his hard thighs. She was breathing faster than normal, and it felt like her whole body was tingling as she stared into his dark eyes. His mouth opened like he wanted to say something, but nothing came out.

The moment hung, suspended… delicate.

A critical juncture. Just like when she'd walked down the hallway to the coat closet to confront Cash.

There were two choices.

Get up now or…

Audrey leaned forward and pressed her lips to his.

For a moment, it was like kissing stone, and she almost pulled away as quickly as she'd pressed forward, but suddenly, he came to life beneath her like Pygmalion's statue, kissing her back with a fiery intensity that took her breath away. Or maybe it was the way he flipped her onto her back so fast, she barely registered the motion before she was on the couch with him between her thighs.

Wrapping her arms around his neck, her inner thighs sliding against his legs, Audrey arched her back, feeling his erection rocking against her and grinding her clit against him. Pure pleasure shot through her, the heat pulsing from her bottom adding to the growing ecstasy as he moved against her, the friction sending her senses soaring higher.

It was the most passionate moment of her life, and they hadn't even taken their clothes off yet.

CHAPTER TWENTY-NINE

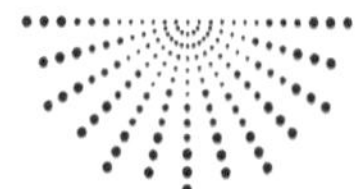

MASON

He'd had it all under control, mostly.

Right up until he hadn't.

Spanking Audrey had been far too enjoyable. Her little movements. Her whimpers. His cock had throbbed every time she wriggled on his lap. Every time his hand had smacked against her butt, he'd been able to watch the impact, to see the imprint left behind until her skin had all turned a pretty pink, and it was no longer possible to see the individual swats.

But he'd had a handle on it. He wasn't going to do anything about it.

But then she'd started to moan. Then she'd started to grind herself against his thigh in a way that made it impossible to ignore how aroused _she_ was. That's when he knew he had to stop because he wasn't going to be able to control himself much longer.

And he was always in control.

He'd hauled her up onto his lap. He was going to tell her that was enough of a demonstration, and they needed to stop. To offer her aftercare. But then he'd felt the heat of her bottom straight through his pants, pressing against his thigh. Seen her parted lips and glassy eyes full of heat and need.

Then she'd pressed her lips against his, and he'd tasted her for the first time. She tasted like vanilla and cookies. That's when his control had snapped. He'd kissed her back because he had to. Because once he got a taste, he needed more. He wanted to devour her.

Platonic! His brain screamed at him as he pinned her down to the couch, kissing her for all he was worth as her lips parted for him and he claimed her mouth.

He might have been able to pull away... but then she put her arms around him. Her legs slid against his, her heels moving to press against the backs of his thighs, pulling him closer.

Kissing. They were just kissing. It didn't count if they were just kissing, right?

Even if she was undulating beneath him. Even if she was rocking her pussy against his body, rubbing herself on his erection, shuddering at the pleasure running through her. Even if he was doing the same, moving over her, against her, in a manner he hadn't engaged in since high school.

Soft breasts flattened against his chest, her cry muffled against his lips as her movements beneath him became more frantic. More needy. Mason groaned into the kiss, sliding his hands down her sides, gripping her bottom so he could lift her to press himself more firmly between her thighs.

His cock was begging to be inside her, but he barely managed to hang onto that thin veil of sanity.

They hadn't discussed sex.

Hell, they hadn't discussed this either, but she'd kissed him first... Kissing was one thing. Fluid exchange was another. She slid her hands into his hair and gripped it hard, tugging, as she cried out in ecstasy. She was climaxing against him, and he was...

He was...

Fuck.

His cock pulsed as he reached his own peak. Fluid spurted as he rocked against her, wet and sticky and making him feel like he really was in high school all over again.

Lifting his lips from hers, he pressed their foreheads together.

"Fuck…" He shuddered as the last spurts of cum leaked out, leaving him in wet boxer-briefs. Thankfully, he preferred to wear some kind of undergarments rather than going commando, or this whole situation would be even more embarrassing.

He'd just jizzed in his pants like a goddamn teenager.

"Oh…"

Mason opened his eyes to meet Audrey's green gaze. She looked horrified.

"Oh my gosh, I'm so sorry… I shouldn't have… we agreed—"

"No." He cut her off. "If anyone should be apologizing, it's me. I lost control."

"I kissed you first. You—"

"I'm the experienced one," he said firmly. "And we didn't discuss… well, this, beforehand. I should have stopped you before you even kissed me."

She blinked, still staring up at him.

"Why didn't you?" The question came out in the whisper, as if she was afraid to ask it.

Mason let out a long, slow breath.

"I didn't want to," he admitted because he didn't have a better reason than that.

Because their faces were so close together, he could see the pink flush that crept along her cheeks.

"If you're wondering if there was enthusiastic consent on my part, there was," she whispered again. "But I didn't… I didn't ask you…"

"Trust me, there was enthusiastic consent on my part, too. But we do need to talk about this." Mason let out a long, slow breath, pulling away from her despite his reluctance. The mess in his pants was already getting uncomfortable. "Where is your bathroom? I'm going to go… clean up, then we can talk. Nothing bad… I promise." The way her face fell when he said they were going to talk meant he felt the need to reassure her immediately.

She didn't look entirely reassured, but she showed him to the bathroom.

While he was taking off his underwear and getting himself re-sorted, his mind was racing furiously.

Boundaries.

That was what they needed.

Clear guidelines for what was going to happen between them.

Yasmine had asked not to see him with another woman for at least a month. That was three more weeks.

Not that he was sure there was anything going on between him and Audrey other than the insane chemistry. Which could easily disappear as soon as it had appeared. Mason gripped the vanity as he stared at his reflection in the mirror.

He didn't look any different, but he felt different.

Everything had been different with her.

Which meant he didn't know what to expect in terms of this attraction. Which was unnerving. He didn't know how long it would last. Would it burn off slowly or go by in a flash?

The urge to keep going was strong. He hadn't felt any less attracted to her after they'd both gotten off, but it wasn't like they'd had sex.

Had Yasmine meant she didn't want to see him with another woman or that she didn't want him to have sex with another woman? He was pretty sure it was the former. Not that she would need to know, regardless. If they weren't together, his sex life wasn't any of her business.

And he'd very quickly forgotten about every other woman, and every other consideration, once he'd gotten his hands on Audrey.

Shit.

What if they started dating, and the attraction wore off? Or he woke up one day, and it was just gone? How was David going to react if Mason started something with Audrey, only to end it just as quickly? And right after ending his engagement… Was this a rebound? Maybe this was a rebound. Maybe that's why the attraction was still so strong.

Okay. Boundaries. Guidelines.

He nodded at himself and straightened up. His eyes caught on where his pants pocket was bulging because he'd shoved his wet underwear into it. Not exactly a confidence-builder, but a good reminder that things with Audrey hadn't been like anyone else. Not from the moment he'd met her.

AUDREY

Taking the opportunity to change her underwear to some she hadn't soaked through, Audrey returned to the couch and smoothed her skirt over her legs. Maybe she should go back to the armchair.

But she didn't want Mason to think she was ashamed of what they'd done.

Because she wasn't.

Although maybe she should be.

That had not been the plan.

But he hadn't let her apologize either.

What was he doing?

What was he thinking?

Maybe he was thinking that she was desperate.

Which she wasn't.

It wasn't like she was yearning for a relationship. Especially after Cash.

She'd just…

She'd never been aroused like that before.

Her bottom was still sore, and just thinking about it made her want to squirm in place. Even though her clit was kind of sore, too.

Dry humping. They'd basically been dry humping. And it had been way hotter than any sex she'd ever had.

Which doesn't speak very highly of my sex life before this.

Although she hadn't thought her sex life was that bad. She just hadn't known what she was missing. Spanking was part of it. But so was the heady attraction between her and Mason.

He said they were going to talk. Nothing bad, but who defined bad? If he told her that it could never happen again, that might not be bad by his definition. Would it be bad by her definition? She honestly wasn't sure. She wanted more. More of this. More like tonight. With Mason, specifically.

But only if he wanted her in the same way. Which was the big question.

The door to the bathroom opened, and Audrey sat up straight, turning slightly to face the hallway where he was coming from. He looked as calm and confident as ever, while she felt like a messy bundle of anxiety. What was she thinking? Why on earth would he want her?

Except that he had…

He smiled when he saw her sitting there, and some of her nerves immediately settled, a few of the butterflies in her stomach coming to a halt.

"Sorry for keeping you waiting," he said as he came over to sit beside her on the couch. Very closely beside her. Close enough that as the cushion dipped down, their legs ended up touching instead of there being a bit of space between them—and he didn't shift away.

That was a good sign, right?

"That's okay. Um, so what did you want to talk about?" Smooth. Real smooth. But if it was bad, she wanted to get it over with.

Mason leaned back against the couch, stretching his arm along the back, which meant it was behind her. Audrey turned her upper body to look at him, rather than leaning back against his arm, even though she really wanted to. He was studying her with that intent gaze that made her feel like he could see so much more than her physical exterior.

"Us," he replied simply, and her heart skipped a little beat. "I think it's clear there's an attraction between us. I'm attracted to you, you're attracted to me, and you have an interest in something I'm experienced in. I want to suggest that if you're going to keep exploring kink, you do it with me. Privately. At least for now."

"For now?" she echoed, unsure of exactly what he meant.

"I don't know what the future holds," he said, his tone frank. "I do know that if we go to the club, anyone who knows Yasmine and I were together will have certain expectations if they see us together next. That's a lot of pressure to put on anyone, much less two people who are still getting to know each other."

Audrey shuddered at the very idea. She'd already experienced people trying to pressure her into marrying someone. Though if she had to choose between Mason and Cash…

"There's also the fact that Yasmine point-blank asked me to give her a month before I start publicly seeing anyone. Not that we would need to date in order to scene together, but I want to honor her request and give her the time she needs." He smiled, a rather crooked smile. "Unfortunately, I think a lot of the highest expectations about my relationship with whoever I'm seen with now will come from her."

Which made sense. From what Audrey could see, Yasmine completely bought into her curse. She really thought that whoever Mason dated next would be his happily ever after.

Yeah. That was a lot of pressure.

Especially since Yasmine had become a friend.

"So, you want to… scene together but keep it a secret for now?" she asked.

Mason hesitated.

"A secret sounds extreme, but maybe… we just don't announce it to anyone. You get to explore kink with someone you've already put your trust in. And we get to explore this chemistry together."

"Like fuck buddies?"

"To put it crudely, yes. Although we don't necessarily have to have sex to enjoy the scenes, maybe we don't have to keep it as platonic as we had originally planned either." He dropped his arm down, reaching forward to cover her hand where it was sitting on her lap and squeezing her fingers. The riot of butterflies exploded in her stomach again at his touch, her heart racing faster. "How far we go is completely up to you."

"Not dating, just scening. I just want to make sure I have this correct."

"Yes. Although I'm sure we'll spend some time together." He hesitated again, then gave a little nod, like he'd made some kind of internal decision. "I'll be honest with you, my reaction to you was nothing like I expected. I'm not normally out of control, even when I'm attracted to someone. Nothing like the way I was tonight. It's possible we might burn through the attraction and come out of this good friends who have had some fun together in the past."

"Right. Friends with benefits." Audrey studied him for a long moment. Men should read more romance. He sounded an awful lot like those heroes who thought they were going to fuck their way through the chemistry, as if it had an endpoint and would eventually be all used up. That never worked. Then again, maybe it was just the genre.

Either way, she knew what she wanted.

"Okay," she said, holding out her hand for him to shake. "Deal."

He took her hand and tugged her toward him.

"That's not how we seal the deal, cupcake," he murmured, and his other hand came up to glide through her hair as he tilted her head back for a kiss.

His lips closed over hers as she fell toward him, her hand pressing against his chest as her head spun dizzily.

This was definitely the better way to close the bargain.

CHAPTER THIRTY

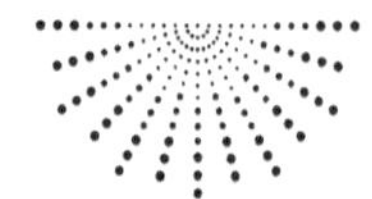

SATURDAY MORNING TEXTS

Mason: My place or yours tonight?

Audrey: Which would be better?

Mason: I have more toys at my place, but I can bring them to yours.

Audrey: Do you live in an apartment?

Mason: No, I'm in a house. On my own. All by myself.

Audrey: Let's do your place, then, so you don't get lonely. Plus, then I don't have to worry about thin walls.

Mason: That's what gags are for 😉

Audrey: I don't know if that's exciting or terrifying.

Mason: It can be both.

AUDREY

Saturday was even busier than the weekdays had been. She wasn't sure the video of Rebecca was still what was bringing people in. Before they opened, Ashley had taken a moment to show her several new videos the bakery had been tagged in, all of which featured different views of members of Black Fox Security.

Which would explain the number of young women who were hanging around inside the shop.

When Harris and Grant walked in, there were audible sighs, and Audrey had to press her lips together to keep from cracking up in amusement as their steps faltered. Clearly, they realized something was going on, but they weren't sure what. She wasn't sure whether she should tell them they were the entertainment.

The fact that a bunch of hot, muscle-y security guys that moved like military—because they were former military—were regulars at the bakery was something she had not considered in her marketing, but clearly it was a selling point. Good to know. Especially since she didn't have to do anything about it except hope they didn't stop coming.

When Harris and Grant swaggered back out of the bakery, she was pretty sure they'd caught on, and neither one of them minded.

Somehow, she got through the day doing a reasonable job of hiding her excitement about meeting up with Mason. Maybe Ashley and Alexis just thought she was excited because of how well the bakery was doing. Which she was...

But she was even more excited about her date with Mason.

Even though it wasn't really a date. Or a hook-up. Meeting didn't sound right, either. Audrey didn't know what to call it.

Thankfully, Yasmine didn't stop by today, or Audrey might have been overcome with guilt. It also helped that Ashley told her that Yasmine had enjoyed a very nice evening with Master Cole. Apparently, Jensen had also eventually shown up, in a bad mood about Dr. Dick, and had spent most of the night brooding and scowling. That was so unlike him from what Audrey knew that she felt bad for the guy.

Ashley seemed more of the opinion that he was suffering due to his own decisions, and if he hadn't been moving like a turtle with Jennifer, he wouldn't be in this situation now. Which was hard to argue.

Finally, the day wrapped up, and Audrey locked the front door with a feeling of satisfaction. No drama. No issues that she needed to be rescued from. Just a good day's work and lots of customers.

If things kept up like this, she would be able to hire more help soon. But she also knew that viral videos could be fickle. She needed to wait and make sure that the foot traffic was going to continue before she jumped to any major decisions. The idea of having to fire someone was among the worst things she could imagine having to do. Even someone like Ashley, who didn't actually need a job and was there more because she wanted to be.

Better to wait it out and be safe instead of sorry.

Audrey's phone buzzed in her pocket as she was finishing up with the end-of-day duties. Alexis and Ashley had already both left. Ashley had offered to drop off the leftovers to the shelter Naomi ran, and Audrey had gratefully accepted. Glancing at her phone screen, Audrey stifled a groan. It was the third time her mother had called that day. If she kept ignoring it, especially now after work hours, there would be hell to pay. Steeling herself, she swiped to accept the call.

"Hello, Mother."

"Audrey." Her mother's tone was frosty. "How lovely to actually hear your real voice instead of being sent to your voicemail."

"I'm sorry." Was she though? She tried to sound sorry, regardless, because her mother wouldn't accept anything less. "The bakery has been really busy, and I haven't been able to answer."

"Really." It sounded more like a statement of dubiousness than a question. "How busy can a bakery be?"

"Very, especially with only three of us working," Audrey answered. Despite her mother's annoyance, she could feel herself getting excited as she explained. "It's been very busy this week and only got busier today, thanks to a video that went viral."

"That went what? Never mind, I don't know what that means, and I don't want to." Even though Audrey couldn't see her, she knew her mother was waving her hand with that brushing motion she made when she wanted to change the subject. "I suppose that means you won't be coming back here to visit any time soon."

"No, mother. I'm too busy here. But as soon as I can, I will come visit."

Apparently, it needed to be said again. Audrey's stomach twisted, and her throat felt clogged, but it got a little easier every time she said it. Practice makes perfect. Maybe one day she wouldn't feel anxiety at all when she had to tell her mother no.

"You know, Cash has been asking after you."

"Really?" Audrey couldn't help the sarcasm that bled into her voice. "I doubt he really cares that much, considering he needs to pass messages through my mother."

"You never take his calls, darling."

Well, that was true enough, but he also hadn't tried in weeks. Not that she wanted him to. She didn't. But she didn't understand why her mother was persisting in trying to pretend that Cash cared about her.

"Is Dad there?" Audrey asked, hoping to divert her mother. Unfortunately, she hadn't counted on the reality of their marriage.

"No, he's on one of his *business* trips. Because he's such a hard worker." The bitterness that infused her mother's voice made Audrey wince. Her dad must have a new mistress. Now she was sorry she'd brought it up.

"Right well, I'm on my way home," she said, hoping her mother would pick up the hint.

"Very well, darling. Please do try to make time for your family soon." The cool tone of her mother's voice said she was highly displeased, and Audrey winced.

"I will." She would try. Maybe she could go back for one night, on a weeknight, sometime soon. Although she had a feeling that the soonest really would be Thanksgiving, which her mom was clearly not going to be happy about. Audrey's stomach twisted again. There was nothing she could do about it. "Love you, Mom."

"Good night, Audrey."

Her mother hung up the phone, and Audrey sighed with relief. That could have gone much worse.

It could have gone a lot better, too.

Another night, she might have felt more let down after talking with her mother, but tonight... tonight she was going to Mason's for the first time. Excitement hummed inside her as she closed down the computer and headed for the back door. Shutting and locking it behind her, she practically bounced her way to her car.

An odd sensation tickled the back of her neck, the feeling that someone was watching her... but when she turned to look, no one was there.

Weird.

<hr>

MASON

Trying to plan out a scene at home was... difficult.

Mason usually kept his kink to the club. Obviously, that wasn't an option right now. It was giving him a lot more sympathy for Jennifer's situation. Though at least she still had the house parties. He wasn't sure Audrey would be comfortable at the house parties.

It was a good thing she had ended up with him.

He didn't like the idea of her alone at some unknown Dom's house, experimenting with kink. BDSM could be wonderful, but there were also people who used it as an excuse for abuse. Audrey was sweet. Innocent. Trusting. It would be all too easy for someone to take advantage of that.

If anything, David should be grateful his sister was in the hands of someone who wouldn't hurt her—other than in the ways she liked.

Yup.

That's what Mason was going to keep telling himself.

Since she'd responded so delightfully to the spanking yesterday, Mason had laid out a number of impact toys on his dining room table for her to try. He'd also picked out a few different options of nipple clamps. His favorite vampire glove. A few vibrators he'd run out to the store for earlier in the day.

He'd also bought two butt plugs. One small and one medium.

They hadn't discussed anal play, but he liked to be prepared. Like a kinky Boy Scout. Even though he'd never actually done scouts.

He did like to play with rope. Which he also had. And cuffs.

Eyeing all the options, he shook his head.

Looked like a hell of a fun night.

Even without sex.

At some point, he was going to have to send her home to sleep, though.

The doorbell rang, and Mason jumped, even though Audrey had texted him that she was on his way.

Everything is fine. No big deal. It's good.

He shook off the nerves and headed for the front door to let her in.

The blast of cold air when he opened the door to see her standing there did nothing to cool off the heat that washed over him. Rosy cheeks over a green coat that matched her eyes, her hair was back in its usual bouncy ponytail, and she was wearing black fuzzy earmuffs that were somehow adorable on her. Mason didn't usually approve of earmuffs. What was the point in covering just your ears? Heat escaped through your entire head.

But on her…

He'd allow it.

"Hi." He smiled down at her, feeling himself soften as the rest of his nerves fled now that she was standing in front of him.

"Hi." She lifted the box she was holding in front of her. "Cupcake?"

"Depends on the flavor," he teased, stepping back so she could come in. He closed the door behind her with one hand, sealing out the icy air, while he took the box from her with the other. "You can put your coat on the hook."

There was a small row of them beside the door, with a couple of his coats hanging from them, but that left plenty empty.

"Thank you." She shivered as she took off her coat to reveal a pair of sensible jeans that hugged her curves and a forest green sweater with a cream print running across it. "I swear, it's colder here than Philly."

"You're not imagining it," he reassured her. "It's because we're closer to the mountains."

"Actually, that does make me feel better. I thought I'd just turned into a wimp."

Mason chuckled and gestured for her to follow him to the kitchen.

"Would you like some hot chocolate? Hot tea?"

"Hot tea would be perfect," she said fervently. "Thank you."

"No problem. It'll give us some time to talk through things." He gestured at the kitchen table and the island, where there were stools. "Pick your seat."

The teapot he kept on the back of the stove already had water in it, so he just had to turn on the burner. Opening the cupboard to the left of the stove, he pulled down the box of options and turned to see where she'd ended up. She'd taken one of the seats at the island, across from him.

Smiling, he placed the box on the counter and slid it in front of her as her eyes widened.

"Wow... that's a lot of tea."

"I like tea, and I like options." He shrugged. "I also have loose leaf, if you prefer."

"Oh, no, please don't go to the trouble," she said, reaching in and plucking one of the small packages. "Orange pekoe is great. It's one of my favorites."

"Perfect." Turning the box back toward himself, Mason picked out a honey vanilla option and set it on the counter before putting the box away. "Sweetener?"

"Sugar or honey."

"I have both." He picked up both options and put them on the counter as well. He preferred honey. Grabbing two mugs, he put them down.

Audrey smiled at him, and his chest tightened.

This wasn't a date.

But it felt... intimate. Maybe even more so than most dates he'd been on.

"How was your day?" she asked.

"Good. We did a lot of team-building exercises. Trust falls and stuff." Things that he'd suggested to Lincoln that they do.

"Because of everything that's going on with Zeus?"

"Exactly. According to him, he and Noelle are now broken up, and he wants nothing to do with her. Which is exactly what he would say if he was a mole still trying to maintain his position on the team."

Audrey eyed him.

"It's also exactly what he would say if he wasn't a mole."

"So, you see our dilemma." Mason shrugged as the tea kettle started to whistle. Picking it up, he poured the water into both mugs.

"Poor Zeus if he's not a mole."

"Well, that's why we did the team-building exercises."

"Did it help?" She cocked her head at him, wrapping her hands around the mug to warm them while the tea brewed.

Mason sighed.

"Not really. Zeus refused to do the trust fall." It was a very middle school exercise, but it was also one of the simplest exercises, and they couldn't even get him to do that with them.

"Why?"

"He didn't want to." No one had wanted to do the exercises; that wasn't the point. It hadn't helped things, though.

It was hard to put faith in someone who wouldn't put at least a little faith in you. Zeus didn't believe the team wouldn't just drop him on the floor, apparently. What would happen in the field now... well, Lincoln had Zeus focused on tech stuff at the moment. "We'll get there. How was today at the bakery?"

"I think the number of Black Fox team members coming into the bakery is increasing my foot traffic," she replied, her eyes twinkling. "Apparently, I'm now known as the hot place to be because of all the hot men who regularly appear."

Mason arched an eyebrow.

"Well... good?"

"It's definitely good. The hot men might be getting the customers into the bakery, but everyone who comes in seems happy with the food, so hopefully, they'll be back."

"And you know we will." He grinned at her. He was definitely going to have to encourage the others to stop by even more. Maybe they could make a schedule.

"I'm okay with that." She lifted the mug to her lips, her eyes glowing as she blew across the hot top and then took a delicate sip. The happy sigh that left her lips as she lowered the mug did all sorts of interesting things to his libido.

Mason took a sip of his own tea before clearing his throat. Might as well get straight to it.

"Well. Let's talk. Is there anything specific you want to try tonight?"

His imagination was already running wild.

CHAPTER THIRTY-ONE

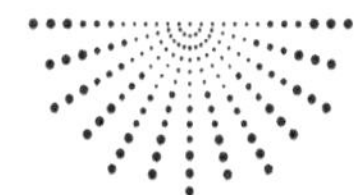

Audrey

Talking kink over tea. Not something she would have expected, but somehow it made sense. The only problem was, she had no idea what she wanted to try. Things that would feel good and lead to orgasms.

"Um... I'm not sure. I wouldn't know where to start." She felt the heat fill her cheeks and told herself it was from the tea.

"If you don't mind picking up your mug, I can show you some things I've laid out," Mason said, getting to his feet. He picked up his mug with one hand while gesturing behind her with his other. Audrey swiveled on her barstool and turned around. Past the kitchen table was an opening to the next room, which appeared to be a dining room.

It wasn't until she got closer that she realized the dining room table was covered in a variety of... things.

"Oh..." The word released on an exhalation, making it sound almost like a sigh. The blush in her cheeks burned even hotter as she looked at everything, and she clutched her mug in front of her chest because she didn't have any pearls handy to grab onto. "Oh, my."

"You don't have to try any of these." Mason moved in beside her, igniting all of her senses by his mere presence. The whole side of her body he was standing on felt like it flared to life. "But I wanted you to see the options."

"That's a lot of options." Which was such a ridiculous thing to say, but her brain felt like it had stopped working.

What did she want?

What did she dare?

Releasing the mug, she reached down to touch one of the... floggers? She was guessing that's what it was. It was made up of multiple long strands of leather that came together in a wrapped handle, and when she touched the leather, it was buttery soft.

"Flogger," Mason murmured, shifting closer to her, so they were almost touching. She swore she could feel the heat of him through her clothes. It was so distracting that it took her a moment to realize she'd guessed correctly on the implement's name.

"This... hurts?" It was so soft.

Mason chuckled.

"Not that one so much. Though it depends on how it's swung. Which is true for everything. That is a very light flogger." He picked it up and held it gently in his grip. "Can I show you, on your arm?"

Her arm. Not sexy, but also a lot less scary.

Nodding, Audrey held out her arm.

The leather falls rose and fell, and whapped against her skin. It didn't hurt, just as he'd promised. There was impact, but it wasn't painful.

"It didn't hurt!" In fact, it had felt kind of good. Her skin tingled where it had landed. Immediately, she wanted to try it on other parts of her body. No wonder people liked getting their butts beat with this. Not just their butts, either.

Mason chuckled. "There are heavier ones, some have knots in them or chain braided in."

Ouch. Okay, a chain sounded like it would hurt.

"Can we try this one to start with?" she asked, reaching up to stroke the soft leather strands. The chain didn't seem like beginner level. But just imagining what this would feel like against her bare skin that wasn't her arm... yes, please.

"Yes. Do you want me to suggest a few things, then you can tell me yes or no?"

Her shoulders relaxed, and she cradled the half-full mug in her hands, nodding enthusiastically. Yes, that sounded much better than having to pick and choose from the array.

"Yes, please."

Mason's hand curved over her shoulder, and she looked up at him. He was so close. Close enough to kiss if she went up on her tiptoes and leaned forward just a little...

"You can start calling me 'Sir', Audrey."

A shiver went down her spine. Her tongue flicked out to wet her lips.

"Yes, please, Sir," she whispered. It should have been awkward, because she didn't normally call people 'sir' unless they were customers, but somehow it fit. It felt right. And it made her stomach do a swoosh-y thing that had her pressing her thighs together as the ache between them began to grow.

Maybe it was all the books she'd been reading.

"A paddle?" He shifted to the side, his hand hovering over the paddle in question. It looked kind of like a ping-pong paddle but without the rubber. Audrey wasn't sure how she felt about it. But that was the whole point of this, wasn't it? To try?

She nodded.

In short order, Mason had gathered the paddle, a crop, another flogger that was more 'thuddy' (in his words), a pair of nipple clamps, some cuffs, a weird glove thing that she had no idea what he planned to do with, then they got to the butt plugs and vibrators. Her face felt like it was on fire, while he seemed completely unfazed. But then again, he would, right?

He did stuff like this all the time.

Audrey had never even thought about putting anything in her butt until she'd read about it. Two months ago, she hadn't known what a butt plug was. Or why anyone would want to use one.

Two months ago, the answer would have been a resounding *hell no.*

Today…

She nodded hesitantly.

"The little one." She wanted to be clear. Not that the larger one was that much larger, and neither *looked* particularly big, especially next to the vibrators, but if romance books counted as any kind of real research, she wanted the smaller one.

The smile that flashed across Mason's lips as he picked up the little package the plug was in made another shiver go down her spine. He set it to the side with the other items they'd picked out.

"Vibrator? Or, if you want an orgasm, I can use my hands and fingers or my mouth. Whatever you're comfortable with."

"Um… any of the above sounds fine." Audrey had to drop her gaze as she answered. She couldn't look him in the face when she admitted that she wanted him to get her off. Truthfully, she would prefer his hands or mouth.

Ok, scratch that, she would prefer his cock, but she also didn't feel like she could come out and say that. Especially since he hadn't offered it. Did that make her slutty? That she wanted to have sex with him?

He had said they were going to be fuck buddies. She'd assumed that meant actually fucking.

On the other hand, working their way up to that made sense. Maybe she was just slutty.

Not that she'd ever thought herself slutty in the past. She tended to take things slow. So, her slutty side was man-specific. She was a slut for Mason.

Audrey pressed her lips together so that none of her thoughts could escape out of her mouth. That was the absolute last thing she needed right now. They were friends with benefits for now. Mason didn't need to know that she had a slutty side specific to him.

<u>*Mason*</u>

Was it possible for a dick to rip through pants like the Incredible Hulk? Because if it was, his pants were going to be shredded any second now. Even though he was trying to keep things educational, the way he would with a regular submissive at the club, his cock wasn't listening.

Nothing for you tonight.

He wasn't trying to keep things platonic, but he didn't want Audrey to think that this was all about sex, either. He was supposed to be teaching her about kink. That was something he could do without getting his dick wet.

It also might be that he was feeling the need to prove that he could control himself after last night's embarrassing out-of-control release.

"Now that we have everything, let's go to my Dungeon," he joked.

"You have a Dungeon?" Audrey's eyes widened.

"Sure. Right over here." He gestured to his living room, which was right beside the dining room. He'd already drawn all the curtains in both rooms in preparation.

Mason didn't usually scene at home, which was why he didn't have a designated play space. Maybe he should make one now… *no, stop.* He wasn't going to set up a play space for one woman when he wasn't even sure how long this would last.

Audrey laughed, relaxing slightly as he led her into the other room. He had cleared out the area around his padded coffee table, which was just the right size to put a woman on. It might not be a real Dungeon, but he had furnished this particular room with a few pieces of very special furniture that he'd bought custom-made from a Dom in D.C.

The coffee table was one of them. One of the cushy chairs was another. There were hidden bolts and hooks and drawers, all of which could turn the furniture into a piece of equipment as desired.

Putting the chosen items on a side table, Mason turned to Audrey, holding the metal cuffs she'd picked out in his hand. Not his favorite for bondage because they could be harsh on the submissive's wrists, especially in certain positions, but there was something about the classic cuffs, and he'd seen the way her eyes had lit up when she'd looked at them.

For tonight, they were a fine choice because he wouldn't be using them to secure her to anything.

Holding up the cuffs, he grinned at her.

"All right, cupcake. If I'm going to put these on you and also use the clamps, you're going to need to take off that shirt and bra."

Her eyes widened again, her blush going from pink to red, and Mason's grin widened. She didn't look scared; she looked excited but also a touch nervous. Perfect.

Taking a deep breath that lifted her breasts, Audrey reached for the hem of her shirt and pulled it over her head. The bra underneath was emerald-green satin, hugging the underside of her breasts while matching lace curved over the tops. Her blush deepened.

"Take your time," he said. "I don't mind a slow tease. And don't forget—you can say 'yellow' or 'red' at any time."

"I don't want to slow down," she admitted in a whisper. "Or stop. I'm just trying to convince myself that you won't judge me for not wanting to."

"Trust me, cupcake, I don't want to slow down or stop, either. Why would I judge you for feeling the same way I do?" But she was brave to admit it. He was definitely going to reward her for that. "Thank you for telling me, though."

She looked like she wanted to squirm. It was a good thing they were doing this here and not at the club. Audrey did not seem to be an exhibitionist, though it wasn't a hard limit for her. He was enjoying being a voyeur, though if it became too much for her, he would step in and help... and enjoy that, too.

Reaching behind her, she undid the hooks of her bra and let it drop away from her body, leaving her naked from the waist up.

"You have beautiful breasts, sweetheart." Large, rounded on the bottom, pale as cream, and tipped with pale pink nipples he couldn't wait to redden.

"Thank you? I mean, thank you, Sir." Her head was still ducked down.

"Look at me, cupcake." At his order, her head jerked up again. The mottled blush across her cheeks was traveling down her neck, and Mason was fascinated by its movement. "Hold your hands out in front of you, wrists together."

Her breasts were large enough that doing so pressed them together, creating a deep cleavage. Stepping forward, Mason held her fists gently in one hand while closing the cuffs around her wrists with the other. *Snick. Snick.* The sound of the latches sliding into place was truly satisfying.

Audrey's breathing was coming a little faster, a little more shallowly as she stared at her cuffed wrists as though she'd never seen them before. The chain between them jingled as she pulled them, like she was trying to see if the cuffs would hold—they did.

"Hands behind your head, cupcake. Feet shoulder-width apart. Present your breasts to me."

Her gaze jerked up to his again, and she let out a huff of air, slowly lifting her arms up and putting them behind her head. Because of the cuffs, she had to place her hands close together. The position thrust her breasts out toward him.

And he had permission to touch all he wanted.

Although if he did as much as he wanted, they would be here all night.

That doesn't sound so bad.

Stepping forward, Mason got into her space, and Audrey's head tilted back to look up at him as he put his hands on her waist and began to slide them up to her breasts. Waiting to see if she would say 'yellow' or 'red'. If she needed a moment to adjust. As his hands moved over her sides, along her silken skin, her pupils dilated, and she sucked in another breath as he palmed her rib cage, then moved up to her breasts.

"Oh..." Her eyelashes fluttered madly.

For the first time, Mason wondered about her past partners. She just looked so *surprised.* Had her previous lovers not taken their time with foreplay? With arousing her?

Oh, my sweet, little cupcake. I am going to enjoy devouring you.

The level of possessiveness that rose inside him as he fondled her breasts, watching her reactions, was shocking. Mason ran his thumbs over her stiff nipples, and she closed her eyes, shuddering as he played with her.

"I'm going to flog these pretty breasts," he told her, his voice husky with need. "Then I'm going to decorate your nipples with the clamps before I turn you over my knee to plug you and spank you. And then I'm going to flog your shoulders and your pretty little bottom, and once you're tingling and sensitive all over, I'm going to use the glove on you until you're begging me to let you come."

And he was going to enjoy every fucking second of it.

CHAPTER THIRTY-TWO

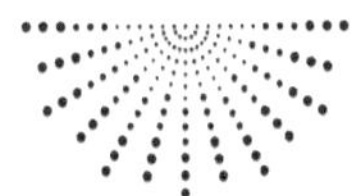

AUDREY

It felt like she was going to spontaneously combust... or melt. She'd never had a man so reverently fondle her breasts, taking his time with them the way Mason was. Like he was enjoying doing so for the sake of doing so, rather than going straight for her nipples or immediately moving on to his next target. Her knees were weak and wobbly, need was pulsing inside her, and she didn't know what to do.

But she wasn't supposed to do anything.

She was just supposed to stand there and let him do what he wanted.

Even if she wanted to do something, with her wrists cuffed, her options were extremely limited.

Which meant she could just relax and enjoy it.

When he went through the litany of what he planned to do with her, it felt like she might form a puddle right there on his living room rug.

"Any objections?" he asked in a low, heated voice, his thumbs running over her nipples again.

Audrey shook her head emphatically.

"Consider this enthusiastic consent," she joked, except it wasn't really a joke. Anything he wanted to do with her, she was in.

Mason chuckled, which made her want to preen. He gave her breasts a squeeze, and she moaned before whimpering with disappointment when his hands dropped away. Stepping back, he turned and picked up the first flogger she'd touched, the soft one.

Nerves flickered through her. It had been really soft. And he'd said it wasn't a painful one. But at the same time, he was going to hit her with it.

Hit her breasts, specifically, which were a very tender area.

Even though she trusted him, even though she was incredibly aroused, even though she wanted to try this... she tensed.

The flogger moved through the air, coming from beneath rather than above, and the ends flicked over her breasts. She sucked in without thinking, an automatic reaction, then relaxed when she realized it hadn't hurt. Maybe a little sting? Not even as much as the first swats he'd given her during her spanking.

"See?" Mason said, smiling. "Not so bad."

"Not so bad at all, Sir," she agreed, feeling her muscles unwinding even more. Now she understood why trust was so important, though. The urge to move away from the *thing* coming at her had been strong.

"Again. Hold still, cupcake."

This time, she knew what to expect, and it was easier to hold still. Being called cupcake didn't hurt, either. She liked the way his voice caressed the endearment. Liked how it also referenced something that was so important to her—her work. Her bakery.

And she knew it was for her.

It wasn't generic like 'sweetheart' or 'honey', although she liked those, too. But 'cupcake' felt special.

So, it wasn't hard at all now to hold still while the flogger flicked over her breasts, heating her skin, adding a little sting to the needy arousal coursing through her. It didn't hurt exactly, but it wasn't all pleasure, either, and somehow, that felt better than if it had been.

The books were right... there's a thin line between pleasure and pain.

"Good girl."

Her insides clenched. Yup. The books were right about that, too. There was just something about being called a 'good girl' that did all sorts of naughty things to her body.

"Now, it's time for the clamps."

Audrey opened her eyes to stare dreamily at Mason. He was so confident as he stepped up in front of her, sliding one palm beneath her right breast. It felt warm in his hand, so much more sensitive than before. His eyes were hot, lit with a fire from within, as his gaze met hers, making her squirm. He closed his fingers around her right nipple. Rolled it. Pleasure rippled, and she moaned…

Then pain flashed through her—sharp, mean, awful pain.

"*Yellow!*" She shrieked, trying to pull back, which just hurt even more. Her whole boob was screaming at her, alarm bells ringing through her. Ow! Ow! Ow! "I mean red! Yellow! Stop!"

Mason wrapped his arm around her as he opened the clamp that he'd put on her nipple, helping hold her up before she could fall flat on her ass. She gasped for breath, as if she'd just run a marathon, tears sparking in her eyes. Why they were coming now that the clamp was no longer on her nipple, she didn't know. Some kind of belated reaction.

Her nipple throbbed.

"Shit, sorry, sorry." He held her tightly with one arm while she trembled. "It's been a while since I did any kind of demo with a total newbie. I should have adjusted the clamps so they wouldn't pinch so tight for your first time."

Or not pinch at all.

Though now that the clamp wasn't *on* her, aggressively biting into her nipple, she would be lying if she said the throbbing didn't feel good. In fact, she felt the urge to make her other nipple match.

So, it wasn't all bad.

"I just wasn't expecting it," she said. "It hurt a lot more than the flogger did."

"I know. And I knew that going in. I'm sorry. It won't happen again." He looked more than contrite; he looked mad at himself.

"It's okay." She didn't want him to beat himself up about it. She was fine. He'd taken them off immediately.

"It's not, and I'll be more cognizant of the fact that you have literally never experienced any of this before. But *you* were a very good girl for using your safeword."

As much as she wanted to make him feel better, she had to admit, being called a very good girl did all sorts of pleasant things to her insides.

Mason released her and looked down at the clamps in his hand, connected by the thin chain. He focused on them as he adjusted them. Because he was so close, she could see how tiny the screws were that he was twisting to force the clamps open, so that they couldn't close all the way. Ouch. No wonder that had hurt; the clamp had been trying to squash her nipple flat.

"Do you still want to try these?" he asked, holding them up so she could see the tips of the clamp were no longer touching. They would grip her nipples, squeeze them, but not try to turn them into pancakes.

Did she want to try them? Not really, but also sort of.

Audrey nodded her head. She was here. The throbbing did feel pretty good now that the clamp was off, and it shouldn't hurt as much this time.

"The other nipple first, though, please, Sir," she said.

He nodded and cupped her left breast. She couldn't help the tension that gripped her as he teased her nipple to hardness. This time, she watched his movements, rather than his face, so she could be prepared for the initial pain.

It did hurt, like a hard pinch, but not like before. The larger opening in the clamp, along with having a better idea of what to expect, helped a lot. Audrey moaned and shivered as she adjusted.

"Better?" Mason asked, his fingers brushing over the tip of her clamped nipple, which sent all sorts of interesting sensations through the tiny bud.

"Yes, Sir."

"I'm going to do the other one now, cupcake. Take a deep breath."

She did. It still hurt—more than her left boob since her nipple was already sore, but it felt good, too. The tight grip made her breasts throb, and she whimpered as he cupped them from underneath, giving the soft flesh a squeeze while his lips hovered over hers.

"Very good girl."

He needed to stop calling her 'cupcake' and start calling her 'puddle' because that's where she was headed right now.

It didn't matter that the pinch on her nipples was going to make her sore tomorrow—she was actually looking forward to that. She wanted to feel it.

Wanted it to last.

A little secret memento that no one had to know about.

"Okay, sweetness. Do you want to take off your own jeans, or can I take them off for you?"

"Um, you can take them off for me, please."

Heat filled her cheeks. She'd enjoyed taking off her shirt and bra while he watched, but she also liked the idea of him undressing her. Touching her more. Plus, that way she didn't have to try to navigate handcuffs and taking off her jeans at the same time.

That seemed like a recipe for disaster, and she'd already face-planted once at his feet, and she wasn't trying to be sexy then. She'd much prefer to let him handle the difficult stuff right now, so she could concentrate on not looking foolish in front of him again.

The slow smile that spread across his lips said he didn't mind at all.

Mason dropped to his knees in front of her, which almost made her jump in surprise. That was not what she'd been expecting him to do. He was now at navel level, starting directly at her soft belly. Crap. Suddenly, Audrey wished that she had handled her jeans on her own.

Except he wasn't looking at her belly in disgust or even like he was trying to hide disdain… His gaze was soft, his lips curved up, and the expression on his face as he reached for the button on her jeans was almost reverent. It wasn't just that he didn't mind her rounder stomach; it looked like he *liked* it. Which she hadn't realized she was concerned about until this very moment, but maybe it wasn't surprising, considering how Yasmine looked.

The button on her jeans popped open, then the zipper, and Mason began to tug her jeans down over her hips. She was not disappointed that he did not take her panties off at the same time. Nope. It wasn't like she wanted to be completely naked while he was completely clothed.

Did she?

As vulnerable as she might feel, there was also something really sexy about the idea.

Which was something to keep in mind for later.

Right now, her brain was fritzing out because with the jeans gone, she could feel the warmth of his breath over the satin and lace of the matching thong to the bra she'd already taken off. Yes, she'd gone for a thong tonight. Because why not?

They might not have sex, but she didn't want anything between his hand and her skin when she spanked her tonight.

"Very pretty." His voice was like a purr.

Yup, she was totally going to melt into a puddle right here and now.

Mason helped her step out of the jeans, then drew her over to the couch. The movement of going over his knee made her gasp as her breasts jiggled, reigniting some of the sensation in her clamped nipples. It was a tiny sting compared to having the clamps applied, but still stimulation that went straight to her pussy.

The chain hung down toward her cuffed wrists, which were right in front of her face, so she couldn't forget she was bound. Just knowing she was somewhat helpless made her feel even more breathless than being over his knees.

She could also now feel his erection digging into her side, just like it had last night. He was as turned on as she was. Her pussy clenched, and she wriggled in place, enjoying the effect she had on him.

"Are you ready for the plug?" His hand caressed her bottom, and she felt her cheeks tighten.

Not because of his caress, but because of his question.

"Is anyone ever really ready?" Did her voice quaver? It might have quavered.

He chuckled.

"Probably not, but I'll be gentle."

He gave her butt another little pat, then she heard the sound of things happening above her. Packages. Things. Lube, hopefully.

Then she felt the butt floss she was wearing being pulled to the side, and she took a deep breath.

"Try to relax," Mason said, rubbing her butt with one hand. It didn't help.

"Yes, Sir."

She couldn't keep the dubiousness out of her voice, and he chuckled again.

"It's a small plug. It shouldn't hurt." He spoke soothingly, but she was still tense. "I'll go slow."

The promise made her shiver in anticipation because it was laden with so much sexual intent. He was going to slowly put something in her butt. Something she'd never let anyone do before. Something she'd never even thought about letting anyone do before she came to Pittsburgh.

Something cold and wet touched her butthole, and she squeaked, automatically clenching. Mason's fingers dug into the muscles of her lower back.

"Relax," he said, in a deep, commanding voice that somehow actually worked on her; she immediately unclenched and went lax over his lap.

Holy fuck. How had he done that?

Audrey stared down at her cuffs, nipples throbbing, as the tip of the plug pushed into her rear entrance.

He was right.

It didn't hurt.

But it felt very odd.

That was not an "in" hole. That was an "out" hole. But he was pushing something into it, anyway. Audrey whimpered. Not because it hurt, but because her brain was struggling to process the sensation. It didn't hurt. Did it feel good?

She wasn't sure.

It felt… raw.

Invasive.

Exciting.

The plug twisted and pushed, going deeper, stretching her open. The stretch burned slightly. A sting.

Then he was pulling it back, retreating, and the sensation made her gasp with the strangeness.

This was nothing like having something in her pussy.

Other than the sensation of being full, she was being filled in the *wrong hole.*

The wrongness, the perversity, only added to her excitement. Her arousal.

She liked that it was wrong. Dirty. The kind of thing that would throw her mother into a faint.

Who knew that putting something up your butt could feel like rebellion?

"Oh!"

He'd pushed it deeper, and Audrey rocked forward, her toes curling. Mason's grip on her tightened, holding her in place as he firmly worked the plug back and forth between her cheeks, stretching her more. She gasped. The sting, the burn was growing as he pushed deeper, and her pussy was getting wetter and hotter with every thrust of the plug into her bottom.

Full.

She felt so full.

Too full.

"Are you sure you're using the small plug?" she asked breathlessly, pressing her hands against the carpet, her muscles clenching again.

Mason laughed.

"Oh, yes. Trust me, you'll be able to take things much bigger than this little plug, eventually."

It might have looked little, but it felt huge.

His cock is a lot bigger.

Oh God.

The thought of his cock pushing into her bottom, stretching her, hurting her, made her entire body pulse.

Now that she had an idea of what that might actually feel like…

I want it.

Even if it did hurt.

Maybe because it would hurt.

I like it when it hurts a little.

Just not when it hurt a lot, out of nowhere. Like with the nipple clamp initially.

But this? Yeah. She liked this a lot.

A whole lot.

The plug pushed deeper, stretching, stretching, and Audrey cried out—then it was inside her. Her tight ring closed around the stem between the bulb and the base, clenching as the intruder filled her. It didn't hurt at all anymore, just felt so very strange.

So very intimate.

She was so *full.*

"Good girl." Mason twisted the base, turning it and making the plug spin, igniting all the little nerve endings around the entrance, and Audrey moaned.

She wasn't sure she could get more turned on from here.

"Time for your spanking."

Oh, hey. She was wrong.

She *could* get more turned on.

CHAPTER THIRTY-THREE

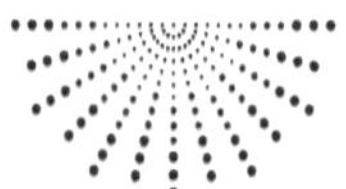

MASON

Fuck, his cock felt like it was going to explode with the way Audrey kept wriggling against it. He was going to need to keep this spanking short, or he was going to embarrass himself the way he had last night.

Seeing the plug nestled between her cheeks wasn't helping.

This was the first time he'd dealt with a complete anal virgin—the submissives he'd played with had never been completely new to anal play—and he'd been nervous he was going to mess it up the way he had the nipple clamps. Instead, she'd responded beautifully. Her pussy was soaking wet, pink and glistening beneath the plug base, practically begging to be filled with cock.

It was an act of pure willpower to move her thong back into place, covering up that tempting view, and focus on the creamy white mounds of her buttocks instead.

His hand came down sharper than he intended, and Audrey hissed in response. It wasn't a bad hiss, more like a noise of surprise rather than protest. She wasn't a pain slut, he could already tell, but she definitely liked pain with her pleasure.

Mason grinned, allowing himself to enjoy the crisp, sharp swats he began to pepper her backside with. He turned the expanse of her bottom the same pretty pink as her pussy before moving his hand down to her sit spots. Audrey gasped, bucking upwards when he did so.

"Ow!"

Immediately, Mason paused, holding his hand in the air. She'd already used her safeword once, so he knew she could… but still. This was their first time scening together.

"Too much?" he asked.

She shook her head.

"I need the words, Cupcake."

Audrey huffed, an adorable little huff. He got the feeling she wasn't used to asking for what she wanted. It might be fun to make her beg sometime.

"Please, Sir, spank me more." She wiggled her butt at him.

Grinning, Mason swatted her other sit spot, and she squealed before lifting her butt for more. He wanted her to be able to feel this tomorrow. Wanted her to think about him when she did.

The possessiveness he felt, the desire to imprint himself on her somehow, was entirely new to him. That wasn't how he normally felt. That wasn't how he did things with submissives.

But it was how he wanted to do things with Audrey.

Fuck.

He moved his hand over her sit spots, down to her thighs, and felt her squirming. She let out soft cries as he turned the backs of her thighs the same bright pink as her delicious ass, and his cock throbbed in response.

That was when he reached for the paddle.

"This is probably going to hurt. Let me know if you need to slow down," he warned her. She hummed in response. "Audrey. Tell me you understand."

"I understand, Sir."

She sounded dreamy.

Someone was enjoying herself.

He wasn't sure she would enjoy this as much… but she might.

Mason didn't use a ton of force behind the first swap with the paddle, but enough to deliver a crisp pop that made her cry out and rock forward on his lap. She whimpered as he rubbed the spot, which was now a much brighter pink than the surrounding area.

But she didn't use her safe words.

"Now the other side."

Another sharp pop. Another cry. A shudder went down her back. Her bottom was warm all over, but now hot where he'd landed the paddle… and he wasn't sure she was truly feeling it anymore. Putting the paddle down, Mason pulled her up to straddle his lap, so he could see her face. He also wanted to check on her nipples.

Make sure he wasn't straining her on her first night wearing them.

Enjoying the view was just a side benefit.

Her breasts were still pink from the flogger, though not nearly as pink as her ass. Her nipples were a dark red hue, much darker than before he'd applied the clamps. Time for those to come off then. Especially because Audrey's expression was dreamy, her eyes glazed.

She wasn't in her right mind anymore.

Whether or not she was fully in subspace was debatable, but she wasn't in a position or headspace to be able to tell when it was time to stop, when her body had had enough, which meant it was his job as the Dom to do so for her. Safe words could only cover so many situations, and this wasn't one of them. She might as well be drunk, which meant she couldn't truly give consent beyond this point.

"Time to take the clamps off," he said gently, watching her face. She blinked, staring at him dreamily. "This might hurt, sweetness."

She smiled at him.

Yup, she was in deep.

So, it might not hurt as much, but it probably would as the blood rushed back into the little buds.

Gently, Mason opened the clamp on the breast that was probably the sorest since he'd done the too-tight clamp on it in the beginning. It took a moment, then her mouth dropped open, and she made a little mewling cry.

Leaning forward, Mason sucked her poor nipple into his mouth, gently suckling to help soothe the pain of her circulation starting up again. She sighed, arching her back, the cuffs on her wrists clinking as she looped her arms around his neck, scooting her bottom closer to him. Her pussy rocked against his dick as she moved.

Fuck, it was a repeat of last night, but with her on top this time.

Mason grabbed hold of her hips as he suckled, trying to hold her in place, but she kept squirming against him. Rubbing herself.

He released the nipple from his mouth and quickly reached up to undo the other one.

Audrey moaned, throwing her head back as he took that one between his lips as well. She was grinding down on him now, shuddering, moaning...

Fuck.

He couldn't help himself; his hips lifted upward, helping her rock against him as he suckled her nipple. Soothing it.

But not soothing her. Or her need.

She moved atop him, trying to ride him even though his cock was tucked away safely behind his zipper. Despite the urge to unzip and thrust up into the wet warmth of her needy pussy, Mason just let her grind on him. Rub herself all over him.

Until she cried out, throwing her head back and creaming herself on his lap... while he embarrassed himself for the second night in a row, unable to contain his own climax while she reached hers.

Fucking hell.

AUDREY

Warm.

She was so, so warm. And comfortable.

Comfortable enough that she didn't want to get out of bed even though her inner alarm clock was telling her that it was time.

She shifted, trying to convince herself that she really was about to get out of bed... and realized she was pressed up against something hard. Something hard and warm. Something that had its arm over her and was snuggled up behind her.

Not something.

Some*one.*

Mason.

What was she doing in bed with Mason?

Last night came rushing back in a flood... until the memories stopped. She'd been over his lap getting her butt spanked, then he'd used the paddle, and it had hurt so much, but she hadn't wanted him to stop. Then... then he'd taken the clamps off. Sucked on her nipples. And...

And they'd gone at it like teenagers. Again.

But why was she in his bed?

"Ow." Shifting again had the shirt she was wearing rubbing against her very sore nipples. Her butt was really sore, too.

"Are you okay?" Mason went from completely still and prone to fully up, dark eyes wide, looming over her. Literally, over her, since one arm had been wrapped around her and the other was on the other side of her. "What hurts?"

"Um..." Her eyes widened as her gaze traveled over his bare chest. His very nice bare chest. It wasn't fair that he could look this good first thing in the morning with his hair all tousled and scruff across his jawline. "Are you wearing any clothes?"

His brow furrowed.

"Yes, I have pajama pants on— Oh, we didn't have sex."

Damn.

Wait. She was supposed to be relieved.

Yay?

That didn't feel right.

"I'm in your bed though, right?" Because that was the only thing that made sense.

Mason nodded. "You were pretty out of it last night. Definitely not in a good enough condition to drive. And I wanted to be able to keep an eye on you. Sub drop after a scene can be pretty brutal, especially if you're not used to it. How are you feeling?"

"I… good? What's sub drop?"

"The drop of emotions." He eyed her. "You might have slept through it. Though you may feel a little off today. Or a little sad."

"Because I didn't get fucked?" Crap. What had happened to her filter? She had one, but it seemed to have gone offline.

The side of Mason's mouth quirked up.

"No. Sex doesn't have anything to do with sub drop. And you weren't in a condition to give consent last night. Sometimes in a scene, a submissive will hit a point where they can't really know what they want. They aren't thinking clearly, and they can't consent. They're too physically overwhelmed to be mentally present."

"So, we didn't have sex because I couldn't fully consent. Because I do remember… um, being on top of you…"

"You still had your thong on, and I still had my pants on."

The bar for men truly was in hell. She was feeling pretty gooey about knowing he hadn't taken advantage of her, even though they'd talked about sex previously. But because she couldn't explicitly consent in the moment… that should be the expectation for all men, but too many of them sucked. It said something about Mason that he'd held firm to that line when a lot of society would not have expected him to nor judged him if he hadn't.

It was another measure of how much she could trust him.

Audrey reached up to twine her arms around his neck before he could pull away. Not that it looked like he was going to pull away, but she wanted to make sure. His gaze met hers and softened.

"I'm in a condition to give consent now," she said softly, before she lost her nerve.

Because she was sore and achy in all the best ways, but at the same time, there was a little part of her that was left unsatisfied. Unfulfilled.

She wanted him.

She was pretty sure he wanted her.

And thankfully, he proved her correct when he lowered his mouth to hers. The kiss was sweet. Gentle.

At first.

Then it changed.

Turning needier.

She was wearing a t-shirt, which she assumed was his because it definitely wasn't hers, and no underwear. He was wearing pajama pants. And she could feel how big and hard he was, even more so because of the thin fabric of his pants and the fact that the t-shirt had fallen up to her hips when she'd lifted her legs to wrap them around him.

The press of his hard body against her breasts made her whimper. Her nipples were still incredibly sore, so much so that even the soft fabric of the t-shirt rubbing over them was almost too much. The clamps had a long-lasting effect.

Mason's kiss moved from her lips to her neck, and Audrey gasped as his hands moved to push the t-shirt up, so he could cup her breasts. She moaned, arching beneath him, trying to rub herself against him. She was so turned on, she didn't want much foreplay.

Didn't need it.

Last night had been like an extended session of foreplay, and she wanted him now... but she couldn't quite get up the nerve to say so.

Which meant that she was in sensual torment as he moved his mouth to her breasts, licking, nibbling, sucking. She whimpered, writhing for him, grabbing at his hair and trying to tug him upwards, to indicate wordlessly what she couldn't bring herself to say.

"What do you need, cupcake?" he murmured, before dragging his teeth over one overly sensitive nipple and making her quiver.

It was like he knew she was struggling to verbalize her desires, and he was going to push her to do it, anyway.

The big jerk.

"Please," she begged.

Please don't make me say it out loud.

"Please, what, sweetness?" He shifted, taking her wrists in his hands and pinning them down on either side of her head, looming above her while their lower bodies connected. She was utterly help-less beneath him, and it made her want him even more.

Audrey's eyelashes fluttered. She couldn't look at him while she said it. A hot blush bloomed across her cheeks. After everything he'd said to her, everything he'd done to her, it was still a struggle.

"Please fuck me," she whispered.

"As you wish."

His voice was a purr, and he pushed both of her hands above her head so he could grasp her wrists with one hand while he leaned over to the side of the bed. Condom. He was getting a condom. At least one of them was thinking clearly.

She didn't hate being pinned beneath him while he attended to the necessary protection. It only took him a moment to rip the package open with his teeth and roll the condom over his dick, then he was back on top of her, his mouth on hers, as he settled between her thighs. Audrey drew her legs up, spreading them wider for him as his cock nudged at her entrance.

Big.

He was *big*.

Thick all around. She cried out into his mouth as he thrust in, her softness opening easily for him. Audrey's hips lifted up to meet his, taking him in greedily, wanting to feel him inside her, to feel him stretching her open. With one hand pinning down her wrists, he looped his other arm around one of her legs, settling the crook of her knee against his elbow, giving him complete access as he started to slowly ride her.

She could feel every inch of him sliding in deep, filling her completely, sending her senses soaring as he rocked against her body before he retreated again… and filled her again. This was no fast fuck; he was taking his time. Using her. Pleasuring her. Making sure she felt every inch of him as he moved inside her.

"Mason," she whispered his name as her pleasure mounted, and he groaned in response.

He began to thrust harder, faster.

The delicious soreness of her clit and nipples, the ecstasy of having him moving within her, the helplessness of being pinned beneath him, all combined in a swirling funnel of pure sensual rapture. Audrey cried out his name again as he filled her, her free leg wrapping around the back of his, trying to hold him closer as her climax peaked.

Pleasure washed over her in pulsing waves, leaving her shuddering beneath him as he continued to move over her, in her. She could hear his low groans as her pussy spasmed around him, gripping him, trying to hold him in place, until he finally buried himself inside her, moaning her name.

Panting, he collapsed on top of her, his weight pressing her into the bed, letting her leg lower as his grip on her wrists loosened. Audrey wrapped her arms around him.

Just... friends with benefits, she reminded herself.

But even as she had the thought, she knew it was already too late. Even if he didn't fall for her, she'd already fallen for him.

CHAPTER THIRTY-FOUR

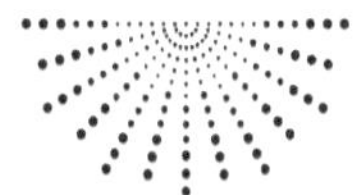

MASON

"I slept with Audrey."

"Who's Audrey?"

Mason paused for a beat. Figured that Asad wouldn't remember that conversation. Sometimes his cousin could be very self-involved.

"Audrey. The woman my ex-fiancée, Yasmine, thought I was attracted to."

"Oh, right, right. Weren't you going to prove that you aren't attracted to her anymore because it was going to go away now that you aren't getting married to Audrey?"

"You mean to Yasmine. I'm not getting married to Yasmine."

No one had said anything about marriage to Audrey. He sure as hell wasn't thinking about getting married to Audrey. They weren't even dating. He couldn't tell anyone up here that they'd slept together. That's why he'd called Asad in the first place; he could tell his cousin since Asad lived a whole state away.

There was no logical reason to feel his chest constrict when Asad said he wasn't getting married to Audrey since that wasn't on the table, anyway.

"Right, you're not getting married to Yasmine, so you had sex with

Audrey. Is the attraction gone yet?" Asad's tone was mocking, clearly thinking he already knew the answer.

It was frustrating that he was right about that.

Mason scowled.

"I don't know why I called you," he muttered.

"Perhaps because you're looking for love advice?" Asad suggested. "From someone who is better at it than you are?"

"I'm not in love with her," Mason said automatically. He wasn't. Was he? Surely it was too soon. They'd just met.

But he was having feelings for her. The protectiveness was understandable. The possessiveness... less so.

"But you're still feeling more for her than you did the woman you were engaged to." His cousin didn't ask it as a question; he stated it as fact.

And Mason couldn't argue with him. He did have feelings for her, and that was why he'd called Asad. He had no idea what to do with those feelings.

"I can't date her openly for a few more weeks. I promised Yasmine she wouldn't have to see me with another woman right away. Plus, David doesn't know that I'm interested at all." Mason turned to face the wall of his hallway, which he'd been pacing up and down pretty much since Audrey had left to go home so she could quickly change and head to the bakery. The urge to follow her there and claim a table for the day was strong, which was why he'd decided to call Asad.

"David her..."

"Brother. You know that. I told you that. What the fuck, Asad, why are you so distracted?"

"Oh, yeah, because it's *my* fault you interrupted my morning blow job. You should feel honored I still picked up the phone in the first—"

Mason hung up on him. For fuck's sake.

He banged his head against the wall, hard enough that it hurt a little.

His phone buzzed, and he rested his forehead against the flat surface as he lifted it up so he could see Asad's text message.

Asad: Stop being a fucking pussy and just go get the girl, dumbass.

So helpful.

It wasn't that easy, but he supposed he couldn't expect Asad to understand. Asad had always been impulsive, and it tended to work out for him. That had never been Mason's style.

His phone buzzed again, but this time when he glanced at the message, he sprang into action.

All hands on deck. Someone had broken into Black Fox.

Which wasn't easy to do, even on a Sunday. There was usually at least one person in the office, regardless of the day, plus the outside security.

His mind raced as he ran to his bedroom and threw on the first clothes he could get his hands on.

This had to be Devlin. Who else would be brazen enough to break in? Who would *want* to?

Had the bakery just been a distraction? One that wasn't working because Mason was handling it and hadn't gone to David with it?

Or was this separate?

Shit.

He quickly sent off a text message to Audrey, letting her know that there had been a break-in at Black Fox and to be on alert. Just in case this was connected to the bakery in any way.

It was pretty busy there, so he didn't take offense when he didn't get a text back before he got to his car, but it did make him a little more worried. Speeding through traffic, he deliberately took a route that would have him passing Cupcakes and Crumbs on his way. Just so he could take a look and make sure everything was going ok.

He had the cameras, of course, which he checked when he was stuck at a red light, but he still wanted an on-the-ground visual. Camera feeds could be hacked.

Thankfully, when he drove by, it was clear that everything was going well there. The place was packed, which was why Audrey hadn't texted him back. She was too busy. He couldn't even catch a glimpse of her.

That was also good because it was unlikely anyone was going to try anything with so many potential witnesses on site. That meant he could concentrate on Black Fox.

He ran into Claudia in the parking lot, both of them exchanging nods as they rushed inside.

"Freaking elevator," she muttered. It didn't take that long, but both of them were bouncing on their feet by the time the doors opened.

Both teams were in the lobby of Black Fox. Grant's head came up when the elevator doors opened, his eyes alight with the alertness that came with action.

Lincoln was sitting in one of the chairs next to Drew, who had Darcie beside him, helping him press what looked like an ice pack against the back of his head. She was helping him hold his locks out of the way. Harris was a little farther away, speaking with David. Jaxon was on a laptop, sitting in another chair, frowning as he looked at the screen.

"What happened?" Claudia demanded to know as soon as she got through the door Grant pushed open for them, Mason hot on her heels.

"We're still figuring it out," Lincoln replied, lifting his head to meet her gaze. His expression was stony.

He was *pissed.*

So was Mason. They'd been attacked on their home ground, and Drew was hurt.

"Drew was here working and headed to the break room when someone got the drop on him," David said, ignoring Drew's unhappy grunt at the description. "We're still not sure what they were here for or if anything was taken. Or who it was."

"Devlin. It has to be Devlin, right?" Darcie asked, frowning. "That's the only thing that makes sense unless there's something you haven't been telling us." She glanced between Lincoln and Harris, the owners, then David and Grant, the team leaders. Her gaze lingered on Grant, who frowned back at her and crossed his arms over his chest.

"You know what I know," he told her.

Darcie sniffed, but she nodded before turning back to Drew and lifting the ice pack. She winced. Her focus on Drew was intent enough that she didn't notice the way Grant was watching her. Those two really just needed to get a room and get it over with. Work out some of that tension.

It was working out well for him and Audrey.

"This is definitely going to be a lump. Please let me test you for a concussion." The request was made with an air of exasperation that told Mason this wasn't the first time she'd made it.

"I'm fine." Drew was focused on a spot on the floor. Shit. Mason sighed inwardly. This was not going to help Drew's feeling that he'd let the team down, even though he hadn't.

"Let her check, Drew," Lincoln ordered.

With orders from the boss, Drew grumbled under his breath but let Darcie run through the tests she wanted. Mason kept one eye on that while going over to see what Jaxon was looking at.

Sensing him, Jaxon glanced up and over his shoulder.

"The cameras were hacked and put on a loop," he said. "I just found the place where the footage was spliced in. It happened right after Zeus left."

"Zeus was here?" Mason asked.

"Yeah, and he left in a hurry." Jaxon pulled up the footage. Now there was an entire crowd behind him. Drew and Darcie remained where they were, but everyone else gathered around, pressing together to all try to see the laptop screen at the same time. Mason didn't bother trying to tell anyone to step back—they all wanted to know what was going on.

They watched the screen as Zeus was walking down the hallway when he got a phone call and answered it. He was talking low enough that the camera didn't pick up what he was saying, and he turned away from it so they couldn't see his face, either. A few minutes later, obviously agitated, he headed out of the office with long, determined strides, moving much faster than he normally did.

Then he was out the doors and in the hallway. He took the stairs instead of the elevator.

But what did it mean?

"He checked in, he's on his way back," Lincoln said.

"This doesn't prove he had anything to do with anything," Claudia pointed out.

"Oh, sure." Drew cast her a dark look. "He leaves in a hurry, the cameras are hacked, and I'm attacked right after, but it has nothing to do with him."

"It looks bad, but it's not proof." Lincoln shook his head. "I'm still not convinced someone isn't setting him up. Did you see him return?"

Drew shook his head, then winced from the movement.

"No," he admitted.

"You don't have a concussion, but stop moving around," Darcie scolded.

He managed a rueful smile for her that resembled a grimace.

"It doesn't mean he wasn't involved either," Mason pointed out. Lincoln was operating under 'innocent until proven guilty' rules right now. That or 'keep your friends close and your enemies closer.' Either could backfire spectacularly.

"He knows," Harris said, and it was clear from his tone that he agreed with Drew and Mason that Zeus was not to be trusted. David was frowning fiercely. What his opinion was, Mason couldn't be sure.

"I'm not firing him unless we have clear proof that he's working with Devlin. So far, we don't." Lincoln shot a look at Jaxon, who nodded.

"He's received no odd payments, he hasn't gone through any files he shouldn't, and he seems to just clock in, do his training and his job, then go home." Jaxon shrugged. "If it wasn't for the way he keeps getting set up, he'd be pretty boring."

From the way Jaxon phrased it, he wasn't convinced of Zeus' guilt. Neither was Mason to be honest, but he wasn't going to presume innocence either.

The elevator doors opened, and the man himself stepped out, along with Jensen and Miguel from Harris' team. All of them looked grim, so Zeus' expression indicated nothing out of the ordinary.

Grant stepped forward to open the door for them, so they didn't have to use their key cards. If Zeus noticed that almost everyone was looking at him, his expression didn't show it. He zeroed right in on

Drew, who had dropped his head down again and was letting Darcie tend to him.

"What the fuck happened?" Zeus asked in apparent bewilderment. "I was barely gone for an hour."

"Someone came in during that time. The cameras looped, so we don't know who, and they got the drop on Drew." Claudia went through the events in a clipped tone, her gaze focused on Zeus, as was Mason's. He wanted to see the other man's reaction.

Drew grunted again, unhappy at being reminded of the fact that someone had managed to get him from behind. On the other hand, going at someone Drew's size made most people take pause, even highly trained operatives. Maybe especially highly trained operatives.

"Why did you leave when you did?" Lincoln asked, and despite the circumstances, he managed to make himself sound curious rather than accusatory.

Still, Zeus stood a little straighter. He was no fool; he realized what it looked like. To be fair, it made it more improbable that he'd have set things up like this, when Mason thought about it.

"Noelle called me. She said she got home and thought there was someone in her house, and she was scared." Zeus' tone was wooden. Flat.

Mason had the feeling he was angry, though it was debatable whether he was angry at Lincoln for questioning him, the situation in general, or Noelle. He would be stupid not to wonder if it was a setup, considering the reason they'd broken up. It could easily be Devlin again.

But she must have sounded convincing.

"I thought you two broke up," Jensen said with a frown.

Zeus shot an exasperated glance at him.

"We did."

"Tell me you wouldn't go check out your ex's house if they called you saying they were scared," Darcie said, frowning at Jensen and then shooting that frown around at everyone else. "Every single one of you."

"Yeah, but… she cheated on him." Jensen was still frowning.

"I told her to call the cops, but she said she had, and it had been ten minutes, and they still weren't there." Zeus' tone still had no inflection. He could have been recounting the weather. It was clear he didn't feel like he should have to share all this information.

"Did she seem truly scared?" Harris asked, frowning.

"She did, or I wouldn't have gone."

"It could have been a double setup," Mason offered. "If Devlin didn't care about scaring her, he could have sent someone to her house to mess with her, figuring she would call Zeus if she couldn't get in touch with him."

Everyone looked at him.

"The way your mind works is scary sometimes," Miguel muttered.

"Only sometimes?" Jensen asked, shaking his head. "That's so fucking convoluted… how could he be sure she would call Zeus?"

"Maybe that's not what happened, and she's just a really good actress." Mason shrugged. "We might never know."

Zeus stood silently. He was watching Lincoln and no one else. While the trust of the team mattered, it was Lincoln who would make the final decision. If he was worried, it didn't show on his face.

In some ways, that had likely been to his benefit for a lot of his service, but Mason wished he was a little easier to read. It would help right now if he wasn't so closed off.

On the other hand, he couldn't really blame the guy.

Either he was being set up and was indignant about being mistrusted, or he was actually working for the other team and needed to act like he was being set up and indignant about being mistrusted.

Sunday turned into a workday.

With the cameras looped, everyone had to check everything. They had no idea what the intruder had gotten into, where they might have gone. The whole afternoon was spent going over the office with a fine-tooth comb. Everyone was grim, Zeus particularly so.

If anything, he'd become more closed off than ever after this incident.

At this rate, even if the guy was innocent, Mason wasn't sure how long he was going to last at Black Fox. This was a hell of a lot of pressure to work under, with everyone mistrusting him.

The most unnerving part was that no one found anything. Nothing had been taken that they could tell. Lincoln and Harris had double-teamed Devlin's old office, even taking the paintings off the walls in case he'd hidden something behind them. No one could figure out why there might have been an intruder, which meant that they were all feeling particularly paranoid.

For all they knew, the only reason had been to set Zeus up.

Which was a suggestion Jensen made while they were eating dinner around the conference room table. It was clear, he wanted to believe in Zeus' innocence. Mason and Drew were more skeptical. David and Claudia were hard to read, though Mason had a feeling they both were swayed more toward his and Drew's skepticism; they just did a good job of hiding it.

"What if—" Claudia was just starting to talk—probably to present another option of why someone might have broken in, since that's all they'd been talking about, round and round—when Mason's phone blared.

Loudly.

His heart jumped into his throat as he jumped to his feet, shoving his chair back and leaving his half-eaten dinner in front of him.

"What the fuck is that?"

"The bakery alarm!" Mason was already on his way out the conference room door when he heard David roar behind him.

"The what?"

CHAPTER THIRTY-FIVE

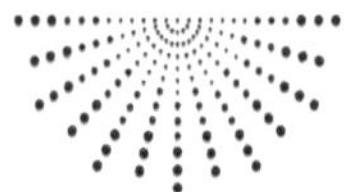

AUDREY

Audrey was just flipping the sign on the door to closed, feeling exhausted to the bone, when a man suddenly appeared on the other side of the glass. She squeaked, jumping back—instead of locking the door, which would have been the smart thing to do. But he'd startled her.

And when she got a good look at him as he came into her bakery, she *really* wished she'd managed to lock the door.

"Cash." She blinked in surprise, shaking her head, like he might disappear if she did so… because surely she had to be imagining him.

"In the flesh." He grinned at her, the way he always did, as if she should be flattered that he was gracing her with his presence.

Or maybe she was projecting, because she used to like the way he smiled at her, but now… that's what it looked like. And maybe that's what it had always felt like, and she just hadn't been able to acknowledge it until now.

He looked exactly how she remembered—wavy blond hair, hazel eyes full of confidence, wearing a navy-blue coat that was fashionable but expensive enough to be functional, too. The Burberry scarf he wore was only partially wrapped around his neck, hanging on like an afterthought—a concession to the weather rather than protection against it.

He dripped with upper-class breeding and arrogance, a reminder of everything she'd run from.

And not just because the last time she'd seen him, he'd been in her mother's coat closet, balls deep in Becky Gray.

"We're closed," Ashley said from behind the counter, sounding suspicious. The fact that Audrey hadn't greeted him with enthusiasm must have gotten her guard up, even though Audrey had never mentioned him before. She didn't exactly like bringing up her ex or how foolish she'd been to have stayed with him for as long as she did.

He wasn't the entire reason she'd fled Philly, but she wasn't sure she would have gotten up the courage to leave if she hadn't discovered his infidelity. It had been her parents' reaction to their breakup, as much as anything, that had finally pushed her out the door to follow her dreams.

"Oh, that's okay, I'm not here to buy anything." Cash grimaced, stretching upward and patting his stomach. "I've gotta protect the integrity of the abs."

Ashley snorted, clearly unimpressed. Which wasn't surprising considering that her husband had a nice set, and he was almost twice Cash's age… plus the whole security firm that he owned could have filled a sexy calendar.

Frowning, Cash settled back into position. With his golden-boy good looks, he wasn't used to people being unimpressed—if not by his looks, then by his name. But Ashley didn't know who he was. And she might not be impressed even if she did.

"Cash, what are you doing here?" Audrey asked, shaking her head. She still couldn't quite believe that he was here at all.

He cleared his throat. Rolled his shoulders back, lifting his chin and sticking his hand in his pocket.

"Audrey Bowers," he said, suddenly very formal. He dropped to one knee as she stared at him, too frozen in shock to react.

"What the fuck?" Ashley's voice was a shrill counterpoint to Cash's as he ignored her and kept going.

"I can't live without you anymore." He pulled the box out of his pocket.

Audrey's heart hammered against her chest. Her palms were sweating, her brain screaming at her to do something, say something, to *stop* him from saying another word, yet she couldn't move. So much adrenaline was pumping through her, she was about to explode, but her jaw and every one of her muscles felt locked in place.

Cash flipped the little velvet box open, revealing a gorgeous sparkling diamond ring. Princess cut. Big. At least two carats, if not three. Her brain catalogued all the things she'd been trained to look for, like a computer's background operating system while the screen remained frozen.

"I don't want to go another day apart from you. Will you marry me?"

Audrey kept staring at him.

He cleared his throat again, lifting the ring toward her, as if maybe she had somehow missed seeing the massive stone or something.

"Uh, Audrey? I just asked you to marry me. You're supposed to say yes." He was looking at her so expectantly, so confidently, she almost said it. Because that was what she was supposed to do. That's what he expected her to do.

It felt like her chest was going to explode. She couldn't breathe. She was sweating. The whole world felt like it was closing in on her.

She couldn't say yes.

Don't cause a scene, Audrey.

Her mother's sharp tones echoed in her head.

But she couldn't say yes.

She just couldn't say no either.

Then the world exploded around her as glass shattered, the alarm blared, and a shrill scream cut through the air.

MASON

It took him less than thirty seconds to make it down the block, yet that was thirty seconds too long, the entirety of both Black Fox Security teams hot on his heels.

He knew they were there, but he couldn't think about anything except getting to Audrey.

Barreling through the door, he came up short, taking in the scene in front of him. Cold air blew in through the front window, which had a massive hole in it, explaining the alarm. Glass shards decorated the tables, chairs, and floor beside the window.

Several feet away, a blond man was holding Audrey in his arms—no, wait, she was trying to push herself out of his arms. Mason strode forward, grabbing the asshole's hand and twisting, making him howl and fall to his knees. He let go of Audrey, which was the point.

"Who is this?" he asked, but his question was lost in the cacophony as the two teams poured in behind him, exclaiming over the mess. Out of the corner of his eye, Mason saw Zeus stride over to between two of the tables and look down at something on the floor before straightening up and raising one arm to draw attention.

Thankfully, the alarm stopped going off—both on his phone and inside the bakery—then Ashley came rushing out from the back, followed by a wide-eyed Alexis. Her eyes widened even more when she saw the group in the main room, and she hung back at the doorframe, while Ashley rushed straight to Lincoln and threw herself in his arms.

"Quiet!" Grant roared, in the way that only he could, his voice cutting through all the noise.

"What the fuck is going on?" David demanded to know as soon as everyone shut up. "Who the fuck is this, what the hell happened to the window, and why the fuck does Mason have the alarm hooked up to *his* phone?"

"I think this brick is why the alarm went off," Zeus said, the hand that had been raised now pointing down at the ground. "If I had to take a wild guess."

"Someone threw it through the window, right after the Ken Doll proposed to Audrey," Ashley said, stepping back from Lincoln's embrace, though still clinging to him. She was as pale as a sheet.

"He what?" David and Mason snapped out in unison, and the Ken Doll in question cried out again as Mason's grip on his wrist tightened.

"Let me go, or I'm going to sue you!" he cried out. "Someone call the police, this is assault!"

"So is throwing a brick through someone's window," Mason snapped out.

"That couldn't have been Cash," Audrey replied, finally saying something. She was standing and hugging herself, only a few feet away from him. Mason immediately let go of the Ken Doll and stepped forward to hug her, only to crash into David, who was coming forward to do the same thing, going by the way his arms were outstretched.

"Shit."

"Fuck."

They managed to get themselves untangled, and Mason stepped back so David could put his arm around his sister. Audrey's eyes were huge, and she looked paler than ever, which made Mason's chest tighten, but when it came down to it, brotherly relationship trumped whatever was between them. He didn't know if she wanted everyone to know that they were... not together, but doing whatever it was they were doing.

"This is Cash?" Claudia asked, nudging the blond with her foot. He cradled his arm as he got to his feet, staring around in confusion. Maybe wondering why no one was calling the cops. Mason didn't bother to tell him that the alarm system would bring them here soon enough. "The douchebag who cheated on you?"

"He what?" Once again, Mason and David spoke in unison, both of them stepping toward the Ken Doll at the same time. Audrey grabbed hold of David, keeping him from moving forward, while Jensen smoothly stepped in front of Mason to block him.

"If you hit him, he'll definitely press charges," Jensen murmured.

That might be worth it now that he knew the douchebag had cheated on Audrey. Who the hell would cheat on a woman like Audrey? A dumbass who deserved to be punched in the face, that's who. But Audrey had grabbed her brother to stop him from doing the same thing, which meant she didn't want the sad sack punched in the face.

Mason would have to settle for hoping the guy's arm hurt like hell right now. He wished he'd twisted even harder.

"I made a mistake, Audrey," Dumbass said earnestly. Mason hoped like hell that Audrey wasn't buying his wide-eyed bullshit. "Losing you is what made me realize how much I love you. Look, I even got you a Cartier ring. You love Cartier."

"I don't want Cartier, Chase. I want to be able to trust my boyfriend not to cheat on me!" Audrey stared at him in pure disbelief.

Claudia broke into a coughing fit that sounded an awful lot like her saying "fuckwad" over and over again.

Dumbass' face heated bright red, but he didn't look at her. He was mostly focused on Audrey, with his gaze occasionally darting to Mason and David.

"He's your friend, right?" Cash said, tipping his head toward Mason. "He was defending you. It's just a misunderstanding. So if you marry me, I won't press charges."

"The fuck?" Jensen asked, turning around, before remembering what he was doing and managing to block Mason from lunging at Dumbass again.

"Are you trying to blackmail her into marrying you, dude?" Grant asked incredulously. His team was hanging back and watching the drama rather than inserting themselves into it, which was probably the smart move.

Darcie let out a low whistle. "Wow, that's pretty desperate."

An ugly expression flashed across Dumbass' face before he managed to bury it under a smile that didn't reach his eyes.

"I am desperate," he said, his voice dripping with poisoned honey as he gazed with intent at Audrey. "Desperate for you, Audrey. Desperate for you to be my wife. Can you send your friends away so we can talk about this privately? I didn't mean for my proposal to turn public like this."

"I... no." Audrey shook her head, digging her fingers into David's arm. She was so pale, her face looked utterly bloodless.

Cash sighed.

"You really want to talk about this with all of them around?" He gestured broadly at the audience, of which Mason was a part of. It felt like his jaw was going to crack, he was clenching his teeth so hard, and he didn't know what he would do if Audrey did try to go off alone with Dumbass.

The wave of possessiveness that rolled over him was impossible to ignore.

Audrey was *his*.

His submissive.

His lover.

And if she said yes to this douchebag's proposal, all hell was going to break loose.

The fact that the asshole was pressuring her when she clearly didn't want to marry him was making him suspicious as hell. Especially considering they were all starting to shiver thanks to the cold blasts of air coming through the shattered window.

"No, I mean no to your proposal," she said, scrunching her shoulders in. Immediately, David stepped closer, putting his arm around her and glaring at Dumbass, who was too dumbfounded to have any sense of self-preservation.

"But... you can't say no."

"She just did. Is he hard of hearing?" Ashley asked, putting her hands on her hips and glaring at him. "She said no. Now, beat it. We need to clean this mess up, and I get the feeling you aren't the kind of guy who gets his hands dirty."

"I..." Cash looked around, but everyone was glaring at him. His gaze finally landed on Mason, and he scowled, straightening up. He lifted his chin and sniffed as he cradled the arm Mason grabbed. "I *will* be pressing charges."

"Good luck with that, considering all these witnesses who saw absolutely nothing," Claudia said casually, leaning her hip against the table she was standing beside. When she smiled at Cash, it was more like a predator baring its teeth at prey in warning—she hadn't decided to take a bite yet, but she could be convinced.

"This isn't over," Cash said, shaking his head. He looked back at Audrey. "Talk to your parents. You'll see. You'll be picking out your wedding dress before you know it."

He stomped out of the bakery, wrapped up in enough arrogance to carry him through Harris' team as they gave him just enough room to go by. If he could have slammed the door behind him, he probably would have.

As soon as he was gone, everyone started talking at once. David's grim gaze met Mason's.

"Let's talk," David said, glaring at him. "I have a *lot* of questions."

CHAPTER THIRTY-SIX

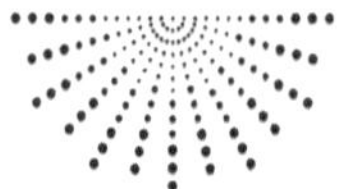

AUDREY

Somehow, Audrey managed to get David to put off asking his questions until the window was boarded up and the glass swept up. Which didn't take nearly as long as she hoped, even though Harris' team returned to Black Fox to do whatever it was they'd been doing before they'd all come running to her rescue. As reassuring as it was to know that she had two teams of trained and terrifying people who would literally dash down the street to save her, it was also somewhat mortifying.

Especially since they'd all witnessed Cash's absolutely disastrous proposal.

What had he been *thinking?*

Scratch that, he clearly hadn't been thinking at all. That, or her parents had put thoughts into his head. Audrey felt positively sick at the thought. She was going to have to call them and confront them, ask them what Cash had meant. Why he was so sure she would marry him. Why he thought she needed to talk to them after she'd said no.

Just saying no had felt like a monumental effort, especially with their audience. Though the audience was also those who had given her the courage to say no in the moment, rather than trying to put him off until later. She hated that she'd had to have the conversation at all.

Especially while wildly distracted by the fact that someone had thrown a freaking brick through her front window! Then, when Cash had just up to try to be protective, all she'd wanted to do was shove him off of her.

She'd wanted Mason.

Not Cash.

Then Mason had appeared, but so had everyone else, and…

She really wanted to go hide in the back office until they all went away, but she knew David would just come looking for her. She could only dodge him for so long, and he wanted answers.

As if the thought had summoned him, he appeared in front of her with his arms crossed over his chest, frowning.

"Okay. Window is boarded up. Police report has been made." He glanced outside, where Lincoln and Ashley were talking to the cops who had shown up only a few minutes after Cash had left. Audrey was glad they'd been a little slow because if they'd shown up while he was there, she wouldn't have put it past him to try to have Mason arrested. "The brick is taken care of. Let's go check the cameras."

And have a talk.

His words hung unspoken in the air, and Audrey winced.

"Do you really need me for that?" she asked. "The office can get kind of crowded."

David just stared at her, arms still crossed over his chest, and Audrey let out a huff of air, her shoulders slumping forward.

"Come on, Cupcake," Mason murmured in her ear, his hand coming down on her shoulder. "Let's go talk to your brother."

The appearance of Mason beside her, his hand touching her, even if it was just her shoulder, had David narrowing his eyes. He wasn't glaring at her, but he was glaring, and Audrey shrank away before he banked his hard look and turned away, stalking toward the office.

As he went past Claudia, she turned to look at Audrey and gave her a thumbs-up.

"You've got this," she mouthed.

While she appreciated the show of support, Audrey didn't feel so sure.

With her brother in front of her and Mason behind her, it felt like she was walking to her doom. As they went into the back, Alexis looked over. She had finished cleaning up but was still standing there, probably wondering what was going on.

"You're good to go home," Audrey said to her.

Alexis nodded, but still looked hesitant.

"Hey, Zeus," Mason called out from behind Audrey. "Can you escort Alexis to her car?"

"Sure."

Immediately, Alexis relaxed, and Audrey kicked herself for not realizing what the other woman was worried about. Alexis had walked to her car plenty of times on her own, but never after a brick had been thrown through the front window of the bakery. Especially when it was dark already.

Having a big, muscular security guy walking with her would help assuage any fears.

Zeus sauntered into the kitchen and gave Alexis a look up and down, as if assessing her. The young woman ducked her head, not meeting his eyes as she put on her coat. He was pretty intimidating.

"I'll see you tomorrow?" Audrey asked. She knew Ashley wouldn't quit over this, but she wasn't so sure about Alexis, and she needed both of them to keep the bakery going with how busy it had been. Plus, she liked Alexis and didn't want to lose her.

Despite her obvious nervousness, Alexis nodded her head firmly, glancing up to meet Audrey's gaze.

"I'll be here," she said softly.

"Good. Thank you," Audrey replied with relief.

Alexis flashed her a quick, shy smile before ducking her head again as Zeus gestured for her to precede him to the back door. Audrey was relieved that he was there. She knew there were some issues with him fitting in with the team, but she trusted him to keep Alexis safe.

As soon as Audrey was in the office with Mason and David, her brother stepped behind the desk, though he was frowning at Mason rather than looking at the computer where the security camera feed would be.

"Why did you ask Zeus to take her?"

"Because it's something I could ask of him that allows him to contribute to the team. Plus, it'll give him a break from Drew."

David's lips pressed together.

"What's going on?" Audrey asked.

"That's what I want to know," David countered, looking between her and Mason.

Yeah, so she'd walked right into that one. The best course of action was denial.

"Nothing." She crossed her arms over her chest.

"I'm teaching her about kink," Mason said, sitting down at the computer chair to boot it up, apparently unbothered that her brother was now glaring at the back of his head.

"What does *that* mean?" David's expression was turning pained.

"Nothing," Audrey said again, contemplating kicking Mason. Not that he was within kicking reach.

"It means exactly what you think it means."

"Weren't you engaged to someone else a week ago?" David ran his fingers through his hair, shaking his head.

"No, I got un-engaged to someone else a week ago." Mason clicked through the programs, pulling up the feed and rewinding to earlier in the evening while they spoke. Audrey considered melting into the floor as her brother looked at her. She turned her gaze to the ceiling.

What she got up to in the bedroom wasn't any of his business. No more than it was her business what he and Cassidy did in the bedroom.

"You know you don't have to use Mason as a teacher; I can find you another Dom," David said, switching his attention to her.

That made Mason's head swing up, and now he was the one glaring at her brother.

"Don't even think about it; she's with me."

Was it wrong of her heart to flutter at his statement? Sure, they'd agreed to friends with benefits, but she couldn't help reacting to what seemed like a show of possessiveness on his part. He cared about her, at least a little. He didn't want to stop teaching her.

"Only if she wants to be."

"I do," Audrey said hastily. "I'm very happy with Mason's, um, tutelage."

"Shit." Mason shook his head, and her heart dropped for a moment before she realized he was reacting to the camera footage. "I think this is the same guy as last time."

The person who had thrown the brick had done so from a motor-cycle—launching it clear across the sidewalk from where they strad-dled the vehicle. Then they took off.

After having been chased by Mason the last time, they were now working from a distance.

Audrey felt her heart drop. Who could be doing this? And why?

Mason

Poor Audrey. Ignoring David, Mason reached out to pull her onto his lap. She needed a cuddle, and David could suck it.

Her brother groaned, but didn't protest.

"What do you mean, the last time?" David asked, sounding resigned.

Mason gave him the full rundown, holding Audrey on his lap. She curled up against his shoulder, trembling. Possibly a delayed reaction to the shock of the brick coming through her window or possibly just overwhelmed from everything that was going on.

It was a lot.

"I can't believe you didn't tell me," David complained once Mason came to the end. "I should have known about this."

"I didn't want to bother you," Audrey muttered.

"You are *never* a bother."

At least David and Mason were on the same page about that. But Audrey wasn't wrong that David had a lot on his plate already.

"I had it handled," Mason said. "She knew that you had a lot going on and didn't want to add to it. Neither did I. Claudia was my backup."

David grumbled and leaned over to examine the footage again. There wasn't much to go on.

"I want to know what Cash meant about Audrey talking to our parents."

Ah. Well. Mason cleared his throat.

"I might have an idea on that." Something he hadn't realized mattered until tonight.

"You do?" Audrey sat up on his lap. She was no longer trembling and seemed a lot calmer, though still upset. Now, she was frowning at him.

"Yes, well. I did some digging on Cash. I didn't come up with the fact he'd cheated on you, but it always makes sense to check out the ex-boyfriend when a woman is being harassed." Mason cleared his throat as Audrey's eyes widened in surprise. "I didn't mention it before because I didn't think it mattered, but apparently he's nearly broke."

"What?" Audrey's mouth dropped open in shock.

"Not just him, but his whole family. However, there's some kind of business deal going down between his father's company and yours…"

"Dad always wanted a piece of that company," Audrey murmured.

"Are you saying our parents made Audrey into some kind of business deal?" David asked, sounding pissed as hell.

"I don't know, but I know it's possible." Mason shook his head. "I didn't really look any further because it didn't seem to involve Cash at all, and it didn't give him a reason to be harassing Audrey. He doesn't have any kind of history of bothering his exes that I could find, so I stopped looking any deeper. I have no idea what the conditions of the deal might be."

"But it gives him a reason to come and propose." Audrey huffed. "Do you think he and his parents could be behind the guy harassing me?"

"Possibly. I think Ashley had him pegged when she said he doesn't seem like the type to get his hands dirty," David said, frowning.

Mason tightened his arms around Audrey's waist. Under the circumstances, having her on his lap wasn't nearly as fun as it could be, but he was still happy to have her there.

After the way today had gone, he didn't want to let her out of his sight.

It made more sense that Cash was the reason someone was harassing her and the bakery than Devlin did, but he still didn't like the timing. What were the odds of two incidents in one day from two separate sources? On the other hand, sometimes when it rained, it poured.

Mason didn't want to make any assumptions and have them blow up in his face because he thought something was too coincidental to be true. Fact was often stranger than fiction, after all.

"I guess I have to call my parents." The sheer amount of reluctance in Audrey's tone made it clear that she did not want to. "I need to find out more about this deal."

"Do you want to do that now?" David asked, reaching out to put his hand on her shoulder. "I can be right here while you make the call."

"Me, too," Mason said firmly, pressing his fingers into her hips to remind her of his presence. "I'm not going anywhere."

The look David gave him said that he didn't know how he felt about Mason's statement, and they weren't done talking about what Mason was doing with Audrey. Apparently, he didn't want to have that conversation with Audrey in the room, though. That was fine. Mason wasn't afraid of David.

He hoped this wouldn't end their friendship, but if David was going to let Mason being with his sister change things between them, that was on him, not Mason. Although if Mason hurt Audrey, he would understand why that would change. Not that David had anything to worry about from him on that score.

He gave David a flat stare in return, doing his best to communicate some of those feelings to his friend.

Something in David's expression changed, though Mason couldn't exactly read what. David looked at Audrey again, who was still sitting tensely on Mason's lap.

"You can't put it off forever, Audrey," David said gently. "I know you. You can't bury your head in the sand over this, not when Cash might be trying to scare you out of Pittsburgh. And if it's not him, then we need to know that so we can figure out who it is."

"I know." Audrey rubbed her hands over her face. "I'm sorry I'm such a coward."

"You're not," David and Mason said at the same time. They were starting to sound like a freaking Greek chorus when it came to her. David's glance at Mason was more measuring this time, as if he was trying to decide how he felt about the fact they were so much on the same page.

"Um, you guys literally served overseas and put your lives in danger." She shook her head, hugging herself, and Mason tightened his grip on her. "I'm chickening out over making a phone call. It's not like I'm in physical danger or anything. I'm just a wuss."

"I would much rather face another enlistment than piss off my mom," Mason admitted. "Trust me. Making the call to let her know that my engagement with Yasmine hadn't worked out was way worse than any mission we went on."

"I don't want to tell our parents anything they'll disapprove of so much that I stopped talking to them entirely," David offered. Audrey didn't look convinced. "Unfortunately, we do need to know."

"Okay." Audrey nodded, squaring her shoulders. "I'm calling them. Right now."

"Good girl," Mason murmured, making her flush.

David gave him a look of death.

CHAPTER THIRTY-SEVEN

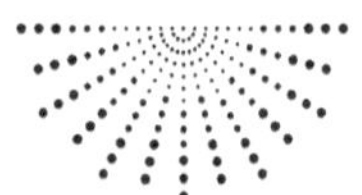

AUDREY

No matter what David and Mason said, Audrey still felt like a coward. It was just a phone call. It was just her parents. They might not even know anything. But the thought of asking made her stomach turn over. Her hands felt clammy. Rubbing them on her pants, she tried to push the discomfort down.

Still, at least David and Mason were there to support her. Plus, doing so kept David from going for Mason's throat. She hadn't missed all the dark looks her brother had been shooting Mason's way. And while she appreciated his protectiveness on some levels, on another, she wanted to tell him that it was none of his business what she and Mason did.

Except that maybe it kind of was, since David and Mason worked together, and Mason was one of David's closest friends. Maybe even his best friend. So, while his was not the most important opinion, it wasn't like he was unaffected by her choices. Especially while the team was already struggling after David's injury and was now trying to figure out if Zeus was trustworthy.

So, yeah.

Better that she keep them focused on her while she made the call to her parents, and hopefully, after that, maybe some of their energy would have dissipated, and they'd be calmer. Maybe David would even forget. Unlikely, but a girl could dream.

Calling her parents and having a long-distance difficult conversation was definitely easier than having a difficult conversation with the two men in the room with her. So, she picked up her phone and found her mother's contact info, pressing the call button, which kept the men focused on her rather than on each other.

I will not throw up, I will not throw up, I will not throw up.

"Hello? Audrey? Is everything okay?"

Her mother sounded concerned, which took Audrey aback for a moment. Did she really not call her parents that often that it was cause for concern when she did?

Well… yeah, maybe. Especially lately. It was just easier not to than to have another conversation about how she wasn't closing her bakery and moving back to Philly.

"Um, hello, Mother. Unfortunately, not really. Cash was just here, and he proposed to me."

"He did? Oh, that's wonderful!" Her mother's gushing tone was genuinely happy, which made Audrey cringe because she knew she was going to have to burst her mother's bubble now. "We can start planning the wedding immediately! It'll be difficult, moving and planning at the same time, but I will be there with you every step of the way."

Well, that sounded awful, and the very idea of having her mother standing over her while she planned a wedding was enough to have Audrey immediately tell her the truth, even though she knew her mother wasn't going to take it well.

"I told him no, mother."

There was a long pause, and Audrey glanced up at David. If he was bothered by hearing their mother's voice after all this time, it didn't show in his expression. He looked completely blank.

"What do you mean you told him no?" Her mother's voice had gone from gushing to shrill. "Why would you tell him no? Oh, he botched it, didn't he? He didn't get the Cartier ring."

Seriously, did everyone think she could be bought off by a Cartier ring? Granted, there may have been one wild moment when she'd been sad that she was saying no to her dream ring, but she needed the ring to come with the right man. Cash was not the right man.

"He had the ring, mother. He had a perfect ring. But he's not the perfect man for me. He cheated on me at one of your parties. And I know you wanted me to forgive him and look the other way, but I can't. I just can't. Marriage is not the answer."

"This is your father's fault," her mother said bitterly. "If he could just keep it in his pants, you wouldn't have such a jaded view of things. Your father sleeping with everything that moves doesn't mean Cash will."

"Ask her about the business deal," Mason murmured into Audrey's ear, making the little hairs on the back of her neck stand up at attention.

Audrey cleared her throat.

"Mom, is the reason you're pushing me to marry Cash because of a deal between Dad and Cash's dad? For the company?"

There was another pause.

"Well, Audrey, you know that in our circles, marriage and business intersect quite often. I won't deny that it would benefit both of our families immensely if you and Cash were to marry."

"Even if his family is broke?"

"They're not broke, they just need to liquidate some assets. Your father and I are more than happy to help Cash and his father out, and they're grateful for our assistance." Her mother said all of this airily, but Audrey knew what she meant. A marriage between her and Cash would allow his family to keep their reputation. Everyone would assume they weren't actually broke, and even if they were, they'd now be bolstered by her family.

They would owe her parents a great deal.

And not all wealth was built on purely money. Having a stable of favors from influential people could be even more lucrative than an actual financial deal.

"It's a wonderful opportunity, Audrey. Not just for yourself, but for the whole family. We can even fund a bakery here for you in Philadelphia if that's what you really want." Her mother's tone managed to somehow be coaxing and judgmental at the same time.

"I don't need you to fund a bakery for me in Philly. I have a bakery here that's doing really well."

"How well can it be doing when people are throwing bricks through the windows?"

Audrey felt Mason go still beneath her, and suddenly, it felt like bile was building up in the back of her throat. It tasted like acid as her stomach turned over. She blinked rapidly, the sting of tears threatening to fill her eyes.

"Mother, how did you know about the brick?"

Because she hadn't known Audrey had said no to Cash. She'd managed to get ahead of him—or maybe he was talking to his parents right now, trying to figure out their next move. If her mother hadn't talked to Cash about Audrey turning down his proposal, there was no way for her to know about the brick, unless…

Her brain tried to turn away from the possibility, but both Mason's and her brother's reactions meant they'd had the same thought. Mason slid his hands up to rub her shoulders, trying to loosen the tension now filling them, while David cursed under his breath and started pacing around the cramped space of the office.

The silence on the other end of the phone stretched on.

"Mother?"

"Excuse me, I hear your father calling for me," her mother replied briskly. "I have to go."

She hung up. Audrey's mother actually hung up without answering the question. On the other hand, what was she supposed to say when Audrey had just realized that it wasn't Cash who had been involved with the incident, but her own mother? Did her father know, too?

Of course, he did. Despite the fact her father was a serial cheater and her mother often seemed to loathe him, on matters of business, they were always a united front. If her mother knew, so did her father and vice versa. Although there was a small part of her, the childish part, that hoped she'd be proven wrong and that one of her parents hadn't betrayed her so horrifically.

Audrey sniffed as the tears welled up, no longer able to be denied. Mason's arms tightened around her.

"Fuck." David kicked the wall. He turned, looking at her like he wanted to hug her, but she was on Mason's lap and in his arms. "*Fuck*. Those assholes. I'm going to find proof, Audrey. I'm going to find proof, and they're going to pay for your window to get fixed, then they're going to leave you the fuck alone to do whatever you want with your life."

With that, he stalked out the door.

Well, she'd hoped the guys would be too distracted to argue after her call. Now, she was regretting that wish.

Burying her head on Mason's shoulder, she turned her face into his soft shirt and cried.

MASON

David and Audrey's mother was a real piece of work. Mason was seething on Audrey's behalf, but he did his best to focus on staying calm and soothing her. David could handle the raging vengeance; he had more reason to than Mason. Mason just wanted to protect Audrey.

Right now, they could split the tasks. Although if Audrey had started crying before David left the room, he doubted the other man would have gone anywhere.

"Just let it out," he murmured, wishing he could tell her that it would be okay, that everything would be alright. But how could he? Her parents had betrayed her on a level that was unfathomable to him. Even though Mason knew there were parents in the world who cared more about themselves and their needs than their own children, it always astounded him when he actually met them.

He was going to have to call his mother later and thank her. As pushy as she could be, she would never hire someone to harass him in hopes that it would galvanize him into doing what she wanted.

Sometimes, the bar for parenting was so damn low…

"We've got you," he said, rubbing his hand over her back as he felt her settle again. "We're here for you." Even if her parents weren't. She still had her brother and grandmother. The team.

"I can't believe they would do this," she said, sitting up and dashing the tears from her cheeks with her fingers. "No, scratch that. I wish I couldn't believe they would do this."

"Is this kind of thing why David went no-contact with them?"

"No." She laughed. A sharp, brittle sound. "They've gotten worse since he did. He knew to get out early. They were always a little controlling, but even so… I didn't expect this of them, yet I'm surprised by not being shocked, if that makes sense."

"It does." Mason kept running his hand up and down her back. She looked pale. Sad. And exhausted. "We should get you home."

"I need to…" Her voice trailed off as she tried to think of something she needed to do and came up blank. If there was something the team was good at, it was organizing in a hurry.

"You need to go home and rest," Mason said firmly, putting a little Dom into his voice. Her shoulders hunched inward, and she peeked at him with a worried expression. "Is there a reason you don't want to go home?"

"No… I guess not."

There clearly was, but not one she was willing to come out and state. Mason tilted his head.

"I could go home with you. Or you could come home with me."

The relief that immediately suffused her features said he'd hit his target. She didn't want to be alone, which wasn't surprising. Having seen the lengths to which her parents would go to get her to do as they wished, he didn't blame her.

"Either one sounds good."

Maybe, but she'd fully relaxed after he'd offered to take her home with him, not when he'd offered to go home with her.

"Let's go to my place."

Still relieved. Eager even. Her eyes were shining with her emotions.

"I do need to swing by my place, though, to pick up some things," she said apologetically.

"Of course. I'll go with you. I can drive you and bring you back here tomorrow morning."

Immediately, she started shaking her head.

"Oh no, I can't ask you to do that. I have to be here way too early."

"You didn't ask me to, I offered," he reminded her. She looked like she wanted to say yes, but was struggling to for some reason. "That's what we're doing. I'll drive you back and forth. I need to be at Black Fox early tomorrow, anyway."

He didn't, but it wouldn't hurt anything, and it allowed her to nod her head in acceptance of his offer.

The only problem with it was the fact she had to get off his lap. Mason kept his arm around her as they went to the front again to see what was going on. The window was fully boarded up, and Claudia and David had their heads together, talking. The rest of the team had already left.

"Hey, how are you doing, Audrey?" Claudia asked sympathetically when she caught sight of them. Her sharp gaze also noted Mason's arm around Audrey's shoulder, but she didn't say anything.

"Um, about as okay as I can be, I guess." Audrey's exhaustion was even clearer now, as was her sadness as her gaze drifted to the window.

"We're going to find out who your parents hired and make sure tonight is the last of it," Claudia said, while David nodded grimly.

"You'll still need to call the insurance company tomorrow, but the police report has been filed. When we find the asshole who did this, he'll be charged. No matter what our parents paid him, I'll make sure it wasn't enough." David raked his hand through his hair, scowling. He glanced at Mason and Audrey.

"Audrey's going to spend the night at my house tonight," he said, and felt her wince as she averted her gaze from her brother's scowl. Not that David was willing to say anything right now, especially in front of her. Mason expected to get an earful tomorrow. "I'm going to drive her."

"Fine," David said shortly. The look he gave Mason said that if any more bricks came Audrey's way, he expected Mason to throw himself in front of them. As far as Mason was concerned, that went without saying. He was getting Audrey a panic button as soon as he could, just in case.

Claudia smirked at both of them, then winked at Audrey, who didn't seem to be paying attention.

Coming forward, David opened his arms, and Audrey left the shelter of Mason's to step into her brother's for a hug. He gave Mason the big stink eye. Mason just let it glance off him. He didn't need to rile David up any more than he already was, and he didn't want to upset Audrey by having a conflict with her brother.

They'd work out any issues while they weren't around her.

Claudia, on the other hand, had no such problem.

"Have a good night," she called after Mason and Audrey as they headed for the back, her voice full of throaty innuendo.

David growled.

Mason tightened his arm around Audrey's shoulder to keep her from turning back.

Tomorrow was going to be interesting.

CHAPTER THIRTY-EIGHT

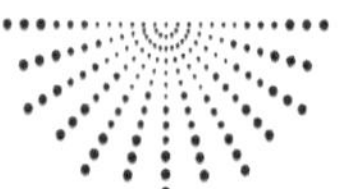

The boarded-up bakery window was a stark reminder of her parents' betrayal every time she looked at it. Fortunately, it didn't seem to have decreased business. If anything, they were busier than ever—according to Ashley, social media was now obsessed with figuring out what had happened to the window.

No one had been in the store, other than Cash, last night, so it was a total mystery.

The most popular theories had to do with the 'big beefy soldier-looking guys' going in and out of the bakery all day.

Ashley's favorite conspiracy theory was the one where the mob had targeted Cupcakes and Crumbs, and now all the muscular men going in and out were security. They were sort of half right, except it was Audrey's parents, not the mob. Though sometimes it seemed like they weren't that far off from each other.

Between the business of the bakery customers coming in and out and the way Audrey's mind kept drifting to Mason and the night before, it was strange but welcome that her parents' betrayal was not at the top of her mind. Keeping up with the steady stream of customers took most of her attention, and the way her body was still humming from Mason's domination took the majority of the rest of it.

Last night, he'd decided that she needed to be distracted from what her parents had done and had gone about providing that distraction in the most delightful ways possible. He'd stripped her naked, covering her in kisses, before laying her down on his bed and explaining 'honor bondage', something she hadn't come across in one of her books before.

Basically, it meant that instead of actually tying her in the position he wanted her in, he wanted her to hold herself in the position he put her in. Which hadn't sounded that difficult until he'd started touching her with his hands and mouth in ways that made her gasp and writhe. He'd had her hands gripping his headboard, so her upper body was stretched out, and her legs spread wide apart.

She'd been completely open and vulnerable to him—and expected to keep herself that way.

He'd started with his lips on hers, his hands on her breasts, and he was kneeling between her spread thighs—which was how he knew when they started to come together rather than remaining splayed in the position he'd dictated. It had been a slow torture of her senses—every time she'd moved out of position, he'd started all over at her lips again.

The first time he'd almost reached her pussy, she'd moved and nearly cried when he'd moved his lips back to hers.

When he finally reached her pussy, she'd stayed as still as she could, able to focus on nothing but keeping herself still as his tongue slid between her sensitive nether lips, toying with her clit. She'd gasped and moaned and managed to stay still... at which point he finally gave her permission to move again.

Then he'd sucked and nibbled and driven her to orgasm after orgasm while her thighs gripped his head. She cried out, her fingers pulling his hair as her head thrashed back and forth in abject ecstasy. Her legs were draped over his shoulders in a manner that made it easy for him to reach up along her sides to fill his palms with her breasts. Squeezing the soft flesh, he'd pinched and tugged her nipples, all while driving her wild with his tongue, until she was literally begging him to stop because she couldn't take any more.

Only then did he lift his head and move up to slide his thick cock inside her, growling 'one more'. That hadn't seemed possible at first, but as he filled her over and over again, rubbing his body against her swollen, overstimulated clit, she'd found herself crying out and creaming all over his dick for a final time.

Today, she couldn't move without feeling how swollen and sensitive her pussy lips were in the aftermath of his torment. At least her nipples had some protection from accidental stimulation thanks to the padded bra she was wearing.

After the lunch hour, there was finally a bit of a lull, so of course, that's when Audrey's grandmother showed up with her friends Mary and Karen from book club. Cassidy was with them, appearing both amused and apologetic as she hung back behind the trio.

"Why on earth didn't you tell me that you'd been attacked?" Grandma asked, putting her hands on her hips and glaring at Audrey. Despite the shirt she was wearing, which declared she liked her books like she liked her men (which Audrey assumed meant 'thick' and knowing her grandmother probably meant 'dick' and not just 'men'), she was pretty intimidating when she got all riled up like this.

"It wasn't an attack," Audrey protested, in a much lower voice, not wanting her grandmother to make more out of things than they were. Especially when she saw the two young women in the corner, thankfully the only customers currently still in the room, swivel their heads around at the statement. "And please, don't shout."

Grandma narrowed her eyes at Audrey, but she did lower her voice.

"I wasn't shouting. And I'm upset. Your cheating rat of an ex showed up, your parents hired some asshole to throw a brick through your window, and you didn't call me about any of it!" She shook her head. "Just because I'm old doesn't mean I don't want the 4-1-1. I can dig it."

"You know that slang is from decades ago, right?" Cassidy asked, amused.

Grandma put her hands out in front of her, palms side up, and moved them up and down in alternating motions.

"Six seven," she said, drawling the second word.

"I don't know what any of that means, and you sound like a demented version of my grandchild. Talk like a normal person," Mary complained.

"I'm going to keep it up until Audrey apologizes."

Three sets of eyes immediately pinged her with begging looks.

"I'm sorry I didn't call you, Grandma," she said. "I was a little distracted."

Grandma wagged her finger at Audrey. "The only acceptable distraction would be if you were getting ridden hard and put away wet by some hot stud."

Audrey knew her grandmother didn't mean it, she was just looking to be outrageous, but she'd hit so hard on the truth that Audrey couldn't help but jolt in a very different reaction than grandma was likely expecting. A hot blush filled her cheeks, and the urge to run almost would have had her bolting, except there was nowhere she could hide that her grandmother couldn't find her.

"Ooh," Karen said, elbowing Grandma. "I think that's exactly what she was doing! Good for you, dear."

"Wait... who was it?" Grandma said, throwing up her hand and frowning at Audrey. Behind Grandma, Cassidy was now staring at the ceiling, because she obviously had a guess and was trying not to draw attention to herself. "It better not have been that dickbag ex."

"No, I didn't sleep with Cash last night," Audrey replied, immediately offended that her grandmother would guess him. She might be a doormat sometimes, but she wasn't *that* much of a doormat. Mostly.

"Then who?"

"None of your business!"

"That's not 'no one'," Mary said, watching her with interest in her dark eyes.

Audrey had no idea how she was going to escape this situation when the door to the bakery opened again. She prayed for divine intervention in the form of a customer, hoping against hope that it wasn't Mason because she was fairly certain her face would give it away…

Worse.

It was so much worse.

She gulped as Yasmine walked through the doorway. Effortlessly chic in her usual winter coat that made her look like she'd just stepped off the runway, her hair was straight down to her shoulders, where it developed a gentle curl. She took off her sunglasses as she walked in. Forget the runway, it was like she was starring in her own private movie.

And having her walk in right at this moment…

For Audrey, it was the worst timing possible. If someone was watching this as a movie, they might be howling with laughter… or cheering for Yasmine to tear her a new one.

Oh God… does she know? Does she not know? Which would be worse? How do I act?

Why is my life like this?

She wouldn't trade this new life for her old life, but sometimes, she wished there was a third option. So far, most of those moments involved Yasmine.

"Hey, Audrey," Yasmine smiled.

She must not know. Crap.

"Hi," Audrey replied weakly, trying to ignore the suddenly suspicious looks her grandmother was shooting between her and Yasmine. "How are you?"

"I've been better." Yasmine eyed the group of women. "Hello, ladies. Can you give Audrey and me a moment? I need to talk to her about something."

That was enough for Grandma to make the wild, and entirely too accurate, leap to the right conclusion. She gaped at Audrey. Mary and Karen appeared confused, but were watching intently.

"It was *Mason?*" she asked in a thunderstruck voice. Then she spun around and caught Cassidy staring at the ceiling. She pointed an accusing finger. "You knew! You knew, and you didn't tell me!"

Yasmine's lips twitched with amusement, but it didn't reach her dark eyes. She cocked her head at Audrey.

"Maybe you have somewhere in the back we could talk?"

"Sure." On the list of people she wanted to be alone with to talk today, Yasmine ranked barely above her parents and Cash, but Audrey didn't have a choice. She owed Yasmine… something. She didn't know what, but something.

If Yasmine wanted to yell at her, she was just going to have to deal with it.

Taking a deep breath, Audrey turned around, giving Ashley a little wave. Ashley gave her a sympathetic look, then greeted Yasmine as they went past. All while Audrey's stomach roiled, and she had to work to keep her shoulders from hunching in.

She closed the door to the office behind them. If there was going to be a confrontation, she was going to need the space and privacy to cry without everyone else knowing about it.

"Do you want to take a seat?" she asked, gesturing to the chairs. "Can I get you something to drink?"

"I'm good, thanks," Yasmine said, settling gracefully into one of the chairs. "I won't be long. I just wanted to come by because Mason called me this morning. He wanted to let me know that the two of you are together, and he wanted me to hear it from him and not the gossip train."

Oh. Well, that was nice of him. Except why hadn't he told Audrey that he was going to do that? Would it have killed him to give her a heads-up?

A little kernel of anger lodged in her gut that he'd set her up like this.

But she couldn't deal with that right now. Yasmine was still sitting right in front of her.

"I'm so sorry," Audrey said, pressing her hands together in front of her as she sank down into the chair across from Yasmine. She was at a loss about what to say after that. Should she offer to stop things with Mason? She didn't want to, even though she was kinda mad at him right now. But maybe she should.

Yasmine blinked.

"About what?"

"About..." Audrey floundered. "About me and Mason. And not telling you. Although he said that you wanted a month before hearing about him with someone else." So it wasn't really her fault; she'd been trying to respect Yasmine's wishes.

"Technically, I asked for a month before *seeing* him with someone else," Yasmine said with amusement. "But you don't have to apologize. I knew you two were going to end up together."

"You did?" Even as Audrey said the words, she remembered how she'd felt like Yasmine had been pushing her toward Mason, maybe even giving her blessing. Though she hadn't come right out and said it like that.

"You two are either very dense or were very much in denial." Yasmine shook her head. "I'll admit, it was beyond me to flat-out say 'go hook up with my ex', but I really did think I was pretty clear."

"You were," Audrey reassured her, even though she hadn't been sure at the time.

Yasmine eyed her but didn't comment on the fact that obviously Audrey hadn't believed her.

"Anyway. Mason assured me that he'd let you know I'm fine with everything, happy for you, actually, but I had a minute and wanted to come say it in person."

Because she was nice. Too nice. So nice it made Audrey's heart hurt for her, knowing her own happiness was coming at Yasmine's expense.

"Thank you." That didn't seem quite right. "I really am sorry, though."

"Stop apologizing." Yasmine shook her head. "It's my own fault. I'm the one who thought I'd found a workaround to the curse. I set myself up for this."

"You couldn't possibly have known that Mason and I would... well... I mean, we didn't do anything before you two broke up, but..." Audrey fumbled over her words before sputtering to a stop and dragging in a deep breath.

"I know you didn't." How could Yasmine be so calm when Audrey was a hot mess, and Yasmine was the one who had been wronged? "But I know how my curse works. I've had enough experience with it."

"Well, we'll do whatever we need to in order to make you comfortable," Audrey said quickly. "More than a month, if you don't want to see us together. And we don't have to go back to the club at all."

Although she wanted to, if only to learn more about kink and be with their friends, but whatever Yasmine wanted, she would do.

"I'm fine, and you guys shouldn't avoid the club. I'm not planning on going back there for a while, anyway."

"But… I thought you had a good scene with Master Cole…" Audrey felt even worse now, no matter what Yasmine said.

"I did. But I also think I need a break from the club. Do you know how many of my exes are there?" Yasmine shook her head. "Too many. I'm going to start doing some of the house parties with Jennifer when I need to scratch the kink itch. I told Mason that, too."

"I'm sorry."

"If you apologize one more time, I'm going to start keeping a count and telling Mason to spank you for each time." Yasmine eyed her.

Audrey pressed her lips together to keep from apologizing for apologizing. She didn't want to make Yasmine have to tell her ex to spank Audrey. Even if it was Yasmine's idea. As threats went, it made for a really good one.

Yasmine's lips quirked up in a small smile.

"Anyway. That's what I wanted to come say. Friends?"

"Of course!" Relief flooded Audrey, and she opened her arms as she got to her feet. Yasmine stood up into her hug and squeezed her back as Audrey hugged her fiercely. She felt a lot lighter than she had before. "Thank you for coming and telling me yourself."

"You're welcome." Yasmine pulled back and smiled at her. There was still sadness in her eyes, but she was clearly trying. Maybe Audrey could try to find someone to set her up with. "I'll see you at book club?"

"I'll be there." Though the reminder of book club made her want to stay in the office and hide, because once Yasmine left, she was going to have to go face her grandmother. She could only imagine that Cassidy would have updated her, Mary, and Karen by now on the triangle of awkward between Yasmine, Mason, and Audrey.

Hopefully, it wouldn't be as awkward after this.

Audrey let Yasmine out of the office, giving her another hug goodbye, then shut the door firmly behind her. She still needed to yell at Mason for not giving her a heads-up. That was a good reason for staying in. It wasn't avoiding her grandma; it was dealing with something else that needed to be dealt with.

Except when she opened her phone, she realized she'd had it on Do Not Disturb, and there were two missed calls from Mason, along with a voicemail and several texts.

He'd tried to get in touch with her.

Which was better, right? Even though it meant she had to go face her grandma sooner rather than later.

But she could put it off a little longer by giving him a call back and telling him that Yasmine had stopped by.

CHAPTER THIRTY-NINE

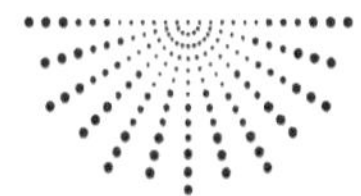

"Do you feel like you've failed the team recently?"

His phone buzzed in his pocket, vibrating next to his thigh, but it was the exact wrong time for him to pull it out and look at it.

Sometimes, Mason pulled his team members in for a talk in his office, but often, it was better to have these kinds of talks outside of it. A lot of them became more talkative when they had something to focus on outside of themselves. And with the amount of time Drew had been spending in the gym or training lately, that was where Mason knew he could catch them.

The question was direct because Mason wanted to see Drew's reaction more than he wanted to hear the other man's response—the wince, the way his gaze averted, the way he hunched in for a moment.

Yeah. He felt like he'd failed them.

"No, I've done everything I was supposed to do," Drew said, as if repeating the words by rote. He'd certainly heard them enough times from Lincoln, David, and Mason. He cast his gaze around the weights in front of him, as though he was focused on trying to decide which he was going to use.

Picking up two of the hand weights, Drew grunted, rolling his shoulders.

Mason felt his phone vibrate in his pocket but ignored it. Drew had been putting this conversation off for a long time now, and Mason wasn't going to let it keep happening.

"You don't sound very convincing when you say that," Mason pointed out, picking up two lighter weights. There was a reason Drew's call sign was 'Sporty', and that was before he'd started his aggressive workout sessions after David was shot.

"What do you want me to say, Mason?" Drew started doing bicep curls, glaring at the wall rather than looking in the mirror. Probably because if he looked in the mirror, Mason would have been able to meet his gaze. "Do you want me to say I fucked up with Cassidy? That I should have reported her flat tire earlier? Stayed on her ass for every second after that, even though we thought her ex couldn't possibly know where she was since we found the trackers? And then maybe David wouldn't have been shot?"

He rolled his shoulders, shaking his head, as his pace picked up. He had perfect form, but he was moving too quickly.

"Do you want me to say that I let some asshole get the drop on me, and now we don't know if we can trust one of our own team members because he might have been the one to knock me out? And we still don't know what Devlin was doing in our office?"

Mason remained silent because he knew if he spoke, Drew would shut down again. Probably for good this time. Right now, he was getting up some steam, the words coming fast and furious and probably without too much thought. His guilt had been pent up for a while now. It was no surprise to Mason that Drew blamed himself for Cassidy almost getting kidnapped and David being shot, even though no one else did. It didn't surprise him that Drew was pissed off and feeling guilty about being knocked out in the office and not even having a glimpse of who his attacker was.

"Do you want me to admit that I've fucked up, over and over and over again now, and that I haven't been able to make it up to the team?"

Puffing, Drew growled as he put the weights back on the rack with a loud clang.

"What do you want me to say, Posh? I fucked up. I failed the team. I can't be relied on. Is that what you want to hear?" He looked away, his mouth shutting, jaw clenching, as he cut himself off from saying anything more.

"I would like to hear you say that you did do everything right and mean it," Mason said gently. "And that it could have happened to anyone, and maybe we were lucky because if not for you, we might not have even known someone was in the office."

"Sure. I did everything right. And it could have happened to anyone. But it happened to me." Grabbing his towel from the side of the rack, Drew flipped it over his shoulder and stalked out of the room without looking at Mason again.

Mason sighed. That could have gone better. Could have gone worse, too.

Reaching into his pocket, he pulled out his phone. One missed call from Audrey. A smile crept across his face, unbidden, which was odd. He wasn't the type of person to smile just because he was getting a call from someone. Especially when he wasn't sure how she was going to feel about the voice message he'd left her.

He'd realized this morning that he wanted Yasmine to hear about him and Audrey from him before the gossip train caught up with her. He didn't have anything to hide, not really, and he was pretty sure she wasn't going to be surprised by the news, but it seemed courteous. But he'd also wanted to let Audrey know he was doing that. Unfortunately, she hadn't answered any of his calls or texts—probably too busy at the bakery—so he'd left her a voicemail about what he was doing.

As much as he'd wanted to wait to be able to hold back from Yasmine, he knew how quickly word of him and Audrey was going to spread after last night. The whole team knew. If Drew didn't go home and tell Naomi, and David didn't go home and tell Cassidy, and Lincoln didn't go home and tell Ashley, Mason would eat the barbells in front of him. There was no way to put the cat back in the bag after last night, and someone was going to say something to Yasmine, probably sooner rather than later.

He'd wanted to be the one to do it, and once he'd had the thought, he hadn't been able to wait.

Hopefully, Audrey would understand. If not, he would apologize and explain why.

She hadn't left a voicemail, so Mason was about to call her back to do exactly that when David came into the gym, closing the door behind him. Raising his eyebrows, Mason put his phone back in his pocket as David faced him and cleared his throat.

"Can we talk?"

"Of course. What did you want to talk about?"

Considering Drew had just left, it could be about him. Or possibly Zeus. But most likely it was about…

"My sister," David said flatly, crossing his arms over his chest.

Mason let out his breath in a whoosh of air. Yeah, he'd figured that was coming, although he still wasn't sure what to do about it. He didn't want to piss off his friend, much less his team leader, but he also wasn't giving Audrey up. She was unexpected, inconvenient, and he was determined to keep her.

"Cassidy has told me it's none of my business, and I see her point, but Audrey is my sister. And she's already been through a lot."

"I know."

"So, I need to know you're serious about her."

Well, shit, was that all?

"I wouldn't have touched her if I wasn't serious about her," Mason said, ignoring the fact that he'd started things off with her by talking about being friends with benefits. Even then, he'd known it was going to be more than that; he just hadn't been ready to admit it yet.

Not that he was going to admit it to her yet, either, not until he was sure she felt the same way about him.

"You were literally engaged to Yasmine less than a month ago; you'll have to excuse me if I have some concerns about that statement." Though from the relief that flickered across David's expression, he did believe Mason; he was just determined to give him a hard time. Mason didn't have a little sister, but he supposed that was David's right as a big brother. He could at least understand being protective of Audrey because he was, too.

"I was. You know me. You know I cared about Yasmine even though I wasn't in love with her. Do you really think I would risk hurting her and angering you just to mess around with your sister?"

David opened his mouth. Closed it. The expression on his face turned decidedly grumpy.

"That's a really good fucking point," he grumbled. "Look, I just don't want to see her hurt again. And I sure as hell don't want her going back to Philly and that viper's nest."

"Then we're on the same page." Mason spread his hands out wide, trying to look harmless. Like the kind of guy a brother would be happy to see his sister with, if that was possible.

"Right. Good." David sighed and then made a face. "Are you guys going to be playing at the club?"

"I think Audrey's more of a private room kind of person."

His friend groaned, raking his fingers through his hair. "I'm not sure I even wanted to know that much."

Before Mason could say anything else, the red light next to the door started flashing. Both he and David exchanged startled looks, then David was yanking the door open, bolting down the hallway with Mason hot on his heels to find out why Jennifer had set off the silent alarm.

They weren't the only ones headed to the front; the whole team was on the move, and Mason skidded to a halt behind David when they reached the front, Jensen right behind him.

Fuck. What was the FBI doing here?

AUDREY

Mason hadn't answered her call and still hadn't gotten back to her. Something must be up at work. She hoped. Which was why she was in the back with Alexis, pounding out her frustration into some bread dough, even though the bakery didn't normally sell loaves of bread. She needed something to do with her hands, or she was going to go nuts.

Alexis kept giving her sidelong looks, as though she was a little worried about her, but she didn't say anything. That was another reason Audrey was in the back. Ashley would have pushed her to talk, customers or no customers. Alexis let her work in peace. Even though Grandma and her friends had finally left, it was safer back here.

A sudden commotion of noise, loud voices, in the front had them both lifting their heads. They looked at each other for a long moment, but it only got louder. Audrey patted her dough and decided it was time for it to take a rest, anyway. Grabbing a cloth to set over it, she headed to the front to find out what the heck was going on.

The bakery was filled with large, muscular, angry men. And Claudia and Darcy. Thankfully, it must have been a lull because there were only a couple of customers seated at the tables and someone else on their way out the door.

"What are you all doing here?" Audrey asked, startled, and her heart did a little hop, jump, and skip when her gaze met Mason's. His jaw was locked, his expression grim, but it lightened a bit when he looked at her. Shouldering his way through the crowd, he made his way to her as David answered.

"The FBI kicked us out of the office." Her brother looked like he was about to explode, he was so pissed off. "They got an anonymous tip about us."

"Oh my God." Audrey covered her mouth with her hands as Mason reached her and put his arm around her. "About *what* though? What could you have done?"

"Nothing."

"Nothing," Lincoln confirmed from behind her counter, where he had just finished giving his wife a greeting kiss. To Audrey's surprise, he was grinning. She felt Mason jerk in surprise as well when he looked over and saw his boss. "But they would have found something if not for Zeus."

Everyone's gaze turned to the muscular bald man who had been hanging back next to the broken front window, a slight space between him and the rest of the teams. He blinked back at them, his neutral expression not changing one iota.

"The break-in wasn't about taking something; it was about leaving something. Namely, some of the files Marshall kept on the side about some of the things he was actually doing under Black Fox's banner." Lincoln's expression hardened, and Ashley leaned into him, offering support and solace for the betrayal of his one-time friend and business partner. "They'd been slightly altered to remove any mention of him and to put the blame solely on us."

"So, they aren't going to find anything?" Drew asked, appearing more worried than ever but also hopeful. Relieved. He kept shooting little glances over at Zeus, who remained utterly nonchalant. Audrey glanced up at Mason, but he wasn't looking at her; he was watching Drew closely.

"No," Lincoln confirmed. "Zeus found it and reported it to me, and we removed it with Jaxon's help. We didn't say anything to anyone else except Harris because we weren't sure what was going to happen or why it had been planted."

Audrey glanced over at her other customers, who were watching everything warily, but Lincoln didn't seem to care if they could over-hear. Thankfully, none of them had their cameras out as far as she could tell. Not that she wasn't grateful for the business the viral videos had brought in, but she had that business, and she didn't want Black Fox to be affected by the social media attention unless she was sure they'd be okay with it.

"Where is Harris?" Ashley asked, looking around.

"He stayed to represent us until Jordana could get there."

"Who's Jordana?" Audrey whispered to Mason, as everyone else nodded as if that made sense.

"Harris and Lincoln's lawyer and Harris' nemesis," Mason murmured, the corner of his mouth lifting. He was watching Zeus now, and Zeus was staring at the ceiling with a bored expression, not doing anything. Audrey couldn't figure out what Mason found so interesting about him. She knew that the team didn't trust him, but he'd just saved the day… right?

"Why is Harris meeting her instead of Lincoln if she's Harris' nemesis?" she whispered back, not sure she could ask about Zeus right now.

"That's why."

She didn't understand, but okay.

"Thanks for saving our asses, Pepper," Jensen said, stepping close enough to Zeus to be able to clap him on the shoulder. "Appreciate it."

Zeus considered him for a moment before giving a slow nod. His mouth may have softened slightly. Not a smile, but not totally emotionless anymore, either.

"You're welcome."

"So, what do we do now?" Darcy, from Harris' team, asked.

"We wait." Lincoln looked at Audrey. "We were hoping you wouldn't mind us waiting here since you're so close by."

"Of course," she replied immediately, as if she would have kicked them out now. Out of the corner of her eye, she saw one of the men in the corner lift his phone up slightly, as if he was taking a picture. Inwardly, she sighed, but at least he lowered it immediately, so it wasn't a video.

And it wasn't like Black Fox didn't know that they were considered desirable sightings to the bakery's customers.

"Great." Claudia was hanging out by the display of baked goods with an anxious-looking Jennifer. Jensen slid over to where they were, putting his arm around Jennifer, and she leaned into him. She'd probably been pretty freaked out when the FBI came in. "Who wants a cupcake while we wait?"

CHAPTER FORTY

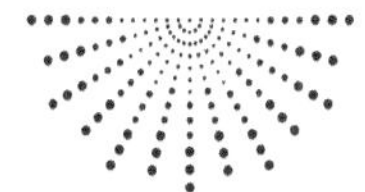

AUDREY

The bakery was flooded with people not long after the Black Fox team sat down to enjoy their food. Word spread quickly that the hot, muscular guys were there. Not just that, but several men had shown up for the gorgeous women as well. Even through the rush, Audrey could see Grant glaring at the two men who were sitting with Darcie, Claudia, and Jennifer. Unlike the other men who had dared to attempt a conversation, these two seemed to know Claudia—one of them looked enough like her that Audrey guessed they were related—and weren't chased off so easily.

At some point, the team started trickling out, either bored and accepting that the FBI search was going to take longer than expected or because they had things they could do elsewhere. Eventually, it was just Claudia and Mason left, and the press of customers had slowed down to a trickle again.

The other two men were still sitting there, and Audrey was curious enough to go say hello.

"Well, hello there," the handsome man who didn't resemble Claudia said, twisting in his seat to give her a flirtatious look up and down. He had blond hair and warm hazel eyes that sparked with intelligence and mischief. His clean-shaven chin showed off his square-cut jaw, and she was pretty sure the way his shoulders filled out his suit jacket needed no padding.

If she wasn't already enamored of Mason, she would have been blushing. She wasn't sure she wasn't.

"I hear you're the owner of this fine establishment."

"I am." Audrey wiped her hands on her apron, bemused, and very aware of the way Mason's eyes were now narrowing at the other man.

"Yes, this is Audrey," Claudia said. "Audrey, this pain in the ass is my brother's best friend, Ian, and this is my brother Miguel." Confirmed. The man who looked so much like Claudia was her brother. He was just as handsome as Ian, though with a browner skin tone and dark hair and eyes, and his smile as he said hello wasn't full of flirtation.

"Hello," Audrey said again with a little wave, starting to sidle closer to where Mason was seated. He was on the other side of the table— he'd been watching her while she was working, and she'd been very aware of his gaze the whole time—but it meant that he was across from her now.

It required her to move past Ian, though, and he grabbed her hand as she did.

"I just have to tell you, I love your buns." He grinned up at her and winked, tilting his head to the side to where half a cinnamon bun was left.

Audrey pressed her lips together to keep from bursting into laughter because Mason was now gripping his plastic knife and looking like he might actually be pissed off.

"Leave the poor girl alone, you walking venereal disease. She has a boyfriend," Claudia snapped, whacking the back of the hand Ian was using to hold Audrey's with the plastic fork she was holding.

"Ouch!" Ian released Audrey's hand and shook his fingers out, still grinning, and apparently, completely as unperturbed by Claudia's insult and minor violence as he was by her rebuke. "Careful, Claudia, you know I like it when you talk dirty to me."

She rolled her eyes and looked between Mason and Audrey as

Audrey scooted closer to him. Immediately, his arm went out and around her waist, pulling her down onto his lap. She squeaked in surprise, but she wasn't unhappy about it.

"Ignore him," Claudia advised. "He'd flirt with a coat rack if it had boobs."

"Hey, now," Ian protested. "I'd want it to have an ass, too." He cupped his hands in front of him, like he was cupping a woman's bottom. "A really nice one."

Claudia eyed him like she'd eye a particularly gross piece of trash on the ground, and Ian grinned back at her. From the way her brother was ignoring them, Audrey assumed this was how they usually were together. There was a little something different about the way Ian flirted with Claudia than he had been with her, though. Something in his eyes.

Were they exes? Or had they hooked up once?

Maybe she'd asked Mason later.

If she dared. Getting into Claudia's business seemed like a dangerous proposition. And Mason might not know, anyway.

But there was something there; she'd be willing to swear it.

"Ignore him," Mason murmured in her ear. "Claudia's not wrong about him."

Actually, what she really needed to ask Mason about was Claudia calling him Audrey's boyfriend and him not correcting her.

She wasn't sure she dared to do that either, though.

Was he her boyfriend? They hadn't talked about that. She would like it if he was. It wasn't like everyone didn't know about them now. And he was acting very boyfriend-y. She liked texting him. She liked sleeping with him. She would like to spend more time with him.

Audrey shifted on his lap, and his grip on her tightened, as if he was worried she was going to get up, which she would need to do, eventually.

"Any word about the office?" she asked.

"Lincoln and Harris are there now with Jordana. They've told us to just do our own things until tomorrow and to come back in then." Claudia shrugged. "I just don't have anything to do."

"I volunteer as tribute," Ian quipped with a wink.

Miguel made a gagging noise. "Bro, you do not want to even go there. You have no idea what she likes to do to men, and I seriously wish I didn't." He shuddered, which made Claudia snicker.

"But you learned your lesson about letting yourself into my house without giving me a heads-up, didn't you?"

"There's not enough bleach in the world to clean out my eyeballs," Miguel grumbled. "I still have nightmares."

"What does she do?" Audrey whispered in Mason's ear. Claudia hadn't really talked much about her preferences during book club or anything. She knew Claudia was the dominant, so she was in charge in her relationships... maybe Miguel had just seen her having sex with someone, but it seemed like more than that.

"She likes cock and ball torture," Mason murmured back, and Audrey felt his tiny shudder, although she wasn't sure if she would have noticed if she hadn't been sitting on him. He hid his discomfort well. She stared at Claudia, fascinated. What would that even look like? "Don't even think about getting any ideas. I get to torture you, not the other way around."

Audrey giggled as he gave her a squeeze.

Maybe he was her boyfriend? She hoped he was.

Mason

The next few days, Mason's life felt like it had changed completely.

The entire team was on edge, but also feeling triumphant after getting one over on Devlin. Of course, Mason couldn't help but wonder if Zeus had been the one to find the planted information because he'd been the one to plant it... He seemed to be the only one who was that paranoid, though. Even Drew was making more of an effort to exchange greetings with the man.

None of that changed Zeus' demeanor. He was the same as ever. At some point, Mason wanted to do a deep dive with him, but short of forcing him into a chair, he wasn't sure how to make it happen. He couldn't *prove* Zeus was avoiding him... but somehow he managed to never be alone with Mason.

Mostly, though, there was a new focus of determination, especially with an upcoming event for the senator where they would be providing her with extra security. MacLeod would be there too, which meant Devlin would most likely be there with him. Hopefully, frothing at the mouth at being thwarted and not smugly satisfied that his trick to make them trust Zeus had worked.

That wasn't the biggest change, though.

The biggest was Audrey.

The daily texts.

The fact that he missed her on the nights they weren't together.

That he couldn't stop thinking about her, even at work, where he'd always been good at compartmentalizing his personal life away from where his focus needed to be.

Part of him was freaked out about it. He'd never been like this with a woman before... but that had been true about her from the beginning. And he couldn't stop. Couldn't get enough of her. It felt like he was a plant and she was the sun, and he finally knew what it was like to bask in its warmth.

But he really couldn't stay away, which was how he ended up at her bakery Tuesday evening, waiting for her to get off work so they could spend the evening together. Brenda was there with her friends when he walked in, and she immediately waved him over. Ashley smirked at him from behind the counter. Audrey was nowhere in sight, which meant she was probably in the back with Alexis.

"Hello, Mason, have a seat." The gleam in Brenda's eye could mean a lot of things, but Mason found himself oddly intimidated.

"Uh, well, I was going to get... something." He waved his hand toward the display case of goodies to his side.

He was met by three gimlet stares.

"Sit," Brenda ordered.

Mason sat. When Brenda was being serious, he wasn't going to mess around.

She reminded him of an old-time gangster with the way she

folded her hands in front of her and leaned forward to give him a hard-eyed look, regardless of the sky-blue sweater with a giant rooster she was wearing. Especially with Mary and Karen on either side of her, also giving him their best stern gazes. Mafia grandmas, all of them.

"I would like to know what your intentions with my grand-daughter are." Brenda arched her eyebrows at him.

"Well, we're still getting to know each other-"

"Skip the flummery, Mason. I expect I don't have much time with you before she comes out," Brenda said, waving her hand.

Well, there was a word he'd never heard used in real life before. But he knew what she meant.

"I like her, Brenda. A lot." He spread his hands wide. "I don't agree with Yasmine that she's cursed, and that's why none of her relationships work out, but as for the person she was with finding *their* person after she breaks up with them... there's a possibility that pattern is holding."

Which was the closest he'd come to admitting out loud how much Audrey already meant to him. Even though it didn't make sense. Even though they hadn't known each other that long. Even though, on paper, he and Yasmine checked more boxes. He didn't know if what he and Audrey wanted out of life aligned.

It was a conversation that would need to happen eventually, but not until he was ready to admit to her that his feelings already went far beyond 'fuck buddy' status and that they were doing this for real. Though he supposed he'd already sort of told her when Claudia had told Ian that Mason was Audrey's boyfriend. But it was important to him to define actual boundaries at some point.

Once he figured out how to do it.

And maybe just a little more time to make sure the emotions were still sticking. Just in case.

Karen, Brenda, and Mary all leaned forward, but toward each other, not him, speaking in low voices, even though he could hear them clearly.

"He doesn't sound very sure," Mary said, sounding skeptical.

"Maybe he's worried about her brother?" Karen suggested. She glanced at him. "I think he can take him, though."

Somehow, Mason managed to keep a straight face.

"He could probably hold his own with David; maybe he's worried he can't keep Audrey satisfied in bed after Yasmine left him." Brenda eyed him as if daring him to say something.

"I never slept with Yasmine," he said, unable to keep himself from interjecting when his sexual prowess was being maligned. "Audrey is perfectly happy with my performance in bed."

At which point, all three women cast him such assessing gazes, he suddenly felt very uncomfortable, as if they could see through his clothes and possibly get a gander at his sexual stats somehow. He crossed his legs, just in case.

"Grandma! What are you doing?" Audrey's voice was slightly shrill and from a bit of a distance. Relief and anticipation flushed through him in equal measure, and he turned in to see her rushing out of the back, wiping flour off her hands with a small towel.

Immediately, Brenda and her friends sat up straight with big smiles on their faces and looks of such completely false innocence that a grand jury would have convicted them by their expressions alone.

"Hi, honey! We're just having a little chat with your man here." Brenda's chirpy voice wasn't fooling anyone, especially Audrey, who moved even faster to come stand by his side.

She looked adorably hot today with her red hair in a low ponytail, rather than a high one, though still tied in place with a polka-dot bow. This one was purple, which matched the purple cable-knit sweater she was wearing under her Cupcakes and Crumbs apron.

Mason wondered if he dared put his arm around her with Brenda's book club watching so closely.

"A chat about what?" Audrey asked suspiciously.

He appreciated her defense of him, though he also cringed inwardly because of what they had been chatting about.

"Oh, you know, this and that," Brenda said, cheerily waving her hand in front of her. For some reason, she didn't want her grand-daughter to know that she'd been questioning Mason about his bedroom prowess, and he chose to be grateful for that. "The boy is a little timid, you know. He should take his cue from Mick. Mick's got a lot of that fat dick spirit."

"It's not fat dick spirit," Mary corrected, rolling her eyes while Mason choked on nothing, and Audrey looked like she wanted to crawl under the table and hide. "It's big dick energy. How do you keep mixing that up?"

"Are you sure?" Brenda asked, frowning. "That seems wrong. How can a dick have energy?"

"The dick doesn't have the energy; the man does. How can a dick have a spirit?"

Mason slipped out of his seat and edged away from the table as the discussion turned to haunted dicks. He slid his fingers into Audrey's, pulling her with him. Either the ladies were too engrossed in their debate to notice, or they didn't care that he and Audrey were leaving.

Just getting out of there, regardless of the reason, was a win as far as Mason was concerned.

"I'm so sorry," Audrey whispered, taking the lead as she pulled him toward the back. Behind the counter, Ashley glanced over and winked at them.

"Not your fault. I should have known better than to go over there." Though he wasn't sure what else he could have done.

They both breathed a sigh of relief as they made it safely to the back. Alexis glanced up from where she was finishing cleaning up her station and smiled shyly at him before ducking her head back down.

"Well, I'm glad you came, even though you had to brave the dragons to do it," Audrey joked. "I feel like most guys would wither away when faced with them."

"It did feel like I had a spotlight on me." He shuddered, following her into the office where she closed the door behind him, then launched herself at him.

Soft curves pressed against him as their lips met, her arms winding around his neck. Desire swelled inside him. She tasted like vanilla and cinnamon, and his cock immediately jerked to attention at the touch of her. Fuck. He really was like a horny teenage boy when it came to her.

When she lowered her heels, no longer on her toes, and their lips parted, she smiled at him with shining eyes that made him feel about ten feet tall.

"Hi."

"Hi." He smiled down at her.

"I'm almost done with work."

"Great. I'm looking forward to you being done with work."

She giggled, but her expression turned a little more pensive.

"Um, so can I talk to you about something?"

A little touch of worry slithered through him, but there was only one answer he could give.

"Of course."

CHAPTER FORTY-ONE

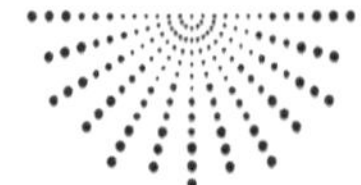

MASON

Mason shouldn't have worried when Audrey said she wanted to talk. In fact, while she was taking a shower and washing off the day, he was very happily setting up for what she wanted.

She wanted what she'd missed out on during her first 'let's try things' scene—namely, the vampire glove.

But also, she'd started reading an age play book called Daddy Devious by Sadie Minx, which she said was 'dark romance' (sounded like kidnapping to him, but he understood the capture fantasy aspect of that), and while she wasn't interested in the age play, she had been intrigued by the disciplinary spankings. She wanted to know the difference between that and the spanking he'd given her.

He was happy to demonstrate, of course.

Add some anal beads to the mix, for his own pleasure, and it should be a fun night. Though maybe a little less for her since it was supposed to be a disciplinary spanking.

He even had a good reason. On the way to his place, she'd admitted that she'd been upset at him for not telling her that he was going to tell Yasmine about them, right up until she'd realized that he *had* tried to contact her. So, he was going to spank her for not putting him on the list of exceptions to her Do Not Disturb.

It wasn't a huge offense, of course, but she wanted a disciplinary spanking, and as far as he was concerned, that meant having a reason to discipline her. Without that, it was just another fun-ishment, no matter how hard he spanked her. The feeling of guilt being absolved was a big part of what made a disciplinary spanking different from a regular spanking, as far as he was concerned.

Maybe someone else would disagree with him, which was fine. They could do things their way. Audrey was his, and that's how he was doing things with her.

While he was waiting, his phone buzzed, and he quickly checked the messages. The tension that had been sitting in his chest for several days eased. Lincoln was confirming that the FBI had found nothing in the 'evidence' they'd gathered.

"What's up?" Audrey asked, walking into the living room.

Mason looked up from his phone and felt his heart do a little jump in his chest at the same time his dick came back to life. She was wearing nothing but his bathrobe, a navy-blue terry-cloth robe that emphasized her curves where she'd tied the belt. It was long enough to cover her down to mid-calf. Something about knowing she was naked under that one easily removed item of clothing—*his* clothing— made the fact that she was completely covered somehow even more tantalizing.

He held up his phone.

"Lincoln says we're all clear at the office. The FBI officially has nothing on us."

"Oh, thank goodness." She let out a sigh of relief, her shoulders relaxing. "I know David will be glad to hear that. He's been trying to hide it, but I can tell he's been internally freaking out."

So could Mason, and she was right on the money.

It was a massive relief and one that was going to allow him to enjoy tonight even more than he was already going to.

Opening his arms to her, he smiled as she came right to him, her eyes alight with anticipation, nothing but trust in her expression.

Mason cradled her face between his hands, sliding the tips of his fingers into her damp hair, and tilted her head back so he could press a soft kiss to her lips.

He lifted away from the kiss and looked her directly in her gorgeous green eyes.

"You've been a very naughty cupcake today," he murmured.

Surprise, followed quickly by arousal and apprehension, sparked in her gaze.

"I have?" Her voice quavered, just a touch. Part of her still didn't believe him, he could tell, but she was already moving toward the mindset of a naughty submissive who needed to be punished, so she could be forgiven.

"You didn't pick up when I called."

"I didn't know you were calling!" Understanding sparked in her eyes. "Oh."

Mason nodded solemnly, still holding her in place with gentle hands around her jawline. He swept his thumb over her lower lip.

"You're going to add me to the exceptions list for when your phone is on Do Not Disturb as soon as we're done here."

"Okay," she said breathlessly.

"And you've just earned ten more swats for not calling me 'Sir.'"

"Sorry, Sir!" The words squeaked out, without a hint of amusement or laughter. Which, to Mason's perspective, meant she was in the right frame of mind to receive a little discipline.

"Good girl. Now, let's get this robe off, so I can punish you properly."

She sucked in a breath, shivering even though she was still wearing the robe. There was a slightly dazed look in her eyes. Yeah, if Mason could put down money on it, he would bet that Audrey was the type who would find catharsis in being truly disciplined.

Letting his hands glide downward, Mason slid the robe off her shoulders, letting it split down to where it was tied at her middle, revealing her breasts and simultaneously trapping her arms. He moved his palms over the heavy mounds, cupping them and lifting, rubbing his thumbs over her nipples so she leaned forward, whimpering at the sensations.

"No punishment for these pretty breasts tonight," he said. "I want you to be able to really focus on the spanking."

"Yes, Sir." Her tongue flicked out against her lower lip, and she sighed in appreciation as he gave the heavy globes a rough squeeze before releasing them. Tugging at the knot she'd made with the tie, he pulled it loose, and the whole robe dropped to the floor in a puddle around her feet. Her arms came up to hug herself, and she shivered.

"Cold?" Mason asked.

"No, Sir."

He raised his eyebrow at her. He could already see the goosebumps forming on her skin. Though her nipples were hard from the stimulation, he doubted that was the only reason.

"Um, I mean, yes, Sir," she admitted sheepishly.

"That's ten more for lying."

AUDREY

"But—" She cut off because she couldn't think of a good argument.

Letting the robe drop *had* left her chilly, but she hadn't wanted to make him feel bad. Or be a bother.

She didn't think he was going to accept either as a reasonable excuse.

Even in her head, it wasn't all that reasonable. Why hadn't she just said she was cold?

"Well, let's warm you up, cupcake." Mason turned and sat down on the couch, gesturing for her to put herself over his lap. The vampire glove, what looked like a bunch of beads on a string that grew in size as they went along, a packet of wipes, and two tubes were sitting on the coffee table in front of him.

"I'm not really cold," she said as she put herself over his lap. "It was just the temperature change from being in the robe to getting out of the robe. That's all. Sir."

"But you were chillier when I took the robe off you." He patted her butt almost affectionately. "You'll learn to speak up when you're uncomfortable, sweetness, or I'll keep warming this pretty little bottom for you."

Audrey squirmed on his lap. Was he being like the Daddy in *Daddy Devious*? No, but at the same time, there was a patient, lecturing tone to his voice that made her think of the book. Maybe she didn't feel like a naughty little girl, but she did feel like she'd been naughty.

Would it have killed her to just say she was a little chilly with the robe off?

Now, she was going to get ten more swats.

That I asked for. Because I asked for a disciplinary spanking. He's just coming up with reasons for it to be actual discipline.

But it didn't feel like pretend. It felt real. Especially now that she was over his lap.

She felt him lean forward, pressing his dick against her side, and heard the sound of plastic moving over wood as he picked something up from the coffee table.

"Now, we're going to start with the beads because I want you totally focused on your ass, which is going to be taking your punishment tonight," he said, still in that lecturing tone. He would make a hot professor. And a dirty one.

His finger, wet and slick, pressed against her anus, and she gasped as he pushed in.

They'd done some more anal play since the first time he'd plugged her, all with his fingers, often while he was going down on her, but it made her gasp and squirm every time. She just couldn't get used to the sensation. It was uncomfortable and arousing at the same time, and she felt her pussy flutter as his finger moved in deeper, twisting inside her.

Then his finger slid away, and something hard and rounded pressed at her entrance. It was smaller than his finger and easily slid inside her. The foreign object wasn't big at all, and it felt very odd. Another one began to push against her and also pushed inside her easily enough, as it about matched the circumference of his finger.

The third one made her rock forward on his lap, gasping a little as he pushed it inside her. That one made her entrance burn a bit, a slight sting pinching her as it popped inside her because it was a little bigger.

"Oh…" She felt her pussy clench as the fourth one began to push in, stretching her wider, making her muscles try to push all of them back out again. They were going in deeper now, too, giving her more of the sensation of being filled in her rear channel, which was perversely unsettling.

"Take a deep breath, cupcake."

She did, doing her best to relax, and moaned as the fourth one joined the three previous. It was big, and the feeling of fullness was almost too much.

"Last one."

The biggest one.

Audrey closed her eyes, her head hanging down toward the carpet, as the tight ring protested being stretched open again. The beads weren't tapered like the plug had been, and being forced open to new dimensions for what hadn't looked like that large a ball but now felt like Mason was trying to push a tennis ball up her ass did actually hurt…

But it felt good, too.

She cried out as it was pushed inside her, panting for breath once it was settled within. Something brushed against the inside of her thigh, and she was pretty sure it was the ring at the end of the string of beads that she'd seen—something he could easily hook his finger into in order to pull them out of her.

Just the thought made her shiver.

What was that going to feel like?

"Good girl," Mason said approvingly, sending a warm flush of heat through her as he patted her bottom. There was a small crinkle of plastic as he got a wipe to clean his fingers. "Now, it's time for your spanking. Let's say, twenty for not answering my call—or for not making me an exception on your DND if you prefer, ten for not calling me 'Sir', and ten more for lying."

"It was only a little lie," she protested, because forty sounded like an awful lot. His hand smacked against her bottom, hard enough to sting, and she squealed.

"That doesn't count as one of them," he warned her. Which meant it was really going to be forty-one.

Audrey wisely bit her lip against saying that *he* was the liar. That would not go well for her, she was sure of it.

"Count them as we go, cupcake."

His hand came down on her upturned bottom, hard. Much harder than he'd spanked her before, not just tonight but previously. Normally, he worked up to this force; he didn't start with it. Audrey's heart jumped into her throat as her butt clenched around the beads, already wondering what she'd gotten herself into.

"Start counting, or you're going to get more that also aren't part of the official count," he warned her.

"Um, one, Sir," she managed to gasp out, just barely catching herself from starting at two.

"Good girl."

Then his hand came down again on her other cheek, and she squealed, bucking forward before she remembered.

"Two, Sir!"

Audrey wasn't sure if it was the counting, the fact he had started at a more forceful spanking, or knowing she really had been a little naughty, but this felt so different. It wasn't as sexy, yet she was becoming aroused as his hand came down again and again, and she counted out each and every swat.

Her cheeks clenched around the beads every time, her toes curled, and her bottom was starting to feel like it was on fire by the time they reached twenty. The halfway mark. Tears stung her eyes and slid down her face, dripping to the carpet beneath her.

A gentle hand rubbed over her burning bottom, surprising her as he paused.

"Halfway there, cupcake, how are you doing?"

"Well, my butt hurts. Sir."

That startled a laugh from him, but really, what else was she supposed to say? It freaking hurt!

"You have twenty more to go," he said, still rubbing her bottom, which both stung a little and felt good, as though he was soothing it. "Do you want to use your safe word?"

He was offering her an out. Reminding her of it, really, just in case she'd forgotten.

Audrey felt the tightness of the skin where her tears had tracked over it. The heat of her burning bottom. The way her muscles clenched around the plug. The throbbing between her thighs.

Did she want to stop?

Get to the more pleasurable stuff?

She'd done the initial twenty.

Did she really feel like she deserved twenty for her little lie and for forgetting to call him 'Sir'?

Maybe.

Maybe part of her just wanted to see if she could handle it; maybe part of her was enjoying this, even though she also thought she was crazy to; maybe part of her just needed the catharsis of getting it all out.

"No, Sir." She took a deep breath, readying herself. "I want to finish it."

"Brave girl. These last twenty won't be as hard."

It didn't matter, though. Her cheeks were already on fire, so every swat felt like burning. She cried out. Squirmed. Counted. Wondered if she was insane for asking him to continue. But she didn't want him to stop. Some part of her craved it.

Needed it.

And when she counted the fortieth, she burst into raw sobbing that had nothing to do with the physical pain.

CHAPTER FORTY-TWO

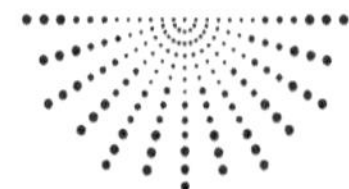

AUDREY

"Hey. Deep breath." Mason pulled Audrey up onto his lap, and she snuggled right in, still weeping onto his shoulder. His hand rubbed her back. "Let it out, sweetness."

"I'm sorry," she replied, hiccupping as she tried to suppress the tears. "I'm sorry."

"For what?" He cradled her against him, one arm wrapped around her back for support, the other over her legs, so he could rest his palm on the hot skin of her ass. Audrey could feel his cock digging into her from the side, so at least she hadn't completely ruined things for him.

"I thought it would be more sexy and less crying." She sniffled.

Chuckling, Mason leaned over to the side of the couch where there was a box of tissues and grabbed it for her. She took two at once and started trying to wipe herself clean.

"I think you needed it," he said. "And I find you plenty sexy. Disciplinary spankings aren't necessarily sexy, you know."

"Well, it was in my head."

That made him laugh again, and he tightened his grip on her as she huffed in annoyance. The steady warmth of his body against hers, the way he held her, made her feel a lot better. Even if he was laughing at her.

"You've had a lot going on. I think you needed to get it out."

He wasn't wrong. Audrey felt depleted but also better. Like a cloud that had gathered up too much moisture and finally let loose with the rain. She still made another 'humph' noise because she didn't like crying. Especially when she ruined something that was supposed to be sexy because she was crying.

His fingers moved over her skin, stroking her, and she shivered. Thanks to the spanking, her butt felt tenderized but also extra sensitive. Which could have been bad, but the way he was touching her right now felt very, very good.

"I think I did, too," she said, even though she felt like she'd been crying too much lately.

Crying over the brick through her bakery window.

Crying over her parents.

But she'd always managed to pull herself back from crying *too much*. At least, that's how it had felt. Now, she realized she might have needed to cry a little more.

As the tears dried up, something else was stirring inside her, helped along by Mason's gentle stroking. Something that made her realize she hadn't ruined sexy time. Just delayed it a few moments. Which Mason didn't seem to mind.

"Feeling better?" he asked, seeming to have noticed that she was more in control. She nodded.

"Good."

Audrey squeaked as the arm behind her moved, taking away her support, so she fell back against the couch.

"Arms up above your head."

Sucking in a breath, she obeyed. Her butt was still across his thighs, hot and throbbing on his lap, but her upper body was now stretched out on the couch, one of her legs on the other side, the other bent at the knee and hanging down over his legs.

All of her was exposed to him, although her legs weren't wide enough for him to really be able to access her pussy. Audrey caught her breath and thanked her lucky stars for that when he reached across her to pick up the vampire glove and pull it on. It suddenly looked even more wicked than it had while it was lying innocuously across from her, as he flexed his hand and met her gaze.

There was a slight curve to his lips, a sadistic gleam in his eye that made her quail and want to whimper. Yet she held herself in position, waiting to find out what he was going to do to her.

Trusting him with her body.

But she still tilted her head back when the claws moved toward her face.

They landed just beneath her neck, over her collarbone, and Audrey whimpered as the sharp tips pricked against her skin and began to slide down between her breasts. Her nipples puckered, hardening, from the sensation, as if begging to be touched by the metal. Her body was just as messed up as her brain, apparently.

It felt like being scratched, so gently, but also with the knowledge that he could probably really hurt her if he wanted to. For some reason, that made it more exciting.

Then he lifted his hand and slapped the side of her right breast, making her cry out and arch upwards as the flat metal studs embedded in the palm of the glove impacted against her soft flesh. It hurt and made her throb, yet when the claws ran over that spot and moved to circle her nipple, she found herself panting for breath, squeezing her thighs together. She whimpered, holding as still as she could to keep him from accidentally stabbing one of her pointed nubs.

When he smacked her left breast, she was more prepared, yet that did nothing to stem the arousal that rushed through her as he circled her left nipple as well.

"Good girl," Mason murmured, as the claws skimmed down to the undersides of her breasts, which felt ultra-sensitive to the pointed tips. If she writhed much more, she was going to end up falling off his lap—then he kept going, over the curves of her stomach and headed toward her pussy.

Oh God… he couldn't possibly intend to use the claws on her pussy, could he?

They dipped lower, moving over her shaved mound, and her clit felt like it was aching, itching for his touch. Even if it did hurt.

"Spread your legs for me, cupcake," Mason ordered.

She didn't want to, but she couldn't stop herself at the same time. She wanted to know how it would feel.

If curiosity killed the cat, then she was dying to know.

Her arousal had overridden her sense of self-preservation in the worst way.

Audrey spread her legs.

The fear, the nerve-wracking wait to see how much it would hurt, made her heart race faster, and she closed her eyes as the claws moved down over her mound. Tracing little circles. Making her wait. Making her writhe.

They slid down on either side of her pussy, against her outer lips, and she went utterly still to ensure that neither finger slipped. Her body hummed with nerves as she panted for breath.

Suddenly, his hand moved away, and she found herself being flipped over onto her stomach. The claws dragged over her heated buttocks, and she squealed, clenching and shuddering in surprise at the stinging lines being drawn on her skin. She'd been so caught up in the sensations on her front, she'd almost forgotten that her butt was hot and throbbing. She'd gotten used to it.

Right up until he was drawing attention to it again.

"Oh God…" Her hands clenched—no, her whole body did—when he found the sensitive spot just underneath her buttocks where the curve met her thighs. Her pussy pulsed between her thighs as she squirmed in place. "Oh…"

It tickled, it hurt, it was unbearably sensitive and yet arousing.

With a chuckle, Mason gave her bottom a couple quick swats, making her yelp as the metal bounced off her hot skin.

Ow, ow, ow.

Her whole body felt flush as he pulled her up onto his lap to straddle him. The heat in his dark eyes made her feel like a sexy goddess, despite the fact that her butt was probably cherry engine red, she was sure her hair was a complete mess, and her cheeks were still streaked from her tears. The way he looked at her made her feel beautiful.

Stripping the glove from his hand, he put it to the side, keeping his eyes on her.

"How do you feel, cupcake?"

His bare hands landed on her thighs and began to rub, back and forth, slowly moving toward her hips, then up her sides, traveling to her breasts.

"Good." She was struggling to think. She wanted sex, but she didn't want to push him. He was the one in charge, right? Audrey sucked in a breath as his hands dropped back down to her hips, going behind them to press his fingers into her hot skin. "Ow!"

"Still good?"

"Yes… just… I don't know how to describe it." It had hurt, but in a good way. A way that made her body pulse with need. She squirmed on his lap. Her ass was full, but her pussy was empty, and she wanted him inside her. He was moving too slowly, like a turtle, and it was pure torture.

Especially as his hands slid back up to her breasts, cupping and squeezing. Sending her senses soaring. Audrey closed her eyes, her head falling back as she moaned, her hips sliding forward.

Please just fuck me.

But she couldn't make herself say it. Not yet. She wasn't sure she was supposed to.

The Dom made the decisions, right? And apparently, the Dom had decided to torment her.

He pinched her nipples, and she grabbed his arms to steady herself, her fingers digging in as the flash of pain and pleasure went straight through her.

"Please…" The word escaped her lips.

"Please, what, sweetness?" He tugged, twisting, and Audrey mewled. Every part of her felt hot and needy, throbbing in time together.

That felt like permission to say it. Like he wanted her to say it.

"Please fuck me, Sir."

Those were the magic words.

Mason was able to get the front of his pants open and a condom rolled over his dick in record time for Audrey to slide down onto him. The sensation of him filling her, jostling the beads inside her, was enough to have her moaning as she worked herself up and down on his cock. It felt even bigger than usual, maybe because of the position, maybe because of the beads inside her—she wasn't sure. All she knew was that it felt really freaking good.

She rocked against him, clenching around him, hands on his shoulders as he gripped her ass, burying his face in her breasts. Kissing them. Nipping them. The little bursts of pain added to her growing pleasure, like adding salt to a recipe to make everything taste sweeter. They coiled inside her, going around and around, tightening and tightening, until she couldn't get any tighter, and they exploded outward in a firestorm of ecstasy.

As she cried out, her body pulsing from the waves of climax, something tugged inside her. Tugged and popped, the sensations catching her entirely off guard as the beads were pulled from her body in the middle of her orgasm, leaving her reeling from the cacophony of rapture.

She was barely aware of Mason groaning beneath her, his grip on her tightening as he joined her in pure erotic bliss.

MASON

Once everything was cleaned up—including him and Audrey—he slipped into bed beside her. She'd insisted on keeping her hair pinned up while they showered, so it was only a bit damp as he nuzzled up behind her, pulling her soft curves against him, and felt her sigh.

He'd thought she'd fallen asleep while he took care of things, but she wiggled around to face him.

"Mmm." As soon as she got turned over, she shoved her face into the spot between his neck and his shoulder and relaxed.

Mason curled his arm around her back, drawing her lower body closer so that she could throw one leg over his. She was pure womanly softness and sweetness against him, settling something in his soul.

"This is nice."

"Yes, it is," he murmured. Mason had never really considered himself much of one for cuddling, but now that he was cuddling Audrey…

Other girlfriends had wanted to cuddle. He'd informed them he wasn't much of a cuddler. Maybe he hadn't been ready. Maybe it just hadn't been right. Because right now, all he wanted to do was hold on to Audrey and never let go.

He'd always held back in relationships before. He could see that now. He didn't want to hold back with her.

He wanted to tell her how he felt.

Which was…

Fuck. Was he in love with her?

Was this what love felt like?

It should be too soon, but at the same time, he couldn't think of any other explanation. At the very least, he was falling in love with her, if he wasn't already there yet.

He should tell her, right?

That would be the right thing to do.

That's what women wanted. That's what he'd always held back from before. But he wanted things to be different with Audrey, so he needed to make them different. By being open with her.

By telling her.

It was supposed to be kind of a big moment, though, right? He should do something special to set it up. To show her as well as tell her.

Or he could tell her right now. Show her in the moment.

Which felt like a lot. But if he put it off, he wasn't sure he wouldn't just keep putting it off. *Be different, Mason. Don't lose her.*

Taking a deep breath, he pulled away slightly so he could see her face.

Her eyes were closed.

Her breathing was even.

"Audrey." He said her name softly. He'd thought she was asleep before, and she hadn't been.

But she didn't stir.

She was out.

Mason let out his breath on a long sigh. Swung his body back toward the nightstand so he could turn off the light before returning to position and pulling her against him again. She snuggled right in. He'd found that she was a bit of an aggressive sleep snuggler. Which he liked.

It was like having his own personal teddy bear. But warmer. And sexier.

"Audrey," he whispered in the darkness. "I'm falling in love with you."

There was no answer other than the soft sound of her breathing.

Next time, he'd say it when she was awake.

Eventually.

CHAPTER FORTY-THREE

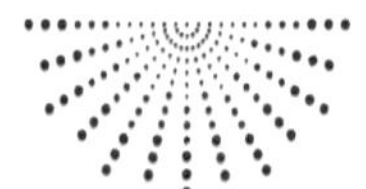

Mason was acting oddly. Not bad oddly, exactly, but oddly. He watched her intently over breakfast. He kept glancing at her when he drove her to the bakery. And for a moment, she thought he was going to say something when he dropped her off, but then he pulled back.

If Alexis hadn't been walking up right at that moment, she might have gotten up the courage to ask what was up with him.

He didn't seem like he'd lost interest in her overnight or anything; he was just... off.

Maybe it was everything at work.

"Good morning," she said to Alexis, getting out of the car after getting a very thorough kiss from Mason that left her cheeks bright pink and not because of the cold slap of air.

"Looks like you're having a very good morning," Alexis joked. She'd gotten a lot more comfortable with Audrey and Ashley during their days working together, and it showed in moments like this.

"I am." Audrey grinned. She'd had an even better night last night. Part of her wished she could have had a similar kind of morning, but she'd slept so hard, they'd woken up too late for fun times.

Eventually, when she had more employees, that might be an

option. And if things kept going the way they were, she might be able to look for more employees sooner rather than later, which would be wonderful. She was just hesitant to rely on the viral videos to keep foot traffic coming in. It would help if they went for a little bit without another viral video, and she could see what regular foot traffic and income looked like.

She and Alexis got to work, heating the ovens and getting started on the various doughs. Ashley came in a couple hours later to prep the front and open things up. Though she put on her usual smile, Audrey could tell she was worried. The FBI thing must have thrown her as much as it had the Black Fox team.

"Hey A-Team," Ashley said, hanging up her coat and grabbing an apron. "All quiet on the bakery front?"

"Thankfully, yes." Audrey had checked the doors and the cameras. Nothing of note was going on.

It was a busy but uneventful day, to her relief. Plenty of customers and quite a few of Black Fox's team stopped in throughout the day to check on her. None of them was Mason, to her disappointment, but she still felt protected. Not just the team, either.

Almost as soon as they opened, Jennifer came in to get a muffin and an order for the office. Cassidy joined David for a quick trip after lunch, and they did not bring Grandma with them. Apparently, she was having lunch with Mick, and it was 'running late'. The way David said the words, he feared what they meant but also didn't want to think about it too hard. Naomi and Yasmine came in mid-afternoon to pick up an order to bring to a special finances class Yasmine was doing for Naomi's shelter.

She felt incredibly supported, which she appreciated. She didn't think it all had to do with Mason, either.

Yasmine definitely hadn't stopped by for Mason's sake.

Some guilt still lingered when it came to Yasmine, but Audrey was trying not to let it affect things. If Yasmine could be friends with Audrey, then surely, she could get past her own guilt to be friends with Yasmine.

By the afternoon, she was feeling pretty good overall. Still a little sore from the night before, but in a good way. Still wishing her parents could be different but happy she had family and a support system here. Still not sure how things would be with her bakery in a few months but feeling like she was on the road to success.

It was good.

Which was why she was humming under her breath when she stepped out of the back of the bakery with the giant trash bag. Even taking out the trash felt like a good task. Because it was *her* trash from *her* bakery.

And maybe she wasn't really paying attention because she was feeling so happy about Mason, and her new friends, and her bakery, which was why she didn't see the man standing on the other side of the dumpster until she was practically right beside him.

Freezing in place, she stared at him, so shocked that she didn't notice the gun until it was pointing at her face.

"Don't scream," he growled.

* * *

MASON

"Hey, Zeus, can I talk to you?" Mason asked, ambling up to the other man in the hallway where he was standing just outside of Lincoln's office, looking over some folders he was holding. He had just finished a meeting with Lincoln, Mason knew, which was why he'd chosen to come talk to him now where he could catch him.

Since he hadn't been able to on the fly, more casually, he'd decided to seek the other man out for a more official invitation to a discussion.

The bald man looked up, his gaze stoic and unbothered as always. He closed the folder.

"Sure."

"My office?" Mason gestured, and Zeus shrugged, falling into step beside him.

He was not a man who was uncomfortable with silence. A lot of the time, just not saying anything could push someone to talk, but not Zeus. He was nonchalant for the entire walk, all the way until he was seated in the chair across from Mason's, giving the office a quick once-over before focusing on Mason and waiting.

Got it. If Mason wanted to talk, he was going to have to kick it off.

Leaning forward on his elbows, Mason cleared his throat.

"I wanted to check in with how you think you're adjusting to your new position," he said. "I know it's been a bit of a rough start."

Zeus shrugged.

"It's been fine."

Mason raised his eyebrows, but Zeus didn't expound upon that.

"You think it's been fine even though Drew revealed that Noelle was cheating on you in a meeting? And it's been clear there have been some trust issues with the team."

"I'm glad I found out." Zeus shrugged again. "And I knew there might be issues. I'll do my job, regardless."

He was so incredibly blasé; he either really didn't care, or he was an incredible actor. Mason studied him, looking for any crack in his armor but not finding one. Maybe he really didn't care what the team thought of him. He was calm, collected, and confident, even if no one trusted him. That, or he didn't care because he was ballsy enough to fool all of them.

Brenda would probably say that he had a fat dick spirit.

Goddammit, he really hoped that would get out of his head, eventually.

"I'd like to help you integrate with the team, if that's something you'd be open to." It was his job, after all, even if he didn't fully trust Zeus yet, either. But he needed to try to make sure they were working well as a team. There was wariness in Zeus' eyes, but maybe something else, too. Hope? Desire for connection? Or maybe Mason was projecting because he wanted there to be something he could do to help.

Before Zeus could answer, Mason's phone started blaring. Loud. Not the bakery alarm.

Audrey's panic button.

He was on his feet, phone in his hand, screen on before he could blink.

She was at the bakery. Behind it, maybe.

"What?" Zeus was already up and bouncing on the balls of his feet, ready to meet whatever the threat was.

"Bakery."

That was the only word Mason could get out before he ran.

Flat-out ran, heart in his throat, terror ripping through him because he couldn't imagine what might have caused her to push it.

Audrey

I'm going to die, I'm going to die, I'm going to die.

"This is a stick-up," the man snarled, brandishing his gun at her. "Gimme all your money."

"I don't have any!" Her voice came out in a squeak as she stared at the gun, unable to look at anything else, even though her brain was telling her she needed to try to look at him. Even though his hat was pulled low over his head and he was wearing sunglasses and a scarf. She should try to get some kind of identifying features in case she lived through this.

God, she hoped that pressing the little button in her apron had worked. There wasn't any kind of notification that, yes, someone was on the way to help.

"You run a bakery! You have to have money!"

"It's all inside!" Tears welled up. Oh God, she was going to die. He wouldn't let her go into the bakery to get money, even though she would. "I can... I can..."

She couldn't think of what she could do.

"Hey! What's going on there?" Someone shouted from the end of the alley. A man. It was a familiar man's voice.

It took her frantic brain a moment for her to place it, and Audrey watched, dumbfounded, as the bad guy turned and pointed the gun at Cash, who was now rushing down the alley, heedless of the danger. He ran straight at the guy and grabbed his wrist, shoving the gun up in the air. Her mouth dropped open as they danced around, ending with Cash between her and the gunman as they grappled over the weapon.

Behind her, the back door to the bakery slammed open.

"Audrey!"

"Mason!" His name burst from her lips with pure relief as she turned toward him.

The gunman let Cash have the weapon and took off sprinting down the alley toward the street. Two men, who had come out of the bakery right behind Mason, took off running after him. Bald with facial hair—Zeus, from Lincoln's team. Full head of hair and a large, fluffy beard—Aiden, from Harris' team. She barely had enough time to recognize them as they went flying past her before Mason was pulling her into his arms.

"Hey! I'm the one who saved her! Audrey, I saved you!" The whine in Cash's voice sounded like a child as he complained.

Astonished—because she couldn't believe Cash had gone running toward an actual gun—Audrey turned in Mason's arms, still clinging to him as her racing pulse finally started to slow.

"Oh my God, Audrey, are you okay?" Alexis had reached their side, her eyes wider than Audrey had ever seen, her normally tanned skin looking abnormally pale as she looked Audrey over. She was gripping a hand mixer, batter slowly dripping onto the ground at her side, though she didn't seem to notice. "The guys just went running through the bakery, they barely paused, and then they came out here and— What happened?"

"That's what I'd like to know," Mason said grimly, holding tightly to Audrey and looking at Cash rather than her or Alexis. When Audrey lifted her arms to hug him, she realized she was still holding the bag of trash and finally dropped it to the ground.

"I saved her, that's what happened." Cash brandished the gun, making Alexis squeak and hide behind Mason, just as Mason shoved

Audrey behind him as well. "She was being robbed, and *I* saved her, not you."

He sounded… sulky?

"Stop waving that around. Give me that." Mason strode forward several steps and snatched the gun away from Cash, quicker than Audrey could blink.

"Hey!"

Ignoring Cash's protest, Mason turned away from him and opened the gun. His shoulders sagged in relief, then his head lifted, and she could see the anger in his eyes when they met hers.

"It's not loaded," he said grimly.

Alexis sidled up to Audrey's side, sliding her arm through Audrey's so they could lean on each other for support. Audrey sagged with relief.

"Oh, thank goodness," she said, though she didn't understand why he looked so grim.

Just then, there was a commotion at the end of the alley. Zeus and Aiden had reappeared, dragging the gunman with them. His hat had been knocked off to reveal light brown hair, and his glasses were askew. He was fighting them, but he wasn't getting anywhere. Zeus had broad shoulders and lean muscle, and Aiden was built like a freaking tank. Two to one—the guy might as well have been a child for all the good his struggles did him.

"You got him!" Alexis cheered. "I'm calling the cops." She reached into her pocket to dig out her phone.

"No, don't!" Cash whirled around, clearly panicked at the idea.

Audrey's jaw dropped as Alexis froze in place. Mason crossed his arms over his chest, glaring at Cash, and she finally caught on to what he had obviously suspected from the moment he'd appeared.

"You set this up!" Fury rose up inside her, replacing the fear, the utter terror she'd felt. A rage like she'd never known before gripped her, balling her hands into fists, and she took a step toward him. Alexis let her go, but moved forward with her, like she was guarding Audrey. "You knew!"

"I'm pretty sure this is the saboteur your parents hired," Mason said, nodding at the man who had now reached them, thanks to Zeus and Aiden.

"I've done nothing wrong! I was just out for a run when these two whackos attacked me!"

Now that she didn't have a gun aimed at her face, Audrey realized what a truly terrible actor the man was. If she hadn't been so freaked out by the gun, his earlier performance would have been as laughable as this one. Since she wasn't terrified, it was easy to see through his bluster.

Now he was the one freaking out. He was the one shaking in fear.

Good.

Satisfaction didn't displace her anger, but it took some of the edge off. Now, it was Cash's turn.

She crossed her arms over her chest.

"You didn't know about the brick," she said. "I believe that. But you can't tell me you didn't know about this."

Cash scowled at her. Alexis stepped forward, suddenly turned into a protective mama bear rather than her usual shy self.

"Talk!" she barked at him, holding the mixer out in front of her. "Or I'll use this on your balls."

"Okay!" Cash stepped back, holding his hands up in front of him in a gesture of surrender. The hired hand looked appalled as he crossed his legs, shrinking between Aiden and Zeus, obviously trying not to be noticed by her. Aiden looked torn between horrified and intrigued as he looked at Alexis, while Mason appeared surprised. Audrey had never heard Alexis sound like that, which meant he hadn't either. Only Zeus' expression didn't change, though he did blink and focus on Alexis for a long moment.

"I... the gun wasn't even loaded, okay? It's not a big deal."

"It's not a big deal?" Audrey repeated slowly. "It's not a big deal. I didn't know that it wasn't loaded. I thought I was going to die. But it's not a big deal."

Cash eyed her nervously.

"I mean, I didn't mean it like that. I just meant... it was your parents' idea!"

Somehow, she'd already known that, but hearing it out loud sent all the air rushing out of her lungs. It was worse than being punched in the gut. She felt like she couldn't breathe. Like she might fall over.

Mason and Alexis were there immediately on either side of her, propping her up.

"It's okay, sweetness," Mason murmured. "We'll figure it out."

But it wasn't okay. None of it was. How could it be?

CHAPTER FORTY-FOUR

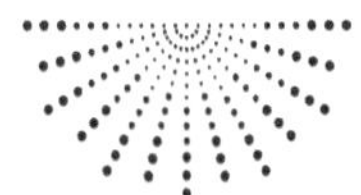

AUDREY

Despite Cash and the PI's protests—a seriously shady PI, considering he'd been willing to act as a hired goon, like something out of a bad movie—Audrey agreed to press charges. They had the camera footage, clearly showing everything that had happened behind the bakery. The PI knew they were there, but apparently had thought his disguise—and Cash—would ultimately protect him.

Instead, the police came and hauled both of them out of there. Cash was already calling for his lawyer, of course, and threatening everyone left and right. She watched as the cops dragged him out of there, doing her best to ignore the people who were videotaping with their phones. Another viral moment. Lovely. At least it would be good for business, but she would much rather not have had any of it happen.

"My parents are going to freak," Audrey said dully; all emotion and color seemed to have been leached from her once Cash had said they were involved. Mason tightened his arm around her. He hadn't let go of her since Cash had revealed that he wasn't the one in charge of today's little show, and he didn't intend to. "They want this deal, and not only did I say no to Cash's proposal, but I just got him arrested.

There's no way his parents will go through with it after this. There's going to be a public record."

"Hey." Mason turned her to face him, letting go of her only so he could hold her face in his hands and make her look at him. "You didn't get him arrested; he got *himself* arrested because of his choices. No one forced him to go along with this delusional plan of theirs."

"It doesn't even make sense," she said plaintively. "How stupid do they think I am? Did they really think I would fall for *Cash* showing up to save me from an attack?"

Maybe she'd fallen for it for a moment when a literal gun had been pointed at her face, but once her adrenaline had faded, she would have realized. There was no way Cash was the type to go running into danger. And the PI's lines had been like something out of a bad movie. She hadn't realized it when she was in a panic, but once she had calmed down, she would have.

The lack of respect her parents had for her intelligence was kind of infuriating. And saddening. But she was clinging to anger, because if she didn't, she wasn't sure she could do what she needed to do.

"It *doesn't* make sense. Maybe they're panicking. Maybe something else. I don't know. It doesn't really matter because, regardless of their reason, it was unacceptable. There is no good reason." Mason's calm, implacable condemnation of her parents' actions helped bolster her. It was a relief to hear him confirming the feelings swirling inside her, completing the half-formed thoughts buzzing around her head. She wasn't alone.

"You are amazing, Audrey, just as you are, and if they can't see that, that's on them."

"Thank you," she whispered, feeling tears spark in her eyes as she gazed up at him, unable to look away because of how he was holding her face. Her hands rested on his chest, and she could feel the beat of his heart through her palm.

Mason studied her face for a moment, a pensive expression on his.

"I completely panicked when your panic button went off," he said in a low voice. The hum of the people around them seemed to fade away entirely as she focused completely on him. "All I could think about was getting to you on time. Whether I'd make it in time."

"You did."

"I did. And you were never in any real danger, thankfully. But just the thought of it…" He closed his eyes, swallowing hard, as a little shudder went through him. "I've been accused in the past of being closed off. I love my family. My friends. But sometimes I've wondered if I'm even capable of falling in love."

She opened her mouth to protest that, of course, he was, and she immediately wanted to go fight anyone who had ever made him feel otherwise, but he put his thumb over her lips.

"I know now that I am because I'm falling in love with you, if I'm not already there."

Audrey's eyes widened; for some reason, that was still the last thing she'd expected to hear from him.

"I don't want to be closed off with you. I don't want to keep myself apart. I want you. All of you. And I want you to have all of me."

Now he removed his thumb so she could respond.

"I'm falling in love with you, too." She moved her hands up his chest to slide around his neck, going up on her tiptoes as she pulled him in for a kiss. He shifted to cradle the back of her neck with one hand, the other going to support the middle of her back.

The sound of applause had them finally breaking apart. Audrey flushed as she realized that everyone was watching—and videotaping —them. Including Ashley. She scowled at her erstwhile employee, though she couldn't make it stick for more than a second before the corners of her lips attempted to lift in a smile. Ashley just grinned and gave her a thumbs-up before stopping the recording and tucking her phone away.

Good grief.

Audrey looked back up at the man who had become her rock through all of this.

"Will you come with me while I call my parents?" she asked.

She wanted him there. While she might not want an audience for this incredibly unpleasant call, she wanted him. And his support. She didn't even want David there, even though he'd been through the same thing, because she knew his anger on her behalf would just make things harder…

But she wanted Mason there.

To lean on. To comfort her. To be there for her. Even though it felt really hard and scary to ask that.

"Of course, cupcake." Sympathy filled his expression, but also pleasure that she'd asked him to be with her. As though he knew how difficult it had been for her to ask.

Giving everyone a wave and Ashley the middle finger, which made her cackle, Audrey headed to the back with Mason. Alexis was still back there, icing some cupcakes while sending nervous little glances at the two muscular men who were hanging back there with her. Aiden and Zeus had made themselves scarce after giving their statements to the police, both trying to avoid the camera phones that had been pointed in their direction.

"Everything good?" Aiden asked.

"As good as it can be," Mason answered, his arm securely around Audrey's shoulders. "You guys can go if you want. I'm going to stay here 'til closing."

Before she could protest, he was already steering her into the office and closing the door behind them.

"You don't have to stay. I'll be fine."

"I know I don't have to."

He didn't bother saying anything more, just went to one of the chairs, taking her with him, and pulling her onto his lap. Audrey pressed her lips together. She shouldn't feel like smiling, considering the situation and what she was here to do, but Mason made her want to smile, anyway.

No, he didn't have to be here, but he was.

And she was so grateful for it.

Leaning against him, she dialed her mother's number. She felt like she should be bracing herself for the conversation, like she always did, but for some reason, the need wasn't there. She felt too empty, too depleted, to care what her mother might say, what she might think.

Maybe tomorrow, or when she had more energy, she'd care more, but right now she felt nothing but relief at the idea of getting this over with.

"Hello, Audrey. To what do I owe the pleasure of you actually taking the time to call me?"

Audrey closed her eyes, her stomach doing a tiny flip. Maybe she wasn't quite as disconnected as she'd thought, but at the same time, it wasn't as bad as it could have been either.

"Mother. I'm calling to tell you that I know you hired a PI to harass me. I know you sent him to threaten me with a gun so Cash could save me." Audrey kept going, her voice quiet but steady, as her mother tried to interrupt her. "I want you to know that I am not coming back to Philadelphia, I will not be taking your calls in the future, and I will contact you when I am ready to talk."

"How dare you!"

"Goodbye, Mother."

Before Audrey could hang up, she heard the click on the other side of the phone. Her mother had hung up first.

Shaking her head, Audrey let her own phone drop into her lap and leaned into Mason. She turned her head into his shoulder and let him hug her. The tears weren't coming, but she knew she would probably cry about it again. Eventually.

Right now, she just focused on the comfort of his arms around her and the warmth of his body against hers.

It felt like home.

---

*M*ASON

"I'm going to fucking kill them."

"Get in line," Mason advised David, though when it came down to it, David probably had the better claim.

Growling, David swung the axe he was holding, the wood splitting with a crack, pieces flying in two directions. They were in Brenda's backyard, and after telling David and Brenda about everything that had gone down today, Mason had dragged David out back to cut fire-wood to help him vent some steam without putting that emotion on Audrey. She seemed pretty even-keeled at the moment, but he didn't want her having to deal with calming her brother down, and David had been about to pop. Brenda, on the other hand, had gone straight into caretaking mode.

So, he let Brenda soothe Audrey, and he got to deal with David.

Mason put another piece of wood in front of his girlfriend's brother.

"I can't fucking believe them."

Chop. *Crack.*

"What the fuck is wrong with them?"

Chop. *Crack.*

"Some people aren't meant to be parents. They have kids because they think they should, not because they actually want them." Mason shrugged. "Although, with your parents, I think it's more that they don't see anyone outside of themselves as 'real'. You're more like dolls, and dolls are supposed to do what you tell them to."

David grunted.

Chop. *Crack.*

"That's a little too accurate for comfort, man. And you never even met them."

"Well, I've gotten to hear a little about your mom. Nothing from your dad, though Audrey seems to lump him in with whatever your mom does."

"She's not wrong to. Our father would have probably dropped both of us when we didn't turn out the way we wanted. Mom at least cared enough to try to manipulate us." David scowled.

Chop. *Crack.*

"What did Audrey do that your dad objects to?" From what Mason could see, she was hardly confrontational, unlike David. Not until she'd been pushed to the end of her limits.

"She's not thin."

Up until that moment, Mason hadn't been holding that much against Audrey's father. After all, it was her mother she was continually interacting with. He wasn't even sure she realized that she constantly talked about her parents as a unit, while never actually talking *to* her father.

If he ever met the man, punching him in the face would be well worth whatever charges were brought forward.

Mason let out a long, slow breath.

"That's it? Seriously?"

"As far as I can tell." David handed the axe over to Mason and stepped back so Mason could take his place.

Chop. *Crack.*

It was very cathartic.

Chop. *Crack.*

Chop. *Crack.*

Chop. *Crack.*

"I keep thinking your parents can't suck any more than they already do, but somehow they keep slithering beneath the bar," Mason said, reaching up to wipe a bead of sweat from his forehead. It was liable to turn to ice on his face otherwise.

"Tell me about it." David shook his head. "Okay. Let's get back inside. Who knows what advice my grandmother is giving Audrey now?"

"Good point."

They gathered up the firewood and headed to the back door.

"You know if you hurt her, I'll have to kill you."

"That was assumed."

"Good."

They came through the door cautiously, not really certain what they would be walking back into, but both immediately relaxed as the first sound they heard was all three women laughing. That was a good sign.

The three were gathered around Brenda's kitchen table, holding mugs of steaming liquid. Cassidy looked up and smiled.

"All done?" she asked, her gaze immediately going to David, checking him over. Despite her smile, there was worry on her face.

David grunted.

"He'll be fine," Mason said, moving over to drop a kiss on the top of Audrey's head and then sliding into the chair next to her.

"Hot cocoa?" she asked, pushing her mug toward him.

"Yes, please." He smiled at her over the mug, their gazes connecting, and he enjoyed watching a pink blush spread across her cheeks.

"So, Mason, Audrey tells me she's meeting your parents next weekend?"

"Yes." Mason put the cocoa back down, the chocolate lingering on his tongue. It was damn good cocoa. "They're looking forward to it."

Warily on his dad's part, hopeful on his mom's. She was still disappointed about his and Yasmine's breakup, but thrilled to hear that he wanted to bring home someone new. His dad had apparently been on his best behavior since Yasmine's comment to him, and he was a bit more reserved, but still supportive. Especially because his mom was so excited.

"Obviously, I won't be introducing him to mine," Audrey quipped, making everyone choke, then laugh. She was giggling, too.

"Sorry," Cassidy said, shaking her head. "I shouldn't be laughing, but…"

"No, no, I meant you to. Gotta laugh so you don't cry, right?" Audrey smiled, taking a sip of her cocoa, placing her lips on the mug in exactly the spot where Mason had put his. "I swear, it's okay."

It did seem to be. She'd started seeing a therapist Mason had recommended, and the fact that she was surrounded by an entire group of people who loved her definitely helped. Especially since two of them were family members who were in the same position.

Charges had not been pressed against her parents, but their deal had fallen apart. He doubted Cash was going to get more than a slap on the wrist, but at least it was having some long-term effects on his life. That was about the best they could hope for.

"Well, I, for one, am very happy you two found each other." Brenda beamed at them. "Mason has almost as much fat dick spirit as Mick. I just hope he knows how to use it, for your sake."

David groaned, falling forward and banging his head on the table.

"Grandma, why?"

"Because you still need to work on removing your butt stick," she answered with ruthless matter-of-factness.

Mason chuckled and leaned over to wrap his arm around Audrey.

"She doesn't have any complaints that I know of," he said.

"Mason!" Audrey hissed, elbowing him in the side.

Worth it, just to watch David try not to completely melt down as steam practically came out of his ears. Mason grinned.

She had no complaints, and he had no regrets.

CHAPTER FORTY-FIVE

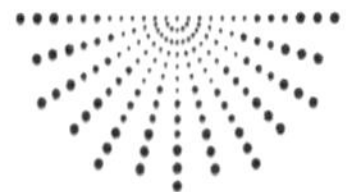

The Outlands was hopping for a Thursday evening. Audrey had closed down Cupcakes and Crumbs a little earlier than usual—she said the evenings weren't her busiest time, anyway—so she could come with them. The gang was all here, except Yasmine, and standing around one of the tables in the bar. Even Zeus was here, though he wasn't very engaged in conversation. Neither was Jensen, and the usually cheerful Baby was very scowly tonight because Jennifer was out on a date with Dr. Grande this evening. Eventually, that girl was going to have to make a choice… but for now, she was still dating both of them.

Mason tried not to feel a twinge of guilt over Yasmine's absence. That was her choice, and he knew he wasn't the only factor in making it. The club really was littered with her exes.

But it was hard not to feel a little guilty when she was absent and hurting, and he was here and incredibly happy with Audrey tucked under his arm. He knew Yasmine was happy for them, though. She'd been her usual self whenever he ran into her, and she'd come into the bakery several times with Claudia. Audrey said that she'd been cheerful at book club. Though, of course, she'd also made several jokes about her curse and giving up on happily ever after.

Eventually, he was going to have a talk with her about that, but… it was too soon.

Right now, he wanted to focus on being here with Audrey.

The woman he'd fallen in love with.

As if she sensed his thoughts, she turned toward him, tilting her head back slightly so she could meet his gaze. The expression on her face wasn't entirely loving, though.

She narrowed her eyes at him, pouting, and leaned in to whisper.

"Do you know how awkward it is to have my boobs half out in front of my brother while there's a plug in my butt?"

"I don't find it awkward at all," he murmured back, and saw her smile before she managed to squash it. His hand drifted down to pat the bottom in question. "Don't worry, cupcake, I'll take it out soon enough, then you'll have much bigger things to worry about."

The bigger thing being his dick, finally buried between his favorite buns—hers.

Audrey scowled at him. She was the one who'd wanted the 'club experience' for this. Mason had the sneaking suspicion she hadn't thought through the fact that her brother would likely be around for it. He leaned forward and gave her a very thorough kiss. Which was fine and not at all awkward in front of her brother since David was very studiously *not looking* at them. And probably doing his best not to think about what Mason and Audrey might be doing soon.

He gave his girlfriend's butt a squeeze, making her squeak and lean in closer to him because he'd chosen to squeeze the cheek that was farther away from him.

Across the bar table, Claudia shot him an amused glance from where she was talking with Lincoln and Ashley. She was the only one really paying attention to them. Drew and Naomi were focused on each other—not surprising, considering how little time they'd gotten together lately—and David was doing everything in his power to ignore Mason and Audrey. Jensen was chatting determinedly with

Zeus, whose contributions to the conversation mostly consisted of nodding.

Mason just smiled.

He glanced up at the clock.

It was time.

His cock jerked in anticipation as he shifted away from their position at the table.

"Our room should be ready by now," he said, pulling Audrey with him. "We'll see you guys later."

"Have fun, you two," Ashley chirped, giving Audrey a wink.

The pained expression on David's face made him want to chuckle, but he angled Audrey away from David, so she didn't have to see her brother's reaction. Everyone else waved them off, including Cassidy, who shook her head in amusement at David's continued pretense that Mason wasn't about to defile his sister.

He was a good boy and didn't grope Audrey's ass again until they were down the stairs into the Dungeon and out of view of her brother. The lower level was quieter than a Friday or Saturday night, but there was still plenty going on.

Several scenes were going on—wax play, a flogging, and three spankings. Audrey's eyes were wide with interest, and her steps slowed as they walked by the wax play, but she didn't stop. Thankfully. Mason was eager to get her *alone*.

But this was also part of the club experience she'd wanted, so if she'd decided to stop and watch, he would have done it.

He was still glad she didn't.

Going into the private room and closing the door shut out all the noise from the club. The moans. The smack of leather against flesh or a hard palm against soft skin. The cries. The sobs. The passion. All of it abruptly cut off.

Leaving them in their own little world.

Audrey had wandered to the middle of the room to where the spanking bench was set up when Mason turned to face her. She was wearing a green and black corset that pushed her breasts up into a shelf, nipping in her waist, and a pair of tight black shorts. Although he'd wanted a skirt, she'd been afraid of the plug falling out or something, so he'd accepted that shorts were the better option for tonight.

Knowing she had the plug inside her, readying herself for him, was much hotter than any skirt she could wear.

"You look delicious, cupcake," he said, stepping away from the door and moving toward her.

"Thank you." She shifted uncomfortably. "You look very handsome."

Mason chuckled, walking up to her and putting his hands on her waist, then sliding them behind her to grip her bottom and pull her lower half toward him. The combination of nervousness and eagerness in her eyes made his cock throb as the stiff panels of her corset pushed against it.

Lowering his lips to hers, he claimed them with a searing kiss. Originally tense in his arms, she softened against him, hands on his chest, leaning into the kiss as if slowly melting into him. Their tongues danced as he massaged her ass, their bodies pressed tightly together, his cock pulsing between them.

Giving her ass one last squeeze, his hands moved up to the laces of her corset, loosening the knots.

He stripped her slowly, moving his lips from hers, so he could kiss every part of her as it was revealed to him. Audrey moaned as his mouth moved over her breasts, pausing at each nipple for a long suck, then dragging his teeth across the little buds before releasing them.

Moving his mouth over her soft curves as he tugged her shorts down, he reached the front of her pussy and pressed his lips to the end of the cleft. His tongue flicked between her lips, teasing her clit, and she cried out as her hands landed on his head, helping her to keep her balance as her knees quaked.

He didn't linger there long, just enough to tease, before getting to his feet again. She was completely naked other than her heels.

"Okay, sweetness, let's get you in position."

He couldn't wait to claim the last part of her.

<u>*AUDREY*</u>

The spanking bench was padded leather and surprisingly comfortable. Though she felt a wave of nerves as Mason began to move around her, using the O-rings to secure her cuffs in place. The helplessness increased her arousal, even as it ratcheted up the slight fear coiling in her belly.

"It's going to hurt, isn't it?" Her butt clenched around the plug as she asked the question.

She wanted to do this. She wanted to try. But she couldn't stop the anxiety.

Mason came around to the front of the bench, dropping down into a crouch so his face was level with hers. Darkly handsome, he was utterly serious as he met her gaze.

"Yes, it is going to hurt, sweetness. And you're going to love it." His fingers brushed back her hair as he pressed a soft kiss to her lips. "You're going to take it for me, aren't you?"

A shudder went through her at the idea of enduring discomfort, even pain, to give him pleasure. The very idea made her hot. She wasn't sure why she was wired like this, but she couldn't deny the truth. And she trusted him. If it was too much discomfort, too much pain, he wouldn't push her. She had her safe words. Even without them, he was always watching her to make sure he didn't push her too far.

"Yes, Sir."

"Good girl."

He kissed her again. The angle was awkward, but it didn't matter. He claimed her lips, conquering her mouth, while his hands cupped her breasts and squeezed hard enough to make her cry out. The sound was muffled by his lips. She jerked against the restraints as he pinched her nipples, hard, making the little buds throb.

Again, she clenched around the plug, her pussy spasming emptily, needily.

Mason was right. His rough fingers on her nipples hurt, but she liked it. And she was going to take it for him, to please him. Because that got her off, too.

Just like it would when he took her ass.

He toyed with her breasts for a few moments longer, still kissing her, still drinking in the sounds she was making. Then he gave her nipples another little tug and twist before releasing them. They were twin points of aching pain on her chest that went straight to her pussy.

Even though he hadn't touched it since teasing the little bud with his tongue, her clit was throbbing in time with her nipples. She pressed her mound against the padded leather beneath her as best she could, needing the pressure, yet unable to move much because of the way she was strapped down.

Mason's fingers trailed over the center of her back to the curves of her bottom as he walked to the other end of the bench.

"Such a pretty ass," he murmured, then he bent down to give her cheeks each a kiss.

Audrey gasped when his teeth sank in, biting the soft flesh hard enough to sting. Then she felt him kiss he spot he'd just nipped. She whimpered.

Whatever he wanted to do to her, he could.

His tongue laved over her clit again, and she moaned, tried to lift her hips to get more of the contact her body craved, but she couldn't do that, either.

She was all tied up. She couldn't pull away. Couldn't lean in.

She'd been immobilized, and there was no escaping whatever he wanted to do to her. With her.

"I've wanted to do that since the moment I met you," he told her.

"Do what?" Audrey asked, slightly dazed. She wasn't sure what part he was talking about.

"Take a bite of this delicious ass," he said, patting the spot where he'd done so. Amusement curled through her and a flush of heat. He had? "And now I'm going to fuck it. Ask me to fuck your ass, cupcake."

Oh, she hated it when he did this. Couldn't he just do it? Take her?

But he liked to hear her ask for it. Maybe even beg for it.

When she didn't respond immediately, his hand snapped against her pussy. The shock of the slap, the stinging bite, followed immediately by wet heat that her body interpreted as pleasure, left her gasping.

"Ask me to fuck your ass, sweetness," he ordered again.

She gasped and tensed as the plug twisted inside her. He pulled it, though not hard enough to actually remove it from the tight hole; he was making sure she felt it. That her focus was where he wanted it to be.

"Please, fuck my ass, Sir," she whispered, closing her eyes because somehow it was easier with her eyes closed.

"A little louder, cupcake."

The plug pulled free as he spoke, and she moaned. Now, both her pussy and her ass were empty, and she craved the feeling of fullness.

"Please, fuck my ass, Sir." A little louder this time.

Something hot and hard and slick pressed at the entrance of her virgin channel. It was much larger than the tip of the plug. Hands splayed out over her cheeks, rubbing them, then moving up to grip her hips.

"One more time, Audrey." His voice was soft. Low. Needy.

"Please, Mason," she begged. "Fuck my ass."

Because she wanted him—needed him—inside her. Needed him to fill her back up. To hurt her. To pleasure her. To use her for his own desires.

"I love you, Audrey."

He'd said the words multiple times since the first time, but there was something extra intimate, yet extra filthy as he spoke them while pushing the hot, slick head of his cock inside her. Audrey's tight ring stretched, and she cried out rather than answering him at the sensation of being opened so wide, so quickly.

The plug had stretched her, yes, but the tip was so much more narrow, and once the bulb was inside her, the stem between the bulb and the base was quite thin. Very much unlike his cock.

It was thick and hard and hotter than the plug. Her entrance was stretched wide, making her pant at the immediate sensation of fullness as she was opened for him. The head popped in, but unlike with the plug, there was no real immediate relief. His shaft was just as thick, and without the slight soft give that his head had.

Audrey shuddered, her muscles clenching around his lubed length, struggling to adjust to the new dimensions as he rocked forward, sliding deeper inside her.

"Oh God, Mason…"

"That's it, sweetness. Just relax." His hands massaged her hips. "Your sweet ass was meant to take my cock. Take it for me."

It did hurt as he thrust in deeper, the slick shaft sliding against her squeezing ring. There was no notch, no relief, it was just thick all the way down, and somehow, it was both painful and wildly arousing. Audrey squeezed and released, over and over, as he worked himself into her ass, until his body finally came to rest against her cheeks.

She was so full. So hot.

"Good girl," Mason murmured, digging his fingers into her back, just above her hips. It felt like his cock must be right next to that spot, he was so deep inside her. "What color are you, sweetness?"

"Green." She was. Yes, it hurt, but she didn't want him to stop. She didn't want him to slow down.

Now that he was deep inside her, her channel fully stretched around him, she wanted to feel him move. Wanted to hear his groans of pleasure. Wanted him to use her.

Wanted him to make her his.

Completely.

CHAPTER FORTY-SIX

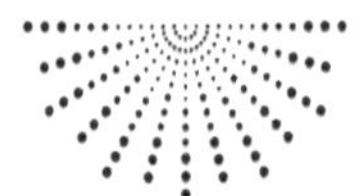

Mason was trying to take things slowly, but Audrey's reactions were testing every inch of his resolve. Gritting his teeth, he ruthlessly gripped his self-control.

Despite the way she was wriggling, despite the way she'd begged, this was still her first time, and he wanted to be gentle with her. He didn't want to hurt her too much. Audrey liked a little bit of pain, and he fucking got off on knowing that she was taking the discomfort to please him, but that didn't mean he wanted to truly hurt her.

He'd deliberately chosen not to focus this scene on her ass, so she wouldn't be distracted by lingering pain from a spanking or flogging or any other sensations. A bit of foreplay, then he'd gone straight to her ass, wanting to make sure she felt every inch of him sinking into her.

Now she had, and it felt better than he could have imagined. Her muscles clasped him, massaging the length of his cock. Taking him in deep while she whimpered and made hot little noises in the back of her throat. He wasn't sure she even realized she was making them.

The stark black of the leather straps stood out against her pale skin, making it impossible for him to forget that she was being held in place. Unable to move. Helpless against his lust.

Which meant that he had to stay in control as best he could.

But she was green. Which meant…

"I'm going to fuck this pretty little ass now, sweetness."

She moaned in response, her muscles clamping down around him and making him groan in return. Fuck she felt like heaven, her tight ass clenching around his dick.

Slowly pulling away, he heard her cry. Felt her fight against the restraints at the sensation. Then he sank into her again, the lube easing his passage through the muscles that were so determinedly squeezing, trying to push him back out.

He moved slowly, shallowly, giving her time to adjust. Enjoying the tight grip of her ass. Letting her get used to both his girth and the sensation of having her ass fucked.

Reining in his own desire was easy until he felt her lifting her hips up to meet his thrusts, using the tiny bit of movement available to do so. Her moans were shifting. Changing. Less pained, more pleasured. Mason began to move harder. Faster. Watching the shiny length of his cock being gripped by her tight ring, which was stretched smooth and white around him, his dick sinking into her no longer virgin ass over and over again.

Because she had given herself over to him… completely.

AUDREY

The wicked feeling of being invaded heightened her pleasure as Mason began to move faster, thrusting harder. It hurt so good. The burning ache of being stretched, the feeling of him moving against sensitive nerve endings that were unused to being touched, was sending her higher and higher.

An orgasm wasn't something she expected from anal sex, yet…

Her body was humming and buzzing, her mound pressing against the spanking bench, over and over again in a manner that made her clit pulse and her pussy flutter. When she clenched around him, she heard his cries of pleasure and felt a kind of exultation wash over her.

His hands gripped her hips tighter as he rode her, fucking her, using her. Audrey cried out as the burn increased, but so did the pleasure.

It was so filthy hot, so wicked, so delicious.

"That's it, cupcake. Take my cock up your tight little ass." He groaned. "Fuck, Audrey, you feel so damn good."

Her insides cramped as he moved harder, faster, and she could feel her clenching muscles sending his pleasure spiraling higher. Pressing back against him, bucking beneath him, held in place by the straps, she cried out as pained ecstasy pushed her senses to their limits.

It was heaven and hell; it was overload and yet somehow not enough.

Audrey writhed in place, right on the edge of climax, yet unable to go over.

As if sensing her dilemma, Mason released her hip and bent forward, burying his cock deep in her ass, his body pressed against her buttocks, as his hand slipped between her and the spanking bench. His fingers barely pressed against her slippery clit when she went off like a rocket, sobbing at the intensity of the erotic storm that drenched her in roiling ecstasy.

She heard him cry out, as if from a distance, felt him harden even further inside her. He felt even thicker, longer, as her muscles clenched around him over and over again.

Even before she felt the wet heat begin to fill her, she could feel the way his cock pulsed inside her, each jet of cum forcing its way past her tight ring on its way to her bowels. Audrey moaned, panting, overwrought from the sensations, the orgasm leaving her breathless and limp as Mason rocked against her, emptying himself into her ass.

His fingers moved in a circle over her clit, leaving her shuddering beneath him as the pleasure finally began to slow. Every part of her felt exquisitely sensitive in its wake, and she whimpered as she felt the last spurts of his pleasure pulse through her.

"Fuck." He muttered the word as his forehead dropped against the center of her back.

It sounded like a blessing and a benediction. Audrey didn't have the energy to respond just yet, but she fully agreed.

Thankfully, Mason rallied fairly quickly, easing himself from her body and getting the straps undone, so he could carry her over to the bed. She felt limply satiated as she curled up with her head on his chest and let out a long sigh.

She felt the same… yet she felt different at the same time.

She couldn't explain it.

Shifting, she felt oddly sloshy inside.

Which made her giggle.

"What?" Mason asked, moving so that he could see her face, brushing long strands of red hair out of his way. Tilting her head back to look at him, Audrey couldn't help but giggle again.

She felt tipsy, as though she was drunk on pleasure.

"Now I'm a cream-filled cupcake," she told him, startling the most amazing laugh from his lips. His grip on her tightened, and she grinned, pleased she'd made him lose control so completely with his astonished reaction.

"Yes," he managed to finally say. "Yes, you are. And I'm going to make you into a cream-filled cupcake as often as possible."

Rolling her onto her back, he kissed her. Gently. Lovingly. Brushing his fingers over her body, cherishing her with his every touch.

"I really do love you," he murmured against her lips.

"I really do love you, too."

Audrey kissed him back with all the love she felt, sliding her arms around his neck to hold him close.

So, this was what love felt like.

And it was utterly perfect.

EPILOGUE

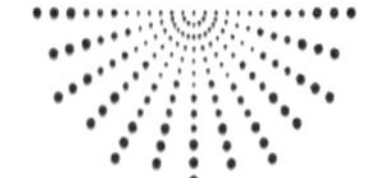

Pausing outside of Cupcakes and Crumbs, Yasmine felt her heart squeeze. Mason was in there with Audrey, his head bent next to hers at one of the tables. She said something that made him laugh, and he turned his head to steal a quick kiss.

The scene was like something out of a movie, and it made her heart ache. Not because she wished Mason was still hers, she didn't, but because she wished that someone would look at her like that. She'd never made Mason laugh like that. She wasn't sure she would know how to. She hadn't even known he could laugh like that. And they'd never kissed like that, either.

Yasmine hurried on before Ashley could look up from the customer she was dealing with at the counter and see her.

Mason and Audrey were right for each other in a way that Mason and Yasmine never had been.

But damn, it hurt to have gotten her hopes up, then crushed once again.

Hope was awful.

And whoever had put this damn curse on her was even worse because they'd stolen her hope.

Not that she really thought she was cursed.

Most of the time.

She'd said it as a joke at first, but at a certain point, it had started feeling real. Yasmine knew Naomi and Claudia thought she was self-sabotaging, but was it really her fault that when she realized a man wasn't the right partner for her, she instantly knew who would be perfect for him?

Every time she did the right thing.

Every time, she ended up alone.

Hope was dead.

Because she couldn't fight it anymore.

She wasn't heartbroken over Mason, but her heart hurt because she'd finally realized the truth...

Even if she wasn't cursed, it didn't matter.

It was time to give up on finding love and accept that the dream was dead.

YASMINE WILL FIND OUT HER FATE IN SECURITY AND SUBMISSION.

To stay updated about my books, for exclusive teasers, and a bunch of freebies, make sure to sign up for my newsletter at www.goldenangelromance.com.

ACKNOWLEDGMENTS

I have a lot of people to thank for helping me with this book.

My amazing beta readers, who are invaluable in helping me catch mistakes, doing the initial grammar and word checks, identifying continuity issues, and working through problems with me. Marie, Candida, Marta, Rara, and Katherine – you all make these books so much better!

My Patreon readers who not only read ahead but are kind enough to give me invaluable feedback as they're reading.

Another extra special thank you to Katherine, who got me started down this career path and has been by my metaphorical side ever since.

And, as always, a big thank you to all of you for buying and reading my work… if you love it, please leave a review!

ABOUT THE AUTHOR

Golden Angel is a USA Today best-selling author of heart and bottom warming romance.

She is a big fan of happily-ever-afters, strong heroes and heroines, and sizzling chemistry.

When she's not writing, she can often be found on the couch reading, in front of her sewing machine making a new cosplay, hanging out with her friends, or wandering the Maryland Renaissance Fair.

www.goldenangelromance.com

BB bookbub.com/authors/golden-angel
g goodreads.com/goldeniangel
f facebook.com/GoldenAngelAuthor
O instagram.com/goldeniangel

OTHER BOOKS BY GOLDEN ANGEL

CONTEMPORARY BDSM ROMANCE

Venus Rising Series (MFM Romance)

The Venus School

Venus Aspiring

Venus Desiring

Venus Transcendent

Venus Wedding

Venus Rising Box Set

Stronghold Doms Series

The Sassy Submissive

Taming the Tease

Mastering Lexie

Pieces of Stronghold

Breaking the Chain

Bound to the Past

Stripping the Sub

Tempting the Domme

Hardcore Vanilla

Steamy Stocking Stuffers

A Sassy Christmas

Entering Stronghold Box Set

Nights at Stronghold Box Set

Stronghold: Closing Time Box Set

Masters of Marquis Series

Bondage Buddies

Master Chef

Law & Disorder

Switch Play

Legally Bound

Shallow Submission

Hidden Away

Secret Submission

Third Wheel

Black Fox Security Doms

Danger and Dominance

Cuffs and Cupcakes

Security and Submission

Whips and Weddings

Rescue and Ropes

Bondage and Bad Guys

Dungeons & Doms Series

Dungeon Master

Dungeon Daddy

Dungeon Showdown

Dungeons & Doms Boxset

Daddies Everywhere

Chef Daddy

Foosball Daddies

Taco Daddy

Cheese Daddy

Garden Daddy

Daddies Everywhere Boxset

Cherry Popping Daddies

Emily by Golden Angel

Lottie by Stella Moore

Titania by Raisa Greenwood

Standalone Daddy Dom

Little Villain

HISTORICAL SPANKING ROMANCE

Domestic Discipline Quartet

Birching His Bride

Dealing With Discipline

Punishing His Ward

Claiming His Wife

The Domestic Discipline Quartet Box Set

Bridal Discipline Series

Philip's Rules

Gabrielle's Discipline

Lydia's Penance

Benedict's Commands

Arabella's Taming

Pride and Punishment Box Set

Commands and Consequences Box Set

Deception and Discipline

A Season for Treason

A Season for Scandal

A Season for Smugglers

A Season for Spies

Desire and Discipline

A Season for Bliss

A Season for Desire

A Season for Christmas.

Indecent Dukes

The Duke's Indecent Scandal

The Duke's Indecent Match

The Duke's Indecent Purchase

The Duke's Indecent Desire

The Duke's Indecent Proposal

The Duke's Indecent Betrothal

The Duke's Indecent Courtship

Bridgewater Brides

Their Harlot Bride

Standalone

Marriage Training

The Duke's Pursuit

Rogue Booty

SCI-FI ROMANCE

Tsenturion Masters Series with Lee Savino

Alien Captive

Alien Tribute

Alien Abduction